CASH OUT

CASH OUT

Jerry Kennealy

SPEAKING VOLUMES, LLC

NAPLES, FLORIDA

2012

Cash Out

ISBN 978-1-61232-865-2

For Emile Dutil and all those wonderful
members of Le Club Des Chasseurs Menteurs:
Al Baylacq, Harold Cereghino, Andre Armand,
Eugene Chaput, Dick Leahy, Barny Ford, et al.
Bon appétit

ACKNOWLEDGMENTS

The author would like to thank the members
of the San Francisco Police Department
who helped him find those dark alleys
and tunnels in the real Chinatown:
Captain Mike Dower, Inspector Daniel Foley,
and Inspector Mike Mullane.

Prologue

The closer Inspector John Tomei came to his house, the more he realized he'd had too much to drink. He slowed the unmarked police car with exaggerated care as he approached an intersection. At one time the Novato Police Department turned a blind eye to traffic violations committed by members of the San Francisco Police Department—who made up an out-of-proportion membership of the town's population. But not anymore. The current chief of police was an ex–San Francisco cop, and he was out to prove that he would be as tough on his former coworkers as he was on everyone else.

Tomei coasted to a stop, looked both ways, then nudged the accelerator. He reached back and scratched the mottled head of a stuffed giraffe that he'd purchased at Toys-R-Us.

The giraffe was so big he hadn't been able to get it into the trunk of the car, so it sat in the back, its elongated neck flopping over the headrest, its beady eyes seemingly staring at Tomei in bewilderment.

The giraffe was a gift for his daughter, Messy. She was seven years of age, and had grown tired of her nickname, and now preferred being called by her full name—Melissa.

He glanced at his wristwatch. Ten minutes past one. That would give him plenty of time to get home, take a swim, then a short nap. He'd be sober by the time he picked up Messy from her after-school day-care center.

Tomei reached between his legs and took a final sip of the "traveler," a now cold mixture of coffee and brandy. The bartender had argued with him when he asked for that last drink. "You've had enough, Tomb. Take it easy."

But Tomei hadn't been in the mood to take it easy. The judge's ruling this morning had been a disaster. The girl. Rosalie. Six years old. Younger than Messy.

The call had come in from Mission Station. He'd responded to the Valencia Street apartment and found the terrified girl crouched in the back of a closet.

The two on-scene uniformed officers hadn't been able to coax her out.

Tomei's nostrils had tightened as he entered the room. The girl was covered in her own waste. Her tattered shorts and T-shirt were molded to her small, emaciated body with sweat and urine.

Tomei had knelt down and began talking to her, telling her that he had a daughter about her age. He took out his wallet and showed her a photo of Messy. The girl's dark, fear-filled eyes bounced from Tomei to the photograph. He slipped his coat off and passed it to her, and after wrapping it around her shoulders, she told him her name. "Rosalie," she had said in a frail, trembling voice.

Rosalie told him that her mother was probably at the Cellar, a bar just around the corner. When he asked about her father, Rosalie pulled his coat around her tightly and began shaking convulsively.

Tomei sent the two uniformed officers to the Cellar, and they came back with the mother, Sonia, a plump brunette wearing a flowered-print dress two sizes too small for her fleshy frame. She'd reeked of stale booze and cigarettes.

At first Sonia acted outraged. "Get out of my apartment. Leave us alone." When Tomei threatened to lock her up and place Rosalie in Child Protective Services, the woman had done a one-eighty, flirting with

Tomei, and then, when that got her nowhere, she blamed everything on her husband. "Rico. That bastard! He's been at Rosalie. I know it. I know it. But there's nothing I can do."

Tomei found Rico later that day, at a Mission District bar known to be a hangout for gangs dealing in Mexican brown heroin.

Rico was short, heavyset, with weight lifter's shoulders and a drinker's paunch that hung over the dragon-shaped brass buckle on his belt.

Tomei knew all about the buckle. The dragon's head slid out along with a razor-sharp three-inch "skinner's blade."

Rico was wearing leather bike jeans and a black tank top exposing ribbons of prison-style heated ball-point pen tattoos across his shoulders and down his beefy arms. His stringy black hair was worn in a ponytail that reached past his shoulders. Long pointed sideburns drooped down and curled around his jawbone.

Rico Moreno had sucked in his stomach and bunched his fists when Tomei showed his badge. A crowd of Rico's friends started to encircle Tomei. When Tomei whispered the name "Rosalie," Rico waved his buddies away and meekly followed Tomei out to the street. Rico hesitated as they reached the unmarked car. Tomei cuffed him behind his back and threw him into the backseat.

All that had taken place seven months ago. This morning in court Ricardo Moreno was "flying the American flag" in a blue business suit, white shirt, and red tie. His hair was short, neatly barbered, his sideburns trimmed at mid-ear. He'd walked into court with an exaggerated limp, telling the judge that he was still in pain from the "unnecessary and uncontrolled beating he had received from the arresting officer, Inspector John Tomei."

Moreno's Brooks Brothers clad lawyer had nodded somberly as his client recited his story without missing a beat. They had rehearsed the speech more than a dozen times that morning.

Sonia Moreno was garbed in a loose-fitting, sober black dress, a Bible clutched in one hand, rosary beads in the other.

Rosalie was spruced up as if for the first day of school—a plaid skirt, maroon sweater, shiny black leather shoes with tiny silver buckles. She glanced at Tomei and gave him a weak smile seconds before the bailiff called the court to order and Judge Oren Thacker entered the courtroom.

The judge had a busy calendar. It didn't take long. Within twenty minutes he ruled that Rosalie Moreno should be returned to the custody of her parents.

Tomei's protests were at first denied by the judge, then the gavel was crashed down on the desk as if Judge Thacker was pounding nails. "One more outburst, Inspector, and I'll hold you in contempt."

Rico Moreno smiled into Tomei's eyes. He ran the tip of his tongue over his lips and then turned to leer at Rosalie.

Tomei made his way over to him, hand outstretched. "No hard feelings," he said, and before Moreno could react, Tomei grabbed Moreno's fingertips and squeezed hard. Moreno tried to keep a calm, macho look on his face as Tomei continued the pressure. He didn't release Moreno's hand until he heard a bone crack.

"Fat lot of good all that did me, huh pal?" Tomei asked the giraffe as he steered into the quiet cul-de-sac where he lived. He was surprised to see his wife's Porsche in their driveway. Joan had left for her office in San Francisco early that morning.

Tomei parked the car, wrestled the giraffe from the backseat, and lugged it across the shadow-checkered lawn.

He dug his keys from his pocket and opened the front door, wondering how Joan would react to his boozy condition. She had been acting jumpy lately. Her job as an executive in a San Francisco Media Gulch software firm was taking more and more of her time. And her energy.

Tomei set the giraffe down and tiptoed toward the bedroom, stopping when he spotted the orange top of a bikini on the hallway floor. Joan's bikini. He stooped to pick it up. It was damp. A few yards down the hall he came across the bottom of the bikini.

There was a loud noise from the bedroom. A woman groaning. Tomei's first thought was that Joan was being assaulted—raped. He freed the .38 snub-nose revolver from the holster at his belt and ran into the room.

A man's broad back was all that he could see, until Joan's flushed face rolled across the pillow. Her arms reached back to grasp the metal headboard. She groaned again, then opened her eyes. When she spotted her husband, she screamed.

The man freed himself from the bed, stumbling, nearly falling to the floor. He stared at Tomei with a mixture of fear and embarrassment on his face.

"Jesus, John, I—"

Tomei raised the gun and fired. The naked man raced barefoot through the open glass door leading out to the pool, Tomei in pursuit. Tomei fired again as the man skirted the pool, then snapped off two more shots as the man used a chaise lounge as a springboard, vaulting over the privet hedge and into the adjoining backyard.

Joan's screams made him turn back toward the house. She was standing alongside the pool, naked, the stuffed giraffe clutched to her chest.

"John," she sobbed. "That was Dave. Don't shoot, for God's sake!"

Dave Holdings. Their next-door neighbor. A fireman. A friend to both of them—he'd thought.

When Joan saw the look on her husband's face she inched backward toward the bedroom, the giraffe squeezed tight against her shivering body. "Please, John. Put the gun away. Don't shoot me. Please."

Tomei raised the weapon to his temple and pulled the trigger. The sound of the hammer hitting an empty chamber sounded like an explosion to him.

Chapter One

Eighteen Months Later
San Francisco
Chinatown

The bundles of money made a soft plopping sound as they hit the table.

Kan Chin smiled briefly as he picked up one of the packets, riffling the bills' edges as if they were a deck of cards.

"You counted it?" Kan Chin asked in Cantonese, his voice soft, gentle, barely audible.

Willy Hon tilted his head and squinted, trying to catch a glimpse of the old man's eyes. The single overhead fixture dangling from the ceiling cast a small pool of circular light on the grimy green-felt tabletop. There would usually be a half dozen men sitting around the table playing cards or mah jongg. The light had been carefully positioned so that all anyone could see were their opponents' hands. There were no gamblers tonight. Tonight there was only Kan Chin.

"Yes, it has been counted," Hon answered solemnly. "Three hundred and eleven thousand dollars."

Kan Chin leaned forward, his balding head momentarily coming into view. He was in his early seventies, with tissue-paper-thin skin that stretched over the bones of his face and hands. His eyes appeared to swim behind thick-lensed, steel-framed glasses.

He scooped the money onto his lap, then said, "Were there any difficulties?"

"No."

Chin snapped the rubber band holding one of the packets of bills. "Rossi was not alone?"

Hon hesitated a moment, then said, "No. The woman was there."

A pleased grin split Chin's face. "Yes. She was not a problem?"

Again Hon paused before answering.

Chin's voice cracked like a whip. "Tell me. I don't want to drag the story from you."

"The man reacted as you said he would. He was so frightened he wet his pants when I threatened him. But the woman, she—"

"Did you kill her?"

"No. But Jimmy and Gim. This was their first job. They—"

Again Chin cut in. "It doesn't matter what they did. She is of no consequence now."

There was the sound of the chair's legs scraping the hardwood floor as Chin rose slowly to his feet.

"Acceptable, Willy. Very acceptable. You did well." He peeled some bills from one of the bundles of money and pushed them toward Willy Hon.

"Distribute the money as you see fit. And tell Jimmy and Gim there will be more work for them soon."

Chapter Two

FBI agent Donald Jamison arched his back and stretched, his crew-cut, ash-colored hair brushing up against the car's cloth headliner. He felt bored. And cramped. And hungry. At six feet three inches and packing two hundred sixty pounds, he just wasn't built for surveillance jobs. Especially jobs that took place in the front seat of one of the Chevrolet Saturns that the Bureau, in its infinite wisdom, had purchased. He wondered idly if someone back in Washington had gotten a kickback from General Motors. He hoped so. Hoped that somebody was getting something out of the deal, although in all honesty there weren't too many vehicles he could sit in for more than fifteen minutes without feeling cramped.

A van was what was needed, Jamison decided. A full-spectrum surveillance van with air-conditioning, two-way mirrors, a computer terminal that could tap into phone lines, and a 360-degree rotating infrared periscope with a fifty-to-one zoom lens. A fax machine, leather bucket captain's chairs, and, best of all, a refrigerator and microwave oven. He knew the Bureau had such vans. He had seen them in Philadelphia. New York probably had a hundred of the damn things. But here in San Francisco, it was just the goddamn Saturns.

Jamison stretched again, crumpled the empty cardboard coffee cup in his hands and tossed it casually over his shoulder into the backseat. His hand wandered toward the dashboard, then stopped halfway and dropped to his lap. There was no sense turning the radio on. His partner, Paul Flowers, didn't like country music. How the hell could a guy not like country? And what kind of a name was Flowers to have to go through life with? What nicknames had he been tagged with as a kid? Daisy? Buttercup?

Jamison studied Flowers out of the corner of his eye. Small, skinny little runt. Flowers had no difficulty in getting comfortable in the Saturn. None at all. He could sleep all night right behind the steering wheel.

"The guy going in now, he looks a little familiar, Donny Boy," Flowers said in that low, juicy, Kentucky drawl that drove Jamison up the wall. It always sounded as though he was chewing tobacco and getting ready to spit. Jamison turned his attention to the restaurant and watched as a man in a tweed sport coat and Levi's stopped at the front entrance, pausing to glance up and down the street before disappearing inside Sully's Bar & Grill.

"Yeah, he should look a little familiar," Jamison said, a frown creasing his forehead as his memory kicked in the vital statistics. "He's an ex–San Francisco cop. What the hell's his name?" Jamison snapped his fingers as if that would help prod his memory. "He had some goofy nickname. What the— 'The Tomb' that's it. John Tomei. Word is he came home one day, found a guy in the sack with his wife, and took a shot at him. Tomei had to quit the job or go to trial and probably do some time in the slam. So he quit."

Flowers unsnapped his seat belt. "Your informant didn't mention anything about an ex-cop, did he?"

"Nope. And nothing about a bookie either."

Flowers pulled the key from the car's ignition.

"The Tomb, huh? Let's go see if he's meeting with our boy."

John Tomei raked a hand through his hair and scanned the room, spotting Billy Rossi sitting alongside an attractive blonde at the far end of the bar. There were several drinks and a set of bar dice cups lined up in front of Rossi. The blonde had a tall, dark drink in her hand. Tomei made a bet with himself that it was iced tea.

He worked his way through the bar crowd, which was two and three deep in spots. Rossi owned a piece of the place, and Sully's was the city's premiere sports saloon, with a dozen TV sets set up around the bar and dining room, broadcasting everything from baseball, to soccer, to basketball, tennis, golf, whatever the digital satellite on the roof could pick up. Because of the sports action, it was also a very popular hangout for bookies.

The bartender caught his eye, and after a moment's hesitation, gave a slight nod, which Tomei returned. It had been a couple of years since Tomei's last visit to Sully's, but bartenders, like cops, have long memories.

Tomei tapped Rossi on the shoulder and the bookmaker spun around on his stool to face him.

"Hey! The Tomb. Jesus Christ. Thanks for coming. Thanks a lot. What are you drinking?"

"Calistoga water will do fine, Billy."

"Another man on the wagon," Rossi said with a scornful shake of his head. "What's happening to this town? Hey, Chris," he called to the bartender, "get my friend a Calistoga." He circled his arm like a rodeo cowboy about to lasso a steer. "And get a round for everybody," Rossi yelled, his voice booming above the bar chatter and the vintage big-band music coming from the old-fashioned neon-ribbed jukebox.

There was a chorus of cheers from the forty-plus crowd at the bar when they realized they were in for a free drink.

The bartender took care of Tomei's order first, then went into full gear filling the rest of the drink requests.

Tomei took a sip of the mineral water, bottled from a spring in the nearby Napa Valley, an area much more famous for its wine than its water. He watched as Rossi peeled off fifty-dollar bills from a bulging money clip, dropping them casually alongside the string of untouched drinks in front of him.

Tomei studied Rossi's companion. Attractive—pushing thirty from one direction or the other—hazel eyes, bland as a cat's, lips extended in a thoughtful pout. The right side of her face was puffed out a bit, the faint outline of a bruise visible through her makeup. The powder-blue V-neck sweater showed off her figure to good advantage.

Tomei tried to remember the last time he'd seen Billy Rossi. It had to have been four years ago, when he was still working Vice. The man hadn't changed much. Still a big spender. He was like most of the old-time San Francisco bookies Tomei had run into. They all had a certain Damon Runyon, *Guys and Dolls* manner about them: the way they talked, the way they dressed, the flashy, trophy girlfriends. And the money. Lots of it, and they liked to spread it around.

Rossi's beef-and-bourbon complexion was a little more toward the rare roast beef side now, and he'd put on some unneeded weight. His suit could have been picked from the pages of *Esquire* or *GQ* magazine. The jacket's cut was Italian, the black material a raw silk, the casual, slightly baggy look of the coat and the jaunty spread of the shirt collar must have done justice to the magazine's sleek model. On Rossi the effect was that of a man who had dressed to please a woman, and hadn't quite pulled it off.

While Tomei was checking out Billy Rossi, the blonde's shopper's eyes raked Tomei professionally, taking in the rumpled sport coat, the frayed collar of the denim shirt tucked into faded jeans. A loser, she thought, a real loser, though she liked his face—broad, careworn, with crow's-feet around the eyes, as if he spent a lot of time squinting into the sunlight. And his hair—long, shaggy, the way it curled up at the back, almost reaching his shoulders. It was a dark brown, without a trace of gray. Why was it that the good-looking ones were always the losers? she asked herself.

"Sherri, say hello to the Tomb," Rossi said, jamming his money clip back into his pants pocket. "The Tomb and his partner Gucci chased me, caught me, and put me behind those nasty bars. Those were the longest three months I ever spent in my life."

Sherri's face remained passive, unimpressed. She leaned forward on her stool and crossed her legs, watching Tomei's eyes follow her hemline. "He's not going to be able to do anything about those guys, Billy."

Tomei rattled the ice cubes in his glass. "What guys, Billy?"

The bookie grabbed Tomei's shoulder, pulled him close, then whispered hoarsely into his ear. "I was robbed, Tomb. Some slants robbed me. And they want to take over. Put me out of business."

Chapter Three

"Let's get away from the bar," Billy Rossi suggested, holding his drink out in front as he pushed his way through the crowd. A waitress in white tennis shorts and an up-collared, mustard-colored polo shirt gave Rossi a friendly wave and pointed to an empty booth at the rear of the restaurant.

Rossi slid into the red imitation leather booth. John Tomei followed, scooting around so he was facing the bar. Rossi picked up the white linen table napkin folded flowerlike in a wineglass and used it to wipe his face.

"Man, I've been sweating like a pig lately. The doc says my blood pressure is high, my cholesterol is high, and if I'm going to fix 'em, I've got to stop getting high." He took a long pull on his glass, draining it, the cubes clicking against his teeth.

"What the hell do doctors know, anyway?" he said irritably, then signaled to the waitress for a refill. "Grand-Dad and water, honey."

"Who robbed you?" Tomei asked, looking over toward the bar. "And how long have the feds been following you?"

"You spotted some feds?" Rossi asked nervously, reaching into his breast pocket for a pair of glasses.

"Billy, anytime you see a pair of bored-looking suits parked in front of a fire hydrant, you can bet your roll they're feds. The city doesn't have the money to handle that kind of surveillance anymore." Tomei wondered if that was still true. He'd been out of touch for a long time.

"Maybe they're after someone else," Rossi speculated, reaching for the drink as the waitress approached. "You ready for another?"

Tomei placed a hand over his glass. "I'm fine."

When the waitress retreated, Tomei said, "The two guys near the front entrance. The big one has a crew cut. His partner is the little guy standing right next to him."

Rossi pushed the glasses down his nose and tilted his head back. "Yeah, I see them. Jesus. That's all I need." He put the glasses back in his pocket. "I've got to get a new prescription. Hell, it seems like all I'm doing these days is seeing docs. Who are they with? The FBI?"

"That's right. So tell me about the robbery."

"Three of them. Slants." He grimaced and appeared embarrassed. "Asians. They came right into my house. Little shits. But they had big, slick-looking guns. The kind those commandos use in the movies. The kind that our government banned. I guess the slants didn't hear about the ban. And a knife. A long-bladed sucker. One of the bastards stuck the tip up my nose. He said he was going to cut it off and make me eat it if I didn't open my safe. I believed him. He acted like he was the boss."

"How'd they get into the house, Billy?"

Rossi's shoulders rose a few inches. "They had to come right through the front door, I guess. I'm really not sure, Tomb."

"Don't you have a burglar alarm?"

"Yeah," Rossi answered sheepishly. "But it wasn't on. I don't activate the damn thing until I go to bed."

"When was this?"

"Monday. About eight o'clock."

"P.M.?"

"Yep. The football game was on."

"The Bears and Forty-niners?"

Rossi picked up the napkin and blotted his face again. "No, Monday the sixth. The Green Bay Packers and the Atlanta Falcons."

Monday-night football. Every bookie and every bettor in town would have been glued to a TV set. "Do you have any idea who they were?"

"Nope," Rossi conceded. "They had these stocking masks. Only the one with the knife did any talking. In English. At least to me. They were Chinese, Japanese, Viets. Who the hell can tell?"

"How old were they?"

"It's hard to say."

"Guess," Tomei insisted. "Fifteen or forty?"

Rossi scratched his jaw thoughtfully. "Well, the one who did the talking, he seemed older than the others. Maybe twenty-five, thirty, something like that. The other two were really skinny. Kids. Teenagers, I'd bet."

The waitress returned with two menus. "Are you ready to order now, Billy?"

Rossi fished a twenty-dollar bill from his roll and handed it to her. "Give us a few more minutes, will you, sugar?" He leaned back and took a leather cigar case from his coat. "Want one?"

Tomei declined with a nod.

Rossi extracted a cigar from the case, ran it under his nose, and sighed. "The doc says I can't have these anymore." He put the unlit cigar in his mouth, then said, "Those little buggers knew what they were looking for, Tomb. They knew about the big safe."

Rossi's safe was a chest high, Wells Fargo, two-ton antique monster that he claimed once housed the gold dust brought in by the early California prospectors at Sutter's Mill. "Anyone who has ever been to your house knows about that safe, Billy. How much did they take you for?"

"More than three hundred big ones, Tomb. Three hundred and eleven thou, to be precise."

Tomei winced. "Good thing they didn't know about the second safe."

"Yeah," Rossi grunted. "Good thing, huh? Nobody knows about that safe. Except you, of course. And your old partner, Gucci, and that posse you brought with you." Rossi picked up a fork and ran this thumb along the tines, remembering the day that then San Francisco Police Inspector John Tomei, along with his partner Elaine "Gucci" Surel, and a Vice Squad crew had come to his house, armed with a batch of search warrants and subpoenas.

Tomei had been suspicious about the prominently displayed Wells Fargo safe. He figured there had to be another one in the house somewhere, and eventually found it, well hidden in the wall behind a bureau. After some legal hassling, Rossi had opened up both of them. Fortunately for Rossi, he'd been expecting the raid and had transferred over a quarter of a million dollars in cash to a safe-deposit box just a few days earlier. All that was in those two safes were cigars. Big Cuban Monte Cristos.

Tomei was certain that someone had tipped Rossi off, but he never did find out just who that someone was. Whoever it was, he was sure that Rossi had shown his appreciation. In cash.

Tomei studied his menu. "It's a sad story, all right, Billy. But why tell me?"

"I certainly couldn't go to the cops, could I?" Rossi asked, turning his palms up in dismay. "I'm stuck for it, Tomb. There are certain losses you have to take in this business. That's just part of the game. But I don't like the way these guys played the game. They got really nasty."

Tomei peered over his menu at Rossi. "Did they rough you up?"

"Not too much. They stuck that blade up my nose, and I caved in. It's only money." He worked the cigar from one end of his mouth to the other. "Hell, my nose is about the only part I've got left that still works fairly well. But Sherri. They got rough with her. There was no need for it. And they slashed some of my paintings. No need for that either. I gave them the money.

That should have satisfied them. They made all kinds of threats. Warned me to get out of the business. They were taking over my territory. Called me a useless, gutless old fuck. No class. You know what I mean?"

"Yes. I know what you mean." Tomei looked for the FBI agents but they were nowhere in sight. He pulled a handful of sugar packets from a glass container and began stacking them like poker chips. "Why are you telling me this? I can't do you any good. You must know my situation."

"Yeah, yeah," Rossi grunted. "I was sorry to hear about you having to quit the department. I heard you were having a tough time, so I thought—"

"Who told you I was having a tough time?" Tomei wanted to know.

"Double G. He said you were living in some cabin up the Russian River and that you needed dough pretty bad."

Tomei tipped over the sugar stack. Double G. Garrett Griffin, a small-time bookie who ran a bar in Rio Nido, less than a mile from Tomei's cabin. He had tried to sell Griffin his boat. That was just before the bank took it away from him.

Rossi picked a piece of tobacco from the tip of his tongue. "Look. You busted me fair and square. There's no hard feelings. Those two hours you gave me were appreciated. Really appreciated."

Tomei nodded. When he arrived at Rossi's the night of the arrest, Rossi had been all decked out in a dark suit, looking more like a prosperous banker than a bookmaker. He'd told Tomei that he was on his way to the wake of an old friend. Tomei checked the obituary column in the newspaper. The name was there, and Tomei told Rossi to take off, but to be back in two hours. There really hadn't been much of a gamble in letting him go. Rossi was too smart to jeopardize what he was sure was going to be a light sentence by trying to make a run for it, like a caricature television crook. So Rossi went to the wake, and returned at the appointed time, armed with boxes of pizzas and beer.

Rossi leaned forward and lowered his voice. "I figure you could use a job, Tomb. These guys. They gave
me two weeks. If I haven't packed it in by then, they'll
come after me."

"That doesn't leave you much time, Billy."

"I know. Just eight days left. I've been going crazy.
Then I thought of you. I need a tough guy, like you,
Tomb. I'd like you to stay with me at the house." The
bookie held up a hand when Tomei started to protest.
"Just a few days. You don't have to hang around me
all the time, but I think it would make Sherri feel
better, you know what I mean?"

"Billy, I can't—"

"Five hundred bucks a day. How's that sound?" He
tapped his breast pocket. "I have an envelope here
with fifteen thousand bucks. Expenses. I'll pay you
wages for as long as it takes. You tell me what's fair,
and I'll pay you. Just take a look, okay? Poke around.
See what you can come up with."

Rossi rolled his hand into a fist. "I need someone
to make a statement for me. To show whoever hit me
that I'm not a toothless old fart who's just going to
lie down like a dog. You know what I mean, Tomb?"

Tomei nodded, then smoothed out a cocktail napkin. "I've been out of the game for a while, Billy. He
began drawing on the paper with a ballpoint pen.
After a couple of minutes, he slid the paper to Rossi.
"Is this the way it still works?"

Rossi looked at the diagram briefly. "That's it,
Tomb. Same old story."

Tomei took back the drawing and stared at his nota-
tions. A few of the original bets were made on the
street, usually at a bar, a restaurant, a dry cleaner, just
about anywhere, but the majority of the bets were
taken by phone, at an office—a small, bare room with
a bank of phones, handled by people called writers,
whose one and only job was to post the bets. To keep
the writers honest, all bets were recorded. Writers
were paid a few hundred dollars a day. Not much,
considering the amount of money they were booking,

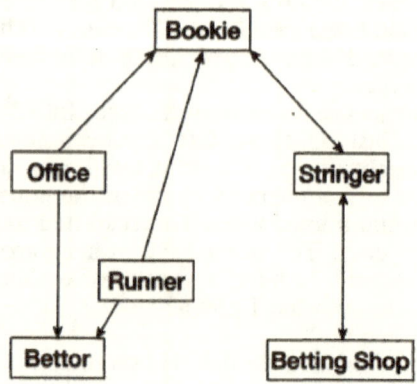

but it was all cash, and they were usually people who were working to pay off their gambling debts. The office would have a manager, someone to make sure the bets were handled correctly and who destroyed the tapes at the proper time.

Each bettor had a code number, usually a combination of letters and numbers: A-16, J-46, PA-33. The individual bets were handled with the same care that the Bank of America gave to a favored corporate client.

The bets from the street were turned over to a stringer, a man most people called a bookie but who was actually a go-between—the connection between the bettor and the bookie.

A stringer would have his own territory, his own list of customers. He would keep a running tab on their pluses or minuses, and would make his collections or payoffs once a week. A stringer's handle of the take would run somewhere between twenty-five and fifty percent of the action, the rest going to the bookie.

For the winners, and one of the things that Tomei had been surprised to learn was that there were consistent winners who might end the year several hundred thousand dollars in the black, the bookie would use a runner whose job it was to deliver the payoffs, though a lot of bookies had turned that job over to Federal Express.

Tomei vividly remembered following a runner who left Billy Rossi's house, drove to a nearby Federal Express office, and dropped off a package the size of a hardcover book. Later that day FedEx delivered that package to a thirty-three-year-old former stockbroker.

The following two Tuesdays, packages of a similar size were delivered to the same address. Going through subpoenaed records, Tomei had been able to identify the man through his betting number. He was a Stanford graduate who readily admitted that he was a "middler," a bettor who used a sophisticated, computer-run system, placing bets in particular situations when the point spread on a game varied slightly from one day to the next.

"Arbitrage. It's like arbitrage in the market," the Stanford man had explained to Tomei. "Only it's more fun."

A good many bookies had moved their operations to South America or the Bahamas, and ran their businesses via the Internet. They concentrated on small-time bettors who paid their losses and collected their winnings via their credit cards. Rossi catered to the cash-and-carry gamblers who bet substantial sums and wanted their winnings paid promptly, and in cash.

"Well, what do you think, Tomb? Can you help me?" Rossi asked, trying to sound casual, bringing Tomei's wandering mind back to the present.

"How many stringers do you have working for you, Billy?"

"Ten."

"Runners?"

"Four."

"Offices?"

"Three. Writers vary. It depends on the season. Maybe ten, maybe a little more."

Tomei rearranged the sugar packets in a neat line.

"That's a lot of people. These punks knew your house, and how to get into it. They knew that Monday night was prime time. They had help. It had to be someone working for you. It would take a lot of time to check them out." He shook his head. "You need half a dozen people. At least."

"But Tomb, I ain't got no Asians working for me. Not a one. And hardly any of my clients are Asians. A few at the most." He pulled the now soggy cigar from his mouth. "Nobody knows nothing about this. I ain't gonna let these guys kick me out of my business. You find out who set me up. You find some way to get that money back, and half of it is yours. No questions asked. What do you say?"

Chapter Four

"Look at them," Mayor Richard Barr shouted angrily, slapping the folded newspaper against his thigh. "Look at them!"

The object of Barr's fury was the expanding population of tents once again filling up the small park directly across from City Hall.

Barr leaned against the gilded balcony railing outside his office. He was a burly, energetic man with a fleshy face seamed with the marks of a lifelong worrier. His high forehead was pebbled with sweat and the veins on his neck stood out like purple cords.

It was one of those perfect late autumn days, sparkling blue skies, a bright sun driving away the slight chill in the air. Stretched out amid the patches of grass and the park benches was a ragtag mixture of tents— some simply blankets or sheets, their ends tied to the arthritic gnarled branches of the sycamore trees geometrically spaced along the park's paved paths.

The homeless were back, claiming the park to be theirs unless the mayor came up with a better alternative. It was the same problem that had caused Barr's predecessor to lose the election. To Richard Barr. Now they were back.

Damn unfair, Barr thought. He'd bent over backwards to find adequate housing, and busted his butt to find money in a stretched-thin city budget. Organized promotions, rock concerts, all with an eye to getting enough money to put in some permanent, low-cost shelters. And it had worked. Some of the old converted buildings didn't look much better than the army barracks he'd remembered from Vietnam. But they were clean. Warm. Safe.

But now the tents were springing up again. And in his own front yard. Right across from City Hall.

"It's that damn Philip Dong. That's who's behind it," Barr fumed, then turned abruptly on his heel, nearly knocking down his aide, Charles Prescott, as he strode purposefully by his secretary's desk, down a spacious hallway studded with photographs of his predecessors, past the huge walk-in safe that covered what legend said was once a secret stairway leading down to the first floor, a stairway that long ago Mayor Sunny Jim Rolph used to smuggle women into his personal office. Barr settled into the leather chair behind his desk, leaned back, looked at the ceiling, and wondered if that had been the late Mayor George Moscone's last earthly vision that fateful day back in 1977, when disgruntled supervisor and former policeman Dan White shot him. White calmly giving Moscone a coup de grâce, then reloading before walking down to the supervisor's chambers and shooting gay advocate Harvey Milk.

Barr dragged his eyes from the ceiling and tossed the folded newspaper to Charles Prescott.

"And what about this article?" Barr demanded.

Prescott, a slender man in his mid-thirties with pointy, foxlike features and neatly barbered glossy brown hair, caught the paper and shrugged his shoulders.

"It's a Phil Dong plant, all right, Mr. Mayor. No doubt about it. And I'm sure Dong has something to do with that damn village of tents across the street." He shrugged his shoulders as if to say, but what can I do about it?

"Of all the pictures of me, they have to pull that one out," Barr's voice rasped irritably. "You like the picture? It looks like a mug shot." He scraped his fingernails across his chin.

Prescott knitted his brow as he unfolded the newspaper and studied the photograph selected for the story. It had to have been taken at some political function years earlier. A late-into-the-evening political function. Barr had one of those beards that had to be shaved twice a day to keep the midnight shadow away. This was one of those times Barr hadn't bothered with a second shave. His features were slack, as if he'd had a few drinks. The thinning hair that was now a mousey-gray color was dark in the photograph.

"Did you read it?" Barr shouted. "Did you read the damn article?"

Prescott nodded, but to satisfy his boss he went over the article again.

"Mayor Accused of Accepting Mafia Money for Campaign" was in bold type. The story went into details of a two-thousand-dollar donation from the Remo Cheese Company, a firm with reported connections to the mob.

"A cheese company, for Christ's sake," Barr proclaimed. "It's your job to check out the donors, Charles. You're supposed to keep me away from these situations."

Prescott accepted the criticism without comment.

"You should have known about this cheese guy, damn it," Barr continued. "It's your responsibility."

"I admit I screwed up. I didn't know of any connections he had with the mob. Hell, Remo was a supporter in the last election. He's damn near ninety years old. Someone should have brought it out four years ago."

Barr leaned forward, the chair creaking in protest. "Yes, but I wasn't running against this *belino* Dong four years ago. He's really sticking it to me. Get a load of that name-change comment."

Prescott turned back to the newspaper article. The reporter made no mention of who had supplied him with the information of the Remo donation, but toward the end of the story he'd quoted Philip Dong, Barr's closest contender in the mayoral polls, as saying, "I know nothing about any association that Mayor Barr may have with organized crime, but I do find it interesting that his family name was Barrera, not Barr. After all, Michelangelo didn't change his name to Mike, or Angelo. One should not be ashamed of his heritage.

"We cannot allow organized crime to obtain a toe-hold in our community, and I promise, as mayor, I will make certain that does not happen. The death threats I have received recently have done nothing but hardened my resolve. I will not tolerate threats. The citizens of San Francisco will not tolerate threats from these hoodlums."

"That son of a bitch," Barr said hotly. "Did you see that crack about heritage? My grandfather sat on Ellis Island for two months, freezing his ass off. Then some lazy customs agent thought it was too much trouble to spell Barrera, so all of a sudden my grandfather was Mr. Barr." He slammed a fist down on the desktop, hard enough to cause a stapler to fall to the carpet.

The election was in eight days and Barr's once formidable lead in the polls had been slipping. It was close now. Too close to call. Barr had worked his way through the maze of San Francisco politics, from assessor to supervisor and finally to mayor. He wanted that second term. Wanted it badly. At least the first half of the second four-year term. As soon as the mayoral election was over, his plan was to start the campaign for state senator, an election just two years away. If he lost this race for mayor, he'd have no chance at the senator's seat.

Barr had learned early that to win in San Francisco you had to have the coalitions behind you: black, white, labor, civil service, and the gay community. They all voted in blocs. Lose one labor organization and all of them were ready to vote against you. Offend one lesbian action group and the whole gay vote was likely to go down the drain.

One bloc that Barr had always counted as being in

his pocket was the Chinese community. The Chinese had never actually voted in heavy numbers before, but the leaders, the kingpins, donated a lot of money to campaigns. Having Chinatown behind you was a big plus. No one had won a mayoral race in the last thirty years without that Chinatown money.

Now some of that money was going to Philip Dong. Worse than that, Dong was getting the Asian community to register to vote. Someone had likened it to the bygone days of Chicago-style politics. All those signatures on the ballot for the first time. Barr was sure that ninety-nine percent of the new registrants had no idea of what they would be voting for. Most didn't speak English. Many of them were no doubt illegals, who weren't entitled to vote. Stacked up like cordwood in dingy one-room units in the Chinatown projects. But who was going to challenge them in time for the election? The bilingual ballots were a joke. The simpletons that drafted the initiatives for the ballots were under the impression that they could have the voter pamphlets printed in English, Spanish, and Cantonese and be done with it. They hadn't counted on the screams of protest from the French and German communities, not to mention the Slavs, the Japanese, the Thais, the Filipinos, and the Chinese: Cantonese, Shanghainese, Mandarin, Hakkas, and a half dozen more that Barr had never heard of. San Francisco was a melting pot that was disintegrating, breaking up into small, hard-nosed groups that wanted things their way and the hell with the other guys.

No, it wouldn't be possible to challenge the voters Philip Dong was loading the rolls with. Not in time for the election. And after, if he complained, Barr would have the noose of racial prejudice hung around his neck for all to see. Another political dead end.

Dong was something of a mystery man, an unknown until two years ago when he ran for supervisor and surprised everyone by garnering more votes than any other candidate, which made him the president of the board of supervisors, the second most powerful job in the city, second only to the mayor himself.

Dong had made millions in real estate in Hong Kong before moving to San Francisco. He was snapping up derelict properties all over town, upgrading them, installing mini-parks, baseball diamonds, and basketball courts. He'd positioned himself as a staunch law-and-order advocate who liked nothing better than climbing into a patrol car and cruising the streets at night.

Four months ago, when Barr's poll numbers showed him thirty points ahead of all four mayoral challengers, Philip Dong was nothing more than a mild pain in the ass.

But the other two men had dropped out of the race, and thrown their support to Dong. Which made him a major pain in the ass now.

Barr rose abruptly, thrust his hands in his pockets and grimaced. "We have to get something on Dong, Charles. Go see Kan Chin. He's probably still pissed off because I didn't give him everything he wanted after the last election. Feel him out. If Chin can give us something we can use against Dong, tell him I'll bend over backwards to accommodate him this time. Tell him whatever you have to, but get me some dirt on Philip Dong."

Chapter Five

John Tomei followed Billy Rossi's progress as he walked over to the blond woman who was still sitting at the bar. Rossi was anything but discreet as he peered though his glasses looking for the federal agents Tomei had pointed out to him.

The fact that the two FBI men had melted into the crowd as soon as they'd noticed Rossi's attention appeared to confirm that Rossi was their target.

Tomei felt no regrets in fingering the two agents. He had come to the conclusion that investigating and prosecuting independent bookies was a waste of valuable police department manpower. It was one of the reasons he'd left the Vice Squad. Or had been pushed out. He had drawn up a rough estimate of the time and money it had taken to make a case against Billy Rossi. He and Elaine "Gucci" Surel had worked six- and seven-day weeks, piling up overtime. There had been three other members of the squad also putting in full-time shifts. The wiretaps, the surveillance teams, the involvement of the district attorney. The court time. His best guess was that the entire operation had cost more than three quarters of a million dollars. And for what? Putting Rossi away for all of three months.

The hypocrisy of it had bothered Tomei from the start. He knew cops, parole officers, even judges who used a bookie on a regular basis. Guys like Billy Rossi never bothered anyone. They weren't connected to the mob. They didn't sideline in drugs, and if their clients ended up owing them a lot of money, there was never any of that "break his legs" stuff. The losers were either carried until their debt was paid off, or else the money was written off, the offender suffering little more than a loss of dignity and the difficulty of finding another bookie to take his money. "You break a guy's arms or legs because of a bad debt, then all you got is a guy in the hospital dumping his guts out to the cops," was the way a veteran stringer had explained it to Tomei. "There's lots of money to be made. Why make waves?"

Tomei's complaints had not gone over very well with his captain, who responded hotly: "If you don't like going after bookies, then get the hell out of here!" Tomei had resisted taking the captain's recommendation, but soon found himself transferred to the Juvenile detail.

If the FBI agents had been narcs from the DEA, or were with the Secret Service, or Alcohol, Tobacco and Firearms, he would have kept silent, but there was a long-standing grudge between the San Francisco Police Department and the FBI. In fact, a long-standing grudge between the FBI and all local and other federal agencies. The old-timers still groused about the days when Bobby Kennedy was attorney general. Kennedy had placed hundreds of illegal wiretaps in Las Vegas hotels and casinos in his attempts to nail Teamster boss Jimmy Hoffa.

The mobsters retaliated by initiating civil suits against the phone company, which in turn shut off everything—including unlisted telephone numbers—to the FBI. Their agents had to come with hat in hand to the Hall of Justice and ask the local cops to pull the unpublished phone numbers.

Other rumors had the tension dating all the way back to the J. Edgar Hoover days when the FBI was King of the Hill. That pompous, "holier than thou" attitude still seemed to prevail.

There were many stories kicking around about Hoover. Tomei's favorite, and one a Secret Service agent swore to him to be true, was when Hoover was in a cost-cutting frenzy and noticed that a lengthy report sent to his attention had wasted space by not using up the full proportions of the pages. Hoover had scribbled a note—"Watch the borders!"—on the side of the report. His minions had interpreted Hoover's concern to be the Canadian and Mexican borders, rather than the margins on letter-sized bond paper, and had dispatched dozens of agents north and south. After a couple of days one weary FBI agent had cabled a question from El Paso, Texas. "What are we watching for?"

It had become a standing joke. Whenever a cop wanted to needle an FBI agent, all he had to say was "Watch the borders."

Tomei tried to put a name to the tall, crew-cut FBI man. Don. Don something or other. Don had stuck his nose into a stolen property sting several years ago, blowing away months of hard work by the Pawnshop detail.

He carefully stacked the sugar packets one on top of the other, reaching a height of twenty packs before they toppled over. It was a game he and his daughter played when they went out to breakfast or lunch. He thought about Billy Rossi's offer of five hundred bucks a day, plus fifteen thousand dollars, for expenses. And half of the money the gang had stolen from Rossi, if he could somehow get it all back. There wasn't much of a chance of that happening. But he could certainly use the money the bookie was offering up front. But could he do Rossi any good? Rossi wanted a show of strength. To hit back. How was he going to get a lead on the three Asians who pulled the heist? The streets were full of punks who would be happy to apply for that kind of work. And it was certainly possible that the men who had ripped off Rossi were working for one of his Caucasian competitors and not an Asian gang.

Sherri Dawson handed Tomei a martini on the rocks. "Billy said you wanted this."

"Thank you," Tomei answered, reaching for the glass. He rose halfway out of his seat. "Please sit down."

She slid gracefully into the booth, sitting up straight, shoulders squared.

Tomei held the drink up to his nose, inhaled the pungent smell of the gin, then said, "Billy thought you might be able to help me get a line on the trio that robbed him and worked you over. Did you get a good look at them?"

"Not their faces," she answered in a deep, bottom of the barrel voice.

"Is Sherry your real name?"

"Yep. Sherri, with an *i*. It's short for Sherrilyn. Sherrilyn Dawson. I guess you want my date of birth and Social Security number, too, huh?"

"Hey. Don't get rattled. I'm just trying to find out what happened," Tomei pointed out. He set the drink down and picked up the cloth dinner napkin and began folding it.

"What did Billy tell you?" she countered.

"Just that they barged into the house. One of them put a knife to Billy's face and he surrendered. He said they got tough with you."

She touched her hair, rearranging a curl. "Yes. You could say that."

"How tough?"

"We were in the TV room watching the game, and they just came out of nowhere. They grabbed me. One of them slapped me and I guess it was stupid, but I slapped him back." She looked into Tomei's eyes to see if he agreed with her assessment.

Tomei gave her a slight shrug of his shoulders.

"Then one of them shoved the barrel of his gun into my stomach. Hard. Hard enough to knock the wind out of me. You know what came next."

Tomei creased the napkin and connected the ends. "Tell me, anyway."

Sherri made a clucking sound with her tongue. "Are you some kind of a voyeur?"

"Tell me about it, Sherri," Tomei replied softly. "I know it was ugly. I know it's not easy going back to it, remembering it, but if I'm going to help, I've got to know it all."

She leaned back, mildly surprised at Tomei's attitude.

"Well, two of them dragged me into the living room and the one that hit me in the stomach shoved the gun into my mouth." Her hand went to her lips. "He damn near chipped a tooth. The other one gestured with his hands. I got the meaning. Take off my clothes. I don't think they could speak English. I heard them say something. I can't remember what it was. Some kind of Chinese, I guess."

She paused, gave Tomei an inquiring glance, then pointed at his untouched glass. "Are you going to drink that?"

Tomei slid his martini across the table to her. "It's all yours."

She took a deep swallow of the drink, then said, "So I did it. Stripped, I mean. They were laughing and giggling. They acted like high school kids. They pushed me onto the couch, one of them held my hands above my head while the other one raped me. They took turns like that. The first one holding my hands while his partner took a turn."

She took another pull at the martini. "Then the third guy came in. The really kinky creep. He had strips of rope with him. He tied my hands and feet— stretched me out so I couldn't move."

"Was it straight intercourse, or did they do other things?"

Sherri stared at the drink in her hand. "Yeah, other things. All the other things. You really want the details?"

"No. Did they keep their stocking masks on?"

"Yeah. Their masks and their shoes. That was about it."

Tomei laughed lightly. The lady had spunk. "Anything unusual about them? Scars. Deformities."

"No. I kept my eyes closed a lot."

"How long have you lived in San Francisco, Sherri?"

"Three or four months."

"Where before that?"

Sherri Dawson moistened her lips with the tip of her tongue. "Why the sudden interest in me?"

"I just want to get the full picture."

She cocked her head to one side, a hand going to her hair, then exhaled deeply, as if she'd come to a difficult decision. "I was born in Texas. Eventually I landed in New York City. I did a few shows. Nothing big. Just the chorus. I spent some time in Florida, then went to Las Vegas. The last few years in Vegas."

"Is that where you met Billy Rossi?"

"No. I've had it with Vegas. I came here, and met him at the track. But what's this got to do with what happened at Billy's house?" She reached for her purse, digging out a pack of cigarettes and a disposable lighter. "What the hell are you doing with that napkin?" she asked irritably.

Tomei glanced down, surprised to see the napkin in his hands. "It's supposed to be a mouse. Force of habit, I guess. My daughter . . . gets a kick out of things like that."

Sherri reached across the table and picked up the "mouse" by its ears. "Hey. That's not bad." She studied it for a moment, then dropped it to her lap.

"Why didn't you call the cops?" Tomei asked. "Did Billy stop you?"

She clicked the lighter several times before it lit, held it to the cigarette with a steady hand, then blew a thick plume of smoke toward the ceiling.

"No. Billy was great. He said it was okay to call the cops."

"Why didn't you?"

Sherri began clicking her lighter, staring into the flame. "Would it have done any good?" she finally said. "The first time I was raped, I was ten years old. By my stepfather. I told my mother about it and all she did was cry. You know what my older sister told me? 'I'm surprised he waited this long.' That's what she told me. Honest to God." She rubbed the glowing end of the cigarette back and forth across the surface of the restaurant's ashtray.

"There were other times when some tough guy wouldn't take no for an answer. It leaves scars, mister. Lots of scars. Face it. You're never going to find these punks. Never."

"How we doing?" Billy Rossi asked, passing Tomei a fresh drink before sliding into the booth.

"There's not much to go on," Tomei said fingering the sugar packets.

"What about the tattoo? Did Sherri tell you about the tattoo?"

Tomei's head snapped up. "What tattoo?"

Rossi glanced nervously at Sherri Dawson and lowered his voice. "One of those punks came back to me. I was tied to the chair. He's the one that slashed all my paintings. He grabbed me by what's left of my hair and stuck the blade up my nose again." He looked at Sherri again and shifted uneasily. "He had his shirt off. The little sucker had a tattoo. Letters. Just two letters. W.G. With a circle around them." Rossi raised his arm and touch the area under his left bicep. "Right here. Does that help?"

Tomei knocked the sugar packets over with a flick of his finger. "It might, Billy. It just might."

Chapter Six

The tattoo meant nothing to Tomei. He had little knowledge of Asian gangs. When he was in the department, just about everything that went down in Chinatown had been handled by the Intelligence Division.

If he could come up with a gang name relating to the tattooed initials, he might indeed be able to earn some of Rossi's money.

"I thought I lost you there for a moment," Billy Rossi said, waving his drink in front of Tomei. "The tattoo helps, huh?"

"Maybe. Did it look professionally done? How big was it?"

Rossi held up his hand, widening his index finger a couple of inches from his thumb. "About like that, I guess, Tomb. I couldn't tell if a pro did it. Now that I think of it, it was kind of wobbly, maybe."

Tomei looked at Sherri Dawson. "Did you see the tattoo?"

"I told you. I kept my eyes closed a lot."

"Could all three of them have had tattoos?"

"Give me a break, will you? I don't know. I don't want to know," Sherri protested, her voice thick with exasperation. She began undoing Tomei's mouse napkin, her long, red-polished fingernails picking at the knots.

Rossi leaned over, pulled an envelope from his coat pocket, and passed it under the table to Tomei.

"Here's the dough, Tomb. Do what you have to do. If you need more, just let me know."

"If I look into this, there's a possibility things could get a little rough. You say these guys warned you off going to the police."

"Yeah. But you're not the police anymore, Tomb."

"I'll do what I can, but no promises."

Rossi sighed, wiped his face and nodded all at the same time. "Good. I appreciate that."

Tomei pushed his drink toward Sherri. "I've got to get going. I have a few things to clear up."

"Here," Rossi said, taking out his wallet and extracting a business card, which showed his name and a telephone number. "You remember where I live. I've got plenty of room. You can stay with me as long as you want." He glanced at Sherri Dawson. "Right, babe?"

"It's your house," she answered dryly.

Rossi patted her on the arm. "Everything okay with you, babe?"

"As good as it's going to get," she answered without enthusiasm, rummaging in her purse for cigarettes.

Tomei rose to his feet. "Let's see just how interested the feds are in you, Billy. Where are you parked?"

"We took a cab," Rossi answered.

"Call for one now. Have it meet you right out in front in twenty minutes."

"Where am I going?"

"Wherever you want. I just want to see if the feds tail you."

"Shit," growled Rossi. "First the slants rob me, then the feds jump on my back." He patted Sherri's hand. "I going to pay those pricks back for what they did to you, babe."

The two FBI agents were sitting in their car when John Tomei exited the restaurant. The name of the big man with the crew cut suddenly popped into Tomei's head. Jamison. Like the Scotch. Don Jamison.

He crossed Union Street, slowly approaching the car. Jamison rolled the window down and gave him a half smile.

"Watch the borders," Tomei called out, not breaking stride.

He heard Jamison's, "Fuck you, Tomei," as he turned the corner onto Fillmore Street.

Chapter Seven

John Tomei walked up Fillmore in long, easy strides, his pace increasing to a jog once he had turned onto Green Street. He turned left again on Webster, running now, occasionally twisting around to see if anyone was following him.

He paused when he got back to Union Street, edging into the doorway of a Mexican restaurant. No one seemed to have any interest in him other than the restaurant proprietor who was waving a menu in his direction.

Tomei crossed the street and made his way slowly through the crowded sidewalks. A Starbucks coffee shop gave him the cover he needed. He ordered a cup of coffee and sat in a chair by the window that provided him a view of the entrance of Sully's Bar & Grill, and, more important to Tomei, of the FBI car.

He sipped at the coffee and checked his watch. Rossi was due out any minute. A Yellow cab pulled up in front of Sully's. The driver double-parked and beeped his horn. A tall, thick-bodied, dark-haired man in a charcoal overcoat exited the restaurant. He looked vaguely familiar to Tomei. Fleshy face, protruding jaw. A cocky, get-out-of-my-way walk. The man went over to the cab, got into a heated exchange with the driver, then opened the back door and climbed in.

The cabbie was throwing up his hands in frustration.

The big man stuck his head out of the cab's window and shouted something. The driver got behind the wheel and took off.

The FBI car pulled away from the curb moments later, driving west on Union Street behind the cab.

Tomei heaved a sigh of relief. So it wasn't Billy Rossi who had drawn the federal agents' interest. Just a coincidence that they'd been following someone when Rossi scheduled their meeting.

Tomei tried placing the big man's face. Where had he seen it? No one he had ever busted. Someone involved in a case years back? Someone— He suddenly slapped his hand on the window counter, loud enough to startle the man reading his newspaper at the next table.

Christ. Dino Lanzoni. Nick Lanzoni's kid brother. Nick Lanzoni, head of one of the five New York crime families, who just months ago had been sentenced to life in prison. The feds had been hitting the Mafia families hard. Tomei remembered one optimistic news reporter saying that the New York families were crumbling. One so-called expert predicted, "The families would be reduced to the level of street gangs within a decade."

Good luck on that, thought Tomei. They'd never go away, but there was no doubt they were hurting. He had followed the progress of the case against Lanzoni in the newspapers. Nick Lanzoni, a soft-spoken, priestly looking man, was a throwback to the old dons. He knew when to open his mouth, and when to keep it tightly shut while he directed the mob's bread-and-butter operations: drugs, loan sharking, prostitution, casino skimming, labor union racketeering. Nick Lanzoni had been trying to drag the mob back to those good-old days, when there was a reverent respect for the top Mafioso. But the old blood was running thin, and there were no replacements willing to put up with the time-honored codes of family-contracted marriages; defined territories; residing in small, lower-middle-class homes with their fathers, mothers, and cousins; living what looked to be a workingman's life, while all that nontaxed cash built up in numbered off-shore accounts.

The new breed was like Dino Lanzoni. Flaunting their money, marrying busty Atlantic City showgirls instead of nice Sicilian maidens who couldn't speak English.

Unlike Nick, who worked behind the scenes, Dino was a known shooter, a killer, a "made man" who bragged about his scores.

What the hell was Dino Lanzoni doing in San Francisco? So far as Tomei knew, there had only been three certified Italian Mafia hits made in San Francisco. The first dating back to 1947 when the body of a Chicago hood named Nick DeJohn was found bound with leather thongs in the trunk of a car, the leather tied in such a way that when DeJohn struggled to get free, he ended up strangling himself.

Joe Barbozza, the second victim, was blown to pieces on a Sunset district sidewalk in 1976. The rumors around at that time were that Barbozza was trying to set up a loan shark business in San Francisco, but had done so without the permission of the Chicago families.

A year later a third confirmed hit was the botched job on a father and son, Orlando and Peter Catelli, both shot and left for dead in the trunk of a car. The father, Orlando, had survived his wounds and pounded on the car's trunk with a hammer until someone heard the noises and called the police.

Of the hundreds of known homicides since then, not one had been attributed to the Mafia.

While the notorious hit man turned federal informer Jimmy "The Weasel" Fratiano had lived most of his life in San Francisco, the killings that he performed for the mob, many of which were thought to be exaggerated by people Tomei considered to be in the know, were all done out of state.

One story was that years ago the old dons had fingered San Francisco as a "neutral zone." Someplace

close to Nevada where they could go and mingle without the cops breathing down their backs.

There were some old retired Mafioso living out the
remainder of their lives in the South Bay and in Marin
County, but they kept to themselves, running profit-
able, legitimate businesses, and, for the most part,
"staying clean."

So what was Dino Lanzoni doing in San Francisco?
Tomei asked himself. Having lunch at the same place
that he met with a bookie who claims he was ripped
off for more than three hundred thousand dollars. Coincidence? God, how he hated coincidences.

Chapter Eight

Charles Prescott was herded into the street-level, grillwork freight elevator under the guidance of two tough-looking young men dressed in black pants and jackets. Prescott could make out the shadowy figures of more of the young hoodlums glaring at him through wooden slats as the elevator groaned and clattered its way up past the second and third floors. After that, all he saw was rough, unfinished cement as they zoomed up to the penthouse.

When the elevator door clanked open, Kan Chin nodded quickly to the young men, who bowed deeply from the waist before closing the elevator's doors.

"It was good of you to see me," Charles Prescott said to his host.

"It is my pleasure."

Prescott had met with Chin several times in the past, but always at a Chinatown restaurant, or in the back of Chin's Mercedes. This was the first time he'd been invited to Chin's residence, the top floor of the tallest building in Chinatown.

"This way," said Chin. Prescott followed the diminutive Chinese down a hallway of polished ebony hardwood floors and pale gray grass-papered walls bare of ornamentation.

Prescott paid close attention to every move Kan Chin made. So small, so thin, so . . . so old-looking. Old and frail, as if a good wind could pick him up and kite him out to the ocean. Only the man's voice gave any hint of his power. Prescott had seen men, powerful men, either physically, politically, or financially, wilt when Kan Chin raised that voice a bare octave.

An intricately carved, orange neolithic tea table was the focal point of the living room. A pair of foot-high cobalt-blue-and-white porcelain Chinese devil dogs silently growled at each other from opposite ends of the table.

"Sit, please." Chin gestured to a pale green sofa set directly across from a wall that was covered with an ornate Oriental mural depicting red-and-gold fire-breathing dragons engaged in combat.

"It was gracious of you to see me," Prescott said, once he was settled on the couch. "Did you read this morning's paper?"

Chin turned, and smiled a mirthless smile. "Ah, yes. I can understand where that might cause Mayor Barr some discomfort."

A doll-faced Asian girl, who appeared to be in her early teens, cloaked in a clinging snow-white gown that reached from her chin to ankles, entered quietly, carrying a tray in her tiny hands.

The tray held a bottle of whiskey, two glasses, and a small silver ice bucket. She bowed to Chin, set the tray on the jade table, then gracefully backpedaled from the room.

Kan Chin picked up a bottle of Knob Creek bourbon from the tray. There was a sharp cracking sound as he broke the sealed cap of the whiskey bottle. He tonged ice into two glasses, then drizzled in some bourbon. Prescott smiled inwardly. He could not remember having had a drink with the man, but Chin somehow knew his favorite brand of liquor.

Prescott accepted the glass, then said, "Your home is beautiful."

Chin bobbed his head in agreement. "How can I be of assistance?" he asked pointedly.

"The mayor misses your support."

Chin removed his glasses and gently massaged the bridge of his nose. "We have been of some support to Mayor Barr."

"Yes," Prescott agreed. Chin had already contributed to the reelection committee.

"But we need more help. Time is getting very short."

Chin took a handkerchief from his pocket and began polishing his glasses. "I don't know if the treasurer would release any more money at this time."

"It's not only money that we seek, Mr. Chin, though we certainly would appreciate any additional donations. What we really need is ammunition."

"Ammunition?"

"Yes. To counter the accusations that are being made against Mayor Barr. The charges are ridiculous of course, but hard to disprove. What we need is something to . . . to counterbalance those charges."

"Ah. I see. Ammunition against Philip Dong."

"Yes, sir. Exactly."

"Ammunition such as that would be quite valuable."

"We're prepared to reward the provider."

"Precisely how?" Chin asked patiently, probing like a dentist.

Prescott took a swig of his drink before replying. "Mayor Barr will be making a great many changes in his new administration. Rearranging his staff, his committees, his commissioners. He would appreciate your input in filling some of those positions."

Chin's voice was soft and eminently reasonable. "Mayor Barr was not that attentive to my suggestions four years ago. How many positions are we talking about, Mr. Prescott?"

"That would have to be negotiated."

When Chin didn't respond, Prescott added, "I'm sure that five or six would not be an unreasonable number . . . if the information is useful."

Prescott thought he had one ace up his sleeve and that this might be the only chance he'd get to play it. "Mr. Chin, from what I hear, Philip Dong plans to make some radical changes in the way business is conducted in the city. I don't think his ideas would be in your best interest. Mayor Barr values your friendship, and he has personally assured me that he will honor all of his commitments this time."

Kan Chin gave a murmur of approval, then said, "I may be able to help you with both of your needs—money and information. I will make some inquiries in Hong Kong and the mainland. No one acquires the amount of wealth Philip Dong has without . . . what is the saying? 'Cutting a few corners.' "

"Your help will be greatly appreciated, sir. I'm sure you can appreciate that we need the information very soon."

Chin gave Prescott a wide grin, exposing a set of small, tobacco-stained teeth. "That is what friends are for. To help each other. I will place some calls, then get back to you."

After Charles Prescott was back in the elevator, Chin poured the remains of his drink into the ice bucket. Out of the corner of his eye he saw the well-polished shoes of Philip Dong approaching.

Chin considered himself a linguist, fluent in English, French, and German. He used Cantonese, the language of Hong Kong, when talking with Willy Hon and the rest of his employees. It was only when he was with Philip Dong that he had the pleasure of conversing in Mandarin, a language he considered superior to all others.

"You heard?" Chin asked, without looking up.

"Yes."

"What do you think?"

"We have hit a nerve. They're worried."

"Indeed they are," Chin agreed. "Things are falling into place, Philip. Mr. Lanzoni is in town, and the FBI found him at the bar, along with Mr. Rossi."

Dong settled down next to Chin and crossed one leg over the other, revealing a section of sock and smooth-skinned leg. "Rossi's business is worth quite a bit to you, isn't it, Kan?"

"Indeed. But not nearly as much as your being elected mayor."

"Do you think Richard Barr will figure out that you're backing me?"

"Yes. He is not an ignorant man. But by then it will be too late."

Dong nodded his agreement. Barr had made a major error in reneging on his promises to Kan Chin. Many of the commission appointments Barr had guaranteed, in return for Chin's support, went to his other backers. Chin had suffered a loss of face.

Kan Chin clapped his hands together and the girl in the snow-white dressed hurried into the room.

"Remove the tray," Chin ordered. "And bring champagne. We have reason to celebrate, Philip."

Chapter Nine

The squawking of blue jays woke John Tomei from a deep, alcohol-saturated sleep. At first he didn't know where he was, then his eyes blinked into focus and he saw the knotty pine ceiling. He was home. Home used to be a three-bedroom, three-bath, thirty-six-hundred-square-foot split-level with a pool, a spa, and a sauna in one of the posher areas of Novato. Now it was a two-room cabin balanced on rotting stilts overlooking the Russian River.

When he and his wife, Joan, bought the cabin, there had been a line, like the ring around a bathtub, etched across the cabin walls, indicating just where the rain-swollen Russian River had crested during one of the floods that seemed to hit the area every six or seven years. They'd gutted the place down to the studs and replaced the decaying walls with knotty pine. Joan loved knotty pine, so the ceilings were paneled also.

Tomei swore at the birds, threw back the blankets, and climbed unsteadily to his feet. He padded toward the kitchen, then stopped in midstride and glanced back at the bed. There had been a woman at the bar last night. They had danced. He remembered that much. He moved back toward the bed. No woman. Just a tangle of sheets and blankets.

He put on his Levi's, wriggled his feet into his desert boots, and headed to the kitchen in a stiff-jointed manner.

Tomei had been a hard-nosed defensive back at U.C. Berkeley, and was good enough, even with a knee injury in his senior year, to have been a late-round draft choice by the Green Bay Packers. He had survived training camp, but was cut before the season got under way. "A Clydesdale chasing racehorses" was the way he described the experience to friends.

Coffee. God, he needed coffee. He tried to estimate how long it had been since he'd gotten drunk. Really drunk. "The incident," as his now ex-wife and both of their attorneys called it, had taken place almost two years ago. After a few false starts, he'd gone on the wagon. And had stayed there for six or seven months. The way his stomach felt, he might just climb aboard that wagon again. His hand shook and the pot clattered against the top of the coffee machine when he poured water into it.

After his meeting with Billy Rossi, Tomei had driven home, seventy-two miles, across the Golden Gate Bridge, to Sonoma County.

He thought about his ex-wife, Joan. Shortly after they were married, she'd gone to work for a small high-tech firm in the Media Gulch District of San Francisco. In less than a year, she was pulling down more money than Tomei was making as a police inspector. There were a couple of years where her salary was double his. Then the company really hit pay dirt and Joan's stock options suddenly made her very rich. She bought a Porsche, put Messy into a private school, and made sure there was a tutor around to instruct Messy in the important things in life, like tennis, equestrian training, and ballet. They'd had tremendous arguments over all of it, Tomei worried that his daughter was missing her childhood.

After the divorce, his visitation rights were set for two days every other weekend. The last time he and Messy were together it had been for three wonderful days at the cabin—fishing, canoeing, walking the trails, swimming in the river. Joan had bargained with him, letting him have the extra day so that she could later take Messy on a trip. So this weekend he'd be with her just the one day. Sunday. And one day wasn't enough.

Joan's company had given up their San Francisco warehouse loft and moved to Gilroy, some eighty miles south of San Francisco. Shortly after that, Joan had married the company's founder, Vernon Gardner, and they purchased a mansion in the hills near their new office complex.

Tomei had been prepared to hate Gardner, but the newly minted multimillionaire had turned out to be a nice guy who was obviously fond of Messy. But Joan's comment that they might be moving to New Mexico had thrown him for a loop. He had a tough enough time coaxing his beat-up pickup truck down to Gilroy to see Messy.

Joan was ready, willing, and financially prepared to take Tomei to court to get permission to move Messy out of state. Tomei had spent every cent he had fighting the civil suit resulting from "the incident." The neighboring fireman Tomei had shot at had filed an action claiming he was entitled to five hundred thousand dollars for his "pain and suffering."

Tomei's attorney had urged him to settle the case. "A hundred grand, and he'll go away."

But Tomei didn't have a hundred thousand dollars. The divorce and criminal trial had eaten up all his money. And now Joan was threatening to take him to court again. Two days ago he'd received a letter from his attorney, Dave Levy. Along with a demand for payment of the fees Tomei still owed Levy was a copy of a letter Levy had received from Joan's attorney. Joan wanted to "come to a comfortable understanding" regarding a revision of visitation and relocation rights. The letter was a cleverly worded legal threat. Give in, give up, or we'll take you to court and bury you. He needed money. A lot of it. And in a hurry.

He pulled the glass coffeepot from the machine while it was not yet half-full, spilling the coffee onto the kitchen counter in his haste to get some of the liquid into a cup. He carried the coffee out to the spare bedroom. The walls were decorated with his daughter's old crayon sketches.

He clicked on the computer and two-fingered his way into the Hotmail website, smiling when he saw that he had mail.

He hurriedly pulled up Messy's e-mail.

hi pop—it's hot down here in florida, but disneyland is great. vern's jet is tight! we got here in a couple of hours. zoom! how's the fishing? say hi to george and gertrude. see you soon.
  love, melissa.

Tomei sipped at his coffee and stared at the computer screen. Disneyland. Florida. Last month Joan had taken Messy to New York. The coming week they were going to Sante Fe, New Mexico, to check out Gardner's new plant site. Next month it was Vale, Colorado, where Gardner had just bought a chalet. In Gardner's jet. A twelve-million-dollar aircraft and his daughter thought it was "tight."

Tomei switched off the computer and walked slowly out to the deck.

He leaned over the redwood railing. It wobbled under his weight. It needed repairing. So did the pilings holding up the deck. He stared down some twenty feet to the sluggish, muddy-green waters of the Russian River. The slope leading to the river was steep, thick with pines, scrub oaks, ferns, and madrone. The air still had a crisp, autumn smell to it. Some of his neighbors had their woodstoves working, sending curly, dark-gray ribbons of smoke wafting toward the slate-colored clouds.

The two blue jays, who Messy had dubbed George and Gertrude, were still at it, hopping from tree to tree, screeching at each other like couples in a TV sitcom.

He went back to the kitchen for more coffee, then took some stale bread out of the refrigerator, breaking it into pieces that he tossed onto the deck floor.

Within minutes the Steller's jays appeared, their crests jet black, their bodies a sleek bluish gray. They suspended their squawking long enough to snatch a piece of the bread and fly off.

"You guys have it made," Tomei protested, watching as one of the birds stabbed at a piece the size of a pack of cigarettes. "Just make enough noise and you get fed." He went back inside and used the phone, dialing the number from memory.

"Vice Squad," answered the booming voice of a young woman.

"Let me talk to Gucci," Tomei said, stretching out a hand for the coffeepot.

"John, you've been a bad boy," Inspector Elaine Surel chided when they were connected. "It's been months. I'm worried about you. You're turning into a hermit. How are you?"

"Hanging in there, Gucci. I need a little help." Tomei provided Surel with Sherri Dawson's full name. "She's thirty-something and says she was living in Las Vegas for the last few years. Run her every way you can think of, Gooch."

Elaine crossed her legs and smoothed her skirt. "Who is she? A new love?"

"Not mine. She belongs to Billy Rossi. Remember him? I also want to find out about an Asian gang. All I know is that they have tattoos, the letters *w* and *g* circled under their biceps. Is Red Vanes still running the Intelligence detail?"

"My, my. You have been away a long time. Intelligence was disbanded and Vanes quit the department. It wasn't a happy parting of the ways." She lowered her voice. "Let's talk about it later. Are you in town?"

"I'm on my way. How about I meet you at church for lunch. Say one o'clock. I have to stop at Rossi's house this morning. Get me Vanes's home address and phone number, if you can."

"Okay," Elaine said, lowering her voice. "I'm bringing someone along. I think you'll like her."

John Tomei pulled up in front of Billy Rossi's address on Pacific Avenue and switched off the Toyota's engine. The fog was thick and low to the ground. Rossi's house was a rambling, half-timbered Tudor with medieval diamond-pane windows that were sheathed by the fine mist. Tomei could barely make out the neighboring properties. He pulled his suitcase from the back of the truck and walked slowly up the shrub-lined path to the front door. The polished silver door knocker was in the shape of a horseshoe.

"Come on in, come on in," Billy Rossi said with a one-sided grimace. He was wearing an unbuttoned plaid flannel shirt. Under the shirt was a black mesh garment. Around his waist was a leather-tooled belt and holster. The holster held a pearl-handled revolver. Both of his hands were clinging to a dog's chain collar. "Sit, Fidel, sit."

Fidel was a huge, gray black German shepherd. His feet made clicking sounds on the tile entry as he tried to free himself from Rossi's nervous grasp.

Rossi yanked on the choke collar. "Ninety-five pounds. Goddamn dog cost me seven grand," Rossi protested, wheezing at the effort of controlling the animal. "You'd think he would behave better. *Kita,* damn it, *Kita!*"

The dog sat, panting, staring up at John Tomei.

"That's the magic word," Rossi explained. "K-I-T-A," spelling it out. "If he gets excited and goes for your throat, you say *kita,* and it's supposed to calm him down."

"Kita," Tomei said softly, slowly moving his hand toward Fidel's head. He knelt down so Fidel could take his time smelling him. "Good boy, Fidel. Good boy." He scratched him behind his ears for a full minute before straightening up.

"Whose idea was it to get a dog?" Tomei asked Rossi.

"Sherri's." Rossi released Fidel's collar. "If I want

him to attack someone, I just point and scream real loud. How about a drink?"

"Does that gun work, or is it just for decoration?"

Rossi slapped his open palm on the holster. "Damn right it works." He removed the weapon and slowly twirled it around his index finger before holstering it. "And I'm ready to use it if those slants come back."

"What's that under your shirt, Billy?"

Rossi scratched his fingers across his chest. "A bulletproof vest. I figure you can't be too careful, right? One size fits all. I bought two of them, one for Sherri, but she wants no part of it. It's upstairs in my room. Help yourself if you want it, Tomb."

"Let's talk outside for a minute, Billy."

Tomei led Rossi toward his car. "I don't know how safe it is talking inside your house. The people that broke in might have planted a bug."

"Hell, that's one thing I don't have to worry about, Tomb. I've got antibugging crap all over the house. Every phone, every electrical contact. If someone tries to bug this place all kinds of bells and whistles go off. I had it swept the day after the robbery, just in case. Nothing there. How about that drink?"

"Coffee is about all I can handle at this time of the day."

Tomei followed Rossi, the dog padding directly alongside the bookie. They entered a large room with brush-swirled adobe walls. A moose-antler chandelier hung from the beamed ceiling. The floors were covered with overlapping Navajo rugs. Oil paintings of western scenes—cowboys on horseback, a cavalry unit riding through a snow-covered meadow, cowhands crouched around an open fire—dotted the walls, and bronze statues of Indians on horseback sat on the varnished hatch-cover coffee table.

Rossi's old Wells Fargo safe was against one wall, its door hanging open, the shelves empty.

Three comfortable-looking burnt ocher chairs were spaced around the room. There was a large empty space near the old brick fireplace.

"That's where the couch was," Rossi said, noting Tomei's interest. "Where they . . . did that to Sherri. I got rid of it."

Tomei examined one of the paintings. It depicted a western fur trader standing in front of a tepee, swapping a horse-load of furs for an Indian bride. Wavy scars from a knife crisscrossed the entire canvas.

"Those bastards did that," Rossi said. "That's by Alfred Jacob Miller. They ruined two more in the dining room. They cost me plenty. I can tell you that. And it's going to cost a lot to get them restored."

"What about insurance?" Tomei inquired.

Rossi wagged his head from side to side. "Nah. I thought the price they wanted for insurance was a rip-off. Who'da thought this would happen, huh? Sherri's in the kitchen. I'll have her bring you that coffee."

"Forget about it," replied Tomei. "I've had enough."

Rossi crossed to a glass-topped drink cart, scooped ice out of a crystal bucket into a heavy tumbler, and sloshed in a double-shot of bourbon. "Got any news?" he asked, after sampling the drink.

"I'm just getting started, Billy. Give me a tour of the place."

Rossi padded down the hallway. "We were in here when they broke in," he said, pointing to a spacious room with four large-screen TVs set into a redwood-paneled wall. Below each TV were VCRs and DVD players. A bank of theater chairs that could have come from a 1920s motion picture palace sat in front of the TV sets.

Tomei followed Rossi and Fidel up a flight of stairs to the upper floor and to his bedroom.

The king-size platform bed was made of dark, polished Burlwood. The matching bed stands had an art deco look, enhanced by frosted-glass tulip-shaped lamps. The two paintings above the bed were of English hunting scenes with red-coated men on prancing stallions.

Sherri Dawson's clothing—red slacks, a matching

blouse, and pale pink bra and panties—were splashed across the bed's white quilt cover.

The bathroom was all copper, brass, and red marble, the centerpiece being an oversized copper bathtub and copper water heater. The water heater was entwined with brass pipes and white enamel knobs. The bottom of the tub was shiny with water spots. A makeup table near the washbasin was littered with jars and tubes of cosmetics. Perched alongside a lightbulb-ringed makeup mirror was a black leather purse.

"Like it?" Rossi asked. "Cost me a fortune. I can tell you that. Those decorators have a license to steal."

"Nice. As long as I'm here, I think I'll use the facilities."

Tomei closed the bathroom door in Rossi's face and immediately went to the makeup table. Sherri Dawson's purse was jammed with tubes of lipstick, a compact, two pairs of sunglasses and Kleenex. Tomei pulled out her wallet, shuffling through a collection of credit cards before finding her ID. A State of Nevada driver's license confirmed she was Sherrilyn D. Dawson. The photo showed her with long blond hair and dangling hoop earrings. He memorized the listed date of birth and address of 19220 Via Perdido, number thirty-six, in Las Vegas, put everything back in the purse and flushed the toilet.

Billy was waiting for him on the balcony just outside the bedroom. Tomei peered over the railing. There was a steep, three-story drop to an area thick with shadowy trees.

Rossi gave a quick tour of two additional bedrooms, one cluttered with packing boxes of all shapes and sizes. Glass-enclosed walnut cases housed an impressive gun collection of western-style revolvers, shotguns, and rifles.

Rossi patted his holster again. "They're all in working order, Tomb. Help yourself to anything you want."

"What got you into the cowboy mood, Billy? The last time I was here the house looked like a Paris boutique."

Rossi gave a lopsided grin. "Yeah. I decorated it for the gal I was with then. The next one wanted everything to be pink. When she left, I just fixed it the way *I* wanted it. I didn't think I'd be having any more women guests. Till I met Sherri."

The third bedroom consisted of a twin-size bed and two matching ornate dressers.

"You can bunk in here, Tomb. I know it's not much, but if you need anything, just let me know."

"Show me the rest of the house, Billy."

Tomei checked the back door leading to the garden. It was secured by a wooden two-by-four slotted into clamps at each end of the door.

"Was this in place the night of the robbery?" Tomei asked.

"Yeah, sure was. No way they got in that way, huh, Tomb?"

Tomei examined the door from the outside, his eyes slowing working up to the bedroom balcony. "No. No way they came in from the back."

"I'm betting they picked the front-door lock, Tomb. I saw some scratches there. I never paid much attention to the damn door, but I don't think those scratches were there before that night. I'll show you."

The scratches were just above the strike plate. Tomei dropped to his knees and examined the lock. It was a Kaba High-Security combination cylinder and deadbolt. He considered himself a capable lock-picker, and knew he could have worked on that baby for an hour and gotten nowhere. Neither would most professional burglars.

"What about the burglar alarm?"

"It's top-of-the-line, but I never set it until I'm ready to go to bed." Rossi pointed to a small plastic keypad on the wall adjoining the front door. "I'll show you how it works." He punched in a series of numbers with his index finger. "That's the code for setting it on and turning it off: one-five-seven-nine. Those are the numbers a guy once used on a four-horse parlay. I'll never forget them. I had to pay off more than thirty g's. You better write 'em down, just in case."

Tomei ran his fingers over the scratch marks. "Do you always throw the deadbolt when you close the door?"

"Yeah, I guess so."

"Don't guess. Do you or don't you?"

Rossi sucked in his lower lip, then grabbed the door knob, shutting the door, then reaching up to throw the deadbolt. "Yeah, I'd say I always do. Habit I guess. Though most times I come in by the garage, then into the kitchen."

"Who was the last person in that night? You or Sherri?"

"We came in together, Tomb. I'm sure of that."

"Okay. Let's take a look at the garage."

Tomei examined the garage door.

"It makes a hell of a racket when it goes up. I would have heard it if they came in that way."

There were two cars in the garage, a white Cadillac convertible and a felony-red Corvette with Nevada plates.

"That's Sherri's car," Rossi said, pointing to the Corvette.

Tomei leaned against the fender of the Cadillac. "Who, besides you, has a key to the house?"

Rossi splayed out his hands. "Just me. And Sherri."

"How long have you known Sherri?"

Rossi's mouth set in a sour grin. "Sherri wasn't involved, Tomb. No way. You know what they did to her."

"I don't think she was," Tomei responded coolly. "But how long have you known her?"

" 'Bout three months, I guess," Rossi said, hitching up his pants. "I met her at the track. Golden Gate Fields. She's a good kid. A real good kid."

A thirty-one-year-old kid shacking up with a sixty-plus bookie, thought Tomei. "What about a maid? A cook?"

"Same woman. She's been with me over twenty years."

"Does she have a key?"

"Sure. She takes care of the place when I go out of

town. But there's no way Mrs. Cleary's involved. I'd bet my life on that."

"I think you should tell her to take a vacation for a week or so. What about your runners? Do they have keys?"

"No. I'm not that dumb."

Rossi screwed up one side of his face, as if he was squinting through a telescope. "So what are we going to do about it, Tomb? I'm running out of time."

"I'm not sure yet, Billy. But I'm working on it."

Rossi reached into his pants pocket and came out with a key. "Here, Tomb. To tell you the truth, I feel a little better with both you and Fidel around. Don't forget the alarm numbers. And if you need more dough, or anything else, just ask, okay? How about a cell phone? You have one?"

"No."

"I've got dozens of the damn things. Couldn't operate in my business without them. I'll get you one."

"There is one more thing, Billy. The day I met you at Sully's bar. The feds that I thought were tailing you went after someone else. Dino Lanzoni. Is there any connection between you and Lanzoni, Billy?"

Rossi held up his hands like a boxer fending off blows. "Dino Lanzoni? Nick Lanzoni's crazy kid brother. You kidding me? I have nothing to do with those people. For Christ's sake, they're gangsters. Just because I have an Italian name doesn't mean I'm connected to the mob. Hell, I'm half-Irish. My mom's name was Doherty."

"And you didn't see Lanzoni at Sully's."

"Tomb, I'm not even sure what the bum looks like. I saw his brother on TV, sure. But not Dino Lanzoni. I don't know him. I don't ever want to know him."

"How about Sherri? She lived in New York once."

"Let's go ask her."

Sherri was in the living room, stretched out comfortably in one of the chairs, drinking coffee and reading the paper. She had on a pink silk robe. Her hair was wet and striated as if she'd just combed it.

Rossi went over and stood behind her, his hands going to her shoulders. "Hey, honey. The day we met the Tomb at Sully's. Do you remember seeing a guy there. Dino Lanzoni?"

Sherri let the paper fall to her knees. "Who? Lanzoni?"

"Nick Lanzoni's brother," Tomei said. "Two FBI agents followed him when he left in a cab. He was in the restaurant. Did you see him?"

"Not that I know of," she answered calmly. "What does he look like?"

"I thought you might know," Tomei answered. "He's a New York mobster. You lived in New York."

"That was ten years ago. I was too busy trying to break into show business to pay attention to mobsters."

"And you never ran into him in Las Vegas?"

"Listen," Sherri said with some heat in her voice. "You can't walk through a casino in Vegas and not pass by some Mafia people. They're all over town. I met a few, sure. But Lanzoni. No. Never. Why? What's the big deal with him?"

"I'm not sure," Tomei said. "I just don't like the coincidence of him being at Sully's that day."

"Cops," Sherri scoffed. "You have to try and make a mystery out of everything."

On the way out of the house, Billy Rossi stopped at a dresser near the front door and chose one of the half dozen cell phones in the drawer. The phone number was imprinted on a white plastic label attached to the phone. Rossi jotted the number on a pad and then pawed through the drawer. "Here's a charger, Tomb. It fits into the cigarette lighter in your car. Keep in touch. And be careful."

Tomei arrived at the restaurant first. "Church" was the code name he and Elaine Surel had dubbed the St. Francis Creamery on Twenty-fourth Street. It was a real old-fashioned creamery, with all the ice cream and candy made right on the premises. "I'm waiting for a friend to join me," he told the cheerful young waitress. "Just a Coke, please."

Tomei had finished the soft drink and was about to order another, when he saw Elaine glide through the front door, an attractive, young, sultry-looking woman beside her.

Elaine strode through the tables as if in a hurry, picking up a lot of admiring glances from the male clientele.

Elaine "Gucci" Surel was forty-seven but looked a decade younger. She was tall and slender. Her olive complexion smooth and wrinkle-free, except for the corners of her eyes. Her makeup accented her high cheekbones. Her hair was the color of pale straw.

Tomei stood to greet her. She slapped him on the back and gave him a wide grin.

"John. It's great to see you. You're looking good. A little shabby, but good." She reached out a hand and stroked his hair. "You do need a haircut. Say hello to my partner, Laura Aguera. Laura, shake hands with the Tomb."

Tomei stuck his hand out. "Nice to meet you, Laura."

Laura nodded, her face passive.

They all sat down and Elaine said, "Are you still working at that bar up the Russian River?"

"A few days a week during the summer, but things are slow now. I'm between jobs, as we unemployed like to say."

"Well, you look like you've been working out, John. I mean, lean and mean." She frowned at Tomei's sport coat. "But the wardrobe. You still need help."

"Everyone can't be a star, Gooch." He turned his eyes to Laura Aguera. She was just an inch or two over five feet, wearing an eye-catching chocolate-brown top and matching skirt. Her eyes were black, almond shaped, her nose arched up slightly. Her skin was shiny, as if it had just been cold creamed. Her dark hair was cut short and matched her eyes.

"How does it feel to be working with a runway model, Laura?" Tomei asked her.

"Well," she answered with a grin. "I have to say that Elaine's worse then my mother about clothes."

It was Tomei who had put the tag "Inspector Gucci" on Elaine shortly after they became partners. She had been a fashion model before entering the police department. It appeared she spent her entire paycheck on clothes: elegant Italian-cut skirts and dresses, rich leather purses and shoes.

Today she was wearing a dove-gray silk jacket and skirt, and a creamy vanilla ruffled blouse. Her current husband, her third, Ross Surel, was an executive at a Montgomery Street brokerage house, and he had been trying to persuade Elaine to quit the department ever since they were married.

"I'm starving," Elaine announced, scanning the restaurant, which was filling up rapidly. "It's been awhile since I've been here, John."

"Me too, Gucci. Long time."

"Try the vanilla milk shake and grilled cheese, Laura," Elaine suggested. "The best in town."

Laura's eyes flicked down the menu then turned to John Tomei. Elaine had raved about Tomei, telling her how handsome he was, and how good a cop he was before he got himself into all that trouble. He was damn good-looking, she had to admit, but with his long hair and beat-up clothes, he looked more like a struggling artist than a cop. There was something about his manner that appealed to her, an honest, no bullshit, no condescending attitude, and when he spoke to you, he looked right into your eyes.

Laura had just about given up on dating. There simply weren't any unmarried, reasonably good-looking, reasonably intelligent men in San Francisco. She and two friends, Sheila, an investigator in the district attorney's office, and Marla, an inspector in the Sexual Assault detail, had banded together, and over a period of several months had gone to all the clubs, bars, and restaurants where they'd heard there were eligible men. The results had been disastrous. They often joked that they should produce a television comedy series—*No Sex in the City.*

The only men with enough nerve to approach them were businessmen in town for a few days of fun, married lushes who had to be half-stoned before they got off their bar stools to make their pitch, and an abundance of pimply faced juveniles who had fantasies about scoring with "older women."

Tomei was single and very sexy. Maybe there was hope.

"What are you having?" she asked him.

Tomei grinned. "I never argue with Gucci about food."

The waitress took their orders, and Elaine said, "How's Messy?"

Tomei's eyes brightened and he brought out a half dozen photographs of his daughter, taken last month at the Russian River cabin.

Elaine studied the photos and passed them over to Laura.

"Pretty girl," Laura said, noting the change that came over Tomei when he spoke about his daughter. The girl was adorable, a bright smile sparkling at the camera while she held a silvery fish by its tail.

Elaine said, "Listen, John. I have that stuff you wanted." She took an envelope from her purse and passed it to Tomei. "I asked around about the W and G tattoo, but I didn't come up with much."

Tomei glanced at the information on Sherrilyn Dawson. A State of Nevada driver's license showing the Vegas address he had found in her purse. She had no criminal record according to the FBI check.

Laura sat back and pecked at her food, while Elaine Surel and Tomei entertained each other with old war stories of their days in the Vice Squad. She studied Tomei. His hands were in constant motion, when he wasn't picking up his sandwich, he was tying straws into knots and folding napkins. She wouldn't want a partner who was that nervous.

When the plates were cleared away and coffee

poured, Elaine asked, "So what's happening now?" while scooping out the last bit of the milk shake with a long-handled spoon.

Tomei's eyes bounced from Elaine to Laura.

Laura patted her lips dry with the napkin, stood up, and opened her purse. "Here," she said, dropping a ten-dollar bill on the table. "That should pay for my share. I'll be out in the car, Elaine."

"She's going to be very good," Elaine said, turning her shoulder to watch as Laura made her way out of the restaurant. "I'm damn happy to have her as a partner. I've gone through three of them since you left, and she's the best. Raw, but she's learning quick. She's tough. And she has the missing ingredient, John. You know what I mean?"

Tomei nodded his head. He and Elaine had often talked about what made someone a good cop. Their simple reasoning was "common sense." The all-too-often missing ingredient.

"How's Ross? Is he still trying to get you to quit the job?"

Elaine twisted the large diamond wedding ring on her finger. "My husband just can't seem to understand why I enjoy this job."

"I'll bet he's a lot happier with Laura being your partner than he was with me."

Elaine smiled ruefully. Ross had been jealous of Tomei. He hadn't liked the idea of the two of them working long hours together, especially those late-at-night cases. There had been a lot of talk in the department about them, too. Gucci and Tomei. She'd once overheard the lieutenant say that he was sure they were "getting it on together."

It somehow amused Elaine. All those tough-talking, hard-boiled policemen, who spent their lives working in life's sewers, investigating homicides, rapes, beatings, yet they were like smutty little schoolboys when it came to sex.

There had never been anything of a sexual nature between her and Tomei. The simple truth was that he'd been madly in love with his wife and worshiped his daughter.

When Elaine first met Tomei, she didn't think they had a chance to make the bond that was so necessary between cop-partners. But Tomei had proved her wrong. He treated her no differently from the men he worked with, and that included the off-colored jokes and rough-and-tumble language that went along with the job. Elaine had easily rolled with the punches, and more than held up her side of the bargain. The police department came in a distant second to her modeling career when it came to foul language, back-stabbing coworkers, and bitchy bosses.

"Ross thinks Laura is just dandy, John. And so do I. You and she have a lot in common."

"Like what?" Tomei asked suspiciously.

"She's divorced. She came home and found her husband in bed. With another man. You can't begin to imagine what something like that does to a girl's ego."

"She looks like she shouldn't have any trouble finding another guy."

"Sure," Elaine said scornfully. "You know how it is. Half the guys in the department want to screw her brains out. The other half thinks she should be at home, cleaning windows and doing the laundry. When she meets someone outside of the department, and they find out she's a cop, they start edging away. Believe me, I've been there. It's not easy. You should give her a call, huh? I think she would like—"

"Listen, Gooch. Right now, I need a little help. And the fewer people who know about it, the better."

"I'll do anything I can for you. You know that."

Tomei did indeed know that. Elaine was the only one who had stood by him after "the incident." She pulled in all the favors she had coming to try and get the police commissioner to keep Tomei on the force. She had found him passed out in his Russian River cabin, had slapped him sober, and dragged him to the department's Stress Unit. Then she'd loaned him money. Money he hadn't been able to pay back yet.

Tomei felt guilty asking Elaine for more help. He told her all about his meeting with Billy Rossi, leaving out only the part about Rossi offering him half of the money if he could somehow recover it.

"Lordy, Lordy," Elaine exclaimed. "Over three hundred thousand dollars. Poor Billy. Somehow I actually feel sorry for the old scoundrel."

"They worked over his girlfriend, Sherri Dawson, too. She says she was raped, and Billy backs her up on that. She still has some bruises."

Elaine pressed her lips into a kiss of worried disapproval. "What's she like?"

"Tough. Edgy. Good-looking. A little on the hard side. I have a hunch she set Rossi up."

"Then she's not very smart, if she got roughed-up as she claims. What does Rossi expect you to do, John?"

"A little digging. He wants me to find out who wants to take over his business."

Elaine's eyes narrowed like a cat's. "John, don't do anything stupid. These Asian gangs are in a league all their own."

"Yeah, I know. But I have to look into it."

Elaine clasped her hands in front of her like a professional mourner. "You could get killed going after these guys, John. Forget it."

"I'm not going to do anything dumb," Tomei declared with confidence. He took a deep breath, then let the air out slowly. "I need the money, Gucci. I need it bad. I'm losing Messy."

"What do you mean you're losing her? She loves you. You know that."

Tomei shook his head slowly back and forth. "You know what Joan gave Messy for her last birthday? A Rolex. 'Just like Mommy's.' I gave her a lousy fishing rod."

"Things like that won't impress Messy, John."

"Joan is being clever about it. Little by little she's showing my daughter what a bum I am. She takes Messy everywhere. They're in Florida now. Joan wants to move to New Mexico. Permanently. I'll never see the kid."

"Can't you stop her?" Elaine asked. "Can't you get the judge to—"

Tomei pounded a fist on the table in frustration. "Damn it. It costs money to fight in court. I owe you money. I still owe my attorney his fee. Joan knows she has me on the ropes. My lawyer got a demand from her lawyer. Cave in, or else. I'm in a box, Gucci. A coffin, and they're nailing the lid shut."

Elaine took a compact from her purse and checked her makeup to stall for time. She had never seen John this way before, and it scared her. "Red Vanes quit when they disbanded the Intelligence detail. He retired rather than accept a transfer. Vanes insists he was forced out. The word is he took a lot of his files with him when he left. There are rumors that Vanes is doing some free-lance work for the FBI." Elaine fished a slip of notepaper from her purse. "Here's his address and phone number. Just don't tell him you got them from me."

"Thanks, Gucci. When I met with Rossi, it was at Sully's on Union Street. Two FBI had the place staked out. That big crew-cut guy Jamison and someone I don't know. Guess who they were following?"

"Someone spot Elvis again?" Elaine inquired dryly.

Tomei picked up the ten-dollar bill that Laura had left on the table and began folding it in crisp angles. "Dino Lanzoni."

Elaine's eyes widened. "Lanzoni? That's all we need around here. Is there a connection between Lanzoni and Rossi?"

He handed her the ten-dollar bill that was now shaped into a bow tie, with Alexander Hamilton's face neatly formed in the center. "He says no. I believe him."

"What about between this Sherri lady and Lanzoni?"

"She claims she knows nothing about him. I'm not sure about her. Maybe Lanzoni showing up at Sully's was just a coincidence."

Elaine snapped her purse shut. "You have to get a real job, John. Something nice and safe. How about putting out oil well fires, or dismantling land mines?"

Chapter Ten

Laura Aguera tapped her fingers impatiently on the edge of the steering wheel as she waited in the car and watched Elaine Surel and John Tomei exit the St. Francis Creamery. She had passed the time by shopping at a nearby produce stand operated by a Mexican family. She had lost her temper when she overheard two young boys, who were unloading crates of lemons and limes, jabber on in Spanish, graphically describing her figure. When the larger of the two made a particularly vulgar comment about the size of her *chichis*, then added that he would like to *"Te voy a hacer la sopa,"* Laura had responded hotly. "You *maletons* should have your mouths washed out with soap. Where is your mother? I would like to talk to her."

The youngsters had apologized profusely, and disappeared into the back of the store.

She watched Elaine give Tomei a chaste peck on the cheek, then walk rapidly toward the car.

Tomei pushed one hand up to shield his eyes from the sun, spotted Laura behind the wheel, and gave a friendly wave.

Laura waved back, wondering what Tomei was up to. Something was bothering him. The "stuff" Elaine had given him. Confidential police documents. She hoped that Elaine wouldn't get into any trouble.

"What do you think of the Tomb?" Elaine asked, sliding into the passenger seat, a wide smile on her face. "I told you he was a hunk, didn't I?" She reached over and dropped the ten-dollar bill folded like a bow tie into Laura's lap. "That's yours. John paid for lunch."

"No," Laura protested, "I don't want—"

"Listen, Laura. John was my partner. He's still my friend. He buys me lunch, he buys you lunch, that's the way it works. Relax. I told you, there's more to this job than red lights and sirens."

Laura quizzically raised her eyebrows as she examined the bow-tied bill. "Why did he do this?"

"John's always working on little tricks and gimmicks like that to amuse his daughter," Elaine explained.

Laura unfolded the bill, slipped it back into her purse, turned on the car's ignition and edged away from the curb. She swung around a pickup truck that was double-parked in front of a market. Three young Latin children, Laura estimated their ages at from five to eight, wearing straw field hats and olive drab jackets huddled together in the back of the truck's cab. They all stared at her with blank eyes. She wondered if any of them had picked the lettuce and onions she'd purchased at the produce stand. "Where to?" she asked.

"Back to the Hall of Justice." Elaine turned her head so she could see Laura's profile. "Well, tell me. What do you think of John Tomei?"

"I don't know, Elaine."

"If we're going to be a team, we have to be honest with each other. Give me a one-word description."

It was a little game that Elaine liked to play. Meet someone for the first time and give a one-word description of him or her. Laura had played along: Tall. Mean. Ugly. Hard. Fat. Lazy. Crazy. Weird. Sick. Dangerous. Stupid.

Laura's one word for Elaine had greatly pleased her partner.

"Savvy," Laura had told her.

"Come on," Elaine coaxed. "What do you say about John?"

Laura pulled to a stop at a red light. "Desperate," she finally said.

Dino Lanzoni was tired of playing tag with the cops. He wasn't sure where or when they had picked him up, but it was time to get rid of them. He had spotted his mark early. The chubby young woman with a baby cradled under her arm. He couldn't tell if the woman's heaviness was due to the arrival of another baby. She looked the type. Big hips, big boobs. A breeder, he thought, definitely a breeder.

He kept his single piece of luggage between his feet, thumbing aimlessly through a *Sports Illustrated* magazine.

The announcement for first-class boarders came over the loudspeaker. He dropped the magazine to the floor, stood up, and lugged his suitcase to the line forming at the ticket counter.

Dumb, he thought. People are dumb. The ones that boarded last always seemed to be the ones up front, blocking the gates. He kept a close eye on the woman with the baby.

"Last call for first-class boarding for Flight eight-four-eight to New York City" came the announcement from the ticket clerk.

Lanzoni showed the clerk his pass and wandered down the jetway leading to the Boeing 747. The moveable corridor took a dogleg left some twenty-five feet from the airplane. Once Lanzoni was sure he was out of sight of anyone in the terminal he stopped and waved the oncoming passengers past him, until he spotted the woman with the baby.

" 'Scuse me, lady, but it looks like you could use a hand."

The woman looked up at the big, dark man and flinched, hugging her child closer to her chest.

Lanzoni's smile did nothing to assuage her fears.

"Look, lady. I just got beeped by my office," he told her hurriedly. "I have to cancel my flight. It's too late for a ticket redemption and it looks like you could use a separate seat for that cute little kid. Am I right?"

The woman tilted her head while reading the first-class boarding pass in Lanzoni's hand.

"Gee. That's awfully nice of you, mister. I'm sorry I was kind of . . ."

Lanzoni smiled down at her. "No problem, lady." He pointed a forefinger at the child. "Cute kid. Here. Take this. I'm sure the stewardess can arrange it so you and the kid are sitting together."

The woman took the ticket, tears forming in the corners of her eyes. "Gee, thanks again. I don't know what to say."

"Don't say nothing. Just get on board. Have a nice trip."

He watched as she boarded the plane, showing her passes to the frowning flight attendant. The last of the passengers streamed by, then an airline employee in white coveralls with green plastic ear protectors dangling around his neck walked up to him. The name "Roy" was stitched in red letters across the chest of the coveralls.

"You better get on board, mister."

"FBI, Roy," Lanzoni said. "Just making sure someone takes off."

Roy was about to question Lanzoni, but there was something in the big man's face that made him hold back. "Okay with me."

"Me too," Lanzoni grunted. He watched as the plane's boarding door was secured. The increase in the engine's pitch as the 747 taxied to the runway apron made him cup his hands over his ears. He waited another five minutes before returning to the terminal area. There was no sign of the cops who had been tailing him.

The airplane would land with a full passenger list in Dallas, then take off again for New York. The cops in New York would think Lanzoni had gotten off at the Texas airport, or that their buddies in San Francisco had screwed up. And they had, Lanzoni thought, allowing himself a tight smile.

Chapter Eleven

Once the neighborhood had been an enclave of upper-middle-class residents: doctors, lawyers, dentists, bank executives. The homes were spacious and detached—unusual for San Francisco—and were built where a racetrack once stood. The street was paved over the track itself and John Tomei could remember his early days as a uniformed officer, chasing hot-rodding kids around the oval circuit.

The residences had gone through a rough period of change in the 1960s and 1970s, but now the mini-mansions were being restored, with new tile roofs, brick pavements, and sculpted yards.

Red Vanes's house was surrounded by an ivy-laced chain-link fence. Bright yellow metal signs staked on the lawn cautioned the passerby to BEWARE OF DOG, and advised any potential burglar that the property was protected by the Modern Systems Alarm Company. Stout wrought-iron grills shielded every visible window, and the roof was littered with odd-shaped antennas.

Tomei looked cautiously over the fence for the dog. He unlatched the gate and hurried across the neatly mowed lawn when a series of snarly barks came from out of nowhere.

Twelve stone steps, the edges recently grouted, led up to the front of the house. A pepper mill–shaped turret encircled the front door. He pushed the doorbell and within seconds a familiar voice boomed out, "What the hell do you want?"

"It's John Tomei, Red."

"I know who it is. What the hell do you want?"

Tomei looked up at the small surveillance camera centered over the carved oak door. "To talk. I need some help."

"Talk about what?"

"An Asian gang. They have tattoos on their arms. The letters *W* and *G*. Open the damn door, Red."

There was the sound of metal sliding against metal, over and over again. The door inched open and Tomei could see one half of a pair of eyeglasses and a shiny bald head.

"You're alone," Red Vanes said in a challenging tone.

"You can see that, Red."

"No one in your car?"

"No. What's the problem?"

The door closed and Tomei heard the rasp of metal against metal again.

"Come on in," Vanes ordered when he yanked the door open.

Tomei entered the house. As he passed Vanes, a beeping sound echoed from the door frame.

Vanes closed the door and leaned against it. He was in his late fifties, well over six feet, with slim, slouching shoulders. His head was completely shaven, just as it had been when Tomei first met him fifteen years ago. The stories on how he'd acquired his nickname, Red, ranged from it having been tacked on from his early school days to go along with his last name, to the time when he was in charge of the around-the-clock stakeout of the Russian embassy. Vanes entered the folklore of the department by once, in the middle of the night, using a chain saw to cut down a series of sycamore trees that were blocking the view of the embassy from the department's surveillance house.

Another theory was that he just couldn't stand his real name—Alonzo—and had been more than happy to be called Red.

Vanes appeared to have lost a good thirty pounds since Tomei had last seen him. His skin had the pale, waxy look of someone who was fighting a serious illness. He forehead was deeply grooved and wattles of flesh hung under the dark stubble of his beard. Shaggy brown eyebrows were partially hidden by oversized black plastic eyeglass frames. He was wearing a baggy safari jacket and worn cords. A red bandanna was tied around his neck. His hands were wedged into two of the jacket's numerous bulging pockets.

"You're packing, right? The monitor picked up something."

Tomei scanned the doorway. "You have a metal detector in your house?"

"I have my reasons." Vanes studied Tomei for a long moment.

Tomei held his hands away from his sides. "I haven't had a gun in my hand since I left the department, Red. It must be the badge."

Vanes frowned with annoyance, then said, "You need a haircut."

"People keep telling me that."

"This way," Vanes instructed, and Tomei followed him down a dimly lit hallway into a cluttered, tobacco-scented room. A powerful opera voice was coming from a stereo. Something sorrowful in Italian. Tomei thought it sounded like Pavarotti, but he couldn't be sure.

Framed photographs of politicians and movie stars dotted the walls. Tomei examined one photo of a younger Red Vanes, his shaven head glistening under the sun, shaking hands with President Ronald Reagan as Reagan boarded Air Force One. The adjoining photo featured a group of six middle-aged men, all dressed in suits and felt fedoras. They were squinting at the camera as if they didn't think it was a good idea to be photographed.

"That's the Chinatown Detail, 1954," Vanes said. "The young handsome guy on the end here is my dad. He used to take me and my mother to Chinatown every Sunday for dinner. Soup to nuts. Or soup to fortune cookies. Dad's hand never went near his wallet."

Tomei had heard stories about the notorious Chinatown Squad. Rumors circulated that most of them became wealthy, their loot sometimes buried in coffee cans in their backyards.

Vanes tapped the glass with his finger. "Dad would prop me on his shoulders sometimes, take me on his beat. We'd make lots of stops. I ended up with pockets full of candy. Dad got envelopes. Ah, the good old days," Vanes sighed. "Have a seat."

When Tomei moved toward an old saddle-colored cracked leather club chair by the fireplace, Vanes was quick to say, "Not that one. Over here."

Vanes slipped into the chair Tomei had attempted to sit in and crossed his legs. "The tattoo you mentioned. The letters W and G. They were inside a circle? Under the arm?"

"That's right. Tell me about the gang."

Vanes switched his crossed knees. "No. You tell me your interest first, then maybe I'll fill you in."

Tomei gave an indifferent shrug, then told Vanes what had taken place at Billy Rossi's house.

Vanes listened intently, his eyes shut, a smile inching across his face when Tomei mentioned that the gang had taken a large amount of money from Billy Rossi.

"How large an amount?"

"More than three hundred thou."

Vanes slapped his hands on his thighs. "Billy never was very bright. And what does he expect you to do? Recover his lost treasure? Punish the perpetrators? Restore the lost virginity of his sweetheart?"

Tomei was getting fed up with Vanes's sarcasm. "He wants to find out who hit him. Who it is that wants to take over his territory, and let them know he's not a pushover. He wants to stay in business. They gave him an ultimatum. Two weeks. One of them is gone. Seven days left. Now, are you going to help me on this, or are you just going to be a jerk?"

Vanes made clucking noises with his tongue. "Don't get so touchy. These are dangerous people, Tomb. I know them. You don't. My best advice to you would be to go home and forget about the whole thing."

"I can't," Tomei responded bluntly. "I need the money."

Vanes leaned back in his chair, the leather squeaking in protest. "Your chances of getting Rossi's money back are nil. Unless I help you. Your chances of getting killed, or hurt very badly, are quite high, whether I decide to help you or not. These people play rough. There are two kinds of bookie operations here on the coast."

"I know," Tomei said. "White and Asian. I never had any contact with Asian bookies when I was in Vice. You had them bottled up."

"That's right. You cross a white bookie, you get cut off from betting more of your money. You cross the Asians and they come after you, chop you to pieces, kill your ass."

"I'll take the risk. Who are they, Red?"

"Wah Ging. That's what the *W* and *G* letters stand for. Kan Chin's men. Chin was behind the robbery."

The name was familiar to Tomei. "Chin. He's a Chinatown businessman, isn't he? Supposedly tied in with the Hong Kong Triads."

"He's *the* Chinatown businessman," Vanes corrected. "A very complicated man, Mr. Chin. He makes a lot of very large donations to charities all over town. There's a wing of the Chinese Hospital that he paid for all by himself. And he is the head of every organized Chinese gang on the West Coast."

Vanes plucked at the sagging skin under his chin. "The three men who hit Rossi's house—two were young, you say?"

"Yes. The woman and Rossi both thought that they were in their teens, early twenties at the most. The third man, the boss, was older."

"The young ones were probably seventeen or eighteen. Hong Kong punks. The older one would be Willy

Hon," Vanes said with a glassy smile. "Hon is Chin's bully boy, and he has a history of hurting women. So does Chin, for that matter. He's an old dude, older than me. He favors young, very young girls, just off the boat from China. Virgins. Once Chin is finished romancing her, she disappears. He doesn't want them blabbing about the fact that he's not quite up to par in the sex game anymore."

Vanes palmed the chair for leverage and raised himself to his feet. "I'm sorry I can't—"

"There's a lot of money involved, Red."

"Yes. Money. And *face*. That's what it's really all about, isn't it?"

"Speaking of face, I saw an odd one the day I met Billy Rossi at Sully's. Dino Lanzoni."

Vanes stiffened as if he'd been hit by a left jab. "Dino Lanzoni. You're sure it was him?"

"Positive."

Vanes's eyes gleamed behind his glasses. "Lanzoni here in San Francisco. What's his connection to Rossi?"

"None, according to Billy. There were two FBI agents staking Sully's out. I thought they were after Rossi, but they followed Lanzoni when he took off. I recognized one of them. Don Jamison. His partner was a short guy with—"

"Paul Flowers," Vanes interjected quickly. "He's only slightly more astute than that boob Jamison."

"I've heard rumors that you're doing some work for the feds, Red."

Vanes rolled his eyes toward the ceiling. "Not for the likes of those two. How about a drink?"

When Vanes left to get their drinks, Tomei moved over to the leather chair. Vanes had been ready to show him the door, but the mention of Dino Lanzoni had really upped Vanes's interest. Tomei ran his hands around the cushion, recoiling when he brushed up against the butts of two revolvers.

Vanes came back minutes later with two icy bottles of Anchor steam beer. He handed one of the beers to Tomei. "There's gin or wine if you prefer."

"This is fine, Red. Tell me more about Chin's gang."

"They're well organized. New people come in all the time from Hong Kong. Drugs are the big money-maker. He's also into extortion, bookmaking, loan sharking, and prostitution. Chin's connected to the Triads on the East Coast and in Hong Kong. His territory runs from Vegas to San Diego and up to Vancouver. Taking over Rossi's business would be a real plum for him. Is Rossi paying you expenses?"

"Yes."

"Good, that information I just provided will cost him five hundred dollars."

"Sherri Dawson said that all three of them were wearing stocking masks."

"Did all three have the tattoo?"

"They could have, but Billy just saw the one. Dawson didn't mention the tattoo. She said she kept her eyes closed a lot."

Vanes took a long swig of his beer, licked foam from his lips, then said, "What's your take on this Sherri? Was she in on the robbery?"

"It's a strong possibility."

"Then you know what that means. If *she* is working for Chin, he will know that *you* are working for Rossi." Vanes pointed the tip of the beer bottle at Tomei. "You had better find out about her for sure."

Tomei flopped into the leather club chair before Vanes could protest. He slipped one of the guns free. "Who the hell are you afraid of Red? You're living in an armed camp. The metal detector. And that baying hound you've got hiding somewhere."

Vanes crossed the room to a ceiling-high cabinet crammed with electronic equipment. He flipped on a switch and the room was engulfed with the sounds of barking dogs. He played with the volume control, causing Tomei to wince.

"Much cheaper than having a real dog," Vanes said, flicking the switch off. "And a lot less work."

"You haven't told me who you're afraid of, Red."

"Kan Chin, for one. He had me kicked out of the department. Hey, don't scowl at me like that! Chin was behind it, believe me."

"I didn't know he had that kind of clout," Tomei said skeptically.

"He does. He has his people in the department. Well-placed people. A few years ago, I had fifteen people working for me in the Intelligence detail. Little by little they were taken from me, transferred to the Gang Task Force, the Hate Crimes Unit, or to the Special Investigations Division. The reason given was efficiency," Vanes scoffed. "What it was all about was control. They took the heat off Chinatown, that's what they did." He moved to the wall with the photographs and tapped a fingernail against an eight-by-ten black-and-white. "That's Chin, thirty years ago. In the middle of the picture. The other little bastards are members of the East Coast Triad. Chin was an up-and-comer back then. He fought some pretty bloody wars in Chinatown. A lot of people were killed, including two cops. One of them was my father."

"Who are you talking about in the department? Who are Chin's men?"

"Find out about this Sherri Dawson, and maybe we can do business, Tomb. I have to know if she's working for Chin before I make a commitment." He pulled a small plastic disk from his pocket and lobbed it over to Tomei. "Know what that is?"

Tomei examined the item, which was round, ivory-colored, with threads of gold and silver running through it. An Asian symbol imbedded in the middle. "It's a poker chip."

"Poker, mah jongg, pan, you name it. Chin runs a dozen or more gambling dens. That ivory chip is worth ten dollars. The reds are fifty, the blues hundred, and the yellow ones five hundred bucks. They're harder to counterfeit than Uncle Sam's money, I can tell you that. You can spend them anywhere in Chinatown, and not just here—in Vancouver, Seattle, Los Angeles, hell, even New York City. Buy groceries, pay

a prostitute, or your dentist. They're as good as gold."
Vanes wiggled his fingers for Tomei to return the chip.
"And you owe me five hundred bucks, my friend."

Tomei peeled off the bills from the roll Rossi had
provided him. "You're sure you're not just a little bit
paranoid about Kan Chin, Red?"

"No. Listen good, Tomb. Chin is the worst kind
of adversary you can think of. Because he's patient.
He's wanted to ruin me for years. He took his own
sweet time about it. He enjoyed destroying me bit
by bit."

Vanes plucked the money from Tomei's hand, then
said, "You spotting Lanzoni. That intrigues me. I believe Rossi. He wouldn't have anything to do with
Lanzoni. Neither would Kan Chin. Lanzoni's nothing
but a dumb thug. Maybe the Dawson woman knows
him."

"Dawson lived in New York for a couple of years.
Then she moved to Florida, finally to Vegas, before
coming out here and moving in with Rossi. She says
she never met Dino Lanzoni, and doesn't even know
what he looks like. I'm going to Vegas to check her
out."

Vanes made a clicking noise with his teeth. "I still
don't like it. Lanzoni being there that day. Was he
alone?"

"I didn't see him until he was outside, getting into
a cab. I don't like coincidences any more than you
do, Red."

"If you're serious about this, really serious, I might
be of some help." He grinned, showing a keyboard of
milky-white teeth. "But help is expensive, these days."
He paused momentarily, pushing his glasses back from
his nose. "Especially for those of us who were forced
to retire before we were ready."

"There should be enough money in this for both of
us, Red."

"Call me when you get back from Vegas. I'll buy
you lunch at one of Chin's places."

*   *   *

Red Vanes stood at the window, parting the drapes and watching as Tomei slid into the front seat of his car, then drove away. No one seemed to be following him.

He hurried to the room he now used as an office. Wanted posters, mug shots, federal bulletins, and aerial maps of San Francisco were thumbtacked directly to the walls. There were three metal desks—two blanketed with computers, scanners, and printers. The third desk held an array of telephones and answering machines. Vanes selected the phone hooked to a digital scanner, which was hardwired to an antenna on the roof. If the scanner picked up any sign of a line breech, the antenna automatically rotated the outgoing call to another of the numerous private phone banks that Vanes contracted with.

He flicked through the coded Rolodex next to the phone, then settled himself into the padded swivel chair and made his first call to New York.

Forty-two minutes later he cradled the phone, relaxed in a comfortable position and stared at the wall. The two calls he'd made, one to the New York Police Department, the other to the New York office of the FBI, had left him with an uneasy feeling.

The men he spoke to agreed on one thing. Dino Lanzoni was a loose cannon. A *reietto*, who was no longer welcomed in New York. There wasn't an official contract out on him—yet. But the families had made it known that he wasn't wanted. The only reason Dino hadn't been hit was because of his brother's influence.

The days of mobsters going to prison and running their business from a cell, where they were wined and dined, were long gone. No one in the Mafia expected Nick Lanzoni to ever breathe free air again. He would die in prison. It would be considered a breech of honor if Nick's brother was killed so soon after the trial.

The New York cop had told Vanes that the word on the street was that everyone figured Dino wouldn't last for more than a year on his own, anyway.

The FBI agent's information had been unsettling. There had been reports of Dino Lanzoni surfacing in Los Angeles. And one report, out of the FBI's San Francisco office, that Lanzoni had been in the city for an unknown length of time, and had been at a bar at the same time a local bookie by the name of William Rossi was present. Lanzoni was followed to the airport, where he boarded a plane that stopped in Dallas, before touching down in New York City. Agents had been waiting at both locations, but there had been no sign of Lanzoni.

The New York Triad continued to supply the East Coast Mafia with a good deal of their drugs. There was lots of competition, especially from the Russian gangs, but the Chinese were still top dog.

Vanes ran a hand across his bald scalp. He knew that Chin was the major supplier on the West Coast. Chin was a careful and selective man. *Would* Kan Chin have anything to do with the likes of Dino Lanzoni? Vanes didn't think so. In fact, he would bet against it, and give good odds to whoever was dumb enough to take such a bet.

His source at the New York FBI office didn't know, or wouldn't tell Vanes, where the original information on Lanzoni being in San Francisco had come from.

"Local agents picked up on him. It might have been just luck."

No. Vanes didn't believe that. The two local agents, Jamison and Flowers, were a couple of lazy clowns with no initiative. They waited until the attorney general swept an investigation away from a local agency and dropped it in their laps, or a paid informer came across with something worthy of his stipend.

Which meant that someone had tipped Jamison and Flowers that Dino Lanzoni was going to be at Sully's saloon. At the same time that a disgraced San Francisco policeman was meeting with a hometown bookie, who had been robbed by Kan Chin's men.

Chin had given Rossi two weeks to give up his business. Why two weeks? He looked at the wall calendar.

Why that date? What was significant about it? There was just a single notation on the calendar. Election day.

Vanes picked up a pencil and drew a triangle on a sheet of yellow foolscap paper. At the tip of the triangle he printed Kan Chin. On the left corner he wrote Dino Lanzoni, on the right corner he added Billy Rossi's name.

He studied the drawing for several minutes. Just before he rose to his feet he scratched a big question mark in the center of the triangle.

Chapter Twelve

Dino Lanzoni sat stone-faced in the backseat, watching the limousine driver jump from the car, run over to the garage door, and slide it shut.

Lanzoni had no idea where he was. The sedan's windows had been darkened and the driver had crisscrossed through the city, up and down hills, obviously trying to confuse Lanzoni. Lanzoni had tried reading street signs at first, but grew tired of the effort. He didn't care where he was, as long as he saw the right man.

The driver opened the car door and Lanzoni climbed out slowly, rolling his neck, like a boxer waiting for the bell to ring.

The garage walls were gray, except where shelves had been ripped away, leaving jagged scars in the Sheetrock. The floor was slick from oil spills.

Three men, all Asians, came thudding down the wooden inside steps leading to the second floor.

Lanzoni watched them closely. Punks. Young punks. Damn near midgets. The oldest probably not yet thirty, with a fat face, wimpy mustache, and oily black hair.

Willy Hon approached Lanzoni on the balls of his feet, his right hand in his jacket pocket, wrapped around the checkered grip of a Walther PPK/S semiautomatic.

Hon gestured with the thumb of his left hand. "Hold them up and away from your body."

"I ain't carrying," Lanzoni grumbled nastily.

Hon gestured again.

Lanzoni scowled and shook his head, but raised his hands.

The two younger men came over quickly and gave him a professional patting down.

"He's not carrying a weapon," Jimmy Kung said in rapid Cantonese.

Hon affirmed the conclusion with a nod. He pointed his chin at Lanzoni and said, "Follow me."

Lanzoni went up the stairs behind Hon, the others tagging along right behind. The weight of the four men caused the wooden steps to groan in protest.

The stairs opened into a small, square hallway. There were five doors. The doors and walls were a dingy cream color and showed long-accumulated grime. The areas above the doorknobs bore heavy fingerprint smudges.

Hon opened one of the doors and they all trooped into the kitchen.

An elderly, frail-looking Asian with thick glasses was sitting on a battered wooden deck chair with cane backing that appeared as if it had been rescued from a sunken ocean liner. He was holding a delicate teacup that was decorated with lavender flowers.

He placed the cup on the nearby rickety kitchen table and rose to his feet.

"Ah, Mr. Lanzoni. So nice to meet you at last."

If someone saw the two men shaking hands, he would have figured that the big Italian, who towered over Kan Chin by nearly a full foot, and whose shoulders were seemingly twice as wide as Chin's, was the one to worry about.

Lanzoni's six feet three inches were clothed in an expensive black cashmere overcoat. Under the overcoat was a Gianni Campagna suit that would retail for more than three thousand dollars. But Lanzoni was not a man to pay retail.

Kan Chin's diminutive figure, birdlike bone structure, and slightly stooped shoulders were swallowed up by a heavy cardigan sweater.

While Lanzoni's full head of hair was so black it had hints of blue in it, Chin's few strands of gray hair looked like pencil lines drawn across his liver-spotted scalp.

Lanzoni took the offered hand into his, fearful that he'd crush it to pieces if he gave his normal squeeze.

Chin bowed his head. "Please, sit down. You would like some tea?"

"No thanks," Lanzoni said. The only other seat in the room was a gray metal folding chair leaning against the wall. Lanzoni snapped it open, twirled it around, and sat facing Kan Chin.

"I'm looking forward to doing some business with you, Mr. Chin. I'm sorry we didn't get together the other day."

"Yes. That was a shame," Chin lied convincingly. "When my men went to the restaurant on Union Street and spotted the police, they thought it best to terminate the appointment."

"Yeah. I don't know how they picked me up so quick."

Chin smiled benevolently, basking in just how naive the man was. Chin had set the time and place for the meeting, knowing that Billy Rossi would be at Sully's. He wanted the police to suspect that there was a connection between the two men. He sighed inwardly, bemused at just how easy it was to direct Lanzoni toward his goals. Dino Lanzoni had been the major player in putting his own brother behind bars. Federal agents had come to the family home, with a subpoena for some of Nick Lanzoni's personal records. The name *Lanzoni* had been misspelled on the document, ending with an e, rather than an i.

The agents were apologetic. Nick was not at home, but the hapless Dino was. He had ridiculed the agents over their mistake, fatally allowing them inside the house to use the phone to call their superiors regarding the purposely mislabeled subpoena. Once inside it had been an easy matter for the agent to drop a bug into the phone.

The Italians never seemed to learn. Electronic listening devices were driving them to prison. Taking them out of the game. Not only had they failed to locate the government bugs, but they had no idea that Chin's counterpoint in New York, the head of the most powerful Triad in the United States, had also planted listening devices in their homes, autos, and places of business.

If the bookmaker Billy Rossi had not been so astute about protecting his home from such listening devices, Chin would have had no need for the Dawson woman.

Chin had heard a tape recording of Dino Lanzoni ranting and raving about his brother's fate. Dino's main concern seemed to be that he was a target of the Mafia families in New York City. The family consigliere had made the matter clear. Leave town. Go west, young man, as the former American newspaperman had so charmingly put it.

Chin took a sip of tea, then said, "How may I serve you, Mr. Lanzoni?"

Lanzoni hunched forward, elbows on knees. "I want to do business. The same business we do with your people in New York." He looked over to the three young Chinese who stood watching him with blank faces.

"Okay to talk?"

Kan Chin snapped his fingers lightly and the two younger men left the room. Willy Hon crossed his arms over his chest and leaned against the edge of the stove.

Lanzoni's voice dropped to a confidential whisper. "Heroin. Cocaine. Large shipments. On a steady basis."

"You already have a customer base on the West Coast?"

"Sure," Lanzoni responded confidently. "And I'm going to expand. Rapidly. Silicon Valley, the whole damn Bay Area. It's been left to the amateurs for too long. I'm also interested in credit cards, and traveler's checks. Your people in Hong Kong do nice work."

Chin nodded in agreement. Hong Kong was now the world's premier counterfeit marketplace.

"Mr. Chin, I figure that the price out here might be a little better than back home. Less travel time, so to speak."

Chin sat back in the cane chair until it creaked, like a hinge in need of oil. "Let us assume for now that I will be able to supply you with everything you need." His lips twisted wryly. "For a price of course. You see, Mr. Lanzoni, we have much the same problems here as you do in New York City. I invest a lot of time and money in placement. People placement. At the present time I have people in all the right places. With promises of more to come."

Dino Lanzoni rubbed the palms of his hands along his trousers. "So what's your problem?"

"Politics," Chin answered softly. "Always politics. We are very comfortable with the present city administration. However, there is an election coming up shortly. Our man in city hall is in danger of losing his position. That would be most inconvenient."

Lanzoni pulled at the knot of his tie and unbuttoned his shirt collar. "So your man loses. Can't you do business with the new people? We do business with everybody back home. Elections don't mean a hell of a lot."

"You are indeed fortunate. The new person, Philip Dong, is a man of my own race, unfortunately. Should he become mayor, he has a very difficult attitude. He's a crusader."

"So what's the problem? Make sure the bastard don't win."

"A simple idea, but there is not a simple solution."

Lanzoni knew when he was hooked and being reeled in. "So what do you want me to do? Break the sixth on the guy?"

Chin narrowed his eyes, his face wrinkling like a fan.

"Break the sixth?" he asked, totally confused.

"The sixth commandment. Thou shalt not kill," Lanzoni explained with a chuckle. "Waste him."

Kan Chin clapped his hands together and laughed. He had heard many different expressions used to describe the act of assassination, but this was a new one. "Not yet. But I thank you for the offer. If it comes to that, you can be certain that I would be very appreciative of your services. What our man needs right now is money. Money from unknown sources. We have contributed a great deal, however, local politics make it difficult to do more."

Lanzoni looked into the old man's eyes in their bed of wrinkles. "How much?"

"A half-million should guarantee success for our candidate."

"As long as we can work out a deal between us, I don't see any real problem with that."

With a knowing wag of a finger, Chin said, "Then I don't see a real problem either."

Chapter Thirteen

After leaving Red Vanes's house, John Tomei used the cell phone Billy Rossi had provided to call Elaine Surel. He gave her the name Vanes had mentioned, Willy Hon. They arranged to meet for a drink after Elaine got off work.

His next call was to a number he hadn't dialed in a long time.

"Four Hair Styling Salon. Can I help you?"

"Styling salon. Does that mean the haircuts cost more than five bucks?"

"Jesus, Tomb," Louie Rodriguez whined, snapping a pair of scissors nervously in one hand. "What happened to you? Who's been cutting your hair?"

"Me," Tomei admitted.

"You? It's going to take me four or five cuts to get it back in shape."

"Just do your best, Louie. Cut it down. Way down."

The barber ran his fingers through Tomei's long locks, a seasick look on his face. "You cut it yourself," he proclaimed sadly. "I work on the man's hair for fifteen years, have it perfect, and then he starts cutting it himself. How could you do this to me?"

Not that many years ago, San Francisco was crowded with "cop bars."

The sight of an on-duty plainclothes detective having a couple of highballs before lunch, while sitting alongside an assistant district attorney, a defense attorney, or a judge, was not an uncommon sight.

Most uniformed officers kept their imbibing hidden from public view, downing their shots and beers in the storage rooms and kitchens of the restaurants and cocktail lounges on their beats.

Both John Tomei and Elaine "Gucci" Surel could remember traipsing around with policemen from other cities, in town to pick up a prisoner, testifying in a trial, or just on a friendly visit. These "friendly little visits" would sometimes last a few days, and the money used for marathon sessions in Cookie's, Shanty Malone's, or the J&B came from slush funds or the hosting policeman's own pocket.

Tomei's favorite town for a "friendly little visit" was New Orleans, back when the Big Easy was big, easy, and friendly.

He and Elaine had once flown down there to pick up a prisoner, arriving late on a Thursday night, getting to court the following morning.

The prisoner, a naive young man who had been persuaded to drive the getaway car for two of his buddies who held up a bank in San Francisco's financial district, had fled for home. The New Orleans cops had found him hiding in his mother's house.

The presiding judge, a bull-necked man with a low forehead almost hidden by thick gray brows, had asked Tomei, "Have you and your partner been able to enjoy the hospitality of our fine city?"

When Tomei answered that due to their late arrival time they had not, the judge responded as if it was a personal affront. "You mean you two haven't been out around town?"

"No, Your Honor," Tomei and Surel had chorused in unison.

The judge pounded down his gavel with authority. "I hereby put this hearing over to Monday morning, at ten o'clock. Now you two inspectors enjoy yourselves, hear?"

And enjoy themselves they did. The New Orleans cops had taken them on a tour ranging from the posh Windsor Court Grill Room and Brennan's to rough, no-nonsense drinking bars on Bourbon Street, across the river to Algiers for Cajun food at Kelsey's, and finally a winding trip on narrow dirt roads, across swamp-edged bridges into the Bayou to an out-of-the-way restaurant at the end of a wobbly, moss-encrusted pier. The centers of the tables were nothing more than large stainless-steel platters. The cooks would come out and pour bucket after bucket of steaming prawns, clams, oysters, lobsters, and spiny creatures the San Francisco cops had never seen before right onto the table.

Neither Tomei nor Surel was able to pay for a single drink or meal, though it seemed to Tomei like the Orleans cops weren't dipping into their wallets that often either.

Even the prisoner enjoyed the benefit of a weekend off. The judge releasing him to his mother's custody, after admonishing him to be in court Monday morning, "Or else!"

By the time Tomei and Surel returned to court they were in no condition to chase the prisoner if he had decided to run for it. Luckily, it appeared that the young man had spent his weekend celebrating as hard and heavy as they had. All three slept through the entire flight back to San Francisco.

But those days were long gone. Both in San Francisco, and New Orleans. Iced tea and soft drinks had taken the place of highballs, martinis, and bottles of beer.

After hours, most city policemen joined in the traffic crush abandoning the city for the promised lands in the suburbs. If they did stay in town for a drink or two, one of the stops was the Double Play, a bona fide eating-drinking establishment described by its owner as serving "Red meat, gravy, and brown booze."

The bar is located in a blue-collar district of the city

and got its name from the fact that the city's minor league ball park, Seals Stadium, was once situated right across the street.

Now, a block-long shopping mall stood in place of the old green-walled stadium.

A popular song on the tavern's jukebox is Sinatra's version of "There Used to Be a Ballpark, Right Here."

"Hi, John," Elaine called out when she spotted Tomei at the bar. "Great haircut," she exclaimed as she ran a hand across his blue blazer. "Ummmm. Italian wool. Very nice. I remember this jacket." She nodded her head as she checked out the gray slacks and blue shirt. "You're getting there."

"Where's your partner?" Tomei said.

"Home. Alone. Waiting for the phone to ring." She took a card from her purse and tucked it in Tomei's breast pocket. "There's her number. Call her."

"Stop playing matchmaker, Gucci."

She responded by sticking her tongue out at him, then ordered a Stoli on the rocks while Tomei nursed a beer. He could never understand how Elaine could cram so much alcohol into her size-nine frame. She regularly drank him under the table when they were partners.

Elaine slipped Willy Hon's rap sheet out of her purse, handed it to Tomei, and said "Ugly little sucker, isn't he?" before tasting her drink.

Tomei glanced at the rap sheet. Hon had more than a dozen arrests, mostly for assault with a deadly weapon. All the charges had been dismissed. The mug shot paper clipped to the report showed a flat-faced Asian with a scraggly mustache that curled downward at the ends. He was smiling at the camera as if posing for his high school yearbook.

"How's Red Vanes?" Elaine wanted to know. "There's talk that he's gone round the bend. Paranoid. And how are you doing with Billy Rossi?"

"Vanes is all right. I checked out Rossi's house. The bad guys apparently came in through the front door.

There were some scratches around the lock's strike plate, but not around the lock."

"So, either they had some super-duper lock picker with them, or someone left the door unlocked for them. Do you think Sherri Dawson's story about being attacked is a phony?"

Tomei drummed his finger on the tabletop. "Rossi found her tied up to the couch. I think they really hurt her."

"So what's that mean, John? If she left the front door unlocked, why would they do what they did to her?"

"I don't know." Tomei waved to the bartender for another round of drinks. "Who do we know in the Las Vegas P.D.?"

"Vegas, Vegas." Elaine closed her eyes, leaned forward, locked her fingers under her chin and appeared as if she might be saying a prayer. "Got it," she said moments later.

"Dick Bostic. A lieutenant in Vice. I talked to him a couple of times about some Vegas high rollers who were roughed up in a Tenderloin card room. The rollers hinted that they were connected with the mob. Bostic said no. They were just wanna-bes. He seemed like a good guy. Do you want to call him?"

"No. I want you to call him. See if they've got anything on Sherri Dawson. Arrests, aided case reports, traffic tags, anything at all. I'll go pay him a visit. And Gucci, it wouldn't hurt if Bostic thought I was still with the department."

"It's good to see you again, Mr. Chin," Charles Prescott said, noticing that a full bottle of Knob Creek Kentucky bourbon sat on the orange jade table. A young doll-faced girl shuffled silently into the room. She wasn't the same one he remembered seeing on his last visit. If anything, she was more exquisite than her predecessor.

She set an ice bucket on the table and Prescott tried to catch her eye. Her skin was creamy white. Flawless.

Chin waved her away. "Thank you for responding so quickly." He handed Prescott a slip of paper. "Those are some suggestions I have for the mayor. I believe you will find they are reasonable."

Prescott examined the neatly typed page, which listed the number of political appointments Chin wanted.

"I will discuss your . . ." Prescott paused momentarily, "suggestions with the mayor. He values your input, and I can assure you that he will listen closely to your recommendations."

Chin bowed his head slightly. He knew that Mayor Barr had already bargained away the appointments to other supporters. "I have something else that will certainly be helpful for Mayor Barr, Charles."

"He will be most appreciative," Prescott answered quickly, taking note of Chin calling him by his first name.

"Yes, I'm sure he will. May I fix you a drink?"

"I could use one," Prescott admitted, waiting until his host had concocted the drink before sitting down.

"You mentioned our support of Mayor Barr at our last meeting," Chin said softly, as if they were conversing in a church. "I have been able to obtain donations from various businessmen who are most anxious to keep Mayor Barr in his post. A sizable amount.

"The sum of money I am talking about is five hundred thousand dollars. Five hundred and fifty thousand, actually. Because of the possibility of repercussions from Mr. Dong, the donation will have to be anonymous." Chin leaned back in his chair and folded his arms across his narrow chest. "In cash."

Prescott had the drink to his lips and pulled it away so fast, some of the liquid dribbled down his chin. He pulled a handkerchief from his pants pocket and patted his face dry.

"In cash you say."

"Exactly. I will have the money delivered to you personally. Should Mayor Barr ever ask about the money, I will give him a figure of five hundred thousand dollars."

Chin waited for the words to take effect.

"But you're giving me five hundred and fifty thousand," was Prescott's guarded reply.

"Exactly."

Prescott took a long sip of the bourbon. "I understand."

I hope so, Kan Chin thought. "There is more, Charles. I think I may have some, what was the term you used? Ammunition. Yes, ammunition to use against Mr. Dong."

Prescott shifted nervously in his chair. "That would be most helpful."

"It is possible that Mr. Dong is guilty of the same type of activity he is trying to smear Mayor Barr with."

Prescott's forehead wrinkled in confusion.

"I have heard a rumor that Philip Dong himself has connections with organized crime. In Hong Kong and on the mainland. I will be able to confirm this in a day or two."

"We don't have much time left. The mayor will be extremely grateful."

"Yes, I'm sure he will be. We have an understanding then, Charles?"

Prescott set his glass down on the table. "I think we understand each other perfectly, Mr. Chin."

Kan Chin nodded his head in what Prescott took as an agreeing gesture.

Chin's true feelings were that the man was a fool. And fools could be dangerous. He leaned forward in his chair and stared directly into Prescott's eyes. "Charles, I have been around for a much longer time then you. There was a politician, some years ago. Mr. Unruh. A crude but very shrewd politician. He was the most powerful man in all of California. More powerful than the governor. He had a saying about politics. 'If you can't eat their food, drink their booze, screw their women, take their money, and then vote

against them, you have no business being a politician.'
Do you consider yourself a politician, Charles?"

Prescott swallowed some of the whiskey to stall for
time. "No, not really. I prefer to stay in the background. Out of sight, Mr. Chin."

Kan Chin rose from the chair and straightened to
his fullest height. "I am pleased with your answer,
Charles. Very pleased. I'm sure we will be able to do
business together for a long time."

Chapter Fourteen

Billy Rossi was yanking on Fidel's choke chain when he opened the door to his house. A lever-action carbine was clamped under one arm. He was wearing a brown-and-black-checked sport coat over a black turtleneck sweater and black pants. His shoes were black-and-brown two-tone.

"Hey, Tomb. I've got to go out and check on some things," Rossi said. He gently set the rifle down, butt first, near the door, then tugged the big dog back into the house. "Sherri's inside. You got anything yet?"

"Maybe." Tomei patted Fidel's head, then handed Rossi the rap sheet he'd gotten from Elaine. "Do you think this could have been one of them?"

Rossi let the leash drop to the floor as he examined the photograph. He screwed up his face, then handed the picture back to Tomei. "I can't tell from that. Who is he?"

"Willy Hon. He's Kan Chin's right-hand man."

"Chin? You think he's the one who came after me?"

"It's a possibility. Have you ever had any trouble with him?"

"No. Kan Chin has never bothered me. No one bothered me up till now. I guess Chin wants to take over the whole damn city. Maybe Sherri can make something out of that photograph. I'll go get her."

Tomei fixed himself a drink and roughhoused with Fidel. The shepherd welcomed the exercise.

When Rossi came back into the room, he said, "Sherri's in the bath. She'll be down in a few minutes." He shot his cuff and looked at his watch. "I've got to go. I won't be back until late. You gonna be here?"

"Yes. I'll be here. You better take Fidel with you. And be careful."

Rossi patted his coat pocket. "I'm packin'." He pulled a double-barreled derringer from his pocket.

"Take Fidel with you. He'll be a lot more useful than the gun, Billy."

Rossi grunted his agreement. "Yeah, I'd probably shoot myself in the foot. Come on, Fidel. Let's go for a ride."

Tomei wandered into the kitchen. Like the rest of the house, it had been redone since his first visit, and he was impressed. Maple cabinets, limestone tile flooring, a center-aisle chopping block the size of his kitchen table at the Russian River cabin. The stainless-steel and brass eight-burner double oven range sat alongside a matching double-door refrigerator and stand-up freezer.

An arched maple door bore the words *Wine Cellar*, the scrawled letters appearing as if they had been put in place by a branding iron.

Tomei had always enjoyed cooking, and when Joan began working late he had taken over the cooking chores, bringing Messy into the process. Once Joan had come home and found the two of them, along with the stove and kitchen linoleum, covered with flour, the result of attempts to make bread or cookies. Joan hadn't thought it the least bit funny, but Tomei and Messy had. They couldn't stop laughing. It was one of those father-daughter bonding moments that he missed so badly.

He rummaged through the refrigerator, finding butter, eggs, Parmesan cheese, and parsley. He had whipped up the ingredients and was about to pour the mixture into a hot frying pan when Sherri Dawson came into the room, a bottle of red wine in one hand, an empty glass in the other. She was wearing a peach-colored, floor-length gown with a V front and back. Her nipples dented the silk. She was barefoot and smelled of lavender.

"I hear you have some pictures."

"Just one," Tomei said. "The photo on the table. His name is Willy Hon."

Sherri poured herself a glass of wine before picking up the photo. She studied it for a moment, then grunted. "I can't tell from this."

"But he could have been one of them?"

She put the drink down, crossed her arms, and hugged herself in a protective, virginal gesture. "I told you they kept their stocking masks on all the time. If this was the leader, he liked to see his friends in action. He got real close and watched. I could see black eyes through his mask, boring into mine. Laughing at me. There were wet marks on the mask by his mouth. He was drooling. The stocking was getting tight on him, I guess. Maybe he was so hot he was having a tough time breathing through the damn thing. But to say this was that man? Sorry. No can do. Who is he?"

Tomei dropped the eggs into the hot skillet. "His name is Willy Hon. He works for Kan Chin, the leader of a gang in Chinatown. Want to split an omelet?"

Sherri walked over to the stove, her hip brushing against Tomei's. "I liked your hair better when it was long." Her voice turned husky. "Billy's gone."

"I know."

"He won't be back for hours."

Tomei rolled the omelet over with a wooden spatula. Sherri pulled his hands away from the stove and moved into him, her breasts pushing into his chest, her arms circling his waist.

"I'm scared. Really scared." She burrowed her head into his shoulder. "Billy and I have an agreement. He doesn't mind if I'm with other men. Billy is . . . having a bad time now. Sex isn't possible."

"How many have there been?" Tomei asked, freeing a hand and dragging the skillet from the heat.

She tilted her head up and stared at him. "None. Absolutely none. Not since I met Billy. Except for those bastards who raped me." She backed off. "Is that what you're worried about? I went to the doctor and got a clean bill of health, so don't—"

"Sherri. You're gorgeous. I like you. But Billy is my client. This is his house. You're his girl."

"My God," she exclaimed. "A man of chivalry. I don't believe it."

Tomei's hands moved as if to explain, then dropped to his side. "How about that omelet?"

"No thanks." Sherri walked to the door, leaning against the frame. She cocked a hip and licked her lips. Her eyes traveled from Tomei's face to his crotch. "Tell your pants it's not polite to point," she smiled, then spun around on her bare foot and strode out of sight.

Tomei glanced down at his pants and swore silently. He carried the skillet containing the now overcooked omelet to the sink and ran cold water over it, telling himself that a cold shower might be a good idea, too.

Chapter Fifteen

After "the incident," John Tomei was advised by the deputy chief of the San Francisco Police Department to take an early retirement rather than face a departmental hearing that would without a doubt result in his being fired. He still remembered the chief's exact words: "Take the drunk's pension or we'll can your ass and you'll end up doing time."

A "drunk's pension" was one third that of a normal pension. Not enough to live on but better than nothing, so Tomei took the advice, signed the necessary papers, and left with as much dignity as was allowed. The only personal item Tomei took with him was his badge. The gun he'd used to shoot at his wife's lover had been confiscated by the Novato Police Department. He'd gotten a letter after the criminal case was dismissed, informing him that he could reclaim the weapon, but he wanted no part of it. Or any gun.

That particular gun had saved Tomei's life. Plain-clothes and off-duty policemen fall into two categories when it comes to their personal firearms. There are those who go for the bulky, high-impact .10mm semi-automatic with clips that can hold up to seventeen cartridges. The others opt for the smallest, lightest weapon they can find. Tomei's choice was an alloy metal snub-nosed revolver with a five-round cylinder. Favoring a tradition that went back to 1835 when Samuel Colt patented the first successful revolver,

Tomei left the round under the gun's hammer empty, to prevent discharge in case the gun was accidently dropped to the floor.

Tomei had admitted to his psychiatrist that he had no idea that he'd fired all four shots that day at his house prior to placing the smoking barrel next to his temple and pulling the trigger.

Like most ex-cops, his badge went everywhere with him, and had saved him from several speeding tags and possibly one drunk-driving charge. There still was a fraternal spirit among police officers and "flashing the badge" opened a few doors. And sometimes kept doors from being slammed in one's face.

The uniformed police officer behind the counter of the Las Vegas Police Department Detective Division had his face frozen in an annoyed, disinterested look that was as much a part of his uniform as the holstered revolver on his belt.

Tomei dropped his suitcase to the floor. "I have an appointment with Lieutenant Bostic."

"Oh, yeah? What's your name?"

"John Tomei."

The officer ran a hand over his bulging stomach and glanced up at the office clock. "What time's your appointment?"

"One o'clock." Tomei pulled his badge from his coat pocket. "San Francisco P.D."

"San Francisco, the land of fruits and nuts." The officer shoved a hefty paw across the counter. "We have our share here in Vegas, believe me. Come on, I'll walk you back to Bostic's dungeon."

Tomei was led through a maze of corridors bordered by six-foot-high vanilla-colored partitions. Gaps in the partitions displayed small cubicles containing a desk, a couple of chairs, and a man or woman talking into a telephone or clicking away at a computer.

The uniformed officer knocked on the wall of one of the cubicles. "Hey, Bostic. You have a visitor." He patted Tomei on the shoulder as he left. "Take care, pal."

Bostic was sitting behind his desk, a phone tucked between his shoulder and chin. He appeared to be in his fifties, with a wind-weathered face; thick, disheveled iron-gray hair; and a square jaw. He waved a hand at Tomei, gesturing to a chair.

"Yeah, yeah, I know, I know," Bostic said into the phone, as his eyes took Tomei in. "What do you want me to do about it? Just pull the bastard in with what I have now? Come to the party, Wally. I've got to have more than that."

Whoever Wally was must have said something to cause Bostic to terminate the call quickly. He dropped the receiver onto its cradle. "Yeah, and screw you, too." He turned his attention to Tomei. "Are you the guy from Frisco?"

It had been sometime since Tomei had heard the word *Frisco*.

"I'm the guy."

"Yeah. Your partner, Surel, called me. I told her all I had on Sherri Dawson was a grand theft report. It must be important to get you up here on a Mickey Mouse report like this."

"It could be important."

Bostic sorted through a pile of papers on his desk, plucking four pages held together by a paper clip from the bottom of the pile. "Here it is. Like I told Surel, it's all we have."

"Gucci told me. I appreciate your cooperation."

"Gucci?"

Tomei explained Elaine's nickname.

"Hey, I like that," Bostic said, leaning back in his chair and locking his fingers behind his head. "What's the big interest in this Dawson lady?"

"I think she let some people into a victim's house. They got away with a lot of money. She claimed she was assaulted and raped."

"You figure the assault's a phony?"

"I think the bad guys got out of control. The owner of the house heard it going down. Saw her get batted around."

"Go ahead, read the report, Tomei. I have plenty to do here."

The Las Vegas grand theft report form was similar in content to the type used by the San Francisco Police Department. The victim's name was listed first: Wong, Arnold. His residence address was in Hong Kong. Suspect, Sherrilyn Dawson—same local address as shown on her driver's license.

The complaint took place at the Casbah Casino, the items listed as stolen were a gold Audemars Piguet Royal Oak watch, with a listed value of forty thousand dollars, eleven thousand in cash, and traveler's checks totaling some fifteen thousand dollars.

"I don't see a follow-up report."

"The guy dropped the charges. We dropped the investigation. Never even booked Dawson."

Tomei tapped the report on his knee. "Somebody made sure he got his stuff back."

"Probably," Bostic agreed. "I vaguely remember the case. I think your lady is a casino hooker. Paid to keep the big spenders happy. She got a little greedy."

"You know anybody at the Casbah Casino?"

"Oh, sure. I know someone at every casino, or I wouldn't be able to do my job."

Bostic began flipping through the Rolodex on his desk. "You want to talk to the man at the Casbah?"

"Yes, I do."

Tomei went back to studying the report while Bostic picked up the phone again.

"Hey, Frisco," Bostic called, catching Tomei's attention. "You're set up for a meeting after midnight tonight." He pointed to Tomei's suitcase. "You have a room?"

"No."

Bostic covered the receiver with one hand. "You want to make it easy on yourself? Stay at the Casbah? I can't get you a comp, but the price will be good."

"I'd appreciate it."

Bostic pulled his hand from the phone. "Yeah. Fix him up with a room, Ben. Thanks." He hung up and frowned at Tomei. "A few years back, I could have gotten you a comp room, the dinner show, and a date with one of those dancers with legs that go all the way up to their shoulders. But *no mas*."

"I know," Tomei said sadly. "It's the same all over."

Bostic raked through his desk drawers, finding a box of business cards with his badge embossed in gold. He scribbled a name on the back of the card. "See this guy, Ben Trane. He's an ex-cop. We have to stick together, right?"

Tomei confirmed the statement with a nod. "No doubt about it."

Tomei hadn't been in Las Vegas since his honeymoon with Joan nearly fifteen years ago. He hardly recognized the famous road known as "The Strip" as the cabdriver crept along in the slow-moving traffic.

Tomei remembered there having been plots of actual desert standing between the casinos. Now there was just one long strip of buildings, everything from soaring casinos, to shopping centers and fast-food restaurants.

He recognized the outline of Caesar's Palace but not much else.

The cabby pointed out the new landmarks: the Mirage; New York, New York; Bellagio; and the Excalibur, the latter looked to Tomei as if it had been constructed by Disney architects who'd been on a three-day drunk.

The Casbah Casino Resort was all pink stucco and towering turrets. The cabbie drove through a series of Moorish arches and pulled up under a red-and-white-striped awning. An athletic-looking man wearing pink-and-red-striped balloon-legged pants and a jewel-laden turban had the taxi's door open before the vehicle had come to a complete stop.

Tomei paid off the cabbie and followed the turban into the lobby. It reminded him of a glorified version of a Warner Brothers sand-and-sex epic seen on late-night television.

Inside the hotel were more turbaned men toting luggage. Attractive women dressed in skimpy harem outfits flitted through the crowd, carrying trays of complimentary cocktails for the gamblers.

To get to the registration desk Tomei had to walk through the middle of the casino itself, where he became instantly aware of the hum of the crowd, the curious pinging noises of slot machines, the spin of the roulette wheel, the occasional triumphant shouts when one of the one-armed bandits coughed up a winner.

Tomei's reservation was logged on the hotel's computer. He was given a key in the form of a plastic credit card, which he was informed could also be used on the room's refreshment center.

Tomei was mildly disappointed that he had to use an ordinary elevator to get to his room, rather than some exotic form of magic carpet.

"Don't those turbans give you a headache?" he asked as he handed the bellboy a ten-dollar bill for his effort at carrying the one piece of luggage to the room and opening the drapes.

The young man cradled the bill, as a vet might handle a fragile bird. "Yes, sir. They sure do." He smiled at Tomei for several moments, then, when he realized that the one bill was going to be the extent of his tip, he jammed the money into the wide silk sash around his waist and without enthusiasm said, "Good luck, sir."

The refreshment center was a waist-high refrigerator stocked with a variety of top-label miniature liquor bottles, splits of wine and champagne, nuts, canned fruit juices, Coke, Pepsi, and a brand of an Italian mineral water Tomei had not seen before. He selected the mineral water and a packet of macadamia nuts, and surveyed the room.

The carpeting, walls, and drapes were all of light blue tones. King-size was not an adequate description for the enormous round bed. The ceiling above the bed was mirrored. A square variegated marble bathtub screened by sheer, billowy drapes was just a few steps from the bed. A sliding glass door led to a narrow terrace with a view of a golf course in the distance. The lush, emerald-green grass seemed misplaced against the background of barren landscape in the distance.

Tomei sipped the mineral water and shook his head, hoping that Lieutenant Dick Bostic of the Las Vegas Police Department had been right about getting the room at a reduced rate. Then he remembered he was operating with Billy Rossi's money. He picked up the phone and called room service.

The turbaned doorman didn't bother looking at the ten-dollar bill John Tomei palmed to him when he asked for a cab. The bill simply disappeared into his balloon-shaped pants. He snapped his fingers and a yellow-and-red taxi pulled up in front of Tomei.

The cabdriver, a short, ruddy-skinned man with a scraggly goatee, gave Tomei a dejected look when given the address on Via Perdido Street. The driver was hoping for a fare to the airport. For some reason customers usually tipped bigger upon leaving town than when arriving. Maybe it was those left-over coins and chips in their pockets. Or maybe it was that they were just glad to leave with enough money to get them back home.

The driver pulled to a curb, reached under his seat for a well-thumbed Thomas Map Book, and found Via Perdido. He leaned over the seat and squinted at Tomei. "It's over on the west side of town, mister."

"I know," Tomei acknowledged. He'd learned long ago never to tell a cabbie you didn't know how far it was to your destination. "Relax. It's a round-trip. You may have to wait a while, but just leave the flag down."

The news cheered the driver, who slotted a Gipsy Kings cassette into the dashboard's tape player and headed west.

The address shown on Sherri Dawson's Nevada driver's license, 19220 Via Perdido Street, turned out to be a biscuit dough–colored apartment complex.

Since landing at the Las Vegas Airport, Tomei had enjoyed a totally air-conditioned environment—the taxis to the police station, to the Casbah Casino, the hotel room, and now the ride to Via Perdido. The afternoon heat hit him like a furnace blast when he left the cab and walked up to the apartment house. It was only a thirty-yard walk, but he slipped his jacket off and was moping his forehead with his shirtsleeve by the time he entered the lobby. The hum and caress of the air-conditioning had an almost sensual feeling.

A sunburned woman in her twenties, her skin the color of cotton candy, with shaggy, sun-blanched hair, wearing a yellow halter top and denim shorts was opening her mailbox.

Tomei strode over alongside her and examined the apartment index. Thirty-six was listed to an A. Avery.

"How do I get to number thirty-six?" Tomei asked the woman.

She gave Tomei a curious look, then began sorting through her mail. "Out that door," she said, nodding her head to the left, "around the pool. Third floor." She stopped her sorting long enough to eye Tomei once again. "Who are you looking for?"

"Sherri Dawson."

The woman shrugged her shoulders. An inch or two of smooth white skin riding up over her halter top.

Tomei thanked her and headed for the pool, thinking that in a few years the woman was going to be sorry she basted so long in the desert sun.

A mirrorlike swimming pool took up most of the courtyard. The pool was surrounded by gaunt palm trees and patches of parched lawn. White plastic tables shaded by orange canvas umbrellas were spaced around the pool area.

Only one person had braved the afternoon sun— a bonily thin middle-aged man with bushy white sideburns. His body glistened with oil and Tomei caught the smell of the tanning lotion, something with coconut in it.

The man lay face-up on a web-backed chaise lounge, eyes closed. Tomei's footsteps caught his attention. He opened one eye, grunted something unintelligible, and went back to his sun bath.

The back of Tomei's shirt was dripping with sweat by the time he reached the door of unit number thirty-six. He pushed the doorbell several times, and was about to return to the waiting cab when the door opened a crack.

"Who is it?" asked a low, sleepy voice.

"John. Is Sherri in?"

The door opened a few inches wider. He could see an oval face draped by wine-dark hair.

"Sherri's not here, John. What was it about?"

"What do you think?" Tomei replied, managing a small smile.

The door swung wide open. "Come on in, John. I'm Ava." She was nearly as tall as Tomei, with an aerobics-firm body fully displayed in a bikini that was nothing more than patches of purple triangles fastened at the neck, back, and hips.

The air conditioner either wasn't on or was set very low. The air was heavy with heat. The carpeting was sand-colored and in need of a cleaning. The walls were upholstered in a pale-blue velvet fabric.

A green-and-white floral-print couch stretched across the center of the room. A half-dozen overstuffed cushions in the same floral pattern were scattered around the floor.

"When did you last see Sherri?" the girl asked, perching daintily on the arm of the couch.

"I haven't been in Vegas for about year. Is she going to be in today?"

"No." Ava's tongue made a slow circle around her lips. "She's gone, John. What was it about her that you liked?"

Tomei winked at her. "Blondes. I'm partial to blondes."

Ava ran her hands through her thick, shoulder-length dark hair. "That's no problem, lover. I can be a blond. I'll look like Sherri's twin sister. It'll only take me a minute to change." She stood up, placed her right index finger on her lips, slowly trailed it down her chin, neck, and then across the sheen of sweat in the hollow between her breasts. She brought the fingertip back to her mouth and licked it. "What did Sherri do for you, John? Tell me what you like. I'm sure we can have fun."

"How much are we talking about, Ava?"

She sauntered over, her hips languidly swaying, her lips back in a pout. "Five hundred, lover, and it'll be the best five hundred you ever spent."

Tomei edged away. "That's a little steep. Maybe I better wait and see if Sherri shows up at the Casbah."

Ava stretched out her arms, encircling Tomei's neck. She pulled him close, grinding her hips against him. "Sherri's not coming back, John. Believe me. She's gone." Her lips came together and she made a kissing sound. "Poof. All gone."

"Where to?" Tomei asked, reaching up and untangling Ava's hands.

"California," Ava said, wrinkling her nose, running her hands down Tomei's back, across the coat jacket he was holding over his shoulder. She stopped suddenly when she felt the outline of Tomei's badge through the material. "Shit. Don't tell me you're a cop!"

"Cops need love, too, Ava."

She pulled away, wheeled around to the couch and flopped down on it, crossing her arms and legs. "You pricks want it all right. You just don't want to pay for it!"

"When's the last time you were busted?"

"Why me? Why the hell are you picking on me?" Ava pleaded, in her poor-little-girl voice. "I've got some friends coming over later. I don't want to waste the afternoon down at county. You know I'll be out in a few hours, anyway. Can't we make a deal?"

"It's not you I'm after. It's Sherri."

"I told you. She's gone. To California. Months ago."

She uncrossed her legs, spreading them wide. "Can we do a deal, John? I'll do anything you want."

"Anything?" Tomei asked, draping his sport coat carefully over the back of the sofa.

Chapter Sixteen

Sherri Dawson glanced over her shoulder every few moments as she widened her stride approaching the Renaissance Park 55 Hotel.

Market Street was crowded with an array of tourists, office workers, and sullen-faced street people. A dark-skinned man in a jaunty porkpie hat was drumming a bossa nova beat on a series of upturned plastic paint cans and old cooking pots. He sounded a lot better than some of the bands Sherri had danced for in New York and Florida.

The Park 55 was located near the corner of Fifth and Market, one of the busier sections of the city. And that's what Sherri wanted. A busy spot. Lots of people. A public meeting place. "Anywhere you wish," Kan Chin had said.

Sherri chose the Park 55 because it reminded her of a Vegas casino. The hotel's granite exterior resembled pyramiding stacks of baccarat chips. Vegas, pure Vegas.

She entered the lobby cautiously. A swarm of people, many with luggage in hand or draped over their shoulders, were congregated around the registration counter.

Sherri's eyes circled the area, looking for Asians. There were plenty of them, mostly Japanese. She stopped and stared at the mylar-mirrored ceiling. The upside-down view of the lobby showed no sign of Kan

Chin. Or the man in the mug shot that Tomei had shown her.

She glanced at her watch. Five on the dot. She took the escalator to the mezzanine floor, where she spotted Chin sitting alone in one of the sofas near the entrance to the Veranda Restaurant.

Chin saw her and rose to his feet. He walked slowly, quietly, as if visiting a sick friend at a hospital.

"Ah, Miss Dawson. Good to see you again," he said solemnly.

"I'll bet," Sherri responded bitterly. "Your men damn near killed me."

"I apologize for their actions." Chin cupped her elbow and led her back to the sofa. "They have been punished. Severely. Most severely."

"Mr. Chin. I know you helped me in Vegas, but this is it. I think I've more than evened up the score."

Chin nodded as he held out an arm, waiting for Sherri to sit before joining her. "Would you feel better if I showed you the graves of the men who disobeyed my orders?" he asked with a sly smile.

"You killed them?"

Chin put a finger to his lips and whispered, "They disobeyed my orders and brought you much pain."

Sherri searched his eyes, wondering if he was telling the truth. "You brought the money?"

"Indeed." Chin drew a buff-colored envelope from his jacket pocket. "The money we agreed on, and a bonus." He passed her the envelope.

Sherri placed it in her purse without checking it. "I'm telling you this because I want you to leave me alone. Forever. Agreed?"

"Agreed," Chin said. "I cannot blame you for your feelings, Miss Dawson."

Sherri took a deep breath, her eyes roaming the room. "All right. Billy's scared. I think he's going to quit the bookie business. He has plenty of money."

"Mr. Rossi does not seem the type of man to quit so easily."

"Billy is mad as hell, but he's scared. He doesn't

want to die. He does want to find the men who stole his money, pushed him around, and cut up his precious paintings." She looked Chin directly in the eye. "The ones who raped me."

Chin's face remained placid. "He will have to look underground to find them, Miss Dawson. At least six feet underground."

"Billy thinks that someone who works for him set him up. He's had a lot of his employees over to the house, grilling them. He even has a rent-a-cop there around the clock." Sherri paused, opened her mouth to say something, then held back.

Chin took note of the gesture. "Has Mr. Rossi's inquiries been helpful to him?"

Sherri took a folded piece of paper from her purse. "Someone gave this to Billy. I don't know who. Maybe the rent-a-cop. I made a copy of it. He thinks it might be one of the men who came to the house that night."

Chin's face was passive as he examined the Xeroxed mug shot of Willy Hon. "I assure you, he is not one of my employees."

Sherri gave him a skeptical look. "I'll tell you one last thing, Mr. Chin. One last bit of information, then we're free of each other. Billy is carrying a gun. And he bought a dog. A big German shepherd, that's supposed to be a killer. An attack dog. There's a word you use, if you think he's going after you."

"And what is that word?"

"Freeze. You say freeze and the dog stops in his tracks."

"Where are you going, Miss Dawson? To Las Vegas?"

Sherri rose slowly from the chair. "I'm through with Vegas. Good-bye, Mr. Chin."

"Good-bye, Miss Dawson." Kan Chin kept his eyes on Sherri's back as she hurried toward the escalator. He slowly raised his hand. The fist was clenched at first, then two fingers popped up.

Willy Hon saw the signal and smiled inwardly as

he began punching out a number on his cellular phone.

Ben Trane was younger than Tomei had expected. An elegantly dressed slender man with the requisite Las Vegas suntan in the prime of his mid-thirties. His prematurely gray hair was cut short and combed forward. His midnight-blue tuxedo had silk-faced lapels. A bright red silk handkerchief flopped elegantly from the jacket's breast pocket.

Trane studied the scribbled message on the back of the business card Lieutenant Bostic had given Tomei.

Tomei noticed Trane's fingernails were trimmed short and well cared for. Gucci definitely would have approved of Ben Trane.

"Nice town, San Francisco. I haven't been there in years."

"It's changing. Not for the better," Tomei said.

"The whole world seems to be going that way. Excuse me for a moment."

They were standing in the middle of a long row of crap tables. Trane took a piece of notepaper from one of the casino employees, jotted his initials on the paper, and a simple notation: OK up to 10G.

"What can I do for you? What's the title? Lieutenant? Inspector?"

"John will do fine." Tomei joined Trane in his slow pacing between the crap tables. Trane's eyes flicked back and forth, gauging the action on the tables, and the body language of the gamblers.

"There was an incident about a year ago. A woman named Sherri Dawson was caught with her hand in a cookie jar. The victim's name was Wong."

Trane arched an eyebrow. "Your interest?"

"Dawson is shacked up with a bookie in San Francisco. He was hit. By three young Asians. She claims she was assaulted."

"You doubt her?"

"Not about being assaulted, I don't. But it looks like she left the front door unlocked for them."

Trane halted and stared at Tomei. "You think she was working with them?"

"Yes. I think it got out of hand. She was there. They used her."

Trane glanced at his wristwatch. Tomei noticed the chunky gold band. It looked expensive and he tried to remember the name of the watch that had been listed on Dawson's grand theft report. An Audemars. Forty thousand dollars. Trane's tuxedo sleeve slipped over the watch before Tomei could see a brand name.

"Let's get a drink," Trane suggested.

The Pepe le Moko Lounge was half filled. The small, circular tables could hold up to six people. Several of the tables were occupied by lone, beautiful, well-dressed women.

"Diet Pepsi," Trane said to the cocktail waitress.

Tomei ordered a mineral water.

"See all those sweet lovely young things at the tables, John?"

"Working girls."

"Right. But not working for us. The casino, I mean. Housewives. Probably from Los Angeles. Maybe Bakersfield. Amateurs. They come in for the day, or just the night, then go home to hubby. Maybe he knows about it. Maybe he doesn't. The pros call them 'hobby-whores.' We don't bother them. There's not much we can do, except get tangled up in a sexual harassment suit if we push too hard. You know why the casinos don't like them?"

"You're not getting a cut."

Trane waved away the answer with his hand. "No, that's not it. They're not reliable. You never can tell if they will be around or not. And you don't know if they see a doctor on a regular basis." Trane dusted the arms of his tuxedo. "You said something about San Francisco changing. Well, Vegas is, too. It's becoming a Disneyland for families. Mom, Pop, the kids. Games for the kids, shows for the parents. Most of the new hotels are catering to the family crowd. We're not. People come to the Casbah to gamble and screw around. We provide the gambling. You have to know good, solid people to provide the rest."

"And Sherri Dawson was a provider."

"Right. Nice lady as far as I knew. Never any trouble. I didn't interfere with her business. She was smart. Professional. Then she hustled Wong. She picked the wrong guy."

"How'd you clear it up? Did she give him his money and merchandise back?"

Trane was about to speak when the cocktail waitress bent down to place their drinks on the table. She performed the operation with stiff knees, so that her breasts almost slipped out of her skimpy diaphanous halter. She gave Trane a big smile, ignoring Tomei.

"Listen," Trane said. "Wong called security. One of my men went up to his suite. They had rented the entire eleventh floor."

"They?"

"These people from Hong Kong." Trane pointed a finger back toward the casino. "We have two shows—dinner and cocktail. The cocktail show finishes around one-fifteen A.M. They booked the showroom for a late-late show. The whole showroom. I won't tell you what that cost, but it was plenty. They brought their own singer from Hong Kong. I can't remember her name. Cute, tiny thing, except for her boobs, which made Dolly Parton look flat. She was so full of silicone she could have floated back to Hong Kong."

Trane took a long sip of his soft drink. "The room was jammed with people from Hong Kong. From all over. The East Coast, and Vancouver. Your town. From what I heard, the busty singer was some Hong Kong heavy-hitter's girl. Anyway, after the show they partied. Wong ends up with Sherri Dawson. When he wakes up, he finds he's been ripped off."

"So what happened?"

"Hell, I called the cops," Trane said emphatically. "I try to settle those things. Keep it quiet. Keep everyone happy. That's my job. But I don't put up with that kind of crap." Trane picked up his glass then abruptly set it down again. "Then Wong took off. Flew back to Hong Kong, I guess."

"So he dropped the charges."

"Yeah. Dawson brought in Wong's watch, his money, and traveler's checks, so the case was closed. There's no way the Vegas P.D. would have gotten Wong to come back here from Hong Kong."

"Did you put the pressure on her to return the goods?"

"I did. I threatened to kick her ass out of here and blackball her from all the casinos in town. She looked through me like I was dirty water. Then this little old Chinese guy from your town talked to her. He didn't look like much, but he had everyone jumping through rings that weekend. He must be a heavy-hitter."

"I think I know his name," Tomei said flatly. "Kan Chin."

"You got it." Trane glanced at his watch again. "Anything else I can do for you?"

"No. Thanks, I appreciate the cooperation."

"I have to get back to work. You want to see a show or something?"

"No. I want to get an early start for home tomorrow."

Tomei's flight back to San Francisco wasn't scheduled to leave Las Vegas until ten-thirty in the morning. He was enjoying a leisurely morning, waiting on the terrace for his room service breakfast.

The desert air hadn't warmed up yet, so he lounged on a well-cushioned recliner, calculating the cost of the Las Vegas trip. Flight, hotel, cabs, meals, a half hour at the slot machines, some eleven hundred of Billy Rossi's expense dollars. And what had he learned? That Sherri Dawson was definitely tied to Kan Chin. She had ripped off one of Chin's Hong Kong associates. Chin had a little talk with her and everyone ended up happy. Sherri was no doubt grateful. Grateful that Chin didn't have her planted somewhere out in the barren Nevada landscape.

As for Ava, the nervous hooker, she'd stared at Tomei in disbelief when he told her that the price for his not arresting her was a look around the apartment.

"You mean you don't want a blow job? Nothing?"

Nothing. And that's about what Tomei found. Sherri Dawson was still getting some mail at the Via Perdido address, but it was all junk. Ava had crammed the mail into a dresser drawer. No phone bills, bank statements, credit card accounts, no letters, nothing more personal then a jumble of catalogs for clothes and accessories.

When the phone rang, he thought it was room service confirming his breakfast order.

"That you, John?"

"Yes. Gucci? How'd you know where to find me?"

"I called Lieutenant Bostic," Elaine Surel explained. "He told me you were at the Casbah."

"What's up?"

"I heard from your client, Billy Rossi. He's nervous as hell. He couldn't reach you on your cell phone. He says that the FBI is harassing him, and now Sherri Dawson's missing."

Chapter Seventeen

Sherri Dawson opened her eyes. Everything was a blur, as if she was looking at the world through someone's prescription glasses. There was a loud sound she couldn't identify, like the magnified buzzing of insects. She tried to scream, but something was lodged in her mouth. She swallowed hard, gagging, choking. She attempted to use her hands but she couldn't move them, or her legs.

She blinked rapidly. Her vision cleared enough for her to make out the surroundings. A ceiling of white fiberglass. She moved her head slowly and saw a double bunk opposite her. The room was rocking back and forth. A boat. Some kind of a boat. The buzzing was the sound of the motor.

She tilted her head toward her feet. There were wide canvas straps crisscrossing her legs, her stomach, her chest. She wiggled her toes to make sure they worked.

The gag in her mouth was unbearable. She gulped several times, trying to fight the panic that was surging through her veins.

Where was she? How did she get there? She remembered meeting with Kan Chin. She had left the Park 55 Hotel, hurried across Market Street, and into Nordstrom's, checking to see if she was being followed, seeing no one. She'd lingered in the department store for over an hour, using a portion of the cash Kan Chin had given her to buy a Ferragamo purse and a Versace leather jacket. She thought the meeting with Kan Chin had gone well. She had lunched at the store's grill, toasting herself with a half-bottle of Schanffenger champagne.

It had been a gamble, not giving Tomei's name to Chin. Chin may have had Billy's house watched. Tomei could have been seen. Her little lie about the rent-a-cop guarding the house had slipped through. Tomei. She hadn't been turned down flat like that before. Never. She thought that he'd change his mind. Come upstairs and slip into bed with her. But her only visitor that night had been Billy Rossi, drunk as sin. Sherri ended up undressing Billy and tucking him into bed. She felt sorry for Billy. He'd treated her straight. Better than straight. With respect, which was something she wasn't all that accustomed to.

She'd finished the wine, then returned to the parking garage at Fifth and Mission Streets, certain that none of Chin's men had followed her. Taken the stairs, rather than the elevator, to her car on the third floor. No one was close by when she slid the key into the Corvette's door.

Then suddenly someone grabbed her ankles, pulled her to the ground. She landed in a bone-jarring crash. A man had been lying under the neighboring car. He was dragging her toward him.

She had screamed, then felt the sharp prick of a needle in her neck, the smoothness of a cloth being lowered over her face. Then there was nothing but darkness.

A door slapped open and a man appeared, drawing her back to the present. He was Asian. Thirty or so. A smirk on his face. He was holding a long-necked bottle of beer in one hand. She mumbled against the gag in her mouth.

The man gave her an insolent smile. "What's the matter, Sherri. Not feeling so good?" He took a knife from his pocket, whipped his hand outward and a blade sprung from the knife's ebony handle.

Sherri tensed as the blade approached her, the flat edge trailing down her forehead, across her nose, the man smiling down at her, his dark eyes glistening in excitement, his lips open, wet. Drooling, Sherri suddenly realized. He was one of the men who had raped her. The one who had tied her with the ropes. His face. He was the one in the picture John Tomei had shown her. Kan Chin's man! Hon. Willy Hon.

Willy Hon curled his tongue against his teeth and whistled softly as he slipped the blade under the dirty rag covering her mouth and cut through the material. He then reached over and pulled the soggy gag from Sherri's mouth.

"Water," she croaked. "Please. Water."

Hon held the beer bottle over her lips and let the liquid trickle out. She gulped it greedily until the trickle became a stream and the beer spilled out of her mouth before she could swallow.

"First you're thirsty, then you spit it out," Hon chided. "You just don't know what you want, do you, bitch?"

Sherri felt that she was going to throw up, but fought against it, because she knew Hon would let her gag on her own vomit.

"Please," she pleaded. "Help me. I'm going to be sick."

"You sure are," Hon agreed. "For a long time. You're going on a trip, Sherri." His round face split into a lantern-size grin. "A slow boat to China. Then back again. And again, and again. I hope you don't get seasick, because you may never set those pretty feet on solid ground again."

He flicked the knife shut, then ran his hand down her neck, pausing at her right breast, squeezing lightly. "Think of it as a Love Boat cruise. And you're the only woman on board." He increased the pressure with his fingers. "Just you and the crew, Sherri. They change the crew after each trip, so you'll make lots of new friends. Think of the—"

The rocking of the boat increased, the engine noise decibeled down. "Looks like we're here," Willy Hon said with a toothy smile.

The cabin door burst open again and another man came into the room. He and Hon had a brief conversation, then Hon grabbed the edge of the stretcher basket and signaled with his head for Jimmy Kung to pick up the other end. They had to fight against the rolling motion of the boat to maneuver the basket through the cabin door and out to the deck.

The cold, salty sea air cleared the cobwebs from Sherri Dawson's head. She didn't like what she saw. The side of a ship. A big ship. A freighter? Tanker? She couldn't tell the difference. The gray paint was peeling and splotched with rust stains. A dozen or so heads peered down at her from the ship's deck. All young. All Asian. All smiling.

Hon and Jimmy Kung lowered the stretcher basket to the small boat's deck and Hon yelled up for the ship's crew to drop the cable.

Sherri watched as a cable with a large iron hook on the end made its way slowly down toward her, like a serpent, a cobra, aiming right for her. Hon grabbed the snap-link hook and made it fast to the stretcher basket's wiring.

He bent down, patted Sherri roughly on the head and shouted, "Bon voyage, bitch."

Sherri felt herself being jerked into the air, the basket swinging free, crashing into the side of the ship. As she rose higher and higher the cheering and laughing became louder. The crew. Waiting for her. She opened her mouth and screamed, the wind carrying her cries out across a vast, empty ocean.

"Cash? Cash? You must be kidding me," Richard Barr shouted. "Kan Chin is going to hand us that much cash?"

Charles Prescott's head did a quarter revolution toward the door leading from the mayor's office to the reception area.

"Don't worry," Barr said. "Everyone's gone. It's just you and me. Now, tell me about the money."

Prescott gave Barr the gist of his meeting with Kan

Chin, leaving out only the fact that Chin had agreed to drop fifty thousand dollars into Prescott's lap.

Barr sat perfectly still, patrolling Prescott's words for a clue of just what Chin was up to.

"Is Chin going to give us anything on that bastard Philip Dong?"

"He said he'll have something in a day or two." Prescott took a leather-bound notebook from his coat and extracted the paper Chin had given him. "Chin said that he would appreciate your considering his choice of appointments to these agencies." He passed the paper to Barr.

Barr read the list, then crumbled it in his fist and threw it across the room. He shot to his feet, jammed his hands into his pant's pockets, and toed at the carpet, like a hitter trying to rub out the chalk outline of the batter's box. Chin was asking for a hell of a lot. Too much.

"Merda," Barr swore. Chin had him by the *coglionis.* The commissions each had five members. Chin already had two of his people on the police and fire commission.

Barr returned to his chair, picked up a pen and began threading it through his fingers. Chin was a shrewd bastard. With three of his toadies on board, Chin could control the inner workings of the police department, be able to appoint his people to positions of authority. He'd know who was in trouble and who was handing out the trouble. He'd have his thumb on all the cases headed for the grand jury. His interest in the fire commission was less obvious, but the firefighters did a lot more than fight fires—they issued permits for alarm systems, and supposedly checked every city apartment, hotel, and business address for fire extinguishers, safety hazards, sprinkler systems.

Barr knew that many of those Chinatown buildings hadn't had a proper fire inspection in years. Kan Chin could pick and choose—keep the buildings he had an interest in off the inspection list. On the others, he could make sure violations were found, and that they would have to be taken care of by contracting firms Chin controlled.

The airport commission was in charge of passing out contracts for the endless construction that went on year after year. And the building inspection commission had an iron grip on just who was allowed to add a light fixture to their house or put up a thirty-story building.

There were commissioners who retired with more money squirreled away in some Bahamas bank account than many of those South American banana boat generals that the newsboys loved to rag on.

Barr stretched his neck to relieve the tension. He had already bartered away most of the appointments Chin was after to other supporters. He'd have to do some juggling to keep everyone happy after the election.

"Didn't Chin give you some kind of a hint as to what he has on Dong?"

"He said that Dong might be connected to organized crime in Hong Kong and on the Chinese mainland."

" 'Might be.' A hell of a lot of good that does me. When is Chin supposed to deliver the money?"

"He'll call me, that's all he said, Mr. Mayor. But I get the feeling it'll be soon."

Barr went to the window and folded the curtain back slowly. The tents were still there. More of them. Every day. Cash. How was he going to launder that much cash? A half-million dollars. Fifteen, maybe even ten years ago, that would have been enough money to cover the expenses for the entire mayoral campaign. Now it cost three or four times that just to run for a city supervisor's job. Time was running short. Six days to the election. It had been a mistake using up most of the money on the early TV blitzes, he admitted to himself. But at the time it seemed a good strategy. Break the backs of his opponents before they developed voter recognition. Only Philip Dong, the dark horse, had hung in there. And when the shadow candidates, the ones with no real chance of winning, dropped out, they all threw their support to Dong. Barr rubbed the back of his hand across his mouth as if wiping away a bad taste. A half million could finish off Dong. He'd find a way to launder the money, shift some into his campaign account, move some into his wife's business account. Cash. Beautiful, crisp, green cash. He'd schedule a fund-raiser at a first-class hotel, pay the bill in cash, and whatever amount of money was raised, he would commingle Chin's cash. Yes, it would be tricky, but he could do it.

He turned back to Prescott, baring his teeth in frustration. "What's your gut feeling on this, Charles?"

"I think we should go for it, Mr. Mayor." Prescott had already mentally spent a good portion of the promised fifty thousand dollars. Clothes, a power-watch, a Caribbean cruise.

"Be careful, Charles. Very careful. Let me know when Chin calls you. I want to know where and when you'll be picking up the money."

Prescott smiled weakly and searched uneasily for the proper words. "Listen, boss. I don't think you should be within a mile of the money when I pick it up. You should be careful as to just how—"

"Yeah, yeah," Barr agreed hastily. "I just want to know, Charles. Call the Fairmont. Tell them we want the ballroom for a fund-raising dinner."

"Another dinner? Mr. Mayor, I don't know if we can squeeze any more people to—"

"Just do it, Charles, I'll take care of drawing a crowd." He pulled his suit coat from the back of the chair and slipped it on. He picked up the phone on his desk and dialed the number for his police body-guard. "I'm on my way. Get the car."

He hung up and patted Prescott on the back on the way out of the room. Good man, Charles, he thought to himself. A good gofer, but not someone he trusted with a half million dollars in cash.

Chapter Eighteen

Kan Chin gazed out the window of his penthouse office. Smoke-colored clouds scudded past the Golden Gate Bridge. Old newspapers darted around in the wind like wounded birds. He heard Willy Hon's footsteps. "You took care of Miss Dawson?" he asked, his eyes drifting over the rooftops of Chinatown, then out to the city's financial center.

"Yes, sir. I'm sure Captain Liu is happy."

Chin nodded his head in agreement. The old pirate, captain of the *Mara Maru*, would make good use of the woman. She was becoming too old to work as a prostitute, at least for the customers that Chin's establishments catered to. He had to either kill her or find a use for her. Her aging beauty would not be a burden for the ship's captain or crew, and if and when she became a nuisance, there was a simple solution. The Pacific Ocean.

Chin lifted a document from his desk. "Miss Dawson presented me with this as a going away present. Your police record, Willy."

Hon studied the rap sheet. He looked like an animal, suddenly alert to prey. "Who gave her this?"

"Billy Rossi. He obviously obtained it from someone in the police department."

"Then Rossi knows that we—"

"The fool believes that he is a knight in shining

armor. He wants to revenge what was done to the fair maiden."

"I should have killed him," Hon said sharply.

"It is not yet the time to kill Rossi," Chin responded. "Talk to our man in the police department. Find the policeman who supplied Rossi with your record. Inflict some pain. Have you heard from Lanzoni?"

"No, not for two days."

"I want to know what he is doing. We can't have that idiot ruin our plans by being arrested, or killed by one of his Mafia enemies."

The salesman eyed the customer over the rim of the morning paper. Money, he thought. Definitely money.

He rose from his desk and strode confidently, with his hands behind his back, his heels clicking rhythmically on the polished tile floor, toward the tall man admiring the gleaming bronze-colored SUV.

"It's a beauty, isn't it, sir?"

Dino Lanzoni ran a thumb across the car's hood then turned toward the salesman, his expression showing that he wasn't impressed with what he saw. Typical California punk, with stringy blond hair, a pink face and pink shirt. Everything except a fucking earring. "Yeah. If you like Jap cars. Is Little Trips in?"

The salesman fingered the knot of his tie. "You mean Mr. Tripoli, sir?"

Lanzoni opened the car's door and slammed it shut with such a force that it shook the entire car. "That's who I mean. Tell him an old friend from New York would like to see him."

The salesman was about to ask for his name, but after Lanzoni opened the car door and slammed it shut again, he decided against it.

Lanzoni grinned at the reflection in the SUV's mirror of the salesman making a hasty retreat back to his desk. He walked over to another car. A sedan. Metallic gray. He was sitting behind the wheel when the salesman approached and gently opened the door.

"Mr. Tripoli has asked you to join him in his office, sir. Right up those stairs."

Lanzoni walked up the theater-aisle-wide staircase to the second floor. A short, bell-shaped woman was waiting for him, teetering on her high heels.

"This way, sir."

She led Lanzoni through a thickly carpeted maze of corridors, to a door with a polished brass PRIVATE sign. She opened the door and held her hand out in a gesture for him to enter.

Anthony "Little Trips" Tripoli was sitting behind a canoe-shaped teak desk. He waited until the door was closed and Lanzoni had moved into the room before standing.

"Dino. I knew it was you from my salesman's description. Good to see you."

Lanzoni grinned. "You're looking good, Little Trips." He wheeled around slowly, taking in the teak-paneled walls, the paintings—bright sprinkles of color in patterns that looked as if the artist had taken his brush and flicked it at the canvas with no idea of where it would end up. Crap, but expensive crap. The chairs were modern—chrome frames with narrow leather strips at the seat and back. More expensive crap.

His eyes settled on the pudgy frame of Anthony "Little Trips" Tripoli. Clocking in on fifty and showing it. The once hard, muscular face was slack, the chin drooping, his neck swelling over his starched collar. His too-dark hair was parted just above his ear and carefully combed across his scalp to disguise the bald spots.

"Prosperous, Trips. You look prosperous. The car business must be good."

Tripoli gave a nonchalant shrug. "How goes it with you, Dino?"

Lanzoni eased himself into one of the chairs, not taking his hands from the arms until he was sure it would hold his weight. "It goes good. How's your father?"

Lanzoni had a lot of respect for Anthony "Big Trips" Tripoli, who was in his eighties now. Retired, living in Carmel, on the 17 Mile Drive. He had been a first-class shooter in his day, though in most of his hits he preferred using an ice pick rather than a gun.

"Pop's doing good. Still playing eighteen holes of golf a day."

Lanzoni shook his head. Golf. What a way to end up.

"You get hold of the people I told you to?"

Tripoli strode over to one of the paintings. Raspberry colored with specks of black, like ants crawling over ice cream, thought Lanzoni.

Tripoli swung the painting away from the wall and fiddled with the dial of a steel wall safe that was just slightly smaller than the Helen Frankenthaler abstract. The safe's door opened on accordion springs. Tripoli extracted a black nylon duffel bag. "This came from your brother's account, Dino." He paused to let that sink in. "No one else."

The implication was clear. His brother had okayed the transaction, but nobody else wanted a piece of it.

Lanzoni patted the case. "And why not? Nick made more money for the family than anyone ever did."

Tripoli leaned his hip against the side of his desk and crossed his arms. "I just wanted you to know, Dino."

Lanzoni bit his lower lip and stared at Tripoli, aching to reach over and squeeze his fat neck until his eyes popped out. The lazy bastard had been living on his father's reputation all his life. Never worked the streets, never made a hit, never scored a deal of any kind. Never did any time. Never had his thumb rolled across a precinct fingerprint pad. Big Trips's good-for-nothing kid. College. Business school. A fucking paper-pusher.

"Thanks, Little Trips. Now I want a favor."

Tripoli clasped his hands in front of him like a professional mourner. He didn't mind calling New York for Lanzoni. Didn't mind being the middle man and handling the transfer of Nick Lanzoni's money, but he didn't want anything else to do with him.

"Look, Dino. Things are a little different out here. I don't know if I—"

Lanzoni heaved himself to his feet. "Relax, Little Trips. I don't want you doing nothing dirty, like killing someone. I want a car. That gray one in the showroom will do. I'll need it for a couple of months."

Tripoli didn't know whether to feel relieved or upset. The sedan retailed at over forty-five thousand dollars. "Look, Dino, it'd be better if you didn't call me Little Trips. At least in front of my employees. As for the car, I've got a beauty in the shop now. Less than a year old. Better than the one downstairs. Sunroof, CD player. The works."

"Nah," Lanzoni said disgustedly, his hands going to Tripoli's shoulder, then to his face, his fingers pinching the bloated cheeks. "The new one, Little Trips. Always a new one. You should know that." He should know that, but he didn't. Whenever Dino had real work to do, he always drove a new car, most often stolen off a dealer's lot. There was no license plate, just the dealer's name tag. All you had to do was put a hat or a scarf on the dash to cover the stamped VIN number, and the cops couldn't write a ticket, couldn't ID it at all. It was damn near invisible. He knew more than one made guy who had been dumb enough to use a car with a license plate on a hit, only to have a witness give the plate number to the cops. One poor *arruso* had wasted three Puerto Rican dealers who were muscling into the wrong neighborhood. Pop-pop-pop. Three shots, three kills. A beautiful job. Only some hooker giving a guy a blow job in an alley sees him peel away from the curb. One of the dead dealers was her pimp. She writes the license plate number in lipstick on the sidewalk.

Dino released his grip, his eyes level with Tripoli's. "I may need a place to stay for a few days. You got a spare apartment where you stash your whores?"

"No, nothing like that, Dino. I'm a happily married man."

"Who you shittin'? I know you, pally. You've got some place where you go and play games. Right?"

Tripoli nibbled at the inside of his cheek, then said, "Well, I've got this boat where I throw a party once in a while. It's nothing big, but—"

"Good. I'll call you. Listen, Little Trips. You ever think of packing it in and just playing golf with your pop?"

Chapter Nineteen

Billy Rossi came to the front door in robe and sorry-looking leather slippers, a cigar clamped between his teeth. His holster with its pearl-handled six-shooter was cinched around his waist.

"Come on in, Tomb, come on in." He opened the door wide and Tomei had his foot across the threshold when he heard Fidel's growl.

"*Kita,*" Tomei said quickly. He dropped to one knee and called the shepherd over. "Fidel, you handsome devil, don't you remember me?"

"He's nervous, I guess, Tomb. Like me."

"Tell me about the FBI, Billy. What did they want?"

"There were two of them. I think they were the same guys you pointed out to me at Sully's. A big guy with a crew cut and a little guy. They started pumping me as soon as I opened the door. I told them to talk to my attorney, Tom Spaulding, and closed the door on them. I think they might have tried to muscle their way in, but Fidel was growling. Nearly foaming at the mouth."

"What did they want to know?"

"They asked about you, Tomb. Just before I slammed the door, they asked about you."

"Did they mention Dino Lanzoni?"

"I didn't give them the chance. I learned that the

only way to handle the FBI is zip the lip, and tell them to talk to my attorney."

"When was this, Billy?"

"Yesterday morning. I tried calling you. Sherri's missing. I'm worried about her."

"Are you sure she just didn't take off?"

Rossi slammed the door shut. "Come on. I'll show you."

Tomei followed him to the master bedroom. The bed was rumpled and a half-empty bottle of Old Grand-Dad whiskey sat on the nightstand, along with a crystal ashtray filled with gnawed cigar butts.

"Look at this," Rossi said, sliding open the mirror-fronted closet doors. "All her clothes." He pawed his way through the neatly hanging garments. "Everything. Fur coats, dresses, shoes." He crossed the room and began opening the drawers of a brass-trimmed mahogany bureau.

"Cashmere sweaters. Tons of them." He reached into another drawer, pulling out a lacy black bra, holding it loosely by a strap, making an up and down movement with his fingers as if dipping a tea bag. "Nothing cheap. All top-class stuff. And look at this."

Rossi let the bra drop to the floor as he flipped open a satin jewelry box atop the dresser. "Her rings, bracelets, earrings. She ain't about to cut out without taking her clothes and jewelry."

He dug a lighter from his robe pocket. "I ain't kidding myself about Sherri. It isn't love, and I know she's going to take a hike one of these days." He paused, using the lighter and puffing repeatedly until the cigar tip glowed red. "But she wouldn't go without telling me, and without her stuff. No way. Especially yesterday."

"What's so special about yesterday."

"It was my birthday. We had a big dinner planned. She wouldn't have missed it. I know that, Tomb. She wouldn't have missed it."

"I could use a cup of coffee," Tomei told Rossi. "We've got to talk."

They headed for the kitchen. The savory smell of freshly brewed coffee perfumed the air. Rossi poured two cups with an unsteady hand. "You want some cream or sugar?"

"No thanks."

"I need a sweetener," Rossi announced, opening a cabinet and bringing out an unopened bottle of Old Grand-Dad.

Tomei said, "I went to Las Vegas. I stopped by Sherri's apartment. She hasn't been back since she moved to San Francisco. I also checked out her place of employment. The Casbah. She was a house hooker, Billy."

"I knew Sherri did some hooking," Rossi said, breaking the bottle's seal, wrestling the cap free and pouring two fingers into his coffee cup. "Hell, no big deal."

"She got herself into trouble. She grabbed a john's wallet and watch. Kan Chin saved her bacon."

Rossi had to use both hands to stop the whiskey bottle from clinking against the coffee cup. "Chin. You're sure she was working for him in Vegas?"

"No. Not for him. But she dipped her hand into the wrong cookie jar. She hustled a friend of Chin's. He saved her from having a few fingers whacked off. She owed him, Billy."

Rossi hooked a chair from the kitchen table with a slippered foot and sat down suddenly, as if his legs had lost their strength. "Owed him," he mumbled softly. "Jesus. She was with me a few months. She learned a lot about me."

"Your phone room? She knows where it is?"

"Where it is now, where it was last month. But not where it'll be tomorrow."

"What else could Sherri pass along to Chin, Billy?"

Rossi blew on his coffee, then took a deep gulp. "Hell, I took her everywhere, once we kinda settled in together. Great-looking woman like that, an old geezer like me. I liked to show her off. You know what I mean?"

Tomei nodded his head in agreement. Rossi parading his trophy girlfriend around. Taking her to see his phone room, his stringers, his runners. It wouldn't take a genius to figure out Rossi's weekly take. And who his big customers were.

"Only thing she never learned about was the other safe, Tomb. I never told her about that."

"Why not?"

"I don't know. That was always my 'fuck you' money." He laughed without humor. "For my old age. What about Sherri? What do you think? Think she's got a chance?"

"Chance at what?"

"Being alive," Rossi shot back with some heat. "I don't want her back. But I don't want her hurt. She's been hurt enough. Think she's got a chance?"

"Sherri could have been involved in an accident. Did you call the hospitals?"

"Yeah. Everyone of them. In town, across the Bay, the peninsula, all of them."

"Billy, maybe she just decided to go away for a few days. To see some friends. She could be calling anytime. Or sending someone to pick up her things. Don't write Sherri off. She's a tough package."

Rossi leaned back in his chair and digested Tomei's news. "Or Chin could have had her whacked. If she was working for him, I don't see why those punks hurt her like that."

"The day I met with you at Sully's. Who picked that spot? You or Sherri?"

"What's the matter? You don't like Sully's?"

"I like it fine. But why there? Why not here at the house?"

Rossi smiled a mirthless smile. "Sherri said we should go out. After what those gooks did to us, I kinda didn't want to leave this place, you know what I mean? Hell, there's no sense denying it. I was scared, Tomb. Damn scared."

"So Sherri suggested Sully's."

"I don't know if it was her idea, or mine. We were

both getting a little cabin fever, you know. So we went out. I go to Sully's a lot. What's the big deal?"

Tomei pointed a finger at the German shepherd. "It might be a good idea for you to take a vacation. But while you're here, you'd better keep Fidel right beside you at all times."

"I want those bastards to know they can't push me around."

"Then we'll have to make a statement. A strong statement. I don't know how Kan Chin will react to it. He won't be happy, that's for sure. It will be easier for me if you're not around, Billy."

"Fuck 'em," Rossi said, reaching down to the dog again. "Fuck 'em, right, Fidel?"

"You're sure about this? Kan Chin is a dangerous man."

Rossi knelt down and patted the dog on its hind quarters. "I didn't tell you this before, Tomb, but that night, when they were here, I pissed my pants. Actually pissed in my pants, that's how scared I was. Sure, I'm old, maybe toothless to them, but I don't like it. Don't like what they did to Sherri. To my paintings. Hell, if I have to live like this, I might as well toss it all in and move to one of those old fart retirement homes and play bridge for the rest of my life. You do what you have to do. I can handle whatever comes up. You need some more dough?"

"No, not now. But it may get expensive."

"There's over two hundred g's in the second safe, Tomb. Find Sherri. Get this bastard off my back and it's all yours."

The phone rang a half dozen times. Laura Aguera glanced around the room. No one seemed to be in a hurry to pick up the call. She grabbed the receiver and said, "Vice, Inspector Aguera."

"Hi. Is Gucci around?"

Laura recognized the voice. John Tomei. "No, I'm afraid she's out at the moment."

"Do you know where?"

Even if she knew, Laura had no intention of passing out her partner's whereabouts. Even to Elaine's ex-partner.

"No. Did you want to leave a message?"

Tomei fluttered his lips in disappointment. "Yes. Tell her I think Sherri Dawson could be in danger. She was driving a red Corvette convertible." Tomei read off the Nevada plate number. "Put it out on the hot-sheet list, will you?"

"On what basis?" Laura asked.

There was a cold silence of several seconds, then Tomei said, "On the basis that I think the lady may be dead. We'll probably find her in the trunk of her car."

"Look, Mr. Tomei—"

"John. We've broken bread together. Just pass that along to Gucci, okay? She'll know what to do with it."

Tomei hung up before Laura could respond. She tore off the top sheet of paper from her notepad, leaned over to Elaine Surel's desk, and speared it onto her message spindle.

"Damn," she muttered softly. Tomei was going to be trouble. She could feel it. Even though she had been intrigued by the man—his looks, his obvious devotion to his daughter, and his genuine affection for Elaine, she just knew he was going to be trouble. She told the receptionist she'd be out for half an hour and took the stairs to the fifth floor.

Laura had been detailed to the Personnel Department for three months of "light duty," the result of an attempted arrest of a Nob Hill burglar who had jumped out off a second-story window and struck Laura before he impacted with the ground. Her shoulder was nearly wrenched out of its socket.

Working full-day shifts in the office had driven her up the wall, but at least she had made some contacts. The detail's secretary, Diane, greeted her warmly.

"Hi, Laura. What's up?"

"I'm just curious about an ex-cop I ran into. Could you pull his file for me? John Tomei."

A curious expression came over the secretary's face.

"Tomei. There was an FBI agent in here yesterday reviewing his file." She rummaged through a pile of folders on her desk. "Here it is. I haven't had the time to put it away." She checked the name on the request slip. "FBI agent Donald Jamison. Do you know him?"

"No," Laura said. "Never heard of him."

"Curious, isn't it? Tomei was Elaine's partner several years ago."

"That's right," Laura said.

"And now Elaine's your partner. Lieutenant Clayton came in and reviewed her file a couple of hours ago." She waved a thick manila folder in her hand. "What's going on?"

Laura's face tightened sharply. Lieutenant Brett Clayton was in charge of the department's Management Control Division, the new, politically correct version of Internal Affairs. "I wish I knew," she said sincerely. "I really wish I knew."

Chapter Twenty

Alonzo "Red" Vanes watched as John Tomei paused in front of the entrance to the Green Dragon restaurant on Jackson Street.

Tomei gave the street a furtive scan before ducking inside. Vanes monitored the pedestrian traffic. No one had paid Tomei any attention, other than the cold looks of disdain that elderly Chinese regularly bestowed on a tall *hun dan*.

Vanes waited a full ten minutes. A delivery truck was double-parked in front of the butcher shop on the corner. Jabbering men wearing blood-blotched coveralls were unloading the truck's contents: fat-coated sides of beef, saddles of lamb, and wooden crates crammed with live rabbits.

The rabbits, seemingly knowing what was in store for them, were racing around the cages, banging into each other. Across the street a man was selling mud-encrusted duck eggs from the back of a battered old VW van.

Vanes slipped through the crowd and entered the Green Dragon.

"Ah, Inspector Vanes, good to see you," the white-jacketed maître d' greeted him. "It has been too long."

"I'm meeting a friend, Henry."

"Yes, yes. Come this way. He is waiting at the table you reserved."

Tomei spotted Vanes and waved a lazy hand in greeting.

"Well, what did you learn about Sherri Dawson?" Vanes asked as soon as he was seated.

"She's dirty." Tomei related the highlights of his trip to Las Vegas while Vanes studied the plastic-coated menu.

Vanes mentally digested the information, weighing its pros and cons. If Dawson was still working for Kan Chin, Chin would have a dossier and photograph of Tomei by now, and he would have been spotted as soon as he entered the Green Dragon.

"You ready to order?" the waiter wanted to know.

Vanes reeled off a burst of Chinese, then turned to Tomei. "They just serve beer and wine. I've ordered the beer. Is that all right with you?"

"Sure." Tomei picked up a chopstick and used the narrow end to make impressions on the tablecloth. "Do you think you waited long enough, Red?"

"For what?" Vanes asked in a confused voice.

"To join me at the table. You had me waiting here like a sitting duck, didn't you? Waiting to see if Chin and his gang were on to me."

Vanes's forehead corduroyed in a frown. "I watched the street," he admitted. "No one was paying you any interest. So it seems your friend Sherri Dawson kept her mouth shut about you. How did Billy Rossi react to what you learned in Vegas?"

"It shook him up pretty good."

The waiter brought their beer, and Vanes engaged him in a conversation in Cantonese.

Tomei shifted nervously in his chair, wondering why Sherri Dawson hadn't told Kan Chin about him. Rossi had been right about one thing. She never would have willingly left her clothes and jewelry behind.

Vanes was reaching for his beer when he spotted a familiar face. "Look who's here."

"Howdy, Inspector," the small, neatly dressed Chinese man said in a southern accent that surprised Tomei. "How you all doin'? Gettin' along good?"

"Texas Joe. How the hell you been?" Vanes asked. "Long time no see."

"I been around. Just ain't seen you."

Tomei stared at the man. He was somewhere in his mid-thirties. He was wearing a western-style hat, the type that southern politicians and Houston oil millionaires favored. His tan suit had a western cut and his white shirt sported a shoestring tie held in place by a large turquoise stone. Greenish gray snakeskin cowboy boots added a couple of inches to his height.

"I've changed employers, Joe. They're keeping me busy," Vanes responded.

"Ah, I see." He smiled at Tomei. "Nice to meet you, mister."

"My pleasure," Tomei replied indifferently.

Texas Joe took note of the two bottles of beer.

"You and your friend want a real drink, Inspector? They don't serve hard liquor here, but I can fix you up."

"Don't worry about it, Joe," Vanes said. "This is just a quick dinner."

Texas Joe clicked his heels together. "No problem. Relax. Gin, right, Inspector? What about your friend?"

Tomei placed his hand over the top of the beer bottle. "I'm fine."

"I'll be right back," Texas Joe promised.

Tomei watched him saunter out of the restaurant. "Is that accent a put-on?" he asked.

"Nope. Joe was born and raised on some cattle ranch in West Texas. He came to San Francisco some ten years ago."

"What does he do?"

"He works both sides of the street. Knows every cop who ever set foot in Chinatown—local, state, feds. He's never been arrested, never gets involved in any hard stuff, himself. But when something's going down, Texas Joe always seems to be right there. He pops up out of nowhere. Talks to the cops, gives us some good information. Talks to all the Triads. You can bet he's giving them a lot better information."

The object of their conversation came back to the table a few minutes later, carrying a plastic tray, waiter-style. He set down a martini in a frosted, stemmed glass in front of both men, then added an ice bucket holding a brimming cocktail shaker.

"Enjoy your meal, Inspector." Texas Joe's eyebrows joined together as he pressed Tomei's face into his memory. "And nice meeting you . . . I didn't catch your name."

"Just a friend who wanted to visit Chinatown," Vanes said. "How's business, Joe?"

Texas Joe gave the universal signal of holding his palm out level and wiggling it. "So, so, Inspector. Anything I can help you with?"

"No, not right now, Joe."

Texas Joe nodded his head and backed away from the table. "See ya now, hear?" were his parting words.

Vanes plucked the olive from his martini. "He'll be spreading the word all over that I'm in the area."

"That's what you want him to do, isn't it, Red?"

"If you're going to do business with Kan Chin, there are rules you have to follow, Tomb. Protocol. What if you and I—"

The waiter returned and began slamming steaming platters and a teapot onto the table. "Texas Joe order this for you," he explained in heavily accented English. "He pay for it, too."

Red Vanes shook his head, then laughed. "What the hell. Bring us two more beers," then started digging into the Kung-Po pepper chicken, pepper steak, Szezhuan scallops, prawns, snow peas, and Ying Yang squab.

When the plates were all cleared away and a fresh pot of tea and fortune cookies were set out, Tomei said, "So, besides putting me on display, what was this all about, Red?"

"If you're still planning to take on Kan Chin, you're going to have to do it in his territory. This is his favorite restaurant. Look over my shoulder and you can see a small alcove, with curtains covering it. That's Chin's personal table. No one else ever eats there. Texas Joe didn't recognize you, which means that Sherri Dawson didn't dump you in Chin's lap.''

"Billy Rossi wants to know where Sherri is. He's willing to pay good money for the information."

Vanes hunched his shoulders and leaned across the table. "My bet is that she's dead. Or Chin has shipped her out of the country and will put her to work in some whorehouse where they change the sheets every other Christmas. Are you still serious about playing hardball with Chin?"

"Dead serious," Tomei confirmed.

"You better be," Vanes warned, "because I'm putting my ass on the line, too."

"I'm doing it for the money. What's your reason, Red?"

Vanes rose abruptly from his chair. "Let's go. I'll give you the cook's tour."

Red Vanes started the tour by wandering up and down Washington Street.

"This is headquarters for the Triads," Vanes said, pointing at the packs of young men in threes and fours, leaning against lampposts, and sitting on the hoods of parked cars.

"Those are the field hands," Vanes lectured. "Punks just over from Hong Kong. Waiting for word from the bosses on who to go after. Of course, if they happen to see a hot target, a drunken tourist with an expensive camera dangling from his neck, they might do a little prospecting on their own."

The groups Vanes pointed out were amazingly similar. All thin, hard-faced young men, dressed in black jeans and casual jackets.

"The bulges under their jackets aren't necessarily guns, kasari-fundo chains, or those razor-sharp star-shaped knives they like to carry," Vanes said. "They're smart enough not to be picked up on the street carrying their toys. No, those bulges are cellular phones. They're in constant contact with their bosses."

Vanes paused at the entrance to a small bar. A faded red neon sign over the entrance blinked the name "Dick's" on and off every few seconds. The place was nearly deserted, just one or two men propped on bar stools. Tomei spotted the smiling face of Texas Joe sitting alone at a table in the rear.

The bartender, a puffy-faced Chinese with lank black hair, called out to them.

"Hey, Inspector Vanes. You come in. I buy you a retirement drink."

"No thanks, Dick," Vanes replied defiantly. "You're going to have to keep that drink on hold for a few more years."

When they had gone a few yards past the bar, Vanes said, "All the Wah Ho boys hang out there."

Vanes continued the tour, taking them through small alleys, pointing out various hangouts of the Triads.

They trooped by a half dozen places that Vanes identified as true gambling dens. They all seemed the same to Tomei. A set of ill-kept concrete steps, protected by a pair of locked wire gates, leading down to a basement. All Tomei could see were the floors, which were either bare concrete or covered with gritted linoleum, and the customers' shoes and pant legs.

"The Chinese have a saying. I can't quote it directly," Vanes said. "But the gist is that money always travels down, not up, which is why the dens are in these crummy basements."

"This is all interesting as hell, Red. But how does it help me get Rossi's money back?"

"Listen, Tomb. I spotted two undercover DEA agents and at least one guy from the Justice Department during our little walk. The streets have eyes, my friend." He jutted his chin to a brick-clad building across the alley. A spotless black Mercedes sedan was guarded by two young Chinese toughs.

"That's Chin's car parked in front of his building's entrance. You go through those doors and an elevator takes you up to his penthouse. Or you can go to the basement and guess what you find? Chin's bank. A vault full of gambling chips that are worth a lot more money than what was taken from Billy Rossi's safe."

"And what am I supposed to do?" Tomei asked in an exasperated tone. "Shoot my way in, grab the loot, fill up the Mercedes, and drive away?"

Vanes gave Tomei an exaggerated wink. "I told you money travels down. So we've got to go down after it." He tugged his jacket sleeve back and checked his watch. "Meet me at three o'clock," he raised his eyes to Tomei. "In the morning, at the corner of Stockton and Sutter. Then we'll see just how much you really want to go after Kan Chin. And Tomb, wear old clothes."

Chapter Twenty-one

Sherri Dawson pressed her fingers together tightly and tried to wriggle her hands through the crude iron cuffs.

She closed her eyes and concentrated on relaxing her muscles, urging herself to go totally limp, to turn her flesh into a soft, flexible jellylike material. And she prayed. But it didn't do her any good. The restraint cuffs had been clamped on too tightly by Captain Liu.

She tilted her head and examined the cuffs. A twelve-inch length of thick, rusty chain separated them. Long enough to wrap around her neck and choke herself, if it came to that. And it damn well *might* come to that. The chain was attached to the steel legs of the bed frame that was welded to the floor. She peered into the lock. A single round hole the size of a cigarette tip. She remembered all those movies she'd seen as a child, where the hero would take a hairpin from his not-too-bright female sidekick and use it to pick locks of every kind, including handcuffs.

But she had no hairpin, and even if she was able to free herself, where could she go?

Kun, the first mate, a big-bellied slob who spoke English better than anyone she'd met on the ship, so far, had made it clear that there was no escape. After being hoisted aboard, Sherri had been carried directly to the captain's cabin.

Captain Liu, a small, shrivel-faced man, had shouted at her in Chinese, while she was still strapped in the stretcher-basket. Kun stood at his side translating.

"You will do as you are told, or you will be thrown overboard. There is no escape!"

Kun began undoing the stretcher straps while the captain unbuttoned his jacket.

"If you displease the captain, or the crew, you will be thrown overboard!"

"We will feed you to the sharks," came at the same time Captain Liu stepped out of his trousers.

When the straps were undone, Sherri was dumped onto the floor.

Liu began shouting again. Kun smiled down at Sherri. "You will please the captain now. I will see you soon."

When Kun returned to the cabin, he had the iron handcuffs. She was paraded through the ship. She counted thirteen men, all Asians, ranging from their early twenties to one gray-haired toothless man who had to be close to seventy. They laughed and grabbed at her, snatching at her clothes. Their eyes were filled with lust. And hate. Sherri could see the hate, smell it, too. They all reeked of unwashed bodies, of confinement, contamination, ready-to-explode aggression.

Kun had shoved her into the filthy ship's galley. The old toothless man was wearing a grease-smeared apron.

"You will work in here when you are not with the men," Kun informed her. He then dragged her outside, his hand entangled in her hair, pushing her toward the railing.

For a moment Sherri thought she was going to be thrown overboard. She peered almost longingly at the salt-waved blue gray water.

Kun shouted a string of orders, and the old cook and two younger men came carrying slop-filled garbage cans. The cans were upturned, the contents oozed down into the ocean.

"Good chum," Kun said, his foul-smelling mouth inches from Sherri's ear.

Captain Liu strode over, carrying a rifle in both hands. The cook came back holding a squealing white bristled, pink-bellied pig, by its ears. The animal's legs flailed helplessly in the air.

The pig was tossed into the ocean. The captain took careful aim and shot it. Blood streamed into the water.

Kun yanked at Sherri's hair. "Look!" he shouted. She blinked through her tears, finally spotting a dorsal fin cruising in the water.

"Shark," said Kun excitedly.

The crew had gathered around. Two more young pigs were thrown into the water. They squealed and paddled in confusion as the dorsal fin approached. The fin submerged, then there was a wild churning of water as the shark's head appeared for a brief moment, its mouth wide open, its teeth flashing in the afternoon sun.

The crew cheered as if they were watching a sporting event.

Sherri closed her eyes and took a deep breath. Her legs wobbled uncontrollably as Kun led her back to the captain's cabin. "You try funny stuff, you join pigs," he warned her.

Sherri could feel the ship slowing down, hear the sound of the anchor being released, the chain rattling through the ship hosel, then the bow anchor crash into the ocean.

Kun had told her that once they were anchored, it was his turn. "Tomorrow you crew. Tonight you me," he boasted.

They still had to be somewhere off the California coast, she reasoned. She had heard Kun say something about San Diego. They were taking on cargo, or maybe delivering something. Then they sailed to Hong Kong. If she was going to try to escape, it had to be soon. Now or never. Either that or the chain, or a knife. Some quick form of suicide.

The cabin door opened with a clang and Kun glared

at her. He closed the door behind him, locking the cleats. He turned to look at her, rubbing his hands together as if he was preparing to enjoy a sumptuous meal.

Kun's dark sweatshirt was ripe with sweat. His jeans were stained and torn in spots. His stomach was cinched by a wide leather belt. On the belt was a ring of keys, and a scabbard holding a bone-handle folding knife. Kun had shown her the knife. Opened the blade, and then the marlin spike, waving the spike in front of her face.

Kun turned a radio on. The music was oriental, lots of clanging bells and harsh voices. He jacked up the volume so loud that if Sherri had not been shackled, she would have put her hands over her ears.

Kun stomped over and removed the key ring, sneering at her while he undid first one cuff, and then the other.

"You be good, or cuffs stay on all time," he warned.

Sherri nodded her head gratefully while she rubbed at her aching wrists.

Kun flopped on the single bunk and beckoned her over. He shook his feet at her. "Take off," he commanded.

Sherri quickly began to untie his shoes. They fell to the floor with a loud thud. The smell of his feet nearly made her vomit.

Kun patted his swollen stomach. "Pants now."

Sherri dutifully undid his belt buckle, then unbuttoned his trousers.

Kun was talking Chinese, soft, fast, his face forming a dark scowl. Sherri closed her eyes and hooked her fingers in the waistband of his underwear and tugged them down.

Kun was laughing now. Sherri nuzzled his knee, using her tongue, while her left hand searched for the belt. She had it.

The knife scabbard was held in place by a snap. How much noise would it make when she undid it? She let out a loud moan at the same moment her thumb popped the snap.

Kun had his hands in her hair, guiding her to his groin, still rattling away in Chinese.

Sherri slowly transferred the knife to her other hand. She fumbled at the blade for a moment, but her fingers kept slipping off the slick metal. She raised her eyes to Kun while she clicked the marlin spike into place.

Kun's eyes were half closed. His mouth slack. Sherri wrenched her head free from his grasp, jumped to her feet, and slammed the spike into his chest.

Kun's scream was drowned out by the loud music. He kicked out, sending Sherri skidding across the room. His two hands pulled at the knife's handle, then he collapsed back onto the bunk, blood billowing from his mouth.

Sherri approached him cautiously. When she was sure he was dead, she used a rocking motion to free the spike from his chest.

She searched the small room for another weapon, finding none. All she had was the knife with the marlin spike. A bottle of Four Roses whiskey stood on the lone metal-topped dresser. She took a long swig directly from the bottle, then approached the door, carefully undoing the cleats. She eased the door open with one hand, the other holding the marlin spike to her chest.

She walked down the cold steel deck on the balls of her feet. She could see the outline of land—mountains and trees and beautiful white buildings. How far away was it? A mile? Two? More? She'd never swum more than a few lengths of a pool in her life, but if she could swim, and then float. If she could find a life ring, or if—

Someone started screaming at her. It was the old cook. He held a garbage pail with both hands. He dropped it and ran toward her. Sherri raced for the railing. She glanced back over her shoulder to see that four men had joined the cook in pursuing her. She didn't slow her momentum as she vaulted over the rail. She kept her eyes closed and legs together. It seemed a long time before she hit the water. It was cold. Much colder than she'd expected. She held her breath as long as she could, then kicked her legs, surfacing near midship.

The men were screaming. She swam to the ship, her hands clutching at the vessel's icy metal skin. The curve of the ship's structure kept her from seeing the crew. Which meant that they couldn't see her either.

The first rays of the setting sun turned the sky a glorious salmon color. Soon it would be dark. A sudden clanging sound startled her. The anchors. They were pulling up the anchors! She would have to swim around to the other side of the ship, the shore side, before they started the engines.

Something hit the water just a few feet in front of her. She held up the knife. The crew. They were coming in after her!

But no. It wasn't a man. A pig! Then another pig plopped into the water, followed by a cascade of garbage. They were chumming for sharks!

Sherri watched in horror as the pigs swam around in circles. There were gunshots. One pig went underwater for a moment, then emerged belly up, blood leaking from its wounds.

She took a deep breath and dove under. When she surfaced, she was at the stern. There was the noise of metal churning against water. The screw! They were starting the engines up. She swam frantically, frightened that any moment the large propeller blades would pick up full power and drag her down to a choppy death.

She kept a steady pace. The tide seemed to be in her favor. She turned on her back and floated. The ship was now at least a football field away. She continued swimming, keeping count of the strokes. When she reached a hundred, she turned on her back again. The ship was under way. Heading out to sea! She was going to make it. Damn, she was going to make it!

The joy she felt fizzled when she looked at the shoreline. It didn't seem all that much closer. Swim and float, she advised herself. Swim and rest. You can do it.

The cold was settling into her bones. If she could just find something. Some drifting piece of wood, anything, if she could just—her mouth opened and she swallowed water. There, straight ahead a fin!

"Oh, dear God. Dear Jesus. No. Not now. Please!"

She swam slowly, with her head out of the water. The fin vanished. Then it appeared again. Off to her right. The shark was circling her!

She shuddered uncontrollably in the frigid water. Her legs were dangling beneath her. She pulled them up, trying to lay as flat as she could. God! The creature could be right below her.

No! It wasn't fair. She didn't deserve to die like this. No one did!

She spotted something off to her right. Something big. White. A boat!

She took off her blouse and waved it over her head, shouting "Help! Help! Please help."

The boat seemed to be coming closer. Was it really a boat? Or just an illusion?

"Help! Please help!" Sherri croaked, her knees now tucked into her chest. She waved the shredded blouse wildly.

The shark fin flashed by, no more than a few yards away.

"Please!" she screamed frantically.

The boat tacked to the left and came right at her. A sunburned man wearing white shorts and a brown San Diego Padres baseball cap was on the bow.

"Slow it down, Danny," he called, leaning over and reaching a hand out to Sherri. "I think we've found a mermaid."

Chapter Twenty-two

John Tomei edged back from the curb as the van chugged to a stop. The windshield was cracked, the roof bird-bombed. The engine died with a jerk and noisy sigh.

The window rolled down and a man with shoulder-length dark hair and a half-smoked cigar clenched between his teeth grinned at Tomei.

"Hey, Tomb. Get in. We haven't got all night."

Tomei hunched down and stared at the stranger.

Alonzo "Red" Vanes tipped the top of his wig up as if it were a hat. "Come on. We've got work to do."

Tomei climbed into the passenger seat. "Why the disguise?"

"Why not?" Vanes countered.

"If we score on Kan, you can use the money to buy a new van, Red."

Vanes reached under the dash, crossed the ignition wires, nursed the clutch, and the vehicle bumped and heaved its way into traffic. "I sure as hell wouldn't buy this thing. I'm sorry I stole it, to tell you the truth." He adjusted the rearview mirror, which was held together by wads of Scotch tape. "Though I don't know how the owner will ever miss it." He puffed at the cigar to get it going.

Tomei studied Vanes carefully. Something was wrong. Not just the wig or the old clothes. "Where are your glasses?"

Vanes tapped the bridge of his nose with a forefinger. "I had laser surgery a few years ago. I have twenty-fifteen vision now. It's great." He glanced over at Tomei. "If someone sees you with glasses all the time, they get used to it. You walk around without them and you're almost invisible."

Tomei shook his head. "You've gone round the bend, Red. Way round the bend."

They traveled through the Stockton Street tunnel. Sleek sedans and sports cars tooted their horns in disdain as they sped past the lumbering van.

"Must be drug dealers on their way home," Vanes said. "Or stockbrokers on their way to work. Either way, they're overpaid."

Vanes turned onto Clay Street, circled the block twice, and finally parked in front of a corner fire hydrant.

"Show time," he said as he climbed out of the van.

Tomei followed him down the street then into a dark alley. Vanes stopped in front of a stout, weatherbeaten garage door. His head pivoted back and forth as he slipped a key into an immense Chubb padlock with bolts of vanadium steel. The warped wood door unlatched with a soft creak. Behind this door was a rust-spotted steel rolling door.

Vanes stooped to his knees and keyed another padlock, sticking his head back into the alley before rolling the door up.

Vanes ushered Tomei inside, locking both sets of doors from the inside. He used a flashlight to find the light switch.

Tomei waited as his eyes adjusted to the fluorescent lighting. They were standing in a small, empty room, barely large enough to hold a single car.

Vanes put his finger to his lips and led Tomei to the rear wall, which was covered with oil-stained plywood. He fiddled with the edge of the wall and it slid backwards a few feet.

Vanes disappeared through the gap, and Tomei followed closely behind him. The room they were in now was half the size of the first one. The walls more of the oil-stained plywood. An unpainted, raw wooden door was centered in one of the walls. Two sets of rubber boots sat on the floor. A pair of heavy canvas turnout jackets hung from fourpenny nails.

"I hope the boots fit you," Vanes said, taking off his shoes and grabbing a pair of the boots. "You're going to need them."

"Just where the hell are we going, Red?"

"I'm going to show you Kan Chin's treasure chest. Come on. Get dressed."

Tomei slipped on the canvas jacket, kicked off his shoes, and worked his feet into the rubber boots.

"There's a knit cap in the jacket pocket," Vanes said as he removed his wig and replaced it with one of the caps. "And gloves. You'll need the gloves." From his own jacket he took out a pair of three-cell flashlights. He handed one to Tomei. "There's a spare in your coat. You wouldn't want to be without a flashlight where we're going."

Tomei expected that they would be going through the door in the center of the room, but before donning his gloves, Vanes unlocked yet one more padlock and the side wall creaked open several feet. "Okay," he said in a whisper. "You stick right next to me. You want to stop, you tap me on the shoulder, okay?"

"Okay," Tomei agreed.

"One more question. Are you afraid of rats?"

"Everyone's afraid of rats, Red."

"Well, you're going to see more than your share. Tuck your pant legs into your boots. If we run into a horde of them, just shine your light right in their eyes and stand still till they get out of the way."

Vanes took a roll of duct tape from his coat pocket and wound a band of the tape around the area where his pant legs met the boot tops. He dropped to his knees and did the same for Tomei.

Tomei grabbed him by the shoulder. "This damn well better be worth it."

Vanes flicked on his flashlight. "Let's go see Kan

Chin's treasure chest. It's a good block and a half away, and we have to go slow."

The air was dank, and reminded Tomei of rotting food and stagnant water. His flashlight beam licked over dark-slimed brick and cement walls. "What is this? A sewer?"

"I don't know for sure," Vanes said in a raspy whisper. "It might have been at one time. It could have been used as an underground cemetery by the old tongs, too. I've come across a few graves. Oh, oh. Here they come."

Tomei waved his flashlight. He saw nothing at first, then there was the sound of movement and a few squeals. He nearly bolted. It looked like a black, lumpy carpet was coming toward him. His flashlight beam reflected off the lead rats' eyes.

"Just stand still. Let 'em go by," Vane cautioned.

Tomei could feel the wave of the rodents brush by his feet. He tried to keep from shaking—literally shaking in his boots.

"Okay," Vanes said. "They're on their way to some crummy restaurant." He chuckled lightly. "I've got some spots in here that even the rats don't know about. Let's keep moving."

At one point Tomei's boots sank at least a foot into a pool of greasy, putrid water. The stench was becoming unbearable. Tomei held his flashlight in one gloved hand, the other covered his nose as he tried breathing through his mouth.

The tunnel's height varied from as much as twelve feet to as little as four, as both men stooped over to worm their way through a narrow crevice in a dilapidated cobblestone wall.

"The worst is over," Vanes announced as he led Tomei over a low-running brick bulkhead.

Vanes wiggled his hands free of his gloves, took a flask from his jacket and handed it to Tomei. "Brandy."

Tomei took a grateful swig from the flask and

passed it back to Vanes. "You come this way often, Red?"

"I sure do. It has paid off big in the past. My father turned me on to the catacomb tunnels that run through Chinatown years ago. A lot of them have been destroyed by street repair, earthquakes, and just plain old mother time settling them into dust. But this one is my own private information highway. I think the rats keep everyone away."

"They sure as hell would keep me away."

Vanes took a sip of the brandy and put the flask back in his jacket pocket. "Okay," he said, his voice soft as if murmuring in church. "We're about a hundred yards from our target." He shined the flashlight beam on his wristwatch. "Chin's men should be coming home with the night's gambling profits." He dropped his cigar to the dank ground. "So keep close, and no talking."

Tomei followed in Vanes's footsteps, pausing when he paused, crouching low when Vanes did. Vanes came to a sudden stop and turned to Tomei, tilting the flashlight beam so that Tomei could see his face. "We're here," his lips mouthed silently.

Vanes slipped the flashlight under one arm and bent down and overturned a crumbling piece of timber, revealing a battery-operated lantern and a clothbound object the size of a paperback book. He switched the lantern on, giving Tomei a view of filthy, scum-encrusted brick walls.

Vanes carefully spread open the cloth. "It's a micro video system," he whispered. He groped around for a minute and came up with a slim electrical cord that he attached to the machine. He flicked on a switch and a four-inch-square video set slowly sputtered on, revealing a dark, blank screen.

"The other end of the cord is attached to a pin-sized camera lens, which I managed to get inside the vault. You can thank our friends the rats for helping me on this. They gnawed their way damn near through the bricks. I just had to drill a half inch or so."

Tomei shuffled over to Vanes, who was pointing a finger at the micro screen. He slipped on a pair of headphones and connected the cord to the micro video system. "It's dark in there now. Make yourself comfortable. The show should start any minute."

"With what?" Tomei said, finding it hard to keep his voice down.

"Gambling chips, and more to come," Vanes promised.

It was twenty minutes before the promised show began. They both heard the distinctive sound of a heavy, well-oiled metal door opening. Tomei leaned over Vanes's shoulder to watch the action. The pin-lens was positioned just above floor level and the distorted fish-eye screen showed a shelf-lined room with a polished concrete floor. There were rows of neatly stacked orange plastic containers the size of shoe boxes on the shelves.

Two men were wheeling in a pair of supermarket shopping carts. The carts were jam-packed with more of the orange plastic containers loaded with gambling chips.

The older of the two men was stockily built, with a droopy mustache. Tomei recognized him from the mug shot Elaine Surel had provided him—Willy Hon—Kan Chin's top dog. Hon took a clipboard from one of the carts and began logging in the containers while the younger man steadily stacked them onto the shelves.

They were talking and laughing as they went about their chores. When the men were through, they rolled the shopping carts from the room. Willy Hon's eyes flicked around the shelves, stopping now and then as his lips moved silently. Then the lights went out and the door shut with a loud clang.

Vanes began disassembling his camera rig. "That guy, the older one, that's Willy Hon."

"I know. I've seen his rap sheet."

Vanes grabbed his flashlight and shined it directly at Tomei. "Who got it for you?"

Tomei waved for the beam to be moved. "A friend, Red."

"Your friend could be in a lot of trouble if it's traced to him."

"You understand Chinese, don't you? What were they saying?"

"Hon was bragging about how much money he'd won at a *pai gow* game earlier tonight. The other guy was new to me. I couldn't pick up a name. Hon kept calling him *tset*."

"Which means?"

"Prick. Did you notice the orange-colored boxes that hold the chips? Orange is a lucky color for the Chinese."

"And Kan Chin believes in luck?"

"I don't think so, but his customers do."

"What about the cash? The chips are stored in the vault, but where's the cash?"

"It goes up the elevator to Chin's penthouse suite, where he counts it, kisses it, and maybe takes a bath with it, for all I know. What do you think, Tomb?"

Tomei rubbed a gloved hand across the blackened brick wall leading to the money room. "I think you want me to break into Kan Chin's money room and haul off those chips, Red. I'm just not sure why."

"You said you wanted to make a statement for Billy Rossi. Can you think of a better way?"

"And what if I do get Kan Chin's chips? He could just pass the word that they were no longer any good. Issue new ones. In the end, they wouldn't be worth anything"

Vanes stamped his boots and grimaced. "No! He couldn't do that. I told you, the chips are good in Vancouver, New York. Anywhere there's a big Chinese community. You just don't get it, do you, Tomb? It's not the money. It's face. If word got out that someone had waltzed off with a load of Chin's chips, he would be humiliated. Nothing you could do to him would be worse than that. He's a proud man. That's his weakness. He'd do damn near anything not to have that story put out on the streets. You'd get Rossi's money back, and Chin's word that he wouldn't lean on you or Rossi again. And as miserable a bastard as Chin is, he is a man of his word."

"I still don't understand your action. What do you get out of it?"

"I'd see Chin squirm. I've been waiting twenty years for a chance to see him on the hot seat." Vanes smiled to cut the tension. "And I'd get a cut of Rossi's money, of course. It's a two-man job, Tomb. I can't pull it off myself. So, what do you say? Are you in or out?"

Tomei felt a sudden chill run through his shoulder blades. Red Vanes was holding something back. "I need some time to think about it. Let's have breakfast and make some plans."

Chapter Twenty-three

"**I** heard from Kan Chin," Charles Prescott said. "I'm picking up the money tonight."

Mayor Richard Barr was at the window, gazing out at the rows of makeshift tents in the park. "Did he have any information on Philip Dong?"

"No, but he says he's working on it, sir."

"When and where do you get the money?"

"Ten o'clock tonight, at the Cabine."

Barr spun around to face Prescott. "The Cabine? Where the hell is that?"

"It's a new club, on Kansas Street. The computer geeks love it. Cabine is French for a telephone booth," Prescott said. "They have phones at the tables and around the bar, so that the customers can ring each other up. It certainly isn't my choice. Maybe Chin has a piece of the place. All I know is that he told me to be there at ten tonight and ask for someone called Sweet Alice."

"Sweet Alice?" Barr's eyebrows shot up toward his forehead.

"That's all I know," Prescott answered defensively.

"I'm having second thoughts about the money, Charles."

Prescott opened his mouth, then snapped it shut.

Barr clasped his hands behind his back and paced the room as he spoke. "Perhaps we'll tell Chin thanks but no thanks on the money, that we'll negotiate the commission jobs with him for the information on Philip Dong."

Momentarily shaken up, Prescott countered with, "Chin would take offense to that, Mr. Mayor. We haven't much time. If Chin thinks we're slighting him, that we don't trust him—"

"Trust him," Barr fumed. "I trust Kan Chin about as much as I trust my first wife's lawyer. But you're right, Charles. We don't have a choice. We do need that money. You can have one of my bodyguards for the night, that way nothing can—"

"Whoever is giving us the money wouldn't want to spot me with a policeman," Prescott protested.

Barr sighed loudly, then said, "You're right again, Charles. But as soon as you have the money, bring it to my house, understood? All of the money."

"Mr. Mayor, you'll get every dollar Kan Chin promised you."

"I'm coming, I'm coming for Christ's sake," Ava Avery shouted at whoever was ringing the bell and pounding on the door. She hoped it wasn't that horny real estate salesman from Denver. He paid top dollar, but he made her work for it.

She checked the wall mirror, seeing she hadn't done a very good job on her makeup. It wouldn't matter if it was Denver. He'd take one look at her lacy bra and thong panties and go for his wallet. She slid the lock free and the door flew open, knocking her back several feet. At first she didn't recognize Sherri Dawson. Her hair was a mess and she was wearing baggy pants and an oversized white cable-knit sweater.

"Jesus, you look like hell. What happened to you?"

Sherri slammed the door shut and slid the lock home. "You don't want to know. I need a bath, some clothes, and a damn big drink."

She strode into the familiar apartment, noticing it looked messier than usual. "Are you alone?"

"Yes. Business has been slow."

Ava followed Sherri down the hall to the bathroom.

She leaned against the doorjamb as Dawson turned on the tub water and upended a bottle of bubble bath into the streaming water.

"Make it Scotch, please," Sherri said as she stripped off her clothes. "A stiff one."

"Okay, okay. But what happened to you? Those bruises look bad. Some kind of weirdo, huh? One of those S and M freaks."

"You *really* don't want to know, Ava. Trust me."

Ava was on her way to the kitchen, when she snapped her fingers. "Hey. I forgot. You had a visitor. Some cop."

Sherri stiffened, with one foot in the tub, the other hovering near the faucet. "A cop?"

"Yeah," Ava said breezily. "A hunky-looking guy. Toomey or something like that. I made him show me his badge. I've had guys try to get a freebie with a phony badge, but his looked legit. From San Francisco. He said he was working with the Vegas cops. He wanted to know all about you."

"When was this?" Sherri asked as she gently lowered herself into the tub.

"Today's what? Saturday. Then it was Thursday. He threatened to bust me. I came on to him. Offered him my whole store, but he turned me down. All he wanted to do was talk about you and go through your stuff. I told him there wasn't much here." She snapped the elastic on her panties. "He turned me down cold. Maybe he's gay. You know him?"

"Yes. I know him. He's not gay, Ava. Just very particular."

John Tomei was sitting in Billy Rossi's front room, a cup of coffee in his hand, Fidel sprawled at his feet. Billy Rossi had listened to his advice and taken a trip out of town, leaving Fidel behind.

"I don't think the people where I'm going would appreciate the animal, Tomb. Fast Eddy Murray will be running my shop while I'm gone. He doesn't know anything about this Kan Chin deal. I'll keep in touch with him and you."

Tomei was happy to have the dog for company. What he wasn't too happy about was his partnership with Red Vanes.

Vanes was a puzzle. He had a long-standing grudge against Kan Chin, but why was he going out on a limb like this? If they went ahead with Vanes's plan, broke into Kan Chin's safe and hijacked the chips, then ransomed them back to Chin, Vanes himself would be exposed. Or would he be? Vanes's elaborate disguises, his knowledge of the Chinatown catacombs—his contact Texas Joe, the strange cowboy-talking character they'd met at lunch. Why would Vanes risk losing all that just to help him? They weren't friends, though Tomei was one of the few members of the police department who the eccentric Red Vanes would talk to. Tomei had done Vanes a favor on a case involving a man who ran rigged poker games in the posher San Francisco downtown hotels. One of the man's pigeons had accused him of using marked cards. The accuser was found beaten to death in a Chinatown alley. Vanes's territory, and he didn't appreciate unwanted visitors. Especially unwanted dead visitors. Tomei had introduced Vanes to several of the gamblers, eventually leading him to the murderer.

Tomei was mulling over his options when Fidel growled and his head snapped up.

A green compact car was pulling into Rossi's driveway. Tomei relaxed when he saw Laura Aguera behind the wheel.

"Easy, Fidel. Easy, boy."

Laura Aguera exited the car and stood motionless for a moment while she got her bearings.

Tomei opened the front door, one hand holding on to Fidel's collar.

"Hi," he called.

Laura placed her hand on her hips and shouted. "Don't you ever answer your goddamn cell phone? I've been calling for hours. Elaine's in the hospital. Someone tried to kill her!"

*   *   *

Laura gave Tomei a brief description of what had happened to Elaine as they drove to the hospital.

At eight-thirty that morning, Elaine was preparing to leave for work. She unlocked the door to her unmarked police car, which was parked in front of her house on Jackson Street, when a truck hit her. The truck, a stolen Ryder rental rig, was later found smashed up against a tree three blocks away. There had been no witnesses. The truck was now in the hands of the crime lab, but Laura held out little hope that there would be any worthwhile clues.

Laura had answered Tomei's follow-up questions with curt, one-word, yes or no answers. She was obviously steamed at him.

The San Francisco General Hospital is a three-block stretch of gawky, red-bricked buildings dating back to the 1930s, surrounded by clogged parking lots, neglected shrubs, and weed-choked lawns. The hospital's newest addition, a seven-story, graceless concrete affair that somewhat resembled an ocean liner's superstructure, housed the patient recovery wards. A gunmetal sky added to the gloom. Gulls wheeled around in circles waiting for rain.

The hospital caters to the have-nots—the homeless, the illegals, the druggies, and those who had never had a chance at climbing aboard the ride to prosperity that a booming economy supposedly provided.

Tomei would not want to have his daughter treated at the hospital for the flu, a skinned knee, or a broken arm. But if, God forbid, Melissa had been badly burned, shot, stabbed, or crushed in an automobile accident, then S.F. General was the place to go. The hospital's emergency ward was understaffed and underpaid, but still provided the absolute best chance for a trauma victim to survive his or her wounds. He hoped that Elaine had gotten there in time.

The pleasant, blue-haired volunteer sitting at the information booth provided them with Elaine's room number.

Tomei and Laura rode the elevator to the sixth

floor, surrounded by sad-faced civilians and doctors who kept their eyes down while they fingered the stethoscopes dangling from their necks. If anything, the doctors seemed more depressed than the visitors.

Tomei spotted Ross Surel, Elaine's husband, pacing back and forth in the hallway. He was of medium height, with neatly barbered hair. Cleft-chinned and long-faced, he looked just like the shrewd, successful businessman that he was.

Tomei offered his hand, which Ross accepted reluctantly.

"How is she?" Tomei asked anxiously.

Ross draped his hand around Laura's shoulder and addressed his answer to her. "The doctor says that Elaine will be all right. They're just not sure how long it will be until she can walk. She'll be in a wheelchair for some time." His hands closed into fists and he looked straight at Tomei. "Do you know anything about this, John?"

"No. Just what Laura told me. When can we see Elaine?"

"The nurses are with her now. I don't think you should bother her." Ross steered Laura down the hall, and his body language made it obvious he didn't want Tomei to join them.

Tomei spotted a cleaning woman pushing a cart down the hall. He asked her where the gift shop was located.

"First floor, sir. But it's closed for repairs."

"Is there a floral shop nearby?"

"Uh-uh. Nothing you could walk to."

Tomei grimaced. Elaine loved long-stemmed roses. He spotted a discarded newspaper in the cleaning cart.

"Mind if I take the paper?"

"You'll save me from dumping it," the woman grinned. " 'Less you drop it somewhere and I have to pick it up again."

Tomei retrieved the paper, rolled it tightly and went to work with his pocket knife.

Laura was waving at him. "Ross went to get a cup of coffee. He looks beat."

"Yes, he does," Tomei agreed.

A nurse with strong, narrow features and crisp black hair peeked her head out of Elaine's room. "Are you both family?" she asked.

"Yes," Tomei said quickly. "Can we see her now?"

"Just for a few minutes. She's still groggy from the medication."

Tomei flinched when he saw Elaine. Her hair was splayed across the pillow, her pale face pinched with pain.

A cast, running from ankle to knee, was elevated above the mattress with chains and weights.

"Hi guys," she said in a thick, groggy voice.

"Hi Gucci," Tomei responded. "What the hell happened to you, partner?"

"It happened so fast. There was no traffic. He was aiming at me." She opened her palm and Tomei gently placed it between his hands. He could feel her pulse. Slow and steady. Thank God for that.

Elaine frowned. "What's that under your arm?"

Tomei stood back and with the flourish of a magician held up the rolled up newspaper, which he began to peel back, turning the paper into a stalk of crisp flowers.

Elaine started to laugh. The laugh turned into a cough, and she bit on her lower lip to keep from crying.

Laura hurried over to the bed, adjusting the blanket and patting Elaine's arm. "We'll come back later. You better get some sleep."

Elaine nodded, then gestured Tomei over. She started to speak, then stopped, closing her eyes, gathering her strength.

Tomei leaned over and whispered, "Take care, Gucci. I love you."

Elaine's eyes opened and she said, "I got a look at the driver, Tomb. He was Chinese."

Chapter Twenty-four

Laura Aguera gave Tomei the silent treatment until they were back in her car. She switched on the engine and stabbed the accelerator.

"Tell me the truth. Did what happen to Elaine have anything to do with those reports she got for you?"

"I don't know," Tomei answered honestly. "But I'm going to find out."

Laura tapped her fingers anxiously on the steering wheel. "The reports Elaine got for you. You know we have to log on, put our star number and a case number on each request that's made on the computer database."

"I'm familiar with the procedure."

"Are you?" Laura challenged. "Then why the hell did you put Elaine in a situation where she could step in shit? Huh? Why?"

"Calm down. We don't know anything about Elaine's accident yet."

"Accident," Laura scoffed. She jammed the shift lever into reverse and the car's balding wheels slithered on the damp asphalt as she steered the car out of the parking lot.

"I'm telling you this only because of Elaine. She's crazy about you for some reason. An FBI agent named Jamison was in the Personnel Department, looking at your file."

"I know Jamison. I saw him at a local saloon. He was tailing Dino Lanzoni. Lanzoni is—"

"I know who the hell Lanzoni is," Laura said heatedly.

"Lanzoni has nothing to do with me. I was meeting with an old bookie, Billy Rossi, who—"

"I know all about Rossi, too," Laura said, slamming on the brakes as a low-slung convertible cut in front of her.

"I doubt that. But Rossi isn't connected to Lanzoni. It was just a coincidence that they were at the saloon at the same time."

"Sure, sure," Laura said sarcastically.

Tomei's voice turned frosty. "Listen, I'm going to find out what happened to Gucci with or without your help. I'd rather do it with you. Can we make a truce?"

Laura gave him a sidelong look, then made a sharp right turn. "I checked on that Nevada license plate you asked about. It was towed from the city garage at Fifth and Mission and then out to the long-term tow yard. The Corvette is still there, as far as I know."

"Thanks," Tomei said sincerely. "Would you mind dropping me off at the tow yard? It's over on Third Street."

"I know where it is. And another thing. Lieutenant Brett Clayton from Management Control was doing some checking into the personnel files, too. He reviewed Elaine's file the day after that FBI agent went through yours." She gave Tomei a thin smile. "Do you think that's just another coincidence?"

Pity the poor drivers who have their cars towed and impounded in San Francisco. The first step in the retrieval process is go to the traffic bureau and pay for the parking ticket. Then it's off to the tow company to settle the towing fee, which can exceed two hundred dollars.

Next, the hapless driver has to somehow make it out to the long-term storage facility, and since the few cabs operating in the city funnel from the airport to the major hotels, finding a cab can be difficult. If the vehicle has been stored for more than four days, it may already be gone. The tow agency can legally start the lien and sale process at that time.

If there was anything of value in the vehicle, the chances of it still being around by the time the owner gets to the long-term storage facility are remote.

Laura Aguera slowed to a crawl as they bumped over a series of railroad tracks and into an area of abandoned industrial buildings and weed-choked open lots. There were dozens of cars lined up on the dirt road that led to a wobbly cyclone fence clogged with fast-food Styrofoam cups and trays.

"Drive around them," Tomei suggested.

Laura pulled up to the fence and a man in grungy sweats came over to them. A smudged silver-colored badge was pinned to his chest.

He stooped over and pushed his wine-flushed face at Laura. "Whatdayathinkyourdoin'?"

Laura could just make out the words *private security guard* on the badge.

Tomei waved his badge. "Open the gate!" he ordered and the man shrunk back.

"Okay, okay. Don't get mad at me."

The gate screeched open and Laura drove down a steep, rutted, gravel-topped road. She kept one foot on the brake, afraid that the wheels would be bogged down in the mud.

"God, this is a depressing place."

"You're right," Tomei agreed.

There were several acres of vehicles of all shapes and sizes jammed together, with barely room for a person to navigate between them. A huge tin-roofed building sat at the end of the road. Stiff-legged pigeons hobbled across the roof.

A long line of ill-tempered-looking men and women, holding redemption forms, stood in front of the cano-pied window of a rusted-out trailer that had a hand-painted OFFICE sign on its side.

Laura coasted to a stop and Tomei said, "Leave it here, but take the keys, or it may disappear."

The air stank of exhaust fumes and spilled gasoline. The broken asphalt ground was pocked with potholes.

She followed Tomei over to the trailer. Several of the men standing in line started to protest when they cut in front of them.

Tomei leaned into the office door. A pimple-faced young man was slouched against the counter near the opened window. The walls were dotted with calendars featuring well-stacked women wearing shorts and halters, smiling and holding wrenches and hand tools as if they were precious objects.

"Where's the boss?" Tomei demanded.

The boy jerked an ink-stained thumb over his shoulder. "Back there."

Tomei turned to Laura. "Would you mind checking for the Corvette in the lot? I'll just be a minute."

Before Laura could protest, Tomei had gently closed the door in her face. He maneuvered through hip-high stacks of cardboard boxes to an open door. He entered the room and kicked the door shut behind him.

"I'm looking for a red Corvette with Nevada plates that was towed from the Fifth and Mission Garage."

The man sitting behind a cluttered desk gave Tomei a menacing look. "I'm looking for one, too, buddy. Get in line."

"The Corvette. Where is it?"

The man stood up. He was in his early fifties and had the boxy build of a former athlete who still worked out once in a while, but didn't let it get in the way of his beer drinking. He had hamlike hands and fleshy arms. A cigarette pack pouched the arm of his T-shirt. "We're short-handed today and I got a lot of customers ahead of you. Fill out a form and wait your turn."

"What's your name?" Tomei asked politely.

"Joe Miller. Why don't you come back—"

Tomei crossed the room quickly. He slammed his fist, with the knuckles extended, right to where he figured the man's belly button would be.

Miller's breath oozed out like air from a punctured balloon. He fell backwards into his chair and stared up at Tomei.

"Joe, I want that Corvette, and I want it now. It's part of a homicide investigation. Unless I get the car right now, I'm calling the crime lab out, and I'll fingerprint you and everyone who works here. You understand that? And while they're being printed, I'm going to run them all for warrants. You think any of your boys might have a record, Joe? I saw a couple of them out there who looked like they just came from a white sale." Tomei brushed his finger across his lower lip. "They had powder marks, Joe. What do you think it was? Sugar? I don't think so."

Miller rubbed his stomach and scowled. "You should of told me you were a cop. You've got no right to hit me."

"Who's going to stop me, Joe?"

Miller thought that over for a few moments then struggled to his feet. "Nevada plates, you say."

"That's exactly what I said. The registered owner is a Sherrilyn Dawson."

"I think I know the car you're talking about. Come on with me."

Dawson's Corvette was in the tin-roofed building. The hood was up, the motor was running and the license plates had been removed.

"What are they doing to it?" Laura asked.

"Either getting ready to sell it to a chop shop for parts or ship it down to Mexico is my guess."

Joe Miller was consulting with two beefy mechanics who had been working on the car. He rubbed his hands on his pants and glanced back at Tomei and Laura every few seconds.

"He's trying to decide whether or not to challenge us," Laura said. "Are you carrying?"

"No."

"Great," she said sarcastically as she slipped her hand into her purse, searching for her gun.

Miller had made his decision. He extended his arms

in a peaceful gesture. "My guys had this one confused with another Corvette." He looked over his shoulder and called, "Danny. Put the plates back on. They found a spare set of keys under the mat. You want to drive it yourself, or you want I should tow it to the Hall of Justice for you?"

Tomei approached the Corvette. When he first saw it in Rossi's garage, it had been dusty, the chrome wheels caked with mud. It was spotless now. The leather interior smelled of Armoral.

"I'll drive," Tomei said. "After I pull the prints, I'll be back to check with you."

He followed Laura to her car. "Thanks for the ride."

"Did I just witness a stolen vehicle incident with my own eyes, Tomei?"

"We have no proof that they were going to steal it."

"I'm talking about *you*. You can't just waltz in here and drive off with someone's car."

"If we leave the Corvette here, we'll never see it again. And if there is a connection between what I'm doing for Billy Rossi and what happened to Gucci, then Sherri Dawson played a role in it. Having the car may help."

"I still don't like it."

"Do you like steak? And Caesar salad?"

Laura was caught off-balance by the question. "You're asking me out for a date?"

"No. But we have to talk. Rossi is gone. I'm staying at his place. Someone has to care for his dog. Come on over at seven. I'd really like your input on this. I'm worried about Gucci."

Laura leaned a hip against her car, then stepped away when she noticed how dirty it was. Damn the man. What was she going to do with Tomei? He pushed people around, acted like he was still a cop. He was going to get her in trouble. But he was right about the Corvette. It would disappear if they left it at the tow yard. And she liked the way he treated Elaine, his feelings for her. That's how partners, even ex-partners, should be. She liked that a lot. "All right," she finally said. "On one condition."

"You name it."

"Show me how you did that flower trick with the newspaper."

Chapter Twenty-five

Willy Hon tiptoed into Kan Chin's office, moving as quietly as he could.

Chin was sitting on the edge of his chair, eyes closed, using the hem of his cardigan to polish his glasses.

It was a gesture Hon was familiar with. It meant that Chin was upset—very upset—about something. Hon hoped it had nothing to do with him.

He stood motionless as a window mannequin, watching as Chin's slender fingers whirled the cashmere across the lens of his glasses.

"I have heard from Captain Liu," Chin finally said, opening his eyes. "Miss Dawson killed his first mate."

"Liu is getting old. Older than an old woman," Hon said, regretting his words as soon as they spilled from his lips. Kan Chin did not appreciate being reminded in any way of his own age. He coughed and cleared his throat. "What did Liu do to the whore?"

"After killing the first mate, Miss Dawson jumped overboard. The *Mara Maru* was at anchor, three miles offshore, near San Diego. Liu says that he personally shot her, while she was in the water, and that the sharks feasted on her."

"A fitting end for the bitch," Hon said with grim satisfaction.

"Yes. If it is true. Miss Dawson, for all her imperfections, has proved to be a survivor."

"She couldn't survive the sharks," Hon asserted.

Chin held his glasses in front of his face, peering through the lenses at Willy Hon as if he were focusing through a magnifying glass. "Perhaps not."

"Do you think Liu lied about shooting Dawson?"

"I want Liu replaced, before the ship arrives in Hong Kong. And I want to know for certain that Dawson is dead."

Hon gave a listless shrug. "Three miles from shore. Even if Liu was lying about shooting her and the sharks, Dawson never would have made it to shore."

"How do you know?" Chin snapped, rocking Hon back on his heels. "Are you an expert on just how far she could swim? Do you know which way the tides were moving when she supposedly jumped overboard? If she is alive and goes to the police, there will be great trouble." Chin pointed a gnarly finger directly at Hon. "It was your responsibility to have her properly disposed of."

Hon sucked in his lips. It had been his idea to give her to Captain Liu as a present. He wanted Dawson to suffer. For the rest of her short, miserable life. Now he regretted not killing her himself.

"I will make certain that she is dead," Hon promised.

"Check with Mr. Rossi. And in Las Vegas. If she is alive, she will seek out friends, and I doubt that she has many. What did you learn of the policeman who supplied Rossi with your photo and criminal record?"

"It was a woman," Hon grunted contemptuously. "Inspector Elaine Surel. She works in the Vice detail. She met with an accident this morning."

"A fatal accident?"

"No. But she won't be bothering us for a while."

Kan Chin replaced his glasses. "She is probably on Rossi's payroll. The old fool is really a toothless tiger. Miss Dawson said that he was ready to abandon his business. Our new associate, Mr. Lanzoni, is delivering the money to Charles Prescott tonight. You have everything arranged?"

"Yes, sir. I'm meeting Lanzoni in an hour. There will be no problems."

"There had better not be any problems, or people will start saying that *you* are getting old, Willy. Older than an old woman."

Dino Lanzoni sat at the bar making interlocking rings on the countertop with the bottom of his highball glass. He shot an impatient glance at the wafer-thin gold watch on his wrist. The watch had been a gift from his brother, Nick. Nick presented it to him in court the day he was sentenced to prison. Nick hadn't said a word. He just undid the leather band and passed the watch to Dino before the bailiff cuffed his hands behind his back. Nick had received a life sentence, and was now doing hard time in the fed's supermax facility in Florence, Colorado. Florence was the only level-six prison in the entire United States. Nick was locked up in a six-by-eight-foot cell twenty-three hours a day. His one hour of freedom was spent alone, in an isolated, high-walled yard, where guards could keep a close eye on him.

Dino had tried to visit his brother, but the feds said no way. Only Nick's attorney, Al Baum, was allowed to see him. Once a month, for half an hour.

Baum had told Dino that Nick was holding his own, and would be free in a few years. "Maybe three, maybe five, but I'll get him out," Baum had boasted.

Dino had grabbed the shyster by his throat and promised to shoot his balls off if he didn't deliver on his promise.

He fingered the watch. Kan Chin's flunky was five minutes late. He'd give him five more minutes, then he'd go calling on Kan Chin himself. He didn't like dealing with flunkies anyway.

The bar was half-filled with slack-jawed middle-aged men gawking at the stripper bumping-and-grinding on the small stand behind the circular bar. A milk-skinned woman with frizzed, hay-colored hair, was holding on to a brass pole, humping her pelvis against it as if it were a ten-foot dildo. She had started her routine in a gaudy pink evening gown and spike-heeled shoes. She was now down to two silver tassels on her nipples and a rhinestone G-string.

She should have kept the dress on, in Lanzoni's opinion. It held up her sagging boobs and covered the bruises on her legs and chunky ass.

She had her head tilted back, grinding away on the pole, moaning in mock orgasm. When she was finished she scooped up her dress, wiggled into her shoes and tottered across the plank leading to the bar, coaxing tips from the drunks.

When she reached Lanzoni she dropped to her knees and said, "Want to show your appreciation, handsome? We can dance together in one of the booths."

"Fuck off," Lanzoni growled.

She sneered and stuck her tongue out at Lanzoni. He reached over and grabbed her upper arm. "Beat it."

She cried out and pulled her arm free. "That's what you can do," she said as she scrambled away. "Beat it raw!"

Lanzoni laughed out loud. It wasn't a bad comeback.

"The woman does not appeal to you?"

Lanzoni spun around on his stool. It was Chin's flunky. Willy Hon. He hadn't heard the little *cazzo* sneak up behind him. He was flanked by the same two young punks that had been at the house the night Lanzoni first met with Kan Chin.

"You're late, Shorty."

Hon hammered his hand against the edge of the bar, like a karate master warming up. "I apologize for the inconvenience. You are prepared for the meeting? You have the money?"

"Yeah, yeah." Lanzoni casually kicked the duffel bag at his feet. "Do you want to count it?"

"I don't believe that will be necessary. You wouldn't be foolish enough to try and cheat Kan Chin."

"Chin said you had something to throw into the pot."

Hon plopped an envelope onto the bar. "This is to be added to the delivery."

Lanzoni picked up the envelope and hefted it in his hand. "How much?"

"Fifty thousand."

"This guy is getting paid real good. I hope he delivers the goods for Chin."

"Oh, I'm sure he will. But Mr. Chin told me to tell you that he may take you up on your offer to 'break the sixth.' "

"Sure, sure." Lanzoni finished his drink then slammed the glass on the bar. "What's the matter, Shorty? You can't handle the tough jobs for your boss? Or even the easy ones. Why aren't you delivering the dough to this Prescott punk?"

Willy Hon's eyes narrowed. He was going to enjoy killing this one. Perhaps a boat ride. Out to the Farallones Islands where the great white sharks gathered. The big Italian would make a tastier meal than the whore. "Mr. Chin will be in touch soon."

John Tomei was rinsing romaine lettuce in the sink of Billy Rossi's kitchen when Fidel scrambled to his feet and growled.

"You're better than the burglar alarm," Tomei praised, drying his hands on a kitchen towel before petting the dog's head. "Let's go see who's here."

Tomei grabbed Rossi's fancy Winchester lever-action rifle as he followed Fidel to the door. He jacked a round into the chamber, just as he'd seen so many cowboys in the movies do, somehow reassured by the sound of the meshing metal parts of the weapon.

He peered through the peephole, then leaned the rifle against the wall when he spotted the diminutive figure of Laura Aguera. He turned off the alarm, and after yanking the door open, said, "Come on in. The dog's name is Fidel, and he's harmless."

"He doesn't look harmless." Laura had always been

wary of dogs, especially large dogs. She was a cat person. She stood tentatively in the doorway as Fidel approached her.

"Just pat him on the head. Let him get the smell of you," Tomei suggested.

"What if he doesn't like my smell?" she queried.

Tomei wrinkled his nose. "Chanel, isn't it? Who wouldn't love it? If Fidel gets too frisky, the key word is *kita*. Just say that and he'll stop going for your throat."

"Thanks a lot," Laura said quickly, sidestepping the dog and entering the house. She scanned the living room, taking in the western paintings, the statues, the leather couch, and the Navajo rug. "Mr. Rossi has rather . . . unique tastes."

"Too many John Wayne movies, I guess. Come on into the kitchen," he invited. "I moved the horses and cattle out to the stables."

Laura started to laugh, then she spotted the rifle leaning against the wall. "Isn't that carrying the decor a little too far?"

"There's a reason for it. Let's have a drink in the kitchen."

Tomei assisted her out of her raincoat. She was wearing a black silk shirt dress, cinched at the waist by a silver chain belt. The top three buttons of the dress were undone, revealing a tantalizing glimpse of décolletage and lacy black bra.

"I stopped by to see Elaine on the way over, John. She's still in a lot of pain."

"I know. I called and spoke to her doctor." Tomei rummaged around in the stand-up freezer, freeing a bottle of Stolichnaya and carrying it to the chopping block. "Vodka okay with you?"

"Yes. That's fine."

"How much did Gucci tell you about me, Laura?"

"Just that you went through a messy divorce. That you're crazy about your daughter, that you're in deep trouble financially, and that she's worried you'll do something stupid to try and make a lot of money in a hurry. She didn't have to tell me what took place at your house when you took a few shots at your neighbor. Just mention your name to any cop who knew you, and that's the first story they mention."

Tomei poured the icy liquid into stemmed glasses, added a twist of lemon and handed Laura her drink. "Did Gucci mention that I'm working for Billy Rossi?"

Laura sipped her drink to stall for time. Elaine had told her about the time she and Tomei had busted the bookie, and how Tomei had more or less been booted out of the Vice detail, and that Rossi had asked him to "settle the score" with the gang who had roughed him up and robbed him. "She didn't go into details," was the answer Laura came up with.

"A Chinese gang. Three men. They cut up some valuable paintings and raped his girlfriend." Tomei paused to sample his drink, then said, "Gucci ran a rap sheet on one of the men who I think was involved. Then she's hit and run. And she told me the driver was Chinese."

"So you think it's the same gang."

"I think, yes. I'm going to find out for sure."

"What did Elaine tell you about me?" Laura wanted to know.

"Just that you had a similar experience. You came home one day and found your husband in bed with his lover."

Lover. That was about as discreet a way as possible to put it, Laura thought. Her husband's lover was his personal trainer, a handsome, muscle-bound bisexual. Laura had encouraged Ron to step up his exercise regimen. Ten hours a day of sitting behind a brokerage desk had taken its toll on his once lean torso. Ron had been reluctant at first, but once he started working out, the gym had become a passion for him. Laura hadn't realized just how passionate until she returned unexpectedly from a training exercise at the department's shooting range. She remembered she smelled of gunpowder and was anxious to jump into the shower for a good scrubbing. She opened the bedroom door to find Ron and his lover thrashing around on the bed—the bed she'd made that very morning, slipping a few Hershey kisses and a pair of silk shorts under his pillow in hopes of sending Ron a message about the lack of romance in their marriage of late.

Tomei brought her out of her reverie. "Getting hungry?"

"Starving. What can I do to help?"

"Pick out some wine." He pointed to a door next to the freezer. "That's the wine cellar. Give me your car keys. I'll put your car in the garage."

"My car? What about the Corvette in the driveway?"

"It belongs here. Yours doesn't. Rossi hired a private security guard to check on the house. If he sees your car, he'll want to check it out."

Laura searched through her purse for the car keys, wondering just what Tomei was up to. She was overwhelmed by the rows of head-high wine racks in the "cellar," which was larger than her bedroom and living room combined. She strolled through the aisles, now and then tugging a bottle loose from its carved oak holder. She really didn't know all that much about wine. Tomei had said they were having steak and she knew she liked red wine, so she selected a bottle that appeared to have the most dust on it. She hesitated a moment, then chose another and carried them back to the kitchen.

"I hope these will do."

Tomei brushed his hands across his apron and examined one of the labels. Chateaux Margaux, one of France's premiere Bordeaux. He had no idea of the actual cost, but knew that any Margaux would go for more than two hundred dollars on a restaurant menu.

"Good choice. Why don't you open one up while I fix the salad."

Laura searched through kitchen drawers until she found a corkscrew. She watched Tomei as she went about her task. He seemed at home in a kitchen. Not many men looked good in an apron, but he did. He used the blade of a chef's knife to squash garlic, then dumped it into a bowl of olive oil.

"How's Melissa doing?" Laura asked, once she had wrested the cork from the bottle.

He gave her a big smile. "Great. I'm seeing her tomorrow."

Talking about his daughter definitely lit Tomei up. He began telling her stories about how bright Messy was. "She's quite an artist. I'll have to show you—" He held up his hands and shook his head. "Sorry. Once I start talking about Messy, I can't shut up. Ready for salad?"

The Caesar was good, the marinated New York steaks cooked to perfection, and the wine superb. "I could get hooked on this stuff," Laura admitted, holding her wineglass up to the dining room chandelier.

"Me too." There was an uneasy moment of silence, then Tomei said, "Gucci told me something else about you, Laura. That you're a good cop. I'm afraid that I've dragged her, and now you, into my troubles."

"The rap sheet Elaine pulled for you. Who was it?"

"A Chinese hood."

"Do I get a name?" Laura asked somewhat testily.

"Willy Hon. My bet is that Hon wasn't driving the truck that hit Gucci. I'd make another bet that whoever the driver was, he's an illegal, so his prints won't be on file with us or the FBI. We'll never be able to ID him."

"Speaking of the FBI, what's Agent Jamison's interest in you? Why would he come to the Personnel Department and go through your file?"

Tomei gave her a rundown of his meeting with Billy Rossi at Sully's saloon. "Jamison must think I'm involved with Lanzoni in some way, or that Rossi is. Billy denies it, and I believe him."

"How about Sherri? She could be mixed up with Lanzoni. Maybe she was filling him in on Rossi's operation."

Tomei sipped the expensive French wine reflectively. "I thought about that possibility. Dawson spent some time in New York City."

"Then she should have recognized Lanzoni," Laura asserted.

"Maybe. But I didn't spot Lanzoni until he was out front, getting into a cab. So it's possible she never saw him." He saw Laura frown. "I know, I know. I don't like coincidences any more than you do."

"Let's play 'what if,' " Laura suggested. "What if Sherri's working for both the Chinese and Lanzoni? What if Lanzoni is out here making a deal with the Chinese?"

Tomei raised his glass in a salute. "Gucci was right when she said you were a good cop. Lanzoni was booted out of New York. He'd want to get as far away from that crowd as possible. What better place than here in San Francisco? He'd need a source. And according to Red Vanes, Kan Chin is *the* source in this area."

"Vanes? Isn't he the guy that made a big stink when they shut down the Intelligence unit?"

"Right." Tomei stabbed the last piece of steak with his fork and ran it through the juices on the plate. The martinis and wine had loosened his tongue. Laura already knew too much. If Kan Chin sent his men after Gucci, there's no reason to think they wouldn't go after her partner, too, so he couldn't keep her in the dark.

Laura said, "When I got back to the Hall of Justice this afternoon, I was summoned to the Management Control Division. Lieutenant Clayton grilled me about Elaine. Not about the accident, but about the rap sheet and mug shot she pulled for you. He acted strange. He wouldn't tell me anything, but he asked a lot of questions."

Tomei frisked his memory for Clayton. He barely knew the man. Clayton had been a sergeant in the Recruitment Division at one time. The Recruitment Division was not an assignment anyone went to if they wanted to do real police work. The Management Control Division was another detail no one Tomei considered to be a good cop wanted to be associated with.

"Clayton is a jerk," Laura continued. "I did what I do best—acted dumb—and asked him how he happened to land on that one rap sheet. He said that it was a 'routine records scan' but I don't buy it. I know there are cops who sell rap sheets and driver's license records to attorneys and private investigators. If Management Control does go after them, they monitor them for weeks, or months before they make a move. One rap sheet? Bullshit. Clayton had to have been told that someone had pulled Hon's rap sheet." She tapped her fist on the tablecloth for emphasis. "Who told him?"

"You're right. And I—"

Fidel suddenly leaped up and galloped toward the front door. Tomei knocked a bottle of wine over in his haste to get to his feet. He reached for the rifle before carefully parting the drapes and peering out the window. He spotted a daub of red taillights just before they disappeared into the fog.

"It was her?" Jimmy Kung asked as the car slithered over the damp asphalt.

"No. Not the whore," Willy Hon answered, the disappointment obvious in his voice. When he spotted Sherri Dawson's red sports car parked in Rossi's driveway, he'd felt a surge of anger and lust run through his body. He would finish her for good this time.

But when he'd peeked through the window, he saw another woman. Younger than Dawson, with dark hair. And a man. It must have been the rental cop that Dawson said Rossi had hired.

Now that he had time to think about it, it made sense. Dawson's car would have been towed away from the garage by the police. Rossi would have gone looking for it.

The dog's bark had frightened him more than he wanted to admit. It was a formidable animal. Then he remembered that Kan Chin had provided him with the key word that would render the dog harmless. "Freeze."

So the dog was of no concern. The man? A low-paid security guard who was probably plying his girl-friend with Rossi's food and booze.

But where was Rossi? Upstairs? Sleeping? Hiding in his bedroom? Hon had thought the bookmaker might die of a heart attack when he threatened him with the knife that night.

Maybe Sherri Dawson was with Rossi, holding his shaking hand. "Drop me off at Chin's place, then get Gim. Come back. I want to know who comes in and out of the house. If someone leaves with the whore's Corvette, follow them."

"You think it was the bad guys?" Laura asked after Tomei had calmed Fidel down.

"I don't know."

"If it was, they spotted Sherri Dawson's Corvette."

"Hell, it could have just been a cat that got Fidel excited."

"Damn it, John. You want them to see the Corvette, don't you?"

"It might shake them up. Make them do some-thing stupid."

"Stupid? Like break into this place again. And that's why you put my car in the garage, isn't it? So, if they did come by, they wouldn't spot it."

Tomei held up the wine bottle he'd tipped over in his haste to reach the front of the house. He divided up what was left into their glasses. "You're in this deep enough as it is, Laura."

Laura picked up her glass and drained the contents in a long, steady gulp. "You realize that they could be out there right now."

"I doubt it. Not with Fidel here. And the house has a state-of-the-art alarm system. We're safe." He shook the empty wine bottle. "I think we should open an-other one, don't you?"

"When you put my car in the garage. Did you notice the small suitcase in the back?"

"I did."

She crossed over to him quickly and wrapped her arms around his neck, pulling him down to her, her open mouth searching for his. She inhaled his tongue. His fingers fumbled with the buttons on her dress as he lowered his head to kiss the hollow of her throat.

Laura broke away, her breasts heaving, her face flushed. "Get the case, John," she said in a husky voice she barely recognized. "And for God's sake, leave Fidel in the garage."

Chapter Twenty-six

Charles Prescott's nostrils tightened when he entered the doors of Cabine. San Francisco had a strong no smoking ordinance for every commercial establishment in the city. It was one of Mayor Barr's pet crusades, though it didn't stop Barr from puffing the occasional cigarette in after-hours city hall gatherings. The rules were supposedly strictly enforced in restaurants and bars. No one at the Cabine was paying any attention to the ordinance. Ribbons of foul-smelling smoke floated up to the tin-plate ceiling and wafted around the strobe lighting. Cigars were the definite poison of choice: thin ones, fat ones, long ones, short ones. The smokers were a fifty-fifty mixture of men and women—well-turned-out dot-commers eager to see and be seen.

Prescott stood his ground for a moment, letting the crowd forge relentlessly around him.

A young woman with a cigarette dangling from her lips was playing Gershwin on an ebony grand piano. The lighting was dim and it took him a few moments to notice that some of the leather-clad women had stubbles of beard blossoming through their makeup.

He headed for the bar, which was at the rear, beyond the piano.

There was a black telephone in front of each stool. The bartender, a dapper man in his forties with a jaunty waxed mustache, cupped his ear to hear what Prescott was saying.

"I'm looking for Sweet Alice," Prescott said.

"A lot of guys are." He pointed to a platform on the opposite wall. "She runs the phones. You want something to drink?"

Prescott ordered a glass of white wine and studied the young woman on the platform. She was sitting in front of what appeared to be an old-fashioned telephone switchboard, with rubbery orange cables and finger-size connectors that plugged into the switchboard. Her bare back was crisscrossed with strips of black elastic that appeared to be suspenders. He craned his neck to get a better look.

When the bartender returned with his wine, he provided Prescott with a cocktail napkin. "Eleven bucks, please. You want to talk to Sweet Alice, just pick up the phone. You see someone at a table, or down the bar you want to hit on, just ask Alice for the number on the napkin."

Prescott had another question ready, but the bartender retreated to fill another order. He examined the paper napkin, which was a diagram of the Cabine's floor plan. There was a number circled in red identifying each telephone and its location throughout the establishment.

He threaded his way through the crowd over to the platform. The buxom switchboard operator turned to face him. She was wearing a winged tuxedo collar and black leather bow tie, but no shirt. The straps of her suspenders were strategically placed across her nipples. Prescott couldn't stop staring, pondering just how the straps stayed in place. Glue? Double-stick tape?

"Can I help you?" she asked in a sultry voice.

"Sweet Alice?"

"Right, honey. What do you need?"

"My name's Charles Prescott. I was told to ask for you, and—"

"Twenty-six, honey."

"I beg your pardon?"

"Table twenty-six." She handed him a phone receiver. "I'll plug you in. Your friend's waiting for you. Don't worry," she grinned. "I won't listen."

Prescott checked the napkin, then tried to locate table twenty-six, but the standing crowd made it impossible.

"Yeah," a strong male voice said when they were connected.

"This is Charles Prescott. I . . . I believe you have . . ."

"The men's room. The one on the second floor. In exactly five minutes. I'm watching you, so don't make any stops. Lock the door behind you. I'll be waiting."

Prescott cursed. He tried to get Sweet Alice's attention, but she was ignoring him. He studied the napkin and found the notation for rest rooms on the second level.

This was all too stupid. Not the kind of thing he expected from Kan Chin. The man's voice. Definitely not Asian. American. The accent—East Coast? Maybe, maybe not. Prescott had been surprised at the number of native San Franciscans whose accents and voice patterns sounded as if they had been born and raised in New York City. He nursed his wine, checking his watch carefully. When five minutes had passed, he edged into the crowd and headed for the stairs.

The men's rest room door was marked with the outline of a man in a tuxedo smoking a cigar. A hand-printed OUT OF ORDER sign was taped to the door. The adjoining ladies' room sported the profiled silhouette of a big-haired nude with her arms stretched over her head.

Prescott's hand hovered for a moment, then he pushed the door open and hurried inside. He squatted awkwardly, peered under the stall doors, and saw the cuffs of a pair of dark slacks and two enormous shiny cordovan tasseled loafers.

"Lock the fuckin' door," the same voice he'd spoken to on the phone ordered. "Then sit down on the can next to me."

Prescott locked the door and hurried into the adjoining stall.

"Sit," the voice commanded.

Prescott followed instructions, perching on the edge of the toilet seat, ready to make a run for it at the first sign of trouble.

"Here you go," the voice said. A black nylon duffel bag was pushed under the metal wall separating the two toilets.

A bulging manila envelope lay on top of the case. He picked up the envelope, undid the hasp and smiled as he ran his thumb across the edge of a thick pack of hundred-dollar bills.

"You wanna count it, pally?"

"I . . . I'm sure Mr. Chin wouldn't—"

"Okay then. Take off. Right now. You're being watched, so get the hell out of here. Go right to your car."

Prescott shot to his feet, nearly dropping the envelope with his fifty thousand dollars into the toilet. He picked up the duffel bag and hurried to the door, his trembling fingers groping for the lock. He wondered what would happen if he disobeyed the order and stopped at the downstairs bathroom. He definitely had to use the facilities.

Mayor Richard Barr listened to Charles Prescott's narration of the events at Cabine with rapt attention.

When Prescott was finished, Barr rubbed his chin thoughtfully. "You never got a look at the guy?"

"No, sir."

"Yet you're sure he wasn't Chinese?"

"He sounded like an American. A loud, vulgar voice, and he was wearing a pair of the biggest shoes I've ever seen."

"That certainly narrows it down," Barr said sarcastically. "There aren't a hell of a lot of big-footed Chinese around." He hitched up his pants and walked over to the kitchen table. The contents of the duffel bag lay spread across the table. Barr had counted the money twice. It was all there.

He randomly pulled one hundred dollar bills out of

the pile until he had a total of a thousand dollars in his fist.

"Charles. The first thing in the morning, I want you to take these to the bank. Your personal bank. Tell the manager that you won the money in a poker game, or a relative gave it to you, or make up whatever story you think best. Just make sure it isn't counterfeit, or marked in some way, understand?"

Goose bumps prickled down Prescott's spine. Counterfeit. He hadn't considered that. "Yes, sir. Good idea." Damn good idea, but instead of the money the mayor was waving at him, he'd give the bank clerk a sampling of his fifty thousand dollars.

Barr handed Prescott the bills, then slapped him on the back, like a coach sending a quarterback into the game late in the fourth quarter. "Good job, Charles. Damn good job. If the money is clean, you're in for a bonus." He kicked the empty duffel bag. "And get rid of that on your way home."

Chapter Twenty-seven

John Tomei gently nudged the accelerator. The Corvette's engine gave out a throaty snarl and his spine was pushed backward into the plush leather upholstery as he zipped past a lineup of SUV's.

The drive from San Francisco to Gilroy usually took him well over an hour, but the light Sunday morning traffic and Sherri Dawson's jazzy sports car was going to cut that down considerably. He turned off the Junipero Serra Freeway and onto Highway 85, heading right into the heart of Silicon Valley.

He laid his head back against the headrest, twisting his neck to relieve the tension. Seeing Melissa would be the best medicine for his aching muscles, but seeing Melissa also meant seeing Joan, his ex-wife, and those meetings guaranteed a headache, at the very least.

Tomei fiddled with the car's radio, trying to find something other than the all-news format and country and western stations' Dawson had programmed into the radio.

He settled the dial on a soft jazz channel. The music somehow reminded him of last night, and Laura Aguera.

He wasn't sure just how much all of the wine they'd consumed had to do with their lovemaking. When he came back from the garage with her overnight bag, Laura moved into his arms again, kissing him gently, softly on the lips. Then it was as if a spark had ignited them. They behaved like teenagers who were taking advantage of the fact that mom and dad were away for the night. Pawing at each other, undoing buttons, pulling down zippers, leaving a trail of clothing along the stairs leading up to the bedroom.

By the time they'd reached Rossi's bed, they were naked, slick with heat. Laura's nails dug into his back, his hands roamed her sensuous body, clutching at her buttocks.

Tomei couldn't recall sex being that desperate, that frantic. It had been impersonal at first, each of them seemingly taking what they wanted of the other, not thinking of their partner, just concerned with their own urgent desires.

They'd fallen asleep with limbs intertwined, bathed in sweat, his face buried in her hair.

Sometime during the night he'd woken up. Laura was lying on her side, her head propped on one hand, staring at him. The moonlight filtered through the window and framed the shape of her shoulders, the curve of her hip, the fullness of her breasts.

He opened his mouth to say something and she put a vertical finger to her lips and whispered, "Ssshhhh," then leaned over and ran her tongue lightly along his forehead, down his nose, and finally plunged her tongue into his open mouth.

This time they made love. Slow, gentle, giving, tender love.

When he woke in the morning, Laura was already up. He found her in the kitchen, feeding Fidel the leftovers from their steak dinner.

"Good morning," she said brightly. "Coffee's on. I have to get going."

Tomei stood there in his slacks and bare feet. There was a long awkward moment, both of them wondering what would happen next.

"I . . . I'm going to see Messy today."

"I know," Laura responded, opening her purse and searching around. "I can't find my car keys," she complained.

"I left them in the ignition when I put it in the garage. Listen. I might not be back until late tonight."

Laura glanced at her watch. "I have to get going." She ran her fingers over the front of her silk dress. "I have to stop at home and change clothes before I go to work." She reached down for her overnight bag. "I don't think what I have in here would be appropriate."

"I never did see what you had in there," Tomei said, moving toward her, arms outstretched.

She tilted her head back and smiled. "You saw everything else, though. John . . . last night was . . . well, last night. I want to see you again, but I know you're busy with Melissa, and then there's Elaine. I want to find out what the crime lab learned about the truck that hit her."

"I'll call you as soon as I get back," Tomei promised. And he'd meant it.

Tomei had been thinking so intensely about last night and Laura that he'd paid no attention to the ululating sound of the siren. He looked in the Corvette's mirror and spotted the revolving red light of a Highway Patrol car.

He maneuvered the Vett over to the shoulder of the road and pulled to a stop, dutifully keeping both hands clamped on the steering wheel in plain sight, as the cautious CHP officer approached, one hand resting on the grip of his holstered gun.

"Roll down the window, please," the officer ordered.

Tomei followed directions, returning both hands to the steering wheel as soon as the chore was completed. All cops get nervous when they can't see a suspect's hands. The officer had his cap tilted up on his forehead. His tinted glasses fit tight to his face. He appeared to be in his forties, which cheered Tomei a bit. Older cops were usually easier to deal with.

"I guess I was going too fast."

"I clocked you at eighty-seven. I'd say that's too fast. Let's see your driver's license, please."

Tomei extracted his wallet. "This is my girlfriend's car. First time I've driven it. I've been a cop for more than twenty years. You'd think I'd know better."

The CHP officer crouched down to take a better look at Tomei. "You have some ID that shows you're a cop?"

"My ID card's in the wallet. My badge is right here," he said, tapping his coat pocket.

"Let's see the badge."

After the officer had examined Tomei's ID and badge, a skeptical grin spread across his face.

"Okay, Inspector, you can take off. But take it easy, huh." He drummed his fingers on the car's roof. "And tell your girlfriend to be careful. A red Corvette with out-of-state plates makes our mouths water."

Tomei merged back into traffic and kept the car below sixty-five for the rest of the trip. He turned west at Hecker Pass. The smell of garlic, for which the town of Gilroy was famous, hung in the crisp autumn air.

Gauzelike clouds curtained a melted-butter sun. He hoped it would warm up enough to put the convertible top down. Melissa would love that.

He drove past a golf course with fairways freckled with bright yellow Modesto ash leaves, then turned into a recently paved road that had no street sign, no identification of any kind. Only the very wealthy could afford that kind of exclusivity.

The road spiraled up a low-lying mountain for two miles. Tomei had gotten lost twice the first time he'd visited Vernon Gardner's mansion. He wondered if Joan had helped Gardner pick the location. She was becoming paranoid about her privacy, wanting no one, least of all her ex-husband, to be aware of her activities. When he called the house, the phone was always answered by Peter, the butler.

He rolled to a stop in front of the massive iron gate that protected the entrance, stretched his hand out the car window and pushed the button on the call box.

"Who is it?" a strong male voice asked.

"John Tomei."

"One second, please."

The iron gates retracted into the walls of the eight-foot-high stucco fence surrounding the property, and Tomei drove six tenths of a mile—he'd clocked it on his last visit—along a path barely wide enough for one car, bordered by towering pines and redwood trees.

He crested a hill and the house came into sight. Tomei had never seen anything quite like it. Ultra-modern, all concrete, glass, and steel in a seemingly haphazard arrangement. Sloping roofs of blue-tinted steel slashed and angled in all directions. More than half of the structure consisted of large, copper-framed windows sans curtains or blinds. It didn't afford much privacy, but then, not very many people got close enough to look.

A half-circle, cobblestone parkway bordered by graceful Italian cypresses fronted the house. He parked alongside one of Vernon Gardner's vintage autos, a magnificent polished green 1932 dual-cowl Packard Phaeton, with huge whitewalls and a matching white top.

If Messy had been driven around in that beauty, the Corvette wasn't going to impress her very much.

Peter, the butler, greeted him warmly. He was middle-aged, with a high forehead and thinning brown hair that had been carefully sprayed in place. He was dressed in what had become "Silicon chic" for domestic help in the Valley: a heavily starched light blue button-down shirt and Chinos, held up by a basket-weave leather belt.

"Good morning, Mr. Tomei. Melissa is upstairs. She'll be down momentarily. Mrs. Gardner asked you to join her in the study for a moment."

Tomei was never sure what to expect when he saw Joan. Always an attractive woman, she was aging more than gracefully. She was standing behind a glass-topped desk that was devoid of anything other than a chrome Danish modern telephone. Her hair had been lightened to a roan color. Her blemish-free skin was lightly tanned. Her nose appeared straighter than it had been, the slight bulge of a double chin had vanished, and her eyes had that narrow look that goes along with a face-lift. She was wearing oversize slacks and a man's-style one-button blazer.

"Good morning," she said formally.

"I hope it stays that way," Tomei responded.

Her expression didn't change. She made a throwaway gesture with one hand. "We have to talk. About Melissa. I hope you can behave like an adult."

"Haven't I always?" Tomei said.

Joan refused to take the bait. "Vernon and I are moving to New Mexico."

Tomei's voice hardened. "No way. I won't allow it."

"It has nothing to do with you," Joan continued in a flat, emotionless voice. "It has to do with our business. Silicon Valley has simply become too crowded. We cannot attract the kind of people we need. They simply cannot afford to buy, or rent a home here, so we have decided—"

"I don't care what you've decided. I'm not giving up my daughter just so you and your husband can make a few more million dollars a year. Messy is not leaving here. I have my visitation rights."

Joan nodded her head in grim agreement. "Yes. You do. That is what I wish to discuss with you. Have you spoken to your lawyer?"

"Not lately. But I read his letter. You're threatening to take me to court again."

"John, I promise that you can continue to see Melissa every other weekend." She held up a hand to stop his protest. "We can fly her here, or Vernon's jet will be at your disposal to come to New Mexico. Funds will be made available so that you and she can be comfortable when you're together. That's eminently fair, don't you agree?"

"No way, Joan," Tomei said between tight-together lips. "You're not going to buy me off."

"I really do wish you'd be less selfish, John, and think of the benefits for Melissa." She slowly brought her hands in front of her, interlacing her fingers. "Vernon is *very* fond of Melissa. He only wants the best for her, believe me. I'm sure he would have no objection to adopting her. That's why I want us to come to some agreement and—"

"Are you crazy?" Tomei shouted. "You think I'm going to sell out to you!" He took a quick step in Joan's direction and she backed away, her hands going up as if to protect herself from a slap.

Tomei pivoted on one foot and marched over to the window. He took in deep breaths, trying to get his temper in check.

"John, I want you to think about this. Really, really give it some thought. If we have to go to court, the expenses will break you. I don't think either one of us wants that. I've had some engineers check the cabin on the river. Their report is discouraging. The whole damn thing could collapse at any time. I think it's dangerous for Melissa to stay there. I'm sure a judge would come to the same conclusion. Be reasonable, John. If we can work this out, I would be happy to pay for restorations at the cabin."

Tomei continued to stare out the window. He could just make out the framed roof of a home being built on the adjoining property.

"You're going to have a new neighbor," he finally said.

"Yes, yes," Joan answered quickly, hoping that the change in subject was an admission that he was going to be reasonable.

Tomei turned to face her. "I wonder if he's a fireman."

Joan's eyes narrowed and her face reddened under her tan.

"Fuck *you*," she hissed.

The door opened and Melissa burst into the room, running to her father and leaping up into his outstretched arms.

They were both laughing as Tomei twirled her around in a circle, her legs outstretched, shoes a foot off the carpet. It amazed him how much she changed in just two short weeks. She was losing that little-girl look. Her hair was cut ruler-straight in a Dutch-boy style. The pink sweater she was wearing was obviously cashmere, and she had that damn expensive watch on her wrist.

Melissa had her mother's raisin-colored eyes, but the shape of her face, her features, were definitely inherited from Tomei, a fact that pleased him mightily.

"Please be careful," Joan cautioned.

"Don't worry, Mom," Melissa said, once she had her feet back on the floor.

Joan stared directly at Tomei. "You *will* be careful, John. I'm worried about that silly roller coaster. And you will please have Melissa back home by seven o'clock."

Tomei had plans to take his daughter to the boardwalk at Santa Cruz. Melissa ran over and gave her mother a big kiss, then tugged at her father's hand. "Come on, Pop. Let's get going."

Sherri Dawson's convertible did make a big impression on Melissa. "Is it yours? It's great!"

While Melissa was fiddling with her seat belt, Peter the butler approached Tomei.

"I'm sorry about this, sir." He coughed into his fist before handing Tomei a sealed envelope. "I believe the proper phrase I'm to use, is 'You're served.' "

Tomei used a thumbnail to open the envelope. Inside was a two-page legal document labeled "Motion to Consider Changes for Custody and Visitation Rights." He jammed the subpoena into his pocket and tried to put on a happy face as he slipped into the driver's seat.

Chapter Twenty-eight

The Russian River

Agent Don Jamison rested the butt of his pistol in the palm of his hand in the approved FBI fashion and carefully sighted in on his target.

"Bang, bang," he shouted at the two squawking blue jays.

"What the hell are you doing?" his partner Paul Flowers wanted to know.

"Those damn birds are driving me nuts," Jamison complained. "They never shut up."

"It was your idea to come up here to Tomei's place, Donny Boy. I told you it was going to be a wasted trip."

Jamison holstered his weapon and walked back into John Tomei's rustic cabin. Flowers had been worried that Tomei would have some kind of alarm or a booby trap set up for intruders, but Jamison had jimmied the front door with a pocketknife in a matter of seconds.

He took a final turn through the kitchen, two small bedrooms and living room. There was nothing. Nothing worth anything to him, or to a thief. Odds-and-ends furniture. An out-of-date kitchen. The computer was an old IBM clone that took forever to boot up. Jamison had worked on the computer for half an hour without finding anything of interest. No wonder Tomei hadn't bothered with an alarm. He went to the bedroom and punched the replay message button on Tomei's answering machine, smiling as he listened to the message once again.

"John. This is Dave Levy. Call me. Joan's attorney is playing hardball on the visitation rights for your daughter. He's talking about going back to court. I'm going to need a payment from you if you want me to continue to represent you in this, so get back to me right away."

Jamison rewound the message then pushed the erase button.

"Good luck, buddy. Your client is a loser."

He stood with his hands on his hips and scowled. The refrigerator's thermostat kicked on, setting off a clattering of vibrating bottles. "I still think Tomei's dirty, Paul. Him being at the restaurant at the same time as Dino Lanzoni and that old bookie Billy Rossi."

"We never saw Lanzoni talk to Tomei or Rossi."

"I still don't like it," Jamison protested.

"The lieutenant didn't like us losing Lanzoni like that either," Flowers said. Lanzoni never arrived in New York, and the FBI office there said there was no sign of him anywhere. He opened the refrigerator, pulled out a bottle of Bud Lite beer and twisted the top off. "I wonder where the hell Lanzoni is hiding. What do you hear from your source?"

"Nothing." Jamison followed his partner's actions, taking a beer from the refrigerator. "Nothing new on Lanzoni at all."

Flowers knew better than to ask Jamison about his precious "source." The big agent protected the informant's ID as if it was priceless property. Flowers had to admit that from time to time, the information Jamison picked up was damn good.

Jamison tilted the beer bottle back and chugged down half in a series of long gulps. He burped loudly, then said, "Did I tell you what I found in Tomei's police department personnel file? The dumb shit tried to kill himself when he found his old lady in the rack with the neighbor. He put his gun to his head, pulled the trigger, but it was empty. Too bad, huh?" He polished off the rest of the beer, and tossed the empty bottle toward the river.

"Come on, Paul. Let's get out of here. We'll go shake Rossi's tree again."

"Okay," Flowers said. "As long as that big dog of his isn't in the tree with him."

Las Vegas

Ava Avery stumbled when one of her high-heeled clogs caught in a crack on the pathway bordering the apartment's swimming pool.

She regained her balance and tightened the nylon robe tie around her waist. She was tired, hoping to go back to bed and sleep the day away. Her morning had been spent fulfilling her bimonthly commitment of having sex with Arnold, the apartment complex's manager.

Arnold was a cute, teddy bear of man in his mid-sixties. A widower for almost a year, he was easy to please, and it paid the rent. There were times when all he wanted to do was talk. But he hadn't been in the mood for much talk this morning.

Arnold liked straight, old-fashioned missionary-style sex. And he preferred blondes, so Ava always wore a long-haired blond wig. Arnold loved to fan the hair out on a pillow while he was getting it on.

She yawned widely as she entered her building. She'd left the door unlocked, as she usually did. There wasn't much chance of a burglary at that time of the day, and besides, there was no place to secure a key in the skimpy bra and thong she had on under the robe.

She was barely inside the apartment when the door was slammed shut behind her. She opened her mouth to scream. A knife blade slashed across her throat so quickly that all that came out was a low, death-rattling gurgle.

Santa Cruz

Santa Cruz is a small coastal community located seventy miles south of San Francisco, on the northern edge of Monterey Bay, nestled close to the majestic redwood forests and the San Lorenzo River. Like the rest of the state, it has been visited by urban sprawl, but there are still a number of finely restored Victorian homes, and the rambling, two thousand acres housing the University of Santa Cruz, which was built on an old cattle ranch.

The main attraction is the mile-long stretch of beach-side Boardwalk, a true, turn-of-the-century amusement park. Within walking distance are dozens of small hotels and boardinghouses that date back to the 1920s, many of which have been gentrified and converted into glitzy bed-and-breakfast establishments.

The temperature was in the mid-sixties. There was no wind, so the beach was crowded with dedicated sun worshipers, many who were brave enough to wade into the icy blue waters of Monterey Bay. Others played volleyball or enjoyed the barking and antics of a colony of mischievous sea lions.

Tomei and Melissa had lunch at a clam house that served its chowder in scooped out loafs of French bread. Then they toured the Boardwalk. The Casino dance hall, built in 1907, now hosts a variety of video games rather than slot machines and jazz bands.

Tomei loved watching his daughter have fun like this, but that didn't keep him from constantly scrutinizing the crowd. "Cops disease," his ex-wife had called it. Wherever they went, Tomei was always on the lookout for trouble. Amusement parks attracted a large number of human predators: flashers, child molesters, rapists. According to crime statistics, which he had no reason to discount, for every one thousand adult males attending an amusement park, rock concert, sports arena, or anywhere young children gathered, four percent would be there for the explicit purpose of committing some type of sexual offense.

Melissa tried her hand at the variety of rides—Tsunami, Orient Express, Whirlwind—and the carnival games such as shooting galleries, coin pitches, and wheels of fortune. She considered herself too old, and sophisticated, to hop onto one of the 1911 carousel's hand-carved horses.

Finally, as Tomei knew they would, they came to the white-timbered Giant Dipper, which had been operating since 1924. The designer, Arthur Loff, had envisioned the roller coaster as a "combination earthquake, balloon ascension and aero plane drop."

After dark it was an impressive site, studded with more than three thousand lightbulbs. During the light of day, it looked to Tomei like a tacked-together giant Tinkertoy that could be knocked down by a strong wind.

He nearly lost his clam chowder when the racketing coaster car crested, then swooped down at fifty-five miles an hour.

Melissa loved it, and begged him to come along for another ride. He bowed out as gracefully as possible, and watched her sitting alone, an exhilarated smile on her beautiful young face, waving madly at him, waiting for the ride to start again.

When she was out of sight, he examined the subpoena thoroughly, then used his cell phone to call Red Vanes.

Vanes answered with a gruff, "Who is it?"

"Tomei. Let's do it tonight."

"I thought you wanted to think this over for a few days," Vanes said.

"Tonight."

"Okay. I've got everything we need. Stop by my house around midnight."

Tomei broke the connection and called San Francisco General Hospital, asking the operator to connect him to Elaine Surel's room.

He was happy to hear Elaine answer the phone herself. "John. I was hoping you'd stop by today."

"I'm down in Santa Cruz with Messy. How are you doing?"

"Good. I'm going home tomorrow. What a blessing that will be. The cafeteria at the Hall of Justice serves better food than this place. Listen, Laura's here. Do you want to talk to her?"

There was a hint of a smile, or maybe even a smirk in Elaine's voice, and Tomei wondered just how much Laura had told her about last night.

"Sure. Put her on."

Laura sounded somber and professional. "How's everything going?"

"Great. What did you find out from the crime lab?"

"Just what we expected. Nothing. The van had dozens of prints, but there were no hits. I was out ringing doorbells all morning. Nobody in the neighborhood saw the driver of the truck."

"Laura. I'm staying down here tonight. With Messy. So I won't be back until tomorrow afternoon."

"I understand. I'll call you if anything turns up. And I—hold it. Elaine wants to say good-bye."

"John. I'm going to throw myself a welcome home party tomorrow night. I hope you can come." She paused for several seconds, then her voice dipped a notch and she said, "Laura will be there."

"You never were any good at being subtle, Gucci. I'll be there."

Chapter Twenty-nine

Sherri Dawson leaned forward and tapped the cab-driver on the shoulder. "Drive around the block again."

"Lady, I been around the block twice already."

"So? The meter's running isn't it? Drive slow."

The driver tugged at his ear. Goofy dame. Good-looking, though. A tall brunette wearing dark glasses, tight, well-packed jeans, a leather jacket, and a Stetson hat.

His eyes bounced from the road to the rearview mirror. She must be hoping to spot her husband, or boyfriend, leaving his lady friend's nest. She kept looking at the cars and the houses.

When they were back in front of Billy Rossi's house, Sherri said, "Pull in here. Park right by the front door."

The cabbie followed orders. He checked the meter. "That's thirty-six bucks, lady."

"Stay right here," Sherri said, opening the door.

"Hey, I got other calls waitin'."

Sherri took a fifty-dollar bill from her purse, tore off one end and passed it to the driver. "Keep the meter running. I'll only be a few minutes."

She approached the front door cautiously. She had called the house a half dozen times. There was no answer. Not even the answering machine.

Sherri had locked herself out of the house a couple

of times, so she'd hidden a spare key under the geranium pot on the front steps. It was still there. She rang the doorbell, her weight resting on her back foot, ready to run for the taxi if anyone other than Billy or Tomei answered the door.

She inserted the key into the lock, worried that Billy may have changed locks again. The key turned and she hurried inside, going directly to the burglar alarm pad, and punching in the code.

She heard a ferocious snarl. Fidel was racing toward her, teeth bared, a ninety-five-pound hairy rocket ready to launch right for her throat.

"Kita!" she shouted. *"Kita*, Fidel!"

Fidel skidded to a halt and sat on his haunches as Sherri approached him slowly, one hand extended in a peacemaking gesture, the other taking off her Stetson. She fanned herself with the hat, then said, "Don't you remember me, boy?"

Fidel sniffed her hand then squirmed and whined softly. She knelt down and petted him. "Good boy, good boy."

Sherri rose to her feet and climbed the stairs leading to Billy's bedroom two at a time.

The bed was a mess of tangled sheets and blankets. She went directly to the closet, hauled out two large suitcases and tossed them onto the bed. Her stash of money, more than thirty thousand dollars, was still in place under the larger bag's lining. She then began filling the cases with her clothes and jewelry. When she was finished, she sat on the bed for a moment, her hand sliding over the sheets, plucking at the mattress buttons. There was a whiff of perfume. Not her fragrance. Had Billy found a replacement for her already?

She carried the two cases out to the hall, then made a quick decision, walking into Rossi's trophy room. The glass doors to the gun case were unlocked. She studied the weapons, then reached in and took a pearl-handled, double-barreled derringer pistol. She broke the breach, saw that it was loaded and slipped it into her purse, alongside the bone-handled knife with the marlin spike.

The cabdriver was watching the meter tick away. When he spotted the brunette lugging the suitcases, he bounced out of the cab and grabbed one of the cases and placed it in the trunk. He'd been right. A husband or boyfriend, and she came back to get her goodies.

Sherri gave Fidel a farewell pat, then shut the door. She retreated into the shelter of the front porch when she saw a sedan pull into the driveway. She jammed her hand into her purse, searching for the derringer. She removed her hand and hugged the purse tightly to her body when two men exited the car. She'd seen more than enough cops in her lifetime, and these two were classics: a Mutt and Jeff team, the big one with an old college-type haircut, the small one had bristly eyebrows and a nose that was too small for his face.

They dressed like cops do when they want you to know they're cops: JCPenney sport coats, shiny-fabric slacks, ties that didn't match their outfits, the shirt collar unbuttoned. And the shoes. Where the hell did they buy those shoes? Scuffed, thick-soled lace-ups that looked like they'd last for twenty years.

The big one rolled his shoulders so that his jacket opened up wide enough to give her a view of his holster.

"Is Billy Rossi home?" the small one asked her.

"Who wants to know?"

"FBI, ma'am," Jamison said. "You a friend of his?"

"He's not home. I don't know where he is."

Jamison strode directly toward her. "You didn't tell me your name, miss."

Sherri grimaced. "Miss." That was a cute touch. From ma'am to miss just like that. "Let's see some ID, fellas."

She examined their credentials, then said, "Don't get too close to the door. The dog in there will kill you if he gets a chance. I told you Billy's not here."

Paul Flowers's face turned sorrowful, as if he'd just

heard terrible news. "That's too bad. We wanted to talk to Billy."

"Yeah. He's a good guy to talk to. Come back later."

Jamison tapped her suitcase with the tip of his shoe. "Where are you going?"

"Somewhere else." She hoisted the case in both hands and started toward the taxi.

"Let me help you with that," Jamison said, flashing his best smile.

"I can handle it."

"I bet you can, honey. What's your name?"

"Open the goddamn door," Sherri yelled at the cabbie.

Jamison held up his arm to block the driver. "I asked you your name, lady."

"I heard you." Sherri dumped the suitcase at the cabdriver's feet. "Can you think of any reason why I should give it to you?"

"We're federal agents," Flowers responded in an authoritative tone.

She pushed past Jamison and opened the cab door. "Big deal. It's still a free country, isn't it?"

Jamison kicked the door shut. "You want to get tough with us, honey? We can get tough with you, too."

"Honey? You called me 'honey'!" She gestured toward the cabdriver who was standing as if he was a soldier at attention, his mouth gaping open. "In front of a witness. I consider that term a form of sexual harassment. Get out of my way."

The two FBI agents looked at each other. Flowers raised his shoulders a few inches and shrugged.

Jamison moved back. "One more question, miss. Do you know a man named John Tomei?"

"The name is unfamiliar to me," Sherri said, picking up the suitcase and climbing into the cab. "Let's go," she shouted at the driver. "I'm in a hurry."

The cabbie waited for Jamison's permission to leave.

"Get going. I've got your cab number. Just make sure you remember where you took her."

Jamison and Flowers watched the taxi until it was out of sight.

"That was one tough cookie," Jamison said.

"Yeah, she's been around the horn a couple of times. Did you get that answer when you asked her if she knew Tomei? She didn't say yes, or no, just 'The name is unfamiliar to me.' A nice way to cover her ass."

"And she has a nice ass. She looked a little familiar to me."

"Her ass, or the rest of her, Donny Boy?"

"She looked just like Rossi's girlfriend. The blonde who was with him at Sully's. The dark hair, the make-up's all different, but I have a hunch it's the same lady. Let's go back to the office and check the film we took at Sully's and see if we can put a name to her."

The cabdriver turned around to look at Sherri. "Where to? Back to the airport?"

"Yes." She'd change cabs there, and come back to town and find a small hotel. Somewhere near Chinatown.

Chapter Thirty

Kan Chin was eating breakfast at his desk when Willy Hon entered the room.

"Good news," Hon said. "Sherri Dawson is dead. She returned to her apartment in Las Vegas. One of Shek Lee's men killed her this morning."

Chin gently wiped his lips with a snow-white napkin. Shek Lee was the head of the Triad in Las Vegas. His men were usually very reliable. "It was rather stupid of her to return to Las Vegas, wasn't it, Willy?"

Hon coughed out a laugh. "She was a stupid slut, nothing more."

"This means that Captain Liu lied to us. You have taken care of him?"

"He has been disposed of," Hon confirmed.

Chin held up his empty teacup and Hon picked up the pot and refilled it. "Texas Joe is waiting outside, sir."

Chin sipped reflectively at his tea. As valuable an informer as he was, Chin dreaded listening to the man. His accent when speaking English was irritating, but when he spoke Chinese, it was unbearable.

"Bring him. And tell him to speak English, Willy."

Texas Joe shuffled into the room, holding his hat in one hand. He was well aware of Kan Chin's feelings toward him, so he kept his speech to a minimum."

"Howdy, sir."

"I want you to call the FBI agent, Jamison, again.

Tell him that Dino Lanzoni is back in San Francisco." Chin turned to Hon. "Do we know where he is now?"

"Living on a boat in the—"

"Enough," Chin said angrily. He settled his teacup gently onto its saucer. "Joe. Tell Jamison that you have heard rumors that Lanzoni has the blessing of his New York family to enter the drug trade. That they are supplying him with heroin, and that Lanzoni is also going to move into the sports betting trade in a large way. Tell him that you will know by tomorrow exactly where Lanzoni is, understood?"

"Yes, sir," Cowboy Joe drawled. "Anything else, sir?"

"Call me tomorrow morning and I will give you further instructions. You may leave us."

Texas Joe stopped at the door, gave Chin a polite head bow, then said, "See ya now, hear?"

Willy Hon made sure the door was firmly closed before turning to face Chin.

"You almost gave away too much," Chin chided. "I don't want that fool knowing where Lanzoni is yet. Where is he?"

"Living on a boat, a yacht, the *Diavolo Mare*, moored at the South Beach Marina, near the new ballpark."

"Who owns the boat?" Chin asked impatiently.

"It belongs to Anthony Tripoli. He is—"

"Yes, yes. I know who Tripoli is. The name. *Diavolo Mare*. Sea Devil. An apt description."

Chin tasted his tea. It was now much too cool for his liking. He approved of Lanzoni's living arrangements. A boat could move quickly, to another marina, or simply anchor in the bay, or sail out the gate.

He stared directly into Willy Hon's eyes, long enough to make Hon uncomfortable. "Acceptable, Willy. Very acceptable."

Hon beamed his thanks. Acceptable was as high a praise as Chin granted to anyone.

*   *   *

They were in a cave, with barely enough light to see. Melissa was running ahead of him. Every time Tomei began to catch up with her, he'd slip and fall, landing in the rank, mushy earth. He called out to his daughter, but she just kept running, swerving left or right as the cave branched out in different directions. He scrambled to his feet and chased after her again, narrowing the gap, but something slowed him down. A black mass of small, huddled bodies squirmed by him, ran over his shoes, nipped at his pant legs. Rats! They were chasing Messy, squealing in a frenzy as they raced by him. He slipped again, landing in their midst. They swarmed over him. He swung wildly and screamed Messy's name.

"Hey. Are you okay?"

Tomei opened his eyes and saw the foreboding figure of Red Vanes looming over him.

"Yeah, sure," he said, lurching up and swinging his feet to the ground. He'd fallen asleep on Vanes's couch.

"You were shouting out somebody's name."

Tomei knuckled his eyes and looked at Vanes again. He was dressed in shabby clothes. His shirt collar was undone and there was a lump the size of a walnut on the right side of his neck. "I was having a crazy dream, Red."

Vanes noticed Tomei's stare. He pulled a bandanna from his pocket and quickly tied it around his neck.

"That's a big lump, Red. Something serious?"

"Yeah. You could say that. A tumor, the kind a doctor could usually cut out with his Boy Scout knife. But this one is wrapped around my carotid artery." Vanes strode across the room and used a mirror to adjust the bandanna. "Radiation hasn't worked. If they try surgery, there's a good chance I won't get off the operating table alive. If I don't have the operation, there's a good chance I just won't wake up one morning." He gestured toward the desk. "Better get dressed. It's show time."

Tomei placed both hands on his thighs and pushed

himself to his feet. Vanes was putting on the black wig, adjusting it just so, staring at his image in the mirror, like an actor getting ready to go on stage.

Next to Tomei's jacket was an assortment of guns—four revolvers of varying barrel lengths, and a half dozen blue-steel semiautomatics.

Lying on the floor were a shovel and pick, as well as three canvas backpacks of the type children used to lug their books to school.

"Grab a gun," Vanes called over his shoulder.

"No thanks. The shovel and pick will be enough for me."

Vanes grabbed one of the pistols, shoved it in his waistband and said, "Okay. Let's go."

The stench in the underground tunnel seemed worse to Tomei this time. He followed at Vanes's heels, trying to estimate just how far they had walked, wondering if he could find his way back to the garage if something happened to Vanes.

His skin chilled when he heard the whirring, rustling sounds of the roaming rats. He stood very still as they streamed by, his flashlight catching the glint of hundreds of beady eyes. Just as suddenly as they'd appeared, they were gone, leaving only the echo of their squealing din.

"They were in a hurry tonight," Vanes joked. "There must be a new restaurant opening up."

They finally arrived at the wall leading to Kan Chin's vault. Vanes uncovered the lantern, switched it on, then connected the micro video and earphone cables to the power source and checked Kan Chin's vault.

"No one's there yet. It shouldn't be long."

Tomei ran his gloves over the slimy bricks.

"The wall is four bricks deep," Vanes said. "All we have to do is open up a hole big enough for you to climb in."

"You're not joining me?"

"It's a young man's game, Tomb. If I could have

pulled this off myself, I would have." He took his brandy flask from his coat pocket and waved it at Tomei. "We might as well get comfortable."

Vanes's idea of getting comfortable was squatting down on the filthy ground and swigging from the flask.

Tomei hunched his shoulders and kept waving his flashlight in the darkness, remembering his dream, and wondering when the rats would make another appearance.

They heard the sound of the vault's door opening.

Vanes tilted the micro video screen so they both could watch. One man, a young Chinese, came into the vault, pushing a shopping cart loaded with orange chip trays. He took his time stacking the chips on the shelves. When he was finished, he ducked his head out the vault doors, then hurried over to the shelves and jammed a handful of blue chips into his coat pocket.

"Kan Chin isn't going to like that," Vanes whispered.

The man exited, slamming the vault door shut behind him.

"I don't like it either," Vanes said, gently laying the micro video on the ground near the lantern. "Just the one guy. Willy Hon should have been with him. Maybe we should call this off and try again tomorrow."

Tomei had no desire to travel through the rat-infested tunnels again. "Have you ever seen this before? One man, and not Hon?"

"Yeah. Once or twice. But I still don't like it. What if Hon comes back to count the take?"

Tomei hoisted the pick over his shoulder. "We're going in now, Red. Right now."

The first two layers of bricks peeled away easily. Tomei worked carefully after that, one brick at a time, until he had a ragged opening at the bottom corner of the wall large enough for him to crawl through.

He edged his way into the opening, pushing the shovel ahead of him. He didn't want to be trapped in there if the entire brick wall came tumbling down. He used his elbows like ski poles to propel himself forward.

The vault floor was cold, smooth concrete.

When Tomei was through the wall, he stood up and waved the flashlight around the room. He spotted a light switch, but didn't want to risk using it for fear it was hooked up to a burglar alarm.

"Shove the backpacks through."

Red Vanes pushed the backpacks into the vault and Tomei began emptying the trays of yellow-colored chips into them. When all three were filled, he squatted down and pushed two of them to Vanes's waiting hands.

There were still dozens of trays of the yellow chips and Tomei decided to fill his pockets before leaving. He was reaching for the chips when the overheard light went on and the steel vault door began to wheel open.

Chapter Thirty-one

John Tomei eyed the opening in the bricks. There was no time to crawl back into the tunnel. He stooped down and grabbed the shovel.

The steel door clicked and clanked, then swung open smoothly. Tomei hugged the wall, the shovel cocked over one shoulder.

Willy Hon had his eyes on the clipboard, preparing to tally the night's gambling proceeds. The dollar amount of the chips varied from day to day, depending on the luck of the customers at Kan Chin's thirteen gambling dens.

Many of the gamblers kept the chips in lieu of turning them in for cash. There was a certain amount of panache, especially for the younger crowd, in paying off your bills with the chips.

It made extra work for Hon, exchanging cash for the chips, when he made his rounds to the Chinatown merchants, collecting their monthly "immunity fees."

The payments guaranteed the merchant immunity from the wrath of Kan Chin, and alerted Hon to any outsiders who may have had the nerve—or stupidity—to poach on Chin's territory.

He stopped abruptly when he saw the empty shelves and chip holders scattered about the floor. He was reaching for his gun when Tomei crashed the shovel over his head.

Hon buckled at the knees and Tomei gave him another whack as he fell to the floor. Tomei then spun around and cautiously peeked out into the hallway to see if Willy Hon had been alone.

Two young toughs were sprinting down the hallway. They shouted loud, undecipherable curses when they spotted Tomei.

He rolled the heavy steel door, leaning against it as it thunked shut. Searching frantically for a lock, and seeing none, he darted to the opening in the bricks, kicked the third backpack into the hole, than scrambled after it. The rough edges scraped against his back as he frantically squirmed through the hole.

Vanes wasn't there! The lantern was on. He could hear voices yelling inside the vault. Then there was a thunderous gunshot, followed by three more shots. The dirt near the backpack absorbed the bullets with muffled, sucking sounds.

Tomei picked up the lantern, hoisted the backpack over his shoulder, and took off, trying to remember the exact path that had led him from Vanes's hideaway garage to Kan Chin's vault.

Where the hell was Vanes?

There was more shouting. He sloshed through a muddy area and over to a low-lying cement bulkhead that seemed familiar. He set the lantern down and swung his legs over the bulkhead. There was another round of gunfire. The lantern smashed to pieces. He was in total darkness.

Tomei crouched down, leaning against the bulkhead, facing back toward the direction of the gunfire. He could hear men shouting in Chinese. How many were there? Did they know about the tunnel? No. Vanes said he was the only one who knew about this tunnel. Why hadn't Vanes waited for him?

He never figured Vanes for a quitter, someone to run away at the first sign of trouble.

One of the men yelled and fired a shot. Tomei saw a brief outline of him in the gun flash.

One thing seemed certain. They had no flashlights. Tomei patted his jacket pockets. His flashlight was there, but he didn't dare switch it on. He edged away from the bulkhead, silently cursing Vanes, stumbling through the dark as if he was blindfolded. His knees banged into something sharp and he fell to the ground in a thud.

His hands landed in some wet muck, and as he tried to regain his footing he heard the low chattering sound of the approaching rats. Tomei tried to stay calm, telling himself that the miserable creatures were probably as terrified of the noise from the gunshots as he was of them.

He lunged out blindly, his fingers making contact with a wall. He hugged the wall, burying his face into the damp cement. He could feel the rats race by him. They must have been scrambling over themselves because they were above the tops of his boots. One scuttled up the wall and ran right across Tomei's chest. He let out a loud, wailing scream of terror, which quickly brought a flurry of gunshots.

Tomei fought the urge to pull out the flashlight, to see just where the hell he was, and how many goddamn rats there were.

There was more shouting, then outright panic, with screams as loud and frightened as his had been. The rats must have reached the gunmen.

Tomei pulled the flashlight from his jacket pocket and was about to switch it on when something touched his shoulder.

"What happened?" Red Vanes asked in a calm, reasonable voice.

"Where the hell did you go?" Tomei rasped. "Willy Hon came into the vault. He has at least two guys with him now. They're doing the shooting."

Vanes grasped one of Tomei's hands. "I took the two sacks of chips back to the garage. Come on, hold on to me and let's get the hell out of here."

They moved slowly, cautiously for several minutes without benefit of a flashlight. There were more gunshots. They sounded as if they came from a long distance away.

*   *   *

Kan Chin's gambling chips were stacked in neat rows on Red Vanes's kitchen table.

Vanes smacked his lips then took a swig of espresso. "That's a lot of money, my friend."

Tomei nodded agreement and ran a hand through his still wet hair. His first order of business after they'd gotten back from the tunnel was to take a long, hot shower. He could still taste the wet cement and his nostrils were filled with the stench of the tunnel muck.

Vanes picked up a stack of ten chips, worth five thousand dollars. "Do you think Willy Hon saw you?"

"It's hard to say. I hit him with the shovel as soon as he was in the vault. I doubt if the two guys in the hallway were close enough to identify me."

"Those last shots we heard. I would bet a good portion of those chips that was Willy Hon, finishing off his comrades. Kan Chin wouldn't want word of what happened tonight to leak out." Vanes stuck his nose over the espresso and inhaled deeply, absorbing the rich Arabic blend. "Did you know that there are actually places in this vast and bountiful land of ours where you can't buy Starbucks?"

"What's the total amount, Red?"

"One thousand and forty-two chips which adds up to six hundred twenty-one thousand dollars."

"And you think Chin will give us that amount of cash for them?"

"He will give *you* the cash," Vanes said sharply. "Remember our deal. I showed you how to steal the chips. It's your job to turn them into cash. I wish I could be there when you meet with Chin."

"Consider yourself invited," Tomei said, pouring himself a cup of the espresso.

"Thanks, but no thanks. Chin will suspect that I'm involved, but I'd just as soon not wave a red flag at that dangerous old bull. When are you going to confront him?"

Tomei looked out Vanes's kitchen window. Sun twinkled through the bare, dew-draped branches of a plum tree. The clouds were steel gray on top, blood-red underneath thanks to the rising sun. What was the old saying? Red skies at morning, sailor take warning. Something like that. He knew he was sailing into dangerous water. Kan Chin's water.

"When are you going to confront him?" Vanes repeated.

"I'll let him think about it all day. Then I'll go to dinner." He stared at his reflection in Vanes's kitchen window, not liking what he saw. "At Kan Chin's favorite restaurant."

Chapter Thirty-two

Willy Hon was in considerable pain. His head was throbbing. His ear was a bloody, bloated mess underneath the gauze bandages. His knees and hands were scraped from crawling through the hole in the wall and banging around in the stinking underground tunnels.

But the physical pain was nothing compared to the mental torture he was being put through. He had been standing, flat-footed, in front of Kan Chin's desk for nearly half an hour, answering Chin's questions, waiting nervously for the next one while Chin polished his glasses with the hem of his cashmere sweater.

"Once again, from the beginning," Chin commanded.

"When I opened the vault door, I—"

"Again. Why were you alone?"

Hon swallowed hard, then said, "I had been gambling. I was winning. I sent Jimmy Kung to the vault—"

"By himself, with the chips."

"Yes. By himself. I arrived no more than a few minutes later, and then—"

"Then you were attacked. By a man you cannot describe. One man. If you had Kung with you, if you had not been alone, perhaps the two of you could have handled the man with the shovel."

"Yes, sir," Hon humbly agreed. "It was an unpardonable error on my part." He hesitated momentarily before expressing his only viable excuse. Either Kan Chin bought it, or Hon knew he was a dead man. "If I had delivered the chips with Jimmy Kung, then I believe the man would have waited until we left the vault before he entered. We would not have known of the theft until this afternoon when we went to the vault again."

Chin held his glasses up to the light, then put them on, staring at Hon over the rims. "So you are telling me that your blunder was a blessing. That it is my good fortune that you disobeyed me, is that it, Willy?"

"No, sir. I just think—"

"Don't think! Just do as I tell you. Always." Chin picked up the miniature video camera that Hon had found just outside the vault's wall. He turned it over in his hand. Hon was right, of course. Whoever was watching through the camera lens could have waited until Hon was through with his nightly accounting duties before entering the vault.

The question that troubled Chin was how long the vault had been under surveillance. The robbery was obviously well planned, well thought out. And how many more cameras were there hidden in the tunnel? How many more of his operations were being monitored this way? And by whom? The FBI? The DEA?

No. Those agencies would never be so bold, or so crude, to actually break into the vault. They would wait, observe for days, months, years if need be. And they certainly wouldn't allow one of their agents to be trapped in a vault with nothing but a shovel.

A rival gang? One he knew nothing about? No. If anyone were to spend the chips in large numbers, they would be giving themselves away.

He looked up at the sad figure of Willy Hon. "You must have gotten some kind of an impression of the man."

"He was a big man. A *hun dan*. I did not see his face."

"Red Vanes?"

Hon's hand went to his bandaged ear. "No. I do

not think so. He wasn't as tall as Vanes, and he moved fast, like a younger man."

Kan Chin removed his glasses, leaned back in his chair and began polishing the lenses again. "Jimmy Kung and Gim. You took care of them."

It wasn't a question. A statement, and Hon replied, "Yes. They are buried in the tunnel. No one else knows what took place."

"Go back to the tunnel, Willy." Chin picked up the mini camera. "Make sure there are no more of these."

"Yes, sir," Hon answered gratefully. He wanted to be far away from Kan Chin. Anywhere. Even that filthy tunnel. "What of the man who hit me? I can have—"

"Do not worry about him," Chin counseled. "He will contact me. And very soon, if I'm not mistaken."

Teresa, the Homicide detail secretary, tapped Laura Aguera lightly on the shoulder.

"There's a cop from Las Vegas on line three. Lieutenant Bostic. He's not a happy camper, Laura. He asked for John Tomei, and when I told him John had retired, he went ballistic. Then he wanted Elaine. You better talk to him."

Laura picked up the phone, and said her name.

"Where's Surel?" Lieutenant Bostic demanded. "Or Gucci, or whatever the hell she calls herself."

"Calm down, Lieutenant. I'm Elaine Surel's partner. She was badly injured. She's in the hospital. How can I help you?"

"You can help me by telling me why Surel lied to me. She sent this Tomei guy up here. She told me he was a cop. She sure as hell didn't say he was a *retired* cop."

"Mr. Tomei was Elaine's partner. Perhaps you didn't understand when she—"

"I'll tell you what I don't understand, lady. I don't understand why Surel and Tomei both lied to me. And I don't know why Tomei was so hot and bothered over a hooker by the name of Sherrilyn Dawson. And

I don't understand why there's a dead woman, a hooker by the name of Ava Avery wearing a blond wig, and damn little else, on the floor of Sherrilyn Dawson's apartment. Where's Tomei?"

"I don't know, Lieutenant, but I promise you—"

"And another thing," Bostic fumed. "The person who found Avery damn near croaked. He opened the door, saw the body, and had a stroke. William Vincent Rossi. DMV shows him with a San Francisco address and he's been busted several times for bookmaking. He's in St. Rose's hospital now. I haven't been able to talk to him. I have a gut feeling that we're going to find Tomei's fingerprints all over the crime scene. Now, what did you say your name was?"

"Aguera. Inspector Laura Aguera."

"Well, Inspector. You better get me some answers or I'm coming to Frisco and, excuse the expression, kick ass. If yours happens to get in the way, too damn bad. Understand me?"

"You do have a way of expressing yourself in a clear and concise manner, Lieutenant," Laura answered calmly. "However, if you get anywhere in the vicinity of my ass, I'll kick your balls so hard you'll be wearing them for earrings. And no one calls it *Frisco* anymore," she said between clenched teeth, then severed the connection before Bostic had the chance to respond.

She immediately dialed John Tomei's cell phone, cursing under her breath when there was no answer. Where was he? And why didn't he ever answer his damn phone?

Dino Lanzoni was impressed with Kan Chin's apartment. He didn't much go for Oriental art and furniture, but it was obvious to him that everything Chin had on display was top-of-the-line stuff.

The Chinese doll-face in the slim persimmon-colored floor-length dress who brought in a tray of glasses and a bottle of brandy was quality stuff, too. She was a little young for his tastes, but definitely a winner. He liked the way she bowed and kept her eyes downcast when she entered the room. She hadn't glanced his way once.

"I hope you approve of the brandy, Mr. Lanzoni. It's a California product. Since you are going to be spending some time here, I thought it would be appropriate."

Chin poured the brandy into one of the glasses and passed it to Lanzoni before dribbling a small amount into his.

"To business," Lanzoni toasted, then took a hit of the brandy, holding it in his mouth, swishing it around his gums before swallowing.

Chin took a birdlike sip of his drink, then settled the glass onto the jade table separating the two men. On the table, lying between the two priceless porcelain Chinese devil dogs, was an inexpensive blue nylon traveling case.

Chin nudged the case in Lanzoni's direction. "Our first delivery. Please examine the contents."

Lanzoni grasped the case and pulled it toward him. Chin's heartbeat raced as the case nearly brushed against one of the thirteen-hundred-year-old Sung dynasty devil dogs.

Lanzoni settled the case in his lap, unzipped the top and used a penknife to prick one of the clear plastic bags. He gently pumped a small portion of the white powder on his index finger, then rubbed it on his tongue. He would have a chemist perform a much more accurate test before he turned any money over to Chin.

"Very nice," he said, smacking his lips.

"The very best China White, I assure you. However, I would suggest that you have your own experts confirm this."

Lanzoni nodded his agreement, then picked up a pack of credit cards. "Very nice," he repeated, then checked out the two American passports and a bundle of traveler's check packets: American Express, Citibank, Credit Suisse, Banque Nationale De Paris, Wells Fargo.

"These are beautiful, Mr. Chin. Now, let's talk price."

"The next time we meet we will have a very detailed discussion about price and delivery, but for now, let us act like friends. The items in the case are yours. A gift of friendship."

Lanzoni took another pull at the brandy, then wiped his lips on the back of his hand. A gift. Bullshit. But if Kan Chin wanted to play games, so be it. "I appreciate that. But I feel that I should give you something in return. Do you have any suggestions?"

"It is not necessary, Mr. Lanzoni, however, you did make mention of performing a service for me. 'Breaking the sixth,' correct?"

Lanzoni eyed the case. The heroin and phony passports, credit cards, and traveler's checks had to be worth a couple of hundred thou. Who the hell did he want hit? The pope? The president?

"Give me a name and the guy's dog meat."

" 'Dog meat.' You do have a way with words, Mr. Lanzoni."

The girl in the persimmon dress entered the room, approached Kan Chin, and bent down, placing her lips next to his ear. "Texas Joe is on the phone. He says that a man wishes to meet with you and that it has to do with gambling chips," she whispered.

Chin waved her away, then said, "I must leave now. A meeting I cannot avoid. I will contact you shortly and provide you with information on the man I wish to have eliminated."

"Yeah, sure," Lanzoni said, zipping the blue traveling bag shut and rising to his feet. He held out a hand to Chin. "I sure like the way you do business."

Chapter Thirty-three

FBI agents Don Jamison and Paul Flowers were seated at their desks, examining the photographs Flowers had taken of Dino Lanzoni, John Tomei, Billy Rossi, and Rossi's blond companion at Sully's Bar & Grill.

"I'm telling you it's the same broad," Jamison said. "The blonde and the brunette in the cowboy hat at Rossi's house."

"I wouldn't argue with you, but what good does it do us? She had her bags packed. She's out of here. I don't want to waste time staking out Rossi's place. We still don't have a positive connection between Rossi and Lanzoni."

"I know, I know," Jamison conceded. "I'd like to put some heat on her. The way she brushed us off. You'd think—" Jamison cut himself off when he heard the soft purring of the telephone locked in his desk drawer.

While Jamison leaned back in his chair and fumbled through his pockets for his key ring, Flowers got up and walked over to the window. Their office was on the twenty-second floor of the federal building and afforded a magnificent southerly view. Crisp stratus clouds towed their shadows across the city and over to the East Bay hills.

The phone call had to be from Jamison's source. Flowers watched a slate-gray peregrine falcon glide past the window and zero in on a pigeon that was huddled on a ledge of the building across the street.

The pigeon made a fatal mistake, fluttering off into the sky when the falcon swooped by. On his next pass the falcon slashed out with his claws. There was a momentary puff of feathers, then the falcon power-dived down toward the street, pulling up in a long, graceful arc, carrying his quarry back to his nest.

Flowers felt no sympathy for the pigeon. The dumb bird got what it deserved. Stool pigeons were an entirely different matter. They had to be carefully nurtured, fed, comforted. He wondered where Jamison was getting the money to keep his source happy. The department had cut its "special contingency fees" to the bone. Jamison was probably using the time-honored system of policemen around the world. Paying for information with more information—running criminal checks, DMV records, or trying to talk judges into handing out lenient sentences for the source's friends.

Flowers turned and watched Jamison. He had his feet up on the desk and a self-satisfied look on his face as he murmured softly into the telephone.

"Lanzoni's back in the city," Jamison crowed, when he terminated the call. "Dino got the go-ahead from the boys in New York to open shop out here. Drugs of course, and guess what else? Sports bets. That's why he was at Sully's with Billy Rossi. And this means that John Tomei's hooked up with both of them."

"Where's Lanzoni now?" Flowers wanted to know.

"My source won't know until tomorrow. I get the feeling that Rossi took a duck. Maybe Lanzoni scared him out of town. And maybe Tomei helped him. I'd like to know where the bastard is right now."

The maître d' at the Green Dragon approached John Tomei with a pained expression. "I'm sorry, sir. But we are full." He held his hands wide apart. "A big party tonight."

"Get me a table. I have business with Kan Chin.

Find Texas Joe and tell him I want to see him right away."

The maître d's face smoothed out and he flashed a welcoming smile. "Right this way, please."

The dining room had several empty tables and Tomei rightly assumed that the reason he was not wanted was that restaurants don't like to cater to lone diners.

He ordered tea and by the time he had finished his first cup, Texas Joe sauntered into the restaurant and over to his table.

"Howdy. Hey. You're Inspector Vanes's friend. How ya all doin'?"

"Tell Kan Chin I want to meet with him. Right now."

Texas Joe took off his hat and fiddled with the crown. "Well now, pardner, I don't know if—"

"Tell him it's about some gambling chips. He'll understand."

"You *sure* you want me to call Mr. Chin. 'Cause, believe me, he can get pissed off mighty damn fast, and if you—"

"Do it. Or Chin will be mighty damn pissed off at you."

"Okay. You got a name, pardner? Who do I tell him wants this here meetin'."

"John. Just tell him John wants to see him."

Texas Joe rolled his fingers around the brim of his hat. "Okay, but I sure hope you know what you're doin', Johnny."

Within minutes the maître d' came to Tomei's table and placed his hands on the back of Tomei's chair.

"Mr. Chin would like you to wait for him at his table, sir. Please come this way."

Tomei was led to the alcove in the rear of the dining room. The spacious table was set with stiff white napkins, sparkling crystal, and sterling-silver utensils.

Two waiters hustled in, one carrying a silver ice bucket, the other pushing a cart loaded with liquor bottles, hors d'oeuvres, and a platter of fortune cookies.

The maître d' arrived and began supervising, ordering the waiters to strip the table to accommodate only two place settings. He then took a bottle of champagne from the ice bucket. He expertly unwired the cork and eased it out. "Iron Horse, 1990 Blanc de Blanc," he said in a hushed voice as he filled a glass. "Mr. Chin's favorite."

Texas Joe poked his head into the alcove. He seemed nervous, moving from one foot to the other. "Mr. Chin told me to tell you he'll be here shortly."

Tomei thanked him and watched as Joe walked off and the diners at the table directly in front of the alcove were ushered from their seats.

A heavyset man in a business suit was reluctant to leave. He got into a heated discussion with the maître d'. He glowered at Tomei as he wiped his face with his napkin and dropped it on the table.

Three young Chinese men settled quickly into the vacant seats, each taking a position so that they had an unrestricted view of Tomei.

Red Vanes had predicted the arrival of Chin's troops. "Be ready for him, Tomb. Texas Joe or one of his stooges will take a Polaroid of you. Chin will fax it to his people all over town, including those in the police department. He won't come until he knows who you are. And before he turns over any money, he'll learn everything there is to know about you."

Tomei tried to appear relaxed as he waited. He resisted the urge to trifle with the napkins and settled for cracking open the fortune cookies.

He kept a close check on the time. It took thirty-four minutes. The three Chinese toughs sitting at the table nearby simultaneously sprang to their feet.

There was an almost audible hush. The sound of diners chatting, of knives and forks scraping plates, of glasses clinking against bottles disappeared, replaced by a low, excited hum, as if a movie star or sports hero had entered the room.

A small, stoop-shouldered old man with sparse hair stopped to talk to the three men now standing at the nearby table. He waved a hand and they moved away in perfect unison, as if they were dancers on a Broadway stage.

Standing next to the old man, glaring directly at Tomei, was Willy Hon, one ear sporting a blood-stained bandage.

The old man entered the alcove with a smile. "Ah. Mr. Tomei. So nice to meet you. I am Kan Chin."

Tomei kept his seat and nodded a silent greeting.

Chin patted Hon lightly on the shoulder. "This is my associate, Willy Hon. I think you met him, or should I say, came in contact with him very early this morning."

Tomei kept his face passive while Hon continued to glare at him.

The maître d' had been hovering outside the alcove. He hurried in and whisked out a chair for Chin.

When he was seated, Chin said something in Chinese and the maître d' bowed his way out of the room.

Kan Chin's eyes seemed to be swimming behind his thick glasses. "Would you be good enough to stand up for just a moment, Mr. Tomei. I apologize for the inconvenience, but in today's world a businessman can never be too cautious."

Tomei stood and Willy Hon approached him. Tomei could see that blood had seeped through Hon's bandage, and the dressing was smeared with dirt. From the tunnel, Tomei guessed. Hon had been poking around down there. Would he ever be able to find Red Vanes's garage? Maybe, but without a lucky break, it could take weeks, or months. Vanes had predicted that Hon would check him for a wire or weapons, so he came in clean.

Hon used his hands roughly, fingering Tomei's clothes from neck to ankles, then turned to Kan Chin, and made a negative gesture by shaking his head.

"Please. Return to your seat," Chin said. "How may I be of service to you?"

Willy Hon positioned himself between the table and the alcove exit. He stood motionlessly, arms crossed, his eyes riveted on Tomei.

"I have some items that belong to you. I want to sell them back," Tomei said casually.

"You are talking about the gambling chips?"

Tomei opened the palm of his left hand, revealing a yellow chip. "Yes." He passed his right hand over his left, rubbed his two hands together and when he opened them the chip was gone.

"Very good, Mr. Tomei. You are a magician?"

"A magician can make things disappear, then reappear." Tomei lifted the napkin in front of Chin's salad plate, exposing one of the chips.

Chin clapped his hands in appreciation. "That is wonderful, truly wonderful." His voice turned sharp. "What is your proposition?"

"I want to return the chips to you, for six hundred and twenty-one thousand dollars."

Chin's eyebrows rode up above the rim of his glasses. "That is an unusual sum."

"That's the amount that I took from your vault. Three hundred and eleven thousand of it belongs to Billy Rossi. The rest is for me and my men."

"Your men? You mean Red Vanes?"

"Vanes was cheap. For five hundred bucks he told me how and where to find you. Through Texas Joe, here, at the Green Dragon."

"How is Mr. Vanes feeling? The tumor on his neck. Life threatening, isn't it? He could die at any moment. Inform him that I know of an excellent surgeon."

"I'll pass that along to him if I ever see him again. Let's get down to business. But first let me tell you this. If I don't walk out of here in half an hour, the chips will be dropped from rooftops all over Chinatown. You will lose something more than just money. You know that."

Chin unbuttoned his suit coat, took off his glasses and began polishing them on the hem of his sweater. "I do not like being threatened."

"I don't like having my friend beaten up, his money taken, his paintings destroyed, and his girlfriend raped."

"My guess is that you do not have any 'men' working for you. That it was just you and Vanes who stole my chips."

"A guess is cheap. A wrong guess is very expensive." Tomei grinned. "I just read that in a fortune cookie."

Chin's jaw moved as if he was chewing gum, his wrinkled cheeks rippling like fish gills. He replaced his glasses. "How much is Mr. Rossi paying you?"

"Not enough."

"I could kill you, Mr. Tomei. Right here. Right now. Mr. Hon could close the drapes, shoot you, dispose of your body. The police would never know. You would simply disappear. You are a young man, with much life ahead of you. Who would mourn your death? Your wife? Perhaps, Mr. Rossi? Friends? Do you have many friends? Ones who would truly miss you?"

"Not a one," Tomei answered. He paused for dramatic effect. "Which proves my point."

"And that point is?"

"I'm not afraid of dying. This is my chance at some big money. It's a gamble I'm more than willing to take. What about you? You're an old man. Your last days must be precious to you. No one is safe from an assassin these days—not presidents, kings, or popes. Certainly not you. I don't care how many of those junior league Bruce Lees you've got guarding you. If I wanted you killed, it would be done. You leave your home, you walk to your car—you're vulnerable. A bomb planted on your car, or nearby. Boom. You're dead." Tomei tapped his wineglass. "I could have poisoned the champagne bottle before you arrived. Killing is easy. So let's knock off the bullshit. I had your vault under surveillance for a week. You probably found the equipment I left behind. I videotaped what went on inside the vault. Not very interesting—to me. But your partners in New York and Vancouver. They might find it interesting that your security was breached so easily."

Chin locked eyes with Tomei for several moments.

Chin considered himself to be a master face-reader, and the ex-policeman had somewhat typical Caucasian features: a high forehead, straight nose, strong chin. His movements were quick, fidgety, the hands of a nervous man, yet his voice was strong, calm, confident. It was Tomei's eyes that Chin concentrated on. Pale gray, clear, unafraid. That's what they were. Unafraid.

Chin blinked first. He turned over his shoulder to look at Hon. He said something in Chinese. Hon stiffened, then turned on his heel and stomped out of the alcove.

"I accept your terms, Mr. Tomei. Be here tomorrow, at this time, with the chips, and I will have your money."

"I was born at night. But not last night. Tomorrow, two in the afternoon, at the United Depository, on Howard Street."

Chin acknowledged the delivery spot with a wry smile. Every policeman and every crook in the city knew of the United Depository, an upscale pawn shop that rented private safe-deposit boxes in the style of Swiss banks—numbered accounts and coded signatures.

Tomei continued. "There are two things you must agree to in addition to the money. Your word that you will not retaliate against me, or my men, including Red Vanes. And that you will not take any further actions against Billy Rossi."

"That is the extent of your demands?"

"No. One more. Sherri Dawson. I want to know where she is, and I want her left alone."

Kan Chin sat very still, his hands gripping his thighs. "I give you my word that neither I, nor any of my men, will bother you, or your associates, including Mr. Vanes. I have no idea what became of Miss Dawson, but I will make inquiries."

Tomei picked up the champagne glass and rose slowly from his chair. He drained the glass and set it carefully on the table.

"Very good. The maître d' said it's your favorite."

"He talks too much."

"By the way. Your man, Willy Hon. You might want to keep an eye on him. He helps himself to a handful of chips every night."

Chin raised his empty glass in a toast. "May you live long enough to enjoy your money, Mr. Tomei."

Chapter Thirty-four

Charles Prescott admired the manner in which Mayor Richard Barr worked a crowd. Barr moved smoothly through the tables of the Fairmont Hotel's ballroom at a steady pace, stopping to shake hands, pat shoulders, bestow chaste kisses, all the while smiling, chatting, shmoozing. It was one of Barr's political assets—face-to-face meetings. It was when he appeared on television that he ran into trouble. The camera was not his friend. He came across as older, sterner, and he had a problem with sweating. The hot studio lighting got to him. Beads of perspiration would form on his hairline and slowly slide downward, carving streaks in his makeup.

Prescott's solution was to have the TV ads produced outdoors, in cooler, natural settings—Golden Gate Park, the Presidio, Fort Point under the Golden Gate Bridge, where Alfred Hitchcock had filmed Jimmy Stewart jumping into the raging bay waters to save Kim Novak in one of Prescott's favorite old movies, *Vertigo*. At least Hitchcock had filmed the initial scenes there. The action sequence had been done in a Hollywood studio. Neither Stewart nor Novak could have survived the real tides, freezing water, and crashing waves of San Francisco Bay.

Fort Point had been the backdrop for the ad Prescott supervised this morning—Barr facing the camera wearing a trench coat, jaw jutting, the wind rustling his hair as he delivered his pitch, which was a negative ad on Philip Dong. All the polls indicated that voters hated negative ads. Prescott didn't believe it, and the results proved him out.

It was one of those situations where the person being polled said what they believed the pollster wanted to hear: I'm against discrimination; I believe in equal rights; I will pay more taxes if it means helping the poor; a person's sex should have nothing to do with their job qualifications, and on and on. Until they entered the voting booth and started thinking about the one thing in life that really mattered—themselves—then they pulled the lever that would save *them* money, keep *their* kids from being bused to another school, or raise taxes on *their* homes.

Someone once said all politics was local. Prescott thought he had a better definition: All politics was personal. What can you do for *me*, baby?

The poll results he just received from Barr's election committee was not going to please his boss. If the voters questioned *were* telling the truth, then Philip Dong had an excellent chance of becoming the next mayor of San Francisco.

Prescott caught Barr's eye and signaled that he had to speak to him.

Barr nodded his agreement but continued shmoozing. He finally freed himself and came over to where Prescott was standing.

"Nice crowd, Charles. You did a good job."

The hotel's staff had done a good job, also. Prescott estimated the attendance at less than three hundred. The tables were spread out and a faux wall had been put in place to narrow the room, make it appear the crowd was larger then it was. Most of those present were die-hard regulars and fringe players who were delighted to have received Barr's invitation, especially since there was no set donation. They would be lucky to pull in five or ten thousand dollars—not nearly enough to cover the cost of the room, food, and liquor.

"I saw the rushes of the commercial we filmed this morning, Mr. Mayor. Dynamite."

"Good, good. Have you placed them?"

A waiter dropped a tray of empty glasses. There was a nervous silence, then laughter rumbled across the room.

"Have you placed the ads?" Barr repeated. "We have the money, let's put them in prime time, Charles."

"I'm working on it, sir." Working hard. Philip Dong's people had already purchased blocks of time on all the local channels. He lowered his voice, slipped a single sheet of paper from his jacket pocket and handed it to the mayor. "The latest poll, sir."

Barr studied the results, then crumpled the paper in his hand, dropped it onto the floor, and stamped on it with his heel. The telltale sweat beads began forming on his forehead. He grabbed Prescott's arm, his fingernails making their presence known through his wool jacket. "Jesus, Charles. I'm only three points ahead! That's a fucking statistical tie. We've got to get something on Dong. What have you heard from Chin? For Christ's sake. I've promised him enough. He'd better deliver. He just damn well has to!"

"He called me, Mr. Mayor. He said he should have something on Dong very soon."

"Good, good. Let me know right away." Barr started to walk away. He stopped abruptly and hurried back to Prescott. "What about the money? You never told me. You had it checked at the bank, right? It's clean, isn't it?"

"Perfectly clean, sir. I hope you have it in a safe place."

John Tomei exited the Green Dragon restaurant onto Grant Avenue and quickly merged into the crowd of tourists and Chinatown locals. He knew that this was his moment of greatest vulnerability. If Kan Chin wanted him dead, a quick knife in the back, right on the street, was a definite possibility.

He threaded his way through a knot of tourists co-cooned around a jewelry store that was advertising an eighty-percent-off sale on the jade rings, pendants, and bracelets in the window.

A string of more than twenty senior citizens, led by a red-capped guide, was shuffling along the sidewalk. Tomei joined the group, a piece of willing flotsam jostled along by the tide of passersby.

When they stopped for a red light at Sacramento Street, he darted into the traffic among a chorus of honking horns and squealing brakes. He broke into a trot when he came to California Street, and hopped aboard a cable car traveling west, up the steep incline.

He spotted another cable car coming from the opposite direction. When the car was abreast, he leaped across, his hands latching onto one of the cable car's outside posts, almost losing his footing and drawing a fifty-fifty response of frowns and smiles from his fellow passengers.

The brakeman pulled the cable car to a lurching stop at Montgomery Street. Tomei jumped off, and started running. After three blocks, he slowed down. There was no sign of a tail. He'd made it. So far. He went over his conversation with Kan Chin as he searched for a public telephone.

What bothered him most was that Chin had too readily agreed to the payoff. How would Chin deal with his telling him that Willy Hon had helped himself to some gambling chips? Violently, Tomei hoped, because it was clear that Hon wanted to settle the score for that shovel to his head.

He used a street-side phone booth to call Red Vanes.

"Chin went for it, Red. He said he'll have the money delivered to the depository tomorrow, just as we planned."

"Did my name come up?" Vanes wanted to know.

"Right away. He knows about your tumor. He says he has a good surgeon for you. And, just as you predicted, he knew my name."

"Did he say anything about your trying to shoot yourself?"

"No," Tomei said, not liking the fact that Vanes knew that particular part of his past. The information was supposed to have been kept confidential, sealed in his police personnel file, but he knew there was no realistic way of preventing the word from getting out, if not from the police file then from the resulting civil action.

"He'll find out. And that could be a big plus for you. Chin would think you're nuts. That you don't give a shit whether you live or die. If he doesn't believe he can scare you, he's left with two choices: kill you or pay off."

"Which way are you betting, Red?"

"I've got my money on you, kid. If he pops you, he'll pop me, too. Call me in the morning. But not too early."

John Tomei's elaborate evasive tactics had been a wasted effort. Willy Hon had been ordered not to follow him from the restaurant. Hon recognized Tomei from the photo that Cowboy Joe had taken as the man he'd seen at Rossi's house. The one he'd assumed was a security guard.

Chin had faxed the photo to one of his men in the police department and learned of Tomei's name.

Now Hon sat alongside Chin in the black Mercedes, parked in front of the entrance to Chin's apartment building.

They had been parked for at least five minutes, the motor running. Chin was leaning forward, his elbows on his knees, his fingers laced together in front of him.

Hon's muscles tightened when Chin opened his mouth to speak.

"I have decided to pay Mr. Tomei, Willy. You will handle that. Make sure that he delivers the chips. All of them. You have made an inventory? You know how much was taken?"

"It's difficult to get an exact amount."

"Difficult? Is that so? I haven't been as attentive as I should have, it seems. Mr. Tomei informs me that he took exactly six hundred and twenty-one thousand dollars, and that you have been helping yourself to some chips every night."

"He lies," Hon said angrily.

"To what purpose? What has he to gain?"

Hon turned away and stared out the car window. "He is trying to make me appear a fool. To lessen your trust in me."

"Perhaps. Perhaps this is his way to make you suffer. Mr. Tomei is an interesting fellow. He claims he is not afraid to die, and I am inclined to believe him. Yet he is protective of Billy Rossi and Red Vanes. Even of the whore, Miss Dawson. There must be someone he loves. Someone he really does not want harmed. We have to find out just who that someone is."

"All he really wants is the money," Hon said.

"Yes, he does indeed want the money. And he will have it. But not for long."

"I will kill him," Hon vowed. "I will—"

"Not until we have the chips. The election is our prime concern. Once that's over, we can concentrate on Tomei and Vanes. Rossi is of no concern and the whore is dead."

A car pulled alongside, then parked directly in front of Chin's Mercedes.

"Here is Lieutenant Clayton," Chin said. "He is delivering Tomei's police file. We will find out what Tomei's weak spots are. Go see Paul Heng. I want a financial check on Tomei. I want to know which bank he uses, how much money he has, who he writes checks to. Everything."

"Yes, sir." Heng was the manager of the Canton Bank. The bank would be closed now, but Heng would not refuse a request made by Kan Chin. "Anything else?"

"Be back here in an hour with the information," Chin ordered, reaching for the door handle.

* * *

A car horn tooted, and a man called out, "Hey, honey. How about a date?"

Sherri Dawson tore her eyes from Kan Chin's Mercedes and glared at the man leaning across the front seat of the silver BMW sedan.

"Beat it," she growled.

The man tapped the horn again. "Come on, honey." He opened his mouth to smile, revealing a string of gold molars that blended in with his tobacco-stained teeth. "How about it? I'm willing to pay for my fun."

Sherri sighed, walked over, and glared at the man. He was in his fifties, with a florid face. There was a bottle of bourbon nestled between his legs.

"Let me get this straight," she said pleasantly. "You want to pay me to have sex with you."

"Yeah. What can I get for a hundred?"

"About two months, you stupid jerk. I'm a police decoy. My partner is filming all of this. He has your license plate, so you'll be getting a notice to appear in court in the mail. Drive off slowly, or we'll book you right now for drunk driving. Get going!"

Sherri strode back to the shelter of the doorway with a view of the alley. Chin's Mercedes was still there. A tan sedan with twin spotlights and a whip antenna pulled in front of the Mercedes.

Two young men appeared from the entrance to Chin's building and bracketed the car, herding it between them to the garage, like two tugs nosing a liner to the dock.

Kan Chin exited the Mercedes and disappeared into the building.

Sherri edged back into the darkness as the Mercedes started coming her way. She knew that Willy Hon was in the car. She had followed the Mercedes earlier, when it left Chin's building little more than an hour ago. She'd followed it on foot, sure she would lose it. There was simply no way for her to keep her rental car on the street—the nearest parking spot she'd found was four blocks away. It had been frustrating, and she was certain it would be a futile effort, but the big car had traveled no more than two blocks, stopping in front of the Green Dragon restaurant.

Sherri had sat at the wine bar and watched Kan Chin and Willy Hon enter the alcove at the back of the restaurant. She couldn't see who was in there with them, but she was rewarded for her wait when John Tomei left the alcove.

It had been a shock to see Tomei there. What the hell was he up to? Tomei had walked right past her at the bar. Within a few feet, paying her no attention. Just like a cop. Always around when you don't need them. Sherri didn't want Tomei anywhere near her until she finished her business with Chin.

Kan Chin and Hon had left a few minutes later. She turned her back, watching them in the bar's mirror. Chin had walked slowly, Hon directly behind him. She'd seen Hon check her out, her legs, her butt, her profile, but his eyes never reached her face, which was protected by the brim of the Stetson, the black wig, and sunglasses.

It was too dark now for the sunglasses. She tilted the tip of the Stetson low on her forehead as the Mercedes purred by, taking a right on Jackson Street.

She followed it again, but stopped when the car surged through a red light, picking up speed as it careened right on Columbus Avenue.

Sherri retraced her steps, turning into the alleyway, picking up her pace as she walked by the entrance to Chin's building. She had been inside once, the day Chin had summoned her from Las Vegas and told her to get close to Billy Rossi.

Chin had given no reason for his request, and she hadn't questioned him. She had expected Chin to ask for something else, too. Sex. But he hadn't. At first she thought he was past the sex game. Too old to play anymore. But then she saw the look in his eyes when the lovely young girl had served them drinks. She remembered a New York hooker once telling her that the older they get, the younger they want them.

Chin was no different. All men were no different, as far as she was concerned.

Chin had never invited her back to his place again. Now she had to figure out how to get inside, without an invitation.

She ducked her chin to her chest when one of the young men huddled in the doorway to Chin's building whistled, and called out something to her in Chinese.

The other man laughed loudly and it sent chills right through her. It was a lewd, derisive laugh, one she had heard all too many times in her life. Like the laugh of the first mate she had stabbed to death on board the *Mara Maru*.

Chapter Thirty-five

"**Y**ou're late," Elaine Surel said over the din of the crowd and the music coming from a string quartet playing Bach cantatas.

John Tomei dropped down into a catcher's stance so that he was eye-level with Elaine. She was in an electrically powered wheelchair, wearing a shimmering, sequined, iceberg-blue dress. Her right leg was encased in a knee-high cast.

Her hair was held back by a narrow headband and the gold bracelets on her wrists clinked as she reached out to him.

"You look marvelous, darling," Tomei said, doing Billy Crystal's Fernando Lamas impression. "Who made the wheelchair? Rolls-Royce?"

"I've worried about you," Elaine said. "Are you all right?"

"Stop worrying about me, and take care of yourself, Gucci. How's the leg?"

She rapped on the cast with a diamond-ringed finger. "It's a bore. A goddamn bore. Now tell me, what's going on? Have you seen Red Vanes?"

"Yes. Several times. Red's helping out." Tomei rose to his feet, his knees making cracking sounds. "Where's Laura?"

Elaine flopped an arm over her shoulder. "She was at the bar awhile ago. Ross's friends are drooling over her, John. You better make up your mind about

Laura. We have to talk. But not now. Come by tomorrow."

"Okay."

She grabbed his hand and squeezed tightly. "I mean it, John. I am worried about you."

"How much has Laura told you?"

"We're partners. She told me everything."

"Everything?" Tomei gave a curt laugh. "That must have been an interesting conversation."

Elaine brought his hand to her face, opened her mouth, and bit down hard. When he pulled away, there was an indentation of her teeth in his flesh. "I mean it. I want to see you tomorrow."

Elaine's husband, Ross, chose that moment to stop by.

"If you're hungry, I'll have someone bring over hors d'oeuvres." He looked at Tomei and added an unconvincing, "Nice to see you, John."

"Great party, Ross. Have you seen Laura?"

"Yes. At the bar. You can't miss her in that dress." He bent down and bestowed a kiss on his wife's cheek. "There are some people I'd like you to say hello to, Elaine."

Elaine gave Tomei a farewell wave and he studied the crowd. Ross's house was a rambling Mediterranean villa with an arcaded entrance court. The rooms were very large, with coffered ceilings and glazed stucco walls.

He estimated there were some thirty elegantly dressed men and women in the living room. Sprinkled among them were casually dressed individuals whose faces he recognized. Cops. He said hello to several of them as he made his way into the dining room, where the bar had been set up.

Laura was standing at the far end of the bar, encircled by four men wearing formal suits. He elbowed his way through the crowd, stopping to pick up a glass of wine from a caterer's tray.

As he got closer, he could see what Ross Surel had meant by "that dress." It was black silk crepe and carved at both the neck and back, her surging breasts split by the deep cleavage.

He waved his wineglass to catch her attention. "Inspector Aguera. You have a phone call."

The men's heads turned in unison, as if they were watching a tennis match, eyeing Tomei, then wheeling back to Laura.

"Excuse me," she said as she pushed through the now frowning quartet. She grasped Tomei's sleeve. "Thanks for saving me. If I heard one more suggestion about where I should invest my money 'for the long haul,' I think I'd scream."

"In that dress, I don't think it was your financial assets they were interested in."

"You like it?" Laura asked, shrugging her shoulders, causing her breasts to jiggle.

"Any man who doesn't like it has serious problems."

Tomei had been to the house several times. He steered Laura down a long hallway and into a room that housed the cleaning supplies.

He kicked the door shut and wrapped his arms around her shoulders, his lips grazing her mouth, moving down her neck.

Laura stepped back. "John. Saturday night. At Rossi's house. It's not something that happens a lot with me."

"I know. It was special. For me. For both of us, I hope."

She grabbed him by his ears and pulled him to the hollow in her breasts. "It was special. I've been trying to get in touch with you. I wish you'd answer your phone once in awhile."

Tomei took his time licking his way back to her lips. "Let's get out of here."

"First I have to tell you something. You're in all kinds of trouble. Lieutenant Bostic of the Las Vegas Police Department called. He's mad as hell. A woman by the name of Ava Avery was murdered in Sherri Dawson's Vegas apartment. Bostic said Avery was wearing a blond wig, so maybe the killer thought she was Dawson. And guess who found the body? Billy

Rossi. He had a heart attack and is in the hospital. Bostic isn't at all happy that you passed yourself off as a cop, John. He says that if he doesn't hear from you, he's coming here to kick ass. I think he means it."

"I'm sure he does," Tomei responded gravely. "Jesus. I met Ava Avery. She was Dawson's roommate. With a blond wig on, she'd look a lot like Sherri. The killer was after Sherri. Poor Ava. Damn it, she was harmless. She had nothing to do with any of this. I'll give Bostic a call."

Laura took a few seconds to respond. "It's not just you. Bostic can make it unpleasant for Elaine, too."

"I'll phone him. First thing in the morning."

"I called the St. Rose Hospital in Las Vegas. Billy Rossi's still on the critical list."

"Thanks for checking. I'll go to Vegas and see him soon."

"John. Elaine told me that you've been talking to Red Vanes. Listen. I was stuck in the Personnel Department at the time they shut down the Intelligence detail. Vanes made veiled threats about having incriminating information on the chief and some of the deputies. He even threatened to sue the department. The chief took him seriously and had a psychological profile done on Vanes. I read the report. It was very spooky. The man has some serious problems."

"I'm being careful," Tomei assured her.

"It's different for you. You're not in the department any more. I am. I'm a cop. A working cop. I just can't act like nothing's happening. I have to know what's going on. What you've been up to."

"Okay. Let's get out of here and we'll talk."

"Where were you thinking of going?"

"Not back to Rossi's place. I was there earlier, and took Fidel for a long walk and made sure he had fresh food and water."

Laura adjusted the straps of her dress. "Why don't you come to my place?"

"I thought you'd never ask," he whispered into her ear.

Chapter Thirty-six

During his career as a policeman, John Tomei had been to the United Depository dozens of times, usually with a suspect who, for a possible reduction in his prison sentence, would allow Tomei access to his safety-deposit box.

The Depository rented the boxes for an annual fee. For a hundred dollars a year you could rent one large enough to hold a few precious legal documents and the family jewels, as long as the family wasn't too wealthy.

The price and size graduated until you reached seven hundred dollars a year for a box that measured three feet in height by four feet in width.

Yesterday morning Tomei and Vanes had rented one such box and stored all of the chips they'd stolen from Kan Chin.

Both Tomei and Red Vanes were well known to Gurbeep Singh, the owner of the Depository, a sharp-faced East Indian with pouchy brown eyes.

The rental procedure was simple. The yearly fee was paid up front. An entry code to the safe room was picked by the renter, then coded into a computer. A single key—or duplicates at fifteen dollars per—completed the transaction. No ID was required, no names or signatures taken. Whoever had the key and the code had access—no questions asked—and there were no records kept as to how often the safety-deposit box was accessed.

After one year and a day, if the contract was not renewed, the owner of the Depository was entitled to sole possession of the box. Harsh terms, but the clientele that migrated to the Depository put up with it because the alternatives—using a bank with all those restrictive procedures and identity clauses, or leaving their treasures with a wife or friend, or simply burying them in the backyard—were worse.

In addition to the safety-deposit boxes, the Depository offered the general services of a pawn shop. There were jewelry cases filled with watches, rings, and gold coins. The walls were festooned with everything from pawned guitars and brass instruments to power tools.

A young man who bore a strong resemblance to Gurbeep Singh, outfitted in a light-blue security guard's uniform, prowled the aisles, now and then covering up a yawn with the back of his hand.

Tomei nodded to the elder Singh, then looked at the Long Case Clock near the front door. One forty-five. Chin's man was due in fifteen minutes to make the exchange.

Tomei had called Red Vanes earlier in the morning from Laura's apartment. Their plan was to have Vanes parked out on the street nearby and to keep in contact via their cell phones.

He kept a nervous eye on the front entrance and called Vanes.

"Are you in place, Red?"

"Yeah. I'm here. Keep the phone on and give me a loud signal when Willy Hon shows up."

"You should see him before me, Red."

"Just in case, Tomb. Just in case."

Tomei slipped the cell phone into his jacket's breast pocket, then began pacing the floor, his hands in his pants pockets, jiggling change, stopping occasionally to eye the jewelry counters.

He'd had a busy day. After Laura left for work, he'd gone to Billy Rossi's house—making sure that none of Chin's men had the place staked out before entering.

Fidel had been happy to see him again. Tomei let the dog out the back door for a romp, then used Rossi's computer to check for e-mail. There was a long message from Messy. She loved New Mexico, especially Santa Fe, with all its shops and Indian artifacts. He wondered if there were any job opportunities in Santa Fe for an ex-cop—a now slightly crooked ex-cop. If Joan was successful with her court strategy, if a judge granted her permission to relocate, then he would have to move to New Mexico. He just was not going to let his daughter slip away from him.

His next call was to his attorney, whose frosty attitude softened when Tomei promised to pay his bill in a few days.

At precisely two o'clock, Willy Hon popped through the front entrance, a black nylon carry-on bag looped over one shoulder. His right ear was still bandaged. There was a plastic insert in his other ear. A thin electric cord ran down the earpiece, disappearing under the front of his shirt.

Tomei angled his head toward the pocket with the cell phone.

"He's here Red. And he's wired—an earpiece. The microphone is probably under his shirt."

Hon stood in place for several moments, his eyes drifting around the room before he moved off in a flat-footed, plodding walk.

"Where are they?" Hon demanded as he approached Tomei.

"In there." Tomei punched the code into the electronic pad by the iron gate leading to a hallway of frayed, inexpensive Oriental rugs. The barred gate silently slid open.

When they were inside, and the gate closed, Tomei held up a hand. "I see the money right now, or the deal is off."

Hon slipped the carry-on from his shoulder and tossed it at Tomei with both hands, as if throwing a basketball.

"The money is there. Give me the chips."

Tomei unzipped the carry-on and hoisted it onto a counter top. "Let's just make sure."

The bills were held together by rubber bands—hundred-count bundles of hundred-dollar bills. He slipped several bills free and, pushing his arm through the iron gate, waved them at the uniformed security guard.

Gurbeep Singh's nephew carried the money to his uncle, who used a jeweler's loupe to carefully examine the bills. When he was finished, he gave Tomei a reassuring nod. They were legitimate.

"Are you satisfied?" Hon asked angrily.

"No. First, I count it."

Tomei took his time, twelve minutes of it, relishing the agitated movements of Willy Hon. When the count was completed, he zipped the case closed and smiled. "Now you can have the chips."

John Tomei unlocked the safety-deposit box and slid it free, taken off guard by how little effort it took. By the time the box was half way out he knew it was empty. He stood there, frozen in place, staring at the emptiness as he lifted the lid.

Hon backed away, one hand cupping the monitor in his ear. He began speaking feverishly in Chinese.

"Listen," Tomei said harshly. "There's been a mistake. I'll have to—"

Willy Hon swore loudly, then, from his waistband, he pulled a gun with a bulb-shaped silencer attached to its barrel.

Tomei yanked the safety-deposit box from the wall and swung it at Hon's head.

Hon ducked and jammed the gun against Tomei's chest as he pulled the trigger.

Tomei careened backward, his head making a smacking sound as it hit the wall.

Hon was right on him, and as Tomei was sliding downward, thrust the gun into Tomei's chest again, drilling his eyes into Tomei's as he once again pulled the trigger.

Chapter Thirty-seven

The blow John Tomei received to the back of his head as he crashed into the wall of safety-deposit boxes had done more damage then the two shots fired by Willy Hon.

Tomei sat at Billy Rossi's kitchen table, a towel-wrapped ice pack on his neck, Fidel at his feet, nursing a hefty jigger of Rossi's Old Grand-Dad bourbon while examining the bulletproof vest that had saved his life. The shooting yesterday in the tunnel had convinced him that Billy Rossi hadn't been overreacting by donning a vest. He had found the vest in Rossi's gun cabinet.

The bullets had blown through his jacket and shirt. One mangled the cell phone in the jacket's breast pocket. The vest's polyethylene ballistic fibers, developed for use in Desert Storm, had swallowed them up. There were visible indentations in the vest's fibers and some broken threads, but no piercing.

The fact that Willy Hon had a silencer on his pistol had helped, too. The silencer not only suppressed the sound but also the velocity of the bullet.

Tomei examined one of the mushroom-shaped bullets, then dropped it onto the table and fingered the two quarter-size bruises on his chest. Kill shots, inches apart, aimed right for his heart.

He had Gurbeep Singh's nephew to thank for saving his life. Rajah had heard Hon screaming, and reacted quickly, running into the vault room, finding Tomei prone on the floor and Willy Hon kicking an empty safety-deposit box drawer.

Hon had bulled his way past Rajah and left, along with the carry-on case full of Kan Chin's cash.

Gurbeep Singh had been relieved when Tomei insisted that he had stumbled and knocked himself out.

Singh didn't believe a word of it, but the police were bad for his business. In gratitude, Singh had confirmed that Red Vanes had been at the Depository when it opened at nine that morning—and that he had left carrying three backpacks. Rajah, ever-helpful, assisted Vanes in taking the packs out to his car.

Tomei picked up the two misshapen bullets, shook them in his hand, and rolled them across the table like dice. "Snake eyes," he said to himself, pondering his next move.

Red Vanes had set him up. But why? What was Vanes going to do with the chips? Was he just after the money? Tomei doubted it. Vanes would have had half of the money, without going through the whole charade at the Depository.

Tomei could imagine how Chin felt. Outraged. Vengeful. He'd lost face. A whole bunch of face. He'd be out for revenge.

Losing face was as important to Vanes as it was to Kan Chin. Vanes held Chin responsible for killing his father. For having him kicked out of the police department.

That tumor growing on Vanes's throat. He claimed he could die right on the operating table.

The operating table would be preferable to falling into the hands of Kan Chin.

Where was Vanes? He wouldn't go back to his house. Kan Chin would have it watched. Even if Vanes was barricaded inside, he'd have to come out sooner or later. If Chin didn't have the patience to wait him out, he just might blow up the whole damn place.

Tomei figured that Vanes would stick close by, so

he could observe Chin's reactions—see him suffer the indignity of losing those gambling chips, of worrying what had become of them.

Vanes must have a safe house in the city. Probably somewhere close to Chinatown. In Chinatown? The garage leading to the underground tunnel. That door in the wall. Where did it lead?

Tomei remembered exactly where the garage was located. Was that it? Was that why Vanes had set him up to be killed? Because he knew about the access to the tunnel?

He wanted to get his hands on Vanes. Around his throat, tumor and all.

Tomei's only advantage at the moment was that Kan Chin and Red Vanes must think he was dead. Vanes hadn't alerted him when Hon had arrived at the Depository for the exchange, because Vanes had undoubtedly been nowhere near the place. But he had been listening on the cell phone. He would have heard the confusion in Tomei's voice when he realized the safety-deposit box was empty. He would have heard Willy Hon's angry banter and understood everything Hon had said. He would have heard the gunshots, and figured that Hon had killed him.

It was an advantage, all right. But how could he use it? And how long would it last? Once Kan Chin found out that he was alive, Willy Hon would be after him again, and so would Vanes.

Tomei tipped the glass and drained the last droplets of the bourbon. He couldn't sit back and wait. He'd have to strike first—and fast.

"I want you to kill Philip Dong tonight," Kan Chin said in a metered tone, stressing each word. "At eight o'clock."

Dino Lanzoni leaned back in his chair and crossed his legs at the ankles. One foot brushed the table and the priceless Chinese devil dogs rattled against the jade. "Tonight? I may need some time to scope the guy out, I mean—"

"He will be at his home. Alone. The side door will be open, unlocked. He will be in his study. It is on the second floor. I have a diagram prepared for you."

"Okay, okay. But what if he's not—"

"He will be there," Chin said emphatically. "He will be waiting for someone. A young woman. She will not arrive. You will."

Lanzoni framed his words carefully before responding. Chin looked pissed. He was rubbing his glasses so hard with his sweater that Lanzoni thought he might break the lenses. "It sounds almost too easy, doesn't it? I'm surprised that you don't have one of your men whack this Dong guy."

"Are you telling me how to operate my business?" Chin said in a voice that caused Lanzoni to sit up straight. "You volunteered your services. I understood that you were a man of your word. Have you changed your mind?"

"No, sir. Not at all. You want Dong whacked tonight, consider it a done deal."

Kan Chin replaced his glasses, then clapped his hands together.

The beautiful China-doll Lanzoni had noticed during his last visit to Chin's place shuffled into the room, carrying a tray, which she gently placed on the table.

There were no drinks this time. The tray held a single item. A long-barreled pistol. Lanzoni recognized the gun right away. A .22-caliber Colt Woodsman. One of the best hit pieces ever produced.

Chin stood up, signaling that the meeting was over. "I hope the weapon is satisfactory. Mr. Hon will provide you with all the information necessary to ensure your mission is successful. I have arranged an apartment for you on the floor below." Chin touched the young girl lightly on her shoulder. "Lia will provide for all your needs."

Lanzoni got to his feet, and once again his leg nudged the jade table, rocking the devil dogs.

After Chin had disappeared through a curtained doorway, Willy Hon approached Lanzoni carrying a slim leather briefcase, which he laid gently on the table.

Lanzoni laughed out loud when he spotted the bandage on Hon's ear. "What happened to your ear, Shorty? Get in a fight with the wrong midget?"

"You should be more careful with those big feet of yours. Those devil dogs are more than two thousand years old," Hon pointed out. "If you knock one over, Kan Chin will have you skinned alive. And I'll be the one doing the skinning."

Lanzoni reached over and picked up one of the porcelain dogs. He examined it briefly, then tossed it in the air, catching it in an open palm as it came within inches of the table. "You worry too much, Shorty."

He turned to the young Chinese girl, who smiled at him before lowering her head to her chest.

Chapter Thirty-eight

Charles Prescott was asleep on his bed, legs spread apart, his arms folded across his chest, as if hugging himself to sleep. A travel folder promoting a Caribbean cruise tented his head.

The ringing of the telephone dragged him from a sun-drenched dream. He brushed the folder from his face and mumbled as he reached for the phone on the nightstand.

Someone had been calling for the last three days. Leaving confusing messages on the machine for a man named Dan.

He grasped the receiver and grunted a harsh "Who is it?," ready to give Dan's friend of a piece of his mind.

"Have you already heard?" asked the agitated voice of Mayor Richard Barr.

Prescott swung his legs off the mattress and elbowed his way to a sitting position. "Heard what, Mr. Mayor?"

"Philip Dong. Someone tried to kill him. Dong shot the guy. Shot him dead. Right in his own house. Do you know what this means?"

Prescott's mind was reeling. "Who . . . who was it?"

"I don't know yet. One of my bodyguards is on his way to pick you up right now. Go to Dong's house. Find out what happened. I want you to make sure you're seen. We've got to be players in this, Charles.

That prick Dong will make a big deal out of it. He'll probably pick up three or four points in the polls. Show some sympathy. Tell the press that I've put the whole fucking police department on the case. Somehow we have to turn this into a plus for us, or we'll both be out of a job after the election. I'm counting on you, Charles. Keep me posted."

Prescott gently put down the receiver and sat staring at it. Who the hell would try to kill Philip Dong? He stood up abruptly and started for the bathroom. His foot hit the slick travel folder and he stumbled, nearly losing his balance and falling to the carpet.

He glowered at the folder. The Caribbean seemed farther away than ever.

John Tomei pulled the tip of his baseball cap down and buried his neck in his shoulders as a wedge of Asian teenagers marched up the alleyway in his direction.

The baseball cap and upturned raincoat collar wasn't much of a disguise. Nothing in comparison to Red Vanes's elaborate wigs and tattered clothing. Tomei had no intention of getting close to Kan Chin's base of operations—at least from the street.

There were eight of them, in a tight formation, dressed in dark clothing. They slowed down when they spotted Tomei. A lone Caucasian walking down a Chinatown alley wasn't all that unusual—in the daylight hours—but at one o'clock in the morning it was rare. A lost tourist? A *tset ha* looking for drugs or some Chinese *hail* at one of the whorehouses that featured very young girls in pigtails and schoolgirl uniforms?

Tomei edged toward the street. He unclenched his fist and a crowbar slid down from inside his raincoat's sleeve. He held the bar away from his side so that the gang could see it. As they got closer, he lowered the bar's curved tip to the sidewalk and let it rasp against the cement.

The teenagers passed him without incident. When

they were a few yards away one of them said something that brought roars of laugher from the others.

Tomei slowed when he approached the garage Vanes had used to gain entry to the underground tunnel, taking in the parked cars, the windows on the narrow, sleepy apartment houses.

This was his third time around the block. There had been no change since his last visit—the same cars, the same lights on in the same apartments.

A sudden movement to his left caused him to duck behind one of the parked cars. He straightened, feeling foolish when he saw a gaunt black cat emerge from the shadows, pause under the yellowish haze of a streetlamp, then disappear into the darkness again.

You're jumpy, he told himself. And you've got damn good reason to be.

His target was the locked garage door adjacent to Vanes's. The doors were nearly identical—warped, weather-beaten, secured with a padlock. The neighbor's lock was nothing like Vanes's—an inexpensive oxidized-steel lock and hasp.

Tomei fitted the lip of the crowbar between lock and hasp, then pushed down hard, rising to his toes to increase leverage. There was a snap and the sound of tearing wood. He waited for an alarm, for an apartment window to slide open. For someone to scream for the police.

The only sound was the electrical fizzing of the power pole's transformer. He squatted down, grabbed the door edge and rolled it up, taking a step backward as the door creaked and yawed on rusty hinges.

An ancient, finned Cadillac sedan dripping with chrome and clouded with dust took up most of the space. Transmission parts, spare fenders, hydraulic jacks, and shop tools were scattered around the floor.

Tomei found the light switch, then closed the door behind him. The spare parts and tools were as dusty as the Caddie. A restoration project put on hold.

He edged around the car and made his way to the rear of the room, again putting the crowbar to use, digging the sharp tip into the plywood separating this garage from Vanes's.

It was an old burglar's trick. If a house, apartment, or office building was too well protected, too hard to enter, break in next door and gain access from there.

There was no way to gain entry without making some noise, so he decided to hurry up and get it over with.

He used his foot to force a section of the plywood free, then gouged the crowbar into a stud post, jumping back when the rotted wood gave way and swarms of milk-colored termites scrambled into sight. He kicked out another stud and a four-foot-wide section of the plywood wall teetered for a moment, then crashed onto the floor.

Tomei hurried through the opening, standing on the fallen plywood, surveying the room. It looked much the same as his last two visits—two sets of rubber boots and turnout coats hanging from nails.

He approached the door at the center of the rear wall, running the beam of the flashlight around the jambs, looking for any sign of an alarm wire or booby trap.

A common brass key-in-handle doorknob was the only visible lock on the door.

He dropped down to his knees. There was a pale slice of light coming from under the door. He put his ear to the floor, and thought he could hear opera music. A powerful tenor. Vanes's kind of music.

Tomei hugged the wall, reached out his hand and placed it lightly on the doorknob. He twisted it slowly, gently, surprised when the latch bolt slipped free of the strike plate and the door clicked open.

Was Vanes so confident of his street-side security system that he hadn't bothered with the door? Or was there something waiting on the other side?

He nudged the door open with the crowbar, counted to twenty then moved quickly.

There was a narrow hallway lined with doorways devoid of doors. The seedy wood flooring was moisture-stained and heel-chipped, the walls and ceiling of moldy plaster that had turned a sooty, gray color. Strings of electrical wire looped down the center of the ceiling, with bare, single-socket lights fastened at random intervals.

Tomei kept the crowbar in his left hand and slipped a .38 revolver he'd borrowed from Billy Rossi's collection in his right. The music was getting louder

He checked each room as he passed. They were identical, square shaped, as moldy as the hallway, the walls lined with grubby wood shelving, the shelves no more than sixteen inches apart. Crude ladders were nailed to the ends of the shelves.

The hall turned right. More rooms, dozens of them, each lined with the same shelves, the same ladders, the same sickish, putrid smell. Beds, he realized. The shelves were bunk beds, or cribs. He remembered reading of the notorious "Chinamen's Rooms" that housed the poor Asian immigrants imported to build the railroads and tend to the rich and mighty in the late 1800s.

Some of the fancier Pacific Heights mansions had cramped Chinamen's Rooms, complete with prisonlike bars, that had been turned into wine cellars.

He tried to envision how many men could be crammed into these rooms. Twenty? Thirty? More?

There was something on the floors. Rat droppings. They appeared fresh.

The warrenlike hallway took another sharp turn. The music stopped, replaced by a melodious feminine voice imploring the listener to join the station's pledge drive.

Something dark and furry scooted by Tomei's leg. A rat. Three more shot past him. There was an overpowering smell. Strong enough to block out the stench of rotting wood and walls. An all too familiar smell.

"Vanes," Tomei called out. "Where the hell are you?"

He charged down the hallway, gun at the ready. He came to an abrupt halt when he entered a large chamber. There was a stove, refrigerator, and microwave oven. A single, tubular-steel bed. A Formica-topped kitchen table on which sat the three backpacks, a bottle of brandy, cartons of Chinese takeout food, and four of the biggest rats Tomei had ever seen.

They stared back at Tomei with their ugly, narrow heads and beady eyes, unafraid, as they chewed at the contents oozing through the bite holes in the takeout cartons.

Tomei raised the crowbar over his head and brought it down on the table. The rats leaped to the floor and scurried away, over to a corner of the room, leaping in among a pile of what must have been a hundred of their brethren—a writhing, frenzied gray blanket of rats. Several of them turned to look at Tomei, revealing blood-smeared faces.

Tomei approached them cautiously, smashing the crowbar on the floor. The rats moved slowly, reluctantly. For a moment he thought they were going to attack him. He fired off several shots from the revolver and the rats scattered, funneling into a hole in the wall, running up each others backs as they squirmed though the narrow opening.

Tomei stopped at the table and took a long pull from the brandy bottle before approaching the lump the rats had been feasting on.

A man, lying on his side. His tweed sport coat chewed to shreds, saturated with blood. Tomei used the heel of his shoe to nudge the body over. A bald skull, the face gnawed to the bone. The ragged, blood-drenched remnants of a blue bandanna tied around what was left of his neck.

What was it that Red Vanes had said that morning in the tunnel? That he knew of some spots in the tunnel that even the rats didn't know about. Vanes had been wrong.

Chapter Thirty-nine

Anthony Tripoli's yacht *Diavolo Mare*, a gleaming white sixty-five-foot sports cruiser with an aerodynamic superstructure, was docked between two sleek sailboats. The sails were neatly rolled and tied. There were no lights in the cabins.

The only sound was the groaning of the mooring ropes as the boats bobbed with the tides.

FBI agent Don Jamison watched the revolving light coming from the fog-shrouded Alcatraz Island lighthouse as he slipped on a pair of rubber gloves. "Come on," he urged Paul Flowers. "Let's get in there and see what's going on."

"Take it slow," Flowers cautioned. "We can't be sure Lanzoni's not in there."

"We've been watching the fucking boat for three hours. Come on. It's freezing out here. No one's on the boat. No one's on those sailboats. We're home free. Let's do it."

Flowers wasn't convinced. He looked out at the bay. A massive U.S. Navy destroyer was heading out to sea. The ship's wake rolled slowly toward the yacht club's dock. Flowers could feel the wooden planking raise and roll under his feet.

"Your source better be right on this one, Donny."

Jamison snapped the rubber gloves at his wrist. "He's never let me down yet."

"Okay. We do it."

Jamison moved swiftly for a man his size. He leaped aboard the *Diavolo Mare*'s teak deck and made for the stern. The stainless-steel-and-glass sliding door leading to the ship's salon was open a crack.

Flowers grabbed Jamison's elbow. "This is too easy. I don't like it."

Jamison slid the door open without replying. When he was inside, he said, "Hey, sometimes you just get lucky. Find a light switch, Paul."

Jamison gave a low whistle when the lights went on. "Look at this. Who says crime doesn't pay."

Ice-smooth varnish covered the rich, rose-colored Cuban mahogany interior walls and curved ceiling. A U-shaped, lime green sofa fit in perfectly between a small galley and wet bar. A bottle of wine lying on its side and plates sticky with gravy and melted ice cream sat on a low-lying table in front of a large-screen television set.

Red wine had dribbled from the bottle making an amoeba-shaped stain on the deep-pile beige carpeting.

"Dino is a sloppy dude," Flowers said. "Little Trips isn't going to like that."

"Little Trips is scared shitless of Lanzoni. He's not going to complain."

The two FBI agents moved through the boat, finding a curved stairway leading to a large bedroom with more of the highly varnished walls. A queen-size bed dominated the room. The spread, blankets, and sheets were jumbled together.

Strewn around the room were men's clothes: pants, jackets, shirts. Flowers picked up one of the suit jackets and examined the label.

"Forty-six long. Made in Rome, for Mr. Dino Lanzoni." He patted the pockets, finding nothing but candy wrappers and toothpicks.

Jamison was on his knees, searching under the bed. He retrieved a suitcase, which he lay on the bed.

Flowers peered over his shoulder at the contents. Six bags of white powder in Ziploc bags and a sheaf of lime green, envelope-size printed forms. He opened one of the bags, dipped his finger in and held it to his nose and inhaled slowly. "Bingo. Top-quality heroin."

Jamison picked up the printed material. "Check this out, Paul. Betting cards—college football, pro football, basketball, golf. No wonder Dino was at Sully's that day. Either he's hooking up with Billy Rossi or he's taking him over."

"Lanzoni's more the takeover type."

"What the hell are you moping about, Paul? We've got the bastard."

Flowers wiped the heroin on his fingertip in a handkerchief. "I still think it's too easy. Dino is dumb. But not this dumb."

"That's why they keep building all those new jails. If they weren't dumb, we'd never catch them."

Philip Dong's house was half-circled by black-and-whites and unmarked patrol cars.

A leather-clad bike cop challenged Mayor Barr's limousine driver for a moment.

"Oh, it's you, Cryder," the officer said when he recognized the mayor's bodyguard behind the wheel. "Is this a zoo, or what? Half the neighborhood showed up."

"It's a zoo, all right. I'm leaving the limo right here."

Inspector Paul Cryder, a beefy former Homicide detective, had been working for Mayor Barr for more than three years. He didn't get the opportunity to visit crime scenes very often anymore. "Stick close," he advised Charles Prescott. "I'll find out what went down."

Portable halogen lights had been placed across the spacious driveway leading to Dong's home. The asphalt was glazed from the fog and reflected the red revolving lights of the police cruisers. Teams of uniformed officers strolled the sidewalk, keeping the gawkers at bay.

Several of the civilians were dressed in bathrobes.

The television crews had muscled their way to the

front of the crowd, cameras and microphones at the ready.

"Hey, Charlie," a deep-voiced, handsome man called out to Prescott. "Give me something, buddy. Is Dong all right? They won't tell us a thing."

Prescott was surprised to see Peter Walker. Walker was the number one rated local news anchor in the Bay Area. Personally, Prescott thought all the hair spray Walker used had penetrated his brain at an early age. Dumb but pretty. His reporting consisted of nothing more than smiling at the camera while reading the TelePrompTer. It must have taken a kick in the pants to get him out at this time of the morning.

Prescott waved at Walker and the rest of the press gang. "I'll let you know as soon as I know. The mayor has made this a top priority."

Inspector Cryder planted a hand between Prescott's shoulder blades and steered him up the terrazzo steps. "Let's get off the street, Charlie."

Cryder stopped to talk to several police officers and crime lab technicians. Prescott tried to work his way into the conversations, but he was ignored.

This was the first time he'd been to Dong's house, which was located in the prestigious St. Francis Woods area of the city. He entered the front door. Sturdy mahogany furniture stood in museumlike arrangements around walls decorated with intricate, delicately colored paintings of potted flowers.

Strips of yellow crime scene tape were strung across a stairway leading to the upper floor.

Prescott twitched when Cryder stuck a finger into his arm. "Dino Lanzoni, Charlie. That's who Dong shot. Dino fucking Lanzoni."

"Lanzoni? I thought he went to prison. How could—"

"Not Nick. His brother, Dino. This is heavy, Charlie. You better tell the mayor right away."

There was a commotion on the stairway. The ambulance crew was coming down with a body on a gurney.

"Where's Dong?" Prescott whispered, wondering why he did so. There was no one close to them.

"Upstairs. We can't get close to him, yet."

The two ambulance attendants carrying the gurney paused when they reached the bottom of the stairs. They were both young men and in good physical condition, but the weight of the body had been a strain.

"He was a big sucker," Cryder said. "Look at the size of those feet."

The dead man's shoes, a pair of enormous tasseled cordovan loafers, hung over the edge of the gurney.

Prescott felt as if someone had kicked him in the stomach. The air went out of his lungs in a long hiss. "Jesus. I'm going to be sick."

"Not in here," Cryder warned. "The crime lab wouldn't appreciate it, Charlie. Hold it till we get outside."

Chapter Forty

"**G**od, that's awful," Elaine Surel said when John Tomei had finished his narration on the death of Alonzo "Red" Vanes. "How— Did the rats just attack him? Was he—"

"I think Vanes died of natural causes, Gucci. He was a ticking bomb, with a tumor in his neck. He died, then the rats found him."

Elaine pressed the motorized switch on her wheelchair and maneuvered over to the double French doors that opened to a stone terrace. "It's still awful. What a way to go. Open these doors for me, please."

Tomei wheeled Elaine out onto the terrace. An armada of motionless, sun-rimmed cumulus clouds was parked over the Pacific Ocean.

"Gucci, there's more to the story." Tomei took several gambling chips from his pants pocket. "These belong to Kan Chin. I stole them."

Elaine stared at him in disbelief. "You stole them?"

"Red Vanes and I did. From Chin's vault in Chinatown."

Elaine selected one of the chips from Tomei's hand and held it up to the sky. "Why did you do this? What are they worth?"

"Five hundred dollars each. They're as good as cash."

"How many did you take?"

"It totals up to a little more than six hundred thousand dollars."

"This is crazy," Elaine said. She bit her bottom lip anxiously. "I can't believe it. You actually stole them."

"Appropriated might be a better term. Chin is . . . was willing to pay to get them back. In good old American currency."

"You stole them," Elaine repeated, dumbfounded. "You were a cop, John. That's a crime. You know what happens to ex-cops like you who go to prison. For God's sake, why didn't you—"

"There's been no crime. No reported crime anyway. Kan Chin isn't going to the police, believe me."

Elaine wheeled her chair around in a circle several times.

"This all has to do with Billy Rossi, doesn't it, John? He hired you to get back at the people who robbed him, and this is what you came up with."

"Yes, it all started with Billy."

Elaine tilted her head back and rubbed her forehead with the heel of her hand. "This is great. I get run down by a truck. Rossi goes looking for his missing girlfriend, finds a dead hooker who was killed because she looks like Sherri Dawson. Rossi has a stroke and ends up in the hospital. Dawson is still nowhere to be found. Red Vanes is eaten by rats. Is that it? Or is there someone else involved in this that I don't know about who's been killed or mutilated?"

"Dino Lanzoni," Tomei replied calmly.

"Lanzoni? For God's sake. Philip Dong shot that son-of-a-bitch to death late last night. Lanzoni was trying to kill Dong. What the hell has he got to do with all of this?"

"I'm not sure, Gucci. But there was a reason for Lanzoni being at Sully's the day I met with Billy. And my hunch is that Kan Chin had something to do with it."

"You're awfully damn calm about this for a guy who has the Chinese mafia after him. What are you going to do now?"

"Trade these chips for the cash Kan Chin agreed to pay."

"Don't you think Chin is going to be mad as hell?

Didn't you consider that when you got into this mess with Red Vanes? Do you really think Chin is going to let you walk away? He's planning to kill you."

"I'll handle Chin."

"Yeah. I bet," Elaine flared. "And what about me? What about Laura? You realize that she's in love with you, don't you?"

"Gucci, I'll take care of things." He bent down and kissed Elaine on her cheek. "It's better if Laura doesn't know too much about all of this."

"I love you both. Don't put me in this position."

"It will be over in a day, Gucci. One way or the other, it will be over."

Tomei parked in a garage in North Beach, six blocks from Chinatown and stayed on the back streets until he reached Broadway, a spacious boulevard that separated the once Italian-dominated North Beach from Chinatown. He zigzagged through the traffic to Grant Avenue. The tourists were out in full force and the local residents were going about their daily activities.

He picked a building on the corner of Grant and Pacific, a four-story building with an elaborate chinoiserie facade featuring gilded iron balconies and colorful ceramic walls.

The building directory listed three dentists, an optometrist, several acupuncture clinics, and a tattoo parlor. There was no elevator.

Tomei first checked the entry hall and found a back door leading to a garbage-can-lined alleyway that exited into Broadway. He climbed up the stairs until he reached the roof.

Like most buildings in the area, the precious roof space was put to use. Clotheslines bowed under the weight of billowing sheets and clothing. A child's mini-playground with bright red, green, and yellow plastic slides and riding horses was encircled by a rusty chicken-wire fence. A fluttering American flag flew from a steel pole at the very front of the building.

Tomei hung on to the pole with one hand and

leaned out and looked down at Grant Avenue. No one in the crowd was paying him any attention. That would change shortly. He reached into his raincoat pockets, came out with handfuls of gambling chips and tossed them into the air.

Texas Joe was sitting at his favorite table at Dick's bar on Jackson Street, savoring his morning coffee along with the newspaper story on the death of notorious gangster Dino Lanzoni at the hands of Philip Dong. A little after three that morning, he had learned that Red Vanes had been found dead in a Chinatown garage.

The information on Vanes had been called into Joe by one of his street people. He had considered it important enough to get out of bed and go to the scene. Vanes's remains had already been transported to the hospital by the time he arrived. A cooperative beat cop had allowed him entrance to the garage and Vanes's mysterious lair. He shuddered when he saw the evidence of what the rats had done to Vanes.

Joe had been tempted to call in the news to Kan Chin at that moment, but wisely decided to wait until a decent time—nine o'clock.

Chin had been most grateful, and had asked one mysterious question: Were any gambling chips found with Vanes?

Why was Kan Chin asking about chips? John Tomei had mentioned the chips at the Green Dragon when he told him to contact Chin. How many chips were there? How would Vanes have gained possession of them?

Willy Hon had bragged to him about killing Tomei. Hon was no doubt responsible for Vanes's death also. Evidently, Hon had not found the gambling chips.

He turned his attention back to the newspaper. The story commanded the entire first page, with photographs of Dong addressing the press and a grainy archives picture of Lanzoni glaring at the camera from somewhere on the streets of New York City.

Texas Joe knew that Dong was Chin's man in the mayoral race. There was no way that Richard Barr could win now. One article in the paper even hinted that there may have been a connection between the shooting and the upcoming election.

Joe had already bet a substantial sum on Dong winning the election. He had learned long ago that there was no reason to bet against anyone backed by Kan Chin.

There was a commotion from outside. A low roar that got louder by the moment. Joe first thought it was some kind of parade, or perhaps a political rally for Philip Dong.

Two young Wah Ho members ran into the bar. Both were panting for breath.

The older of the two leaned over the bar and helped himself to a bottle of beer. "Some crazy man threw gambling chips from a roof on Grant. Five-hundred-dollar chips!"

Texas Joe hustled out onto the street. When he reached Grant Avenue the commotion had already died down. A gap-toothed woman in her seventies smiled widely at him as she waved a yellow gambling chip in front of her face as if it were a fan.

"Hey, Joe. Telephone," the bartender called out to him from the entry to Dick's bar.

Texas Joe strolled back to the bar, figuring the call was from the FBI agent Jamison, to thank him for the tip that Lanzoni was living aboard Anthony Tripoli's yacht. He had tried to imagine just what Kan Chin had planted on the boat to implicate the unfortunate Lanzoni.

He picked up the phone and turned his back to the bartender before speaking. "This is Texas Joe."

"This is John Tomei. Tell Kan Chin that I am sorry for the misunderstanding we had yesterday. Tell him I still have what he wants and I want to deal. If he's not interested, the rest of the chips will be spread all over Chinatown. He can call me at this number."

Joe took a ballpoint pen from his shirt pocket with

one hand and frantically searched for a cocktail napkin with the other. It was Tomei! There was no doubt
about it. Willy Hon had lied about killing him. Kan
Chin was going to be furious.

"Okay, partner," Joe said when he had written the
number down. "I'll tell Mr. Chin right away."

Chapter Forty-one

Willy Hon was still on an emotional high. The amount of cocaine and alcohol he'd consumed during the night and early-morning hours seemed to have barely affected him.

What had affected him was killing Dino Lanzoni. He savored the thoughts of that special moment—Lanzoni entering Dong's house, following instructions, taking the stairs to the second floor, slipping into Dong's den, his gun targeted at the back of the head of the man in the chair sitting in front of a computer.

"Turn around, Dong," Lanzoni had taunted. "I want to see your face."

When the chair spun around Lanzoni saw Willy Hon, his gloved hands holding a revolver.

Lanzoni's face morphed from confusion to rage in a split second as he pulled the trigger. There was no sound of gunfire. Just hollow clicks.

"You're supposed to be a professional. You should have checked the weapon," Hon said. "Those are blanks. These are not." He had taken his time. Risen to his feet then calmly shot the big Italian twice—one bullet directly into his heart, the second into his neck. The sound of the explosions echoed around the room.

Philip Dong had charged into the room, his features clenched in anxiety. Hon handed him his weapon. It was important for there to be gunpowder traces on Dong's hands.

"Shoot the wall. Over there," Hon ordered.

Dong squeezed his eyes shut as he pulled the trigger.

Hon then took a pistol with a silencer on the barrel from his waistband, sighted it carefully on the wall above the computer and fired. He then dropped down next to Lanzoni's body, pried from Lanzoni's hand the gun Kan Chin had given him, and replaced it with the silenced weapon. He raised Lanzoni's arm and fired up at the ceiling.

"Call nine-one-one now," he had instructed Philip Dong.

Hon was miles away by the time the first patrol car arrived at the house.

It had been perfect. Hon felt he had every right to be pleased with himself. Kan Chin had been greatly pleased. The press was having a field day. The election was going to be a triumphant victory for Philip Dong.

The news that the corpse of the crazy old policeman, Red Vanes, had been found in an old cavelike Chinatown chamber was an added bonus.

When Willy Hon stepped into Kan Chin's office, he knew that something was terribly wrong. Chin was standing near the window, talking to Texas Joe. Joe was twirling his hat in his hands and rocking back and forth on the heels of his snakeskin boots.

When Chin turned to face Hon there was rage in his eyes.

"Are you sober?" Chin demanded.

Hon's chest gave a jerk, as if he'd gotten a sudden chill.

"Yes, sir."

"Go," Chin told Texas Joe. "And wait for me in the next room."

Joe kept his eyes down as he passed Willy Hon.

When the door had clicked solidly shut, Kan Chin approached Hon, standing so close that Hon could see the smudge marks on Chin's glasses.

"Willy. You told me that you killed John Tomei."

"Yes. I did. You heard the shots."

Chin struck out, sending the edge of the palm of his hand across Hon's nose. Hon staggered back, surprised at both the speed and the force of Chin's blow.

"Tomei is alive," Chin said, biting off the words, making each one sharp and emphatic.

Hon knew it was better to remain silent. He stood statue-still, blood streaming from his nose, coursing through his mustache, over his lips, joining at the tip of his jaw and trickling to the floor.

"Tomei was in Chinatown, Willy. He threw five-hundred-dollar gambling chips, *my chips*, onto the street. For a man you shot dead, he is amazingly agile. Wipe your nose! You're soiling my carpet."

Hon blotted his face with a handkerchief. He was still too frightened to speak.

"Tomei called Texas Joe. He told Joe he wants to deal." Chin scooped a bar napkin from his desk and hurled it at Hon. "This is Tomei's telephone number. It is obvious that only Tomei and Vanes were involved in the theft. Vanes took off with the chips. That is why the safety-deposit box was empty. Tomei murdered Vanes and now he has them. I want those chips back, Willy. And I want Tomei killed."

"I vow that I will kill him, sir. On my life."

"Your life is not worth very much at this moment. If you had not performed well with Lanzoni, you would not be here now. Understood?"

"Yes, sir."

"Texas Joe is not to leave the premises. Tomei knows him. Perhaps he can be of some use to us."

Laura Aguera was on the phone when she spotted John Tomei chatting with Teresa, the detail secretary. They were sharing some kind of joke. Teresa was giggling, fawning over him.

Tomei stopped to speak and shake hands with several inspectors as he navigated through the haphazard arrangement of desks and filing cabinets that made up the Vice detail.

Tomei gave Laura a shy smile as he settled into

Elaine Surel's chair, which was directly opposite Laura's.

"Okay. Thanks very much," Laura said ending the conversation. She cradled the receiver and frowned at Tomei. "That was the coroner. Red Vanes died of a massive stroke. He was dead when the rats found him."

"I figured something like that happened. I called Lieutenant Bostic in Las Vegas and smoothed things over. He won't be bothering you, or Gucci. Billy Rossi is still in the hospital, and he's out of intensive care."

"Elaine called me an hour ago, John."

"She filled you in, did she?"

Laura gathered up her purse. "Let's go somewhere we can talk."

They were silent in the elevator and on the way out of the Hall of Justice. Tomei followed Laura across Bryant Street, past a blinking neon sign for Dad's Bail Bonds, and into a narrow alleyway to a restaurant that was new to Tomei. The Gin Joint.

"Of all the gin joints in all the world you had to take me here," Tomei lisped à la Bogart in an attempt to break the ice.

Laura was having none of it. She strode past the bar to a high-back booth against the exposed brick wall.

It was between lunch and dinnertime. They were the only customers. The waiter greeted them apprehensively.

"The chef is working on dinner. None of our lunch specials are available."

Tomei was hungry. "How about a hamburger?"

"Yes, sir. And you, ma'am?"

"A martini."

"Make it two," Tomei advised the waiter.

The silence resumed until the drinks were brought. Laura took a sip of the martini, then said, "Goddamn you, John. How could you do something that stupid?"

There was yet another long silence. The scent of gin drifted across the table.

Laura sampled the martini again, then said, "You've

put me in a terrible position. You know that, don't you?"

"I don't see it. You're not involved. It's my problem."

"Your problem!" She had more of the martini. "You keep forgetting that I'm a police officer."

Tomei leaned across the table and lowered his voice. "Listen. You're still new to the game. Things happen. Things that don't get reported, that get swept under the rug, filed in a back drawer, erased from the computer's hard disk. This is one of those things. If I went into the chief's office right now and spilled my guts, they'd find a way to tell me to get lost. They know they'd have no chance of pinning any of this on Kan Chin. The brass wants no part of him. If I went to the FBI, they'd put me in a rubber room for a few weeks, 'debrief' me with doses of high-tech truth drugs, and when they were through, they'd kick me out onto the streets. Everything I told them about Chin would go into a sealed file that no one would ever read. Chin's bulletproof, Laura. Do you know why Red Vanes was able to operate on his own in Chinatown all these years? Because he spoke the language. Sure, we're getting more and more Asian police officers, but they're mostly third- or fourth-generation Americans. They know nothing about their ancestors' tongue.

"If you arrest one of Chin's gang, he'll claim he can't speak English, whether it's true or not. The police will have to hire an interpreter. His court-appointed attorney will hire an interpreter. The prosecuting D.A. will hire an interpreter. That's all expensive as hell and very time consuming. Sitting judges don't want any part of a trial where every question to the defendant has to be translated. It's hard enough keeping a jury awake as it is. So the cases end up being pled down to nothing or just plain dismissed.

"So this is *my* problem. It could have been settled, but Red Vanes screwed that up. Screwed me up. I can't get out of it now. I've got to see it through."

"Elaine said that you're doing it for the money. So

you won't lose your daughter. That's bullshit. There's got to be a better way."

"I can't think of one. If I could, I'd do it, Laura."

"So what are the options?"

Tomei placed his finger on the rim of the glass and ran it around a few times. "I don't have many. I have to get Kan Chin off my back."

"Which means giving him back the gambling chips."

"Gucci really did fill you in, didn't she?"

"You weren't going to tell me?" Laura challenged.

"I . . . I was hoping to tell you after it was all over."

Laura finished her drink and pointed at Tomei's. "Are you going to finish that?"

Tomei's eyebrows arched. He seemed to remember Sherri Dawson asking him that same question that day at Sully's. "Help yourself," he responded.

The waiter arrived with Tomei's hamburger. It was smothered with caramelized onions and Gorgonzola cheese. He ordered another martini to replace the one Laura had confiscated. He offered to share the sandwich, but she shook her head negatively.

"I stopped to see an old friend in Homicide, Lieutenant Jim Cullen, before coming to your office, Laura. The Dino Lanzoni killing. It has a strange smell about it."

"What kind of smell?"

"Lanzoni is a professional killer. He had his gun in his hand. A silenced twenty-two semiautomatic. A pro's gun. It had been fired twice. Yet Philip Dong killed him. With a forty-four-Magnum revolver. Dong purchased the gun six weeks ago, after he alleges he began receiving death threats. He shot Lanzoni once in the heart, once in the neck. Kill shots. You have to be a damn good shot to do that, especially with a Magnum. Dong claims this was the first time he fired the gun, outside of a trip to the police firing range. His third shot missed Lanzoni by a mile and buried itself in the wall. A neighbor says that she heard two shots—bam, bam—one right after another. Then a pause of ten seconds or so before the next shot."

"Which means?"

Tomei took a bite of the hamburger while Laura concentrated on her second martini.

"It has all the earmarks of a setup. The odds of a novice like Dong taking down Lanzoni are so low, Las Vegas wouldn't post the bet. Cullen told me that the FBI, my buddy Don Jamison, was tipped that Lanzoni was living aboard Anthony Tripoli's yacht. Jamison found a stash of heroin on the boat, and some betting cards. The kind of cards Billy Rossi uses."

"So what is Lieutenant Cullen going to do, John?"

"Nothing. Everything checks out at the lab. Dong definitely fired the Magnum. Lanzoni's prints are the only ones on the twenty-two."

"Is this one of those *things* you were talking about? The ones that get swept under the rug?"

"If it was just Joe Citizen who shot Lanzoni, the investigation might proceed. But not with Philip Dong. He's a local hero and a cinch to win tomorrow's election. No one in the department is going to go after him."

"Maybe they shouldn't. Maybe Dong just got lucky."

"Kan Chin's mixed up in this. My bet is he sucked Lanzoni in. Used him as a patsy."

"For what purpose?" Laura asked. "I don't get it."

"It took me a while to figure it out, but I think I've got it. Chin wanted to be sure that Philip Dong was elected mayor of San Francisco."

Laura's hand crept across the table and plucked a thick, hand-cut potato chip from Tomei's plate. She dipped it in the martini and chewed thoughtfully. "No. That's too complicated, John."

"Kan Chin's a complicated man. Red Vanes described him as a sort of chess master who enjoyed moving his pawns around the board. If Dong is his man, it makes sense. Richard Barr had the election locked up a few months ago. Chin had to do something dramatic."

"But Lanzoni? Would Chin risk getting in a war with the New York Mafia?"

Tomei pushed his plate closer to Laura and she picked up another chip. "There was no danger of that. New York had no love for Dino. The sooner he got his, the better." He paid careful attention to Laura while she mulled the information over. Her eyes narrowed, her forehead creased, but her eyes remained clear as she sipped at her martini.

Laura finished the drink, turned the glass upside down and said, "Did you tell Lieutenant Cullen about your theory."

"No. He wouldn't want to hear it."

"So what's your next move?"

"I'm not sure yet. I'll have to meet with Chin, but I haven't figured out where. Tell me, did Gucci teach you how to drink, or is it a natural talent?"

"I shouldn't have had the second one. Gin does things to me."

"What? Makes you sleepy?"

"No. Horny. Let's go to my place, John."

Chapter Forty-two

Kan Chin's voice in no way revealed the anger he was feeling. He had called the number that John Tomei had provided to Texas Joe more than a dozen times before it was answered.

If Tomei wanted to play the patience game, Chin was more than willing to join in.

"John Tomei speaking."

Chin clicked on the phone's speaker button and fixed Willy Hon with an unblinking stare. "You should be ashamed of yourself, Mr. Tomei. Two elderly women were nearly trampled to death when you threw those chips down to the street."

"I wouldn't want to be responsible for anyone's death. Would you?"

"Not even Mr. Vanes's?" Chin countered slyly.

"That was unfortunate," Tomei said. If Chin thought he'd killed Vanes, so be it. "Do we still have a deal?"

"There are fewer chips now," Chin pointed out.

"Make it an even six hundred thousand dollars."

"Agreed. Where and when?"

"Tonight. Ten o'clock. That's . . . two hours and ten minutes from right now. At Rossi's house. Willy Hon won't have any trouble finding the place. He's been there before."

"Mr. Hon is unavailable."

"What happened? Something serious, I hope. Did

Dino Lanzoni manage to do some damage last night at Philip Dong's house?"

Willy Hon flinched. The muscles in his neck and shoulders were drawn into knots.

"I suggest a replacement," Chin proceeded calmly. "Someone you are familiar with. Texas Joe."

"Fine. I want him to be alone. I won't be. If anyone comes with him, the deal is off. I vanish and you know what happens to the chips. After the exchange, we're finished. No reprisals. Do I still have your word on that?"

"You do indeed."

"If you play any games with me, if the money isn't legit, then I'm sending those videos I took of the vault to your associates in New York. Red Vanes supplied me with their names and addresses. You play straight, and I destroy the tapes. You have my word on that."

"How is Mr. Rossi?"

"He's out of town, on a vacation."

"Give him my regards." Chin broke the connection and wagged a finger at Hon. "I underestimated Tomei, Willy. So did you. It won't happen again."

"How could he know what happened at Dong's house last night?"

"He doesn't. It is a guess, that is all. But a shrewd one. I am having Tony Lum deal with Tomei."

Hon swallowed a sudden bile taste in the back of his throat. Lum was one of Kan Chin's favorite body-guards, and he had made it plain that he thought that he should be Chin's right-hand man.

"I can take care of Tomei," he said adamantly.

"I don't doubt that, Willy. But the experience will be good for Tony. You may go. Tell Lum and Texas Joe that I want to see them."

John Tomei rubbed his gloved hands together and wished there was more coffee in the thermos. He had been wedged into a gap in the towering copper-and-green photinia hedge separating Rossi's house from his up-street neighbor since taking the call from Kan

Chin. He had one of Rossi's rifles in hand, and revolvers in both pockets of his jacket. Fidel was huddled next to him.

He had an excellent view of the street and the entrance to Rossi's house, some thirty yards away. The porch light was on, the front door open a crack.

The fog had penetrated the tops of nearby trees and darkness oozed out between their trunks. The bright beams of headlights and the swishing of tires announced the approach of a vehicle. After it passed, there was a hushed, sullen silence. Not a sound of a bird or critter of any kind, other than Fidel's deep breathing.

He petted the dog and whispered kind words. The well-bred German shepherd was worth every cent Billy Rossi had paid for him. He obeyed every command Tomei gave, including sitting quietly in the damp, cold night air for more than two hours.

Tomei tensed. A sound. A car motor? No headlights. No swishing of tires. Another sound—the soft, cloaked clack of a car door closing.

The thick canopy of fog muffled the sound and it was impossible to tell from which direction it had come.

"Shhhh," he whispered to Fidel.

Tomei focused on the silence, imagining he could hear the ticking of his wristwatch. Nothing. Then Fidel's ears sprang up. A branch cracked—silence again.

A shadow moved among the trees. Darkness against darkness. Another movement. The shadow had a head. A man, moving slowly, making less noise than a cat, on the opposite side of Rossi's property.

Tomei blew a relieved stream of air through his lips. There was just the one moving shadow. If the man had decided to gain access to Rossi's house by following the hedge line, there was no way he could have missed spotting him and Fidel.

Headlights! The whining of a car engine. The headlights turned into Rossi's circular driveway and Tomei edged back into the shelter of the hedge.

The car was a nondescript white sedan. The driver parked alongside Sherri Dawson's Corvette and killed the engine. The door opened, the car's interior lights blinked on, giving Tomei a clear view of Texas Joe, cowboy hat and all. He was carrying a tan-colored satchel in one hand.

Tomei kept watching the spot where the shadow was last seen. When Joe slammed the car door shut, the shadow moved again, ten, fifteen yards, then melted into the blackness of the trees.

Texas Joe sauntered up to Rossi's house. He stood uncertainly on the porch for a moment, then ripped loose the envelope Tomei had taped to the door. He clamped the satchel between his legs before opening the envelope.

He studied the message for longer than was necessary. All Tomei had written was that the front door was unlocked, the suitcase full of chips was inside. Joe was to take the case, leave the money, and get out of there right away. "You're being watched" was the final sentence.

"Do it, Joe," Tomei whispered to himself. "Follow orders."

Texas Joe glanced over his shoulder, then with a quick, jerky movement, opened the door.

The shadow moved at that precise moment, and Tomei was able to get a better look. He was short, stocky, dressed all in black. Wearing a knit cap of some kind. Willy Hon. It had to be Hon.

Tomei scanned the tree line, looking for any movement as Texas Joe opened the door slowly, then dropped his satchel, scooped up the suitcase, and quick-stepped back to his car.

The engine turned over and Tomei ducked to the ground as the headlights swept past him.

Silence again.

Tomei kept his eyes on the last place he'd seen the shadow. Fidel was getting testy, murmuring softly, his paws clawing at the dirt.

The man emerged from the shadows and raced

across Rossi's clipped, damp lawn before disappearing from sight.

A window, Tomei guessed. He was figuring to shoot me through a window.

It was a good ten minutes before the stocky figure appeared again. He was standing tall now, moving swiftly, seemingly unafraid. When he darted through the front door, Tomei made his move. Patting the side of his leg to indicate to Fidel to stay close, he jogged up to the front door. He could see the satchel Texas Joe had left in the hallway. There was the sound of doors opening and slamming shut. Hon was upstairs.

Tomei slipped into the house, the carbine cocked and at the ready.

More slamming of doors. Tomei ducked under the stairs. There was the sound of shoes clumping down the stairs.

The man was holding a gun down at his side. His head was covered by a ski mask, with slits for his eyes and mouth.

"That's far enough, Willy," Tomei shouted, pushing the rifle barrel through the stairway balusters. "Drop the gun."

The man balked at first, swinging his arms to the right, but Tomei dug the rifle barrel into his leg. "Drop it!"

The handgun hit the carpeted stairs with a thunk and tumbled to rest on the floor.

"Now, take the mask off, Willy."

The man raised his arms slowly and peeled the mask off.

Tomei was caught off guard. The man's face was small and narrow. He was clean shaven and had thin lips.

"Where's Willy Hon?" Tomei said, gesturing with the rifle for him to come down the stairs.

"Right behind you, *tset ha tset ha*. Put rifle on floor!"

Tomei let go of the rifle and turned to see the ominous figure of Willy Hon in the doorway, an automatic weapon clutched in his hands. Hon barked out an order in Chinese and the man on the steps took a cell phone from his pocket and turned his back to them as he spoke into the receiver.

When he turned back to face them, Hon's weapon made a soft, coughing sound. The bullet streaked past Tomei and blew a hole in Tony Lum's forehead.

Fidel snarled and leaped forward.

Hon kept his gun pointed at Tomei and shouted out, "Freeze."

The dog kept coming. "Freeze," he screamed. The Dawson whore had told Kan Chin that was the animal's command word. Before he could swivel the gun in the dog's direction, Fidel was on him.

Fidel had been trained to go for the throat or groin of an attacker, whichever was closest. He sank his teeth into Hon's groin. The force of the collision knocked the weapon from Hon's hands.

Hon howled wildly. Bent over in pain, he stumbled to his knees, hands groping wildly for his weapon as Fidel went for his throat, clamping his jaws into the soft flesh. Hon's face rattled back and forth like a rag doll.

Tomei yelled *"Kita!"* Fidel released his grip and backtracked a few paces, looking to Tomei for a sign of approval.

Tomei bent over the body. Hon's throat was an open, gaping wound. His head was twisted at an odd angle, his neck broken.

There was a long, whining scream of tires and brakes. Tomei retrieved the carbine and ran to the door. The white sedan Texas Joe had been driving was parked in front of the house.

Texas Joe climbed out of the driver's seat. He came to an unsteady halt when he saw Fidel racing toward him.

"Kita!" Tomei yelled and Fidel skidded to a stop at Texas Joe's feet.

"Who's with you?" Tomei demanded. "Where are they?"

Joe had his hands up in the air, his eyes riveted on Fidel's bloodstained teeth. "Holy sheeeeit. It's just me. Ain't nobody else."

Tomei gestured with the rifle. "Get in here. Quick."

Texas Joe marched with his hands up. When he was inside the house he let out a low whistle and said, "Jeeeesus H. Cheeerist! Are they both dead?"

"Yes. And you will be, too, unless you tell me where the rest of Chin's gang is."

"I ain't shittin' you, pardner. It's just me. Kan Chin told me to drive that fellow there, Tony Lum, out here. Then give that there satchel to you. Take whatever you give me, then drive away and wait for Lum to call me. That's what I did, 'cept you kind of screwed me up with that note. I was waitin' for Lum's call when Willy Hon drove up by me. He wasn't supposed to be a part of this. He just told me to sit tight and follow orders."

Texas Joe's arms were getting tired. He started to lower them, then shot them straight up again when Fidel growled.

Tomei snapped his fingers and Fidel trotted over to him.

"If there are any more men out there in the dark, I'm going to set the dog on you, Joe."

"I ain't lyin'. On my daddy's grave, I ain't lyin'!"

Tomei opened the satchel. It was stuffed with cash. "All right. Lower your hands and tell me exactly what Kan Chin plans are."

"Mind if I sit down, pardner? My legs are about to go out on me."

It took Texas Joe less than five minutes to tell his story, a story that Tomei believed. Joe was too frightened to lie.

"How long have you been working for Kan Chin, Joe?"

"Well, I don't work directly for him, ya know, but when he asks me to do something, I do it right quick."

"Chin is not going to be a happy camper when he finds out what happened tonight."

Joe craned his neck to look at the corpses of Willy Hon and Tony Lum. "I reckon he's gonna be right pissed."

"At you."

"Yep. But at you, mostly."

"Mostly," Tomei agreed. "But you work for Chin. You screwed up."

"Hey, I never did—"

"He's going to blame you. There's no one else to blame. They're both dead."

Joe creased the crown of his hat with the palm of his hand. "Could be. You got some kinda plan?"

"My plan is to disappear. With that satchel of money you brought with you. The case you picked up is full of gambling chips. Is it still in the car?"

"Yep."

"Well, we're going to load those two bodies into the car, then you can take off. You can keep the gambling chips. I don't care where you go, Joe. But if I were you, I'd dump the bodies somewhere, pick up whatever money you've salted away and vamoose."

Texas Joe's eyes were narrow slits in his face. He took a long look at the bodies, the dog, then returned his gaze to Tomei. "I never heard anyone actually say vamoose before. But it ain't a bad idea, pardner."

Chapter Forty-three

"Mayor Barr. You do me an honor. Welcome to my home."

Richard Barr looked over Kan Chin's living room, mentally cataloging the value of the artwork. He came close to gasping when he spotted the orange jade table and the porcelain devil dogs.

"Are those Sung dynasty?" he asked pointing at the dogs.

"You have a keen eye, Mr. Mayor. Congratulations."

"I worked at the Asian Art Museum while I was going through college. I wish you could have congratulated me on winning the election."

"Please. Sit down." Chin clapped his hands and a lovely young girl with waist-length braided hair brought in a tray of champagne.

"How is Mr. Prescott?" Chin asked while the girl poured them drinks.

"He quit as soon as the results came out. Said he was going on an around-the-world cruise."

"Charles seemed to be an intelligent young man."

"A frightened man. I sent him over to Philip Dong's house the night of the shooting. Did you know that Dino Lanzoni had enormous feet?"

"I know nothing of Mr. Lanzoni."

"Really big feet," Barr said, holding his hands wide apart. "When Prescott went to Cabine to pick up that five hundred thousand dollars that you—"

"Not I. Some of your supporters who wish to remain anonymous."

"Yeah. Sure. Well, all Prescott saw of the man who passed him the money were his feet. He was wearing cordovan loafers. The same shoes Lanzoni was wearing when Dong shot him."

"I assure you that the men who provided you with that money would have nothing to do with a man such as Mr. Lanzoni."

"What was it?" Barr asked. "The appointments I promised you and didn't deliver? Was that it?"

Chin remained silent.

Barr picked up his glass and watched a thin line of bubbles rise through the pale gold wine. "Do you follow baseball, Mr. Chin?"

"Baseball? No," Chin responded, wondering why Barr asked the question and hoping that he would get to the real point of his visit.

"There was a manager in the old days. The tough-old days, by the name of Leo Durocher. He had a saying: 'Show me a good loser, and I'll show you an asshole.' I never did agree with Durocher. A good loser," he raised his eyes to Chin's, "an intelligent loser, wants to win again. He forgets all about his loss and thinks of the next game. Or the next election. I'm going to run for the state senate in two years. I'd value your support."

Chin laced his fingers together. "Yes. I see. I, too, disagree with your baseball friend. And I think we could find mutual interests in your quest. We must get together soon and plan out a strategy. There would have to be certain guarantees."

Barr extended his hand across the jade table. "Then we have an agreement?"

"It is a pleasure doing business with a realist, Mayor Barr. There are not enough of us around anymore."

Laura Aguera relaxed her grip on the airplane seat's armrests when the jet touched down at the Santa Fe Muni Airport.

The pilot reversed engines and she was pushed back into her foam-packed seat.

"That wasn't bad, was it?" John Tomei asked.

Laura looked out the executive jet's window at the red-brown New Mexico hills. "I've never flown in this small a plane before. I like the ones with four engines hanging from the wings."

Tomei unbuckled his seat belt. "I could get used to this kind of treatment. No wonder Melissa is getting spoiled."

When the plane had taxied to the terminal, the co-pilot came back from the cabin and said, "I hope you enjoyed the flight. Mrs. Gardner will be meeting you in the terminal."

Tomei thanked him, grabbed their bags, and toted them out onto the tarmac. The weather was warm and dry. Watercolor clouds smudged against the sky.

He spotted Joan as soon as they entered the terminal. She was standing with Melissa, and Peter, the butler who had served him with the subpoena in Gilroy.

"There's the dragon lady. The brunette over by the wall, wearing the red pants suit."

"Is that your ex-wife?" Laura asked. "She's beautiful."

"That's her. And that's Melissa."

His daughter was running toward him, gracefully weaving her way through a crowd of passengers disembarking from a United Airlines commercial jet. She was dressed in jeans rolled up to mid-calf and a white sweatshirt with University of New Mexico printed across the front.

Tomei dropped the luggage as Melissa jumped into his arms.

"Hi, Daddy."

He hugged his daughter to his chest, kissing the top of her head. "Messy, say hello to my friend Laura."

"Hi, Laura. Are you daddy's girlfriend?"

"She's a cop. So be on your good behavior, kiddo."

Laura extended her hand. Melissa was prettier than she photographed. There was no doubt that she was John's daughter.

"Hi, Melissa."

"See, Daddy. She calls me by my right name. You should, too. Are we going out to dinner? I found this really great place. Mexican food. Really authentic, not that stuff you get in California."

"My daughter, the nine-year-old gourmet. How's your mother?"

"Fine." Melissa turned around and waved to her mother.

"She likes it here. So does Vern. You should see the place he's building. We've got our own helicopter pad and everything."

"Hello, John."

Tomei nodded to Joan and introduced her to Laura.

"We're going to La Casa Sena for dinner," Melissa said. "Why don't you come along, Mom?"

"I'm sure your father would rather have you to himself, darling. John, can we talk a minute?" She gave Laura a forced smile. "Peter will take your luggage to the car."

"Messy seems happy," Tomei said when he and Joan were alone.

"Yes. She loves it here. I'm glad that you're being reasonable. Our offer stands. Vernon's jet will be at your disposal every other weekend. When we're finished with the house, you can stay with us, if you wish."

By her tone, Tomei knew it wasn't what Joan wished.

"I'll find a place nearby. I'm thinking of moving here."

The news obviously surprised Joan. "Are you? I must say you seem to have come into some money. Your friend certainly made an impression with Melissa, though he was way off on her birthday. It's not till March. Surely you remember that, John."

"My friend? What are you talking about?"

"He sent her a beautiful jade bracelet. It's exquisite."

Tomei grabbed Joan roughly by the arm. "What friend?"

Joan wrested her arm free and rubbed at it with a hand. "Damn you. That's going to leave a bruise. What the hell's the matter with you?"

"What friend?"

"Mr. Chin. I had the bracelet appraised, and I can tell you—"

Tomei whistled sharply. Laura, Melissa, and Peter turned to look at him. He waved to Peter to bring back the luggage.

"Joan, I need the jet again. I've got to get back to San Francisco. Right away."

Chapter Forty-four

"It's like Chinese New Year, Mr. Mayor," Inspector Paul Cryder said as he nursed the mayor's limousine down Grant Avenue.

The sidewalks were swarming with people, the mob spilling into the street. Many were carrying signs and banners featuring Philip Dong's smiling features. Others held homemade posters with splashy red-and-black Chinese characters.

Cryder had to hold at the corner of Grant and California as a thirty-foot-long nylon and pasteboard mock-dragon serpentined down the street.

"They better celebrate now," Barr said bitterly. "Dong's going to pick their pockets clean. Use the siren, Paul. I might as well enjoy the perks of this job while I can."

Barr leaned back in the limo seat and lit up a cigarette. He blew a smoke ring that wobbled through the air and broke apart against the headliner. Let Dong have the damn car cleaned, he thought peevishly.

He had decided to accept Philip Dong's invitation to his victory celebration at the Chinatown Hall. A quick "hello-and-good-bye" for the cameras. A few handshakes, then he'd get the hell out of there.

Barr wondered how much Kan Chin had to do with the invitation from Dong. Plenty, he guessed. One of the earliest things he learned in politics was that there were times, all too many times, when a man never stood so tall as when he stooped to kiss someone's ass. And kissing Chin's wrinkled old butt was something he was going to have to get used to if he wanted that state senate office. And he wanted it badly.

Cryder tapped the siren lightly and was waved to the sidewalk in front of the Chinatown Hall by a trio of hyperactive young men with bright yellow bands around the sleeves of their black jackets.

"Keep the car right here, Paul," Barr said. "If Dong's crossing guards want you to move, tell them to get stuffed. I won't be long."

John Tomei spotted half a dozen sharp-eyed young men positioned in front of the Chinatown Hall that could have been Kan Chin's men. They moved out of the way as a long black Cadillac parked in front of the hall.

He recognized Inspector Paul Cryder as he hopped out of the limo and held the back door open for Richard Barr.

The commotion gave him the opportunity he'd been waiting for. He crouched down and plunged into the crowd, pushing his way into the narrow doorway at the side of the building that accessed the hall's kitchen.

A heavyset man in a white chef's cap was sneaking a cigarette at the door. He challenged Tomei. "No can come. No can come."

Tomei showed the man his badge. "I'm with Mayor Barr. We have to check the kitchen."

The man backed away grudgingly and Tomei climbed the stairs to the second floor where the kitchen was in full swing. White-hatted chefs were slaving away in front of hot stoves. Tuxedoed waiters were milling around, waiting for their orders. The steam from the cooking pots created a foglike effect.

Tomei received a few annoyed glances as he shouldered his way toward the swinging doors leading to the dining hall.

He had been trying to get close to Kan Chin for

two days, and had run various scenarios through his mind. Killing Chin was one of his options, but he did not know if he could go through with it. He wished he could. He sincerely wished he could.

He settled on a plan. To prove to Kan Chin that he was a vulnerable target. To somehow walk up to him. Touch him physically. Shove the jade bracelet Chin had sent to Messy in his face and warn him that if Chin ever threatened his family, he'd kill him the next time.

He had to put some fear into Chin. He had his speech prepared. It was like a scene from a corny mystery movie: I've put a contract out on you. A hundred-thousand-dollar contract with a professional hit man. If I die, the money is sent to him, the contract goes into effect.

God, it was *so* corny. But Chin would have to think about it, worry about it.

For his plan to work, he not only had to get close to Kan Chin, he had to be able to get away safely. That meant a crowd, a distraction. Philip Dong's victory party seemed to be the answer.

One of the waiters rudely bumped into Tomei, then growled *"Jo med gwai,"* as he bumped open the swinging doors and carried a tray of steaming dishes into the ballroom.

Tomei backed away as a line of waiters followed suit. He waited until the last man had passed him, took a deep breath, and pushed through the swinging doors.

The room was cavernous, rimmed by a high-perched balcony. A rainbow of balloons and streamers hung from the balcony railings.

A twelve-piece orchestra, complete with a male vocalist and floor-shaking amplifiers, was wailing away, much to the delight of a young crowd on the dance floor.

There were rows of dining tables, enough to accommodate several hundred people, Tomei estimated. The tables were half-filled, mostly with women and children. The men were lined up around a bar or clustered in groups, drinks and smokes in hand.

The newcomers entering the ballroom had to stand in a long line, marked by a purple velvet rope, to meet their host. The rope was threaded through brass stanchions every few feet. Philip Dong greeted them warmly, passing on the tribute envelopes that were handed to him to a stunning Asian woman who flicked her jet-black hair back over her shoulders before dropping the envelopes into a hip-high wicker basket at her side.

Tomei wondered if any of the envelopes contained gambling chips in lieu of cash. The men on the balconies worried him. How many of them were Chin's men?

He finally spotted Kan Chin sitting at a table just down from Dong's reception line. He was bracketed by two attractive young women who looked as if they could be the offsprings of the woman to whom Dong was passing the tribute envelopes. The woman was Dong's wife, the girls their daughters, Tomei guessed.

There was a stir as Mayor Richard Barr entered the ballroom. He was pausing to smile and shake hands as he skirted the reception line.

Tomei made a quick decision. Barr was his ticket to Kan Chin. He hurried across the room and, while Barr was grab-handing his way through the crowd, tapped him on the arm.

"Mr. Mayor. Paul Cryder sent me to stay with you. There's a disturbance outside. It may get a little rough."

Barr squinted at Tomei, not recognizing him, but taking it for granted he was an undercover policeman.

"Okay. Okay. Hang close."

Tomei ducked behind the mayor's broad back, peering over his shoulder at Kan Chin every few seconds. Chin seemed to be enjoying himself, chatting with the girls and drinking wine.

A momentary hush came over the gathering when Mayor Barr reached Philip Dong. The two men exchanged pleasantries and then Dong held out his arms and they embraced. The room exploded in cheers and whistles.

Tomei ducked under the purple velveteen rope, drawing an accusing look from the woman at Dong's side. He hurried toward Kan Chin, who looked up at the last moment, his eyes widening when he recognized Tomei.

Tomei dug the tip of his index finger into the back of Chin's neck. He bent down and whispered in his ear. "Bang. You're dead. This is how easy it is. Don't bother me or my family again, or I'll kill you. There's already a contract out on you. You kill me, and it goes into effect. Either way, you fuck with me, and you're dead." He dropped the jade bracelet onto Chin's lap and strode away.

Kan Chin struggled to his feet. He looked around frantically for his men. Since Willy Hon and Tony Lum had disappeared, he'd had to put up with inferiors—young, ambitious, but untrained soldiers. He waved up to the balcony, but no one paid him any attention. He craned his neck to see where John Tomei had gone. He had vanished into the crowd. Damn the man! It had been a very long time since anyone had the courage to challenge him personally. Tomei had actually touched him! He flung the jade bracelet across the table, startling Philip Dong's daughters.

Dong and Richard Barr were walking toward him, so engrossed in conversation that they had not noticed the interplay with Tomei.

"Cho bok," he screamed at the man who had replaced Willy Hon.

Cho bok was ten yards away, his back to Chin, talking with a young white woman.

Chin angrily began walking in the direction Tomei had taken. Tomei must be captured. Captured, not killed. Chin wanted that pleasure himself. There he was! Near the kitchen doors. A line of waiters pushing carts were blocking the door. He was trapped!

Chin looked around frantically for his men. Where the devil were they? Tomei turned back and for a moment their eyes met. Chin could see the fear! He yelled at the waiters. "Hold that man! Stop him!"

A tall woman with black hair moved in front of him. Chin swore at her in gutter Cantonese and pushed her aside. But she didn't move. Instead she bumped directly into him. Then, with one hand, she swept the wig from her head.

Chin glared at her for a second before the face registered. Sherri Dawson. The whore.

"Remember me?" Sherri asked, then drove the tip of the marlin spike into Kan Chin's narrow chest. She wrapped her left arm around his waist, as if they were dancing, her right hand screwing the spike in deeper and deeper as she dragged him toward an unoccupied table. She lowered Chin's convulsing body into a chair, then turned smartly on her heel and walked directly into a waiter.

The waiter's tray crashed to the ground. Hot tea and steaming food spread across the floor, drawing the attention of the nearby diners. No one, other than John Tomei, paid any notice of Kan Chin as he slumped across a table, his head twisted to one side, a puddle of blood forming at his feet.

Sherri Dawson edged into the throng of dancers. She glanced around nervously, looking for Kan Chin's bodyguards. She saw Tomei. Their eyes locked for a brief second. He looked startled, the proverbial deer in a headlight. She hesitated, wondering if he'd seen her kill Kan Chin—and if so, what he would do about it. Her hand slipped into her purse, clutching the derringer pistol.

Tomei dropped his gaze, turned abruptly, and pushed his way through the kitchen's swinging doors.

Chapter Forty-five

"This is not what I expected when you said you were taking me to Las Vegas," Laura Aguera said when Tomei drove the rental car they'd picked up at the airport through the gates of the St. Rose Convalescent Hospital.

"Ten minutes. At the most," John Tomei promised as he hopped out of the car. He slipped a stuffed manila envelope from the suitcase in the car's backseat. "Come on in. Billy Rossi would love to meet you."

The hospital grounds were spacious and well-maintained, islands of emerald lawn, manicured shrubbery, and groomed trees.

The receptionist took his name, checked her chart, and informed him that Mr. Rossi was waiting for him in the game room.

Tomei followed her directions, down a polished mosaic hallway to a large, airy room with potted plants and floor-to-ceiling windows looking out onto a garden with a fountain and swimming pool.

There were glass-topped tables scattered around the room. All of the tables were occupied with up to six people, mostly well into their Social Security payment years. All of them were wearing white terry-cloth robes.

The women outnumbered the men by a six-to-one

ratio, Tomei estimated. He spotted Billy Rossi sitting by himself at a table near the window.

"There's Billy. I won't tell him you're a cop. He might have another stroke."

"Thanks a lot," Laura huffed.

"Billy. Say hello to a Laura Aguera."

Rossi raised his head. The left side of his face appeared as if it was stiff and frozen. He was sitting in a wheelchair, playing a game of solitaire. The wheelchair reminded Tomei of Elaine Surel. Gucci's diagnosis was encouraging. Her doctor had assured her she'd be out of the chair in two weeks. Rossi looked like he might never get out of his.

"Hi, Laura. Tomb. Good to see you."

"I think I'll take a tour of the garden," Laura said. "Nice to meet you, Billy."

"Likewise," Rossi said, and Tomei noticed that he slurred his words. He sat down on the chair next to the bookie. "How are they treating you?"

Rossi moved a black ten over to a red queen with a shaky hand. "Not bad. See that old gal over there? The one with the woolly gray hair?"

That described about half the people in the room, Tomei noticed.

"That's Ester. She's the absolute best pinochle player I ever came across, Tomb. She'll clean out that bunch of losers she's with, then come over here and whip my ass in gin rummy."

Tomei placed the envelope on the table. "You can afford to lose, Billy. This is half of the money that Kan Chin's gang took from your house."

"I read about Chin, Tomb. You're a tougher bastard than I thought you were. Keep the money. Keep it all. You earned it."

"I didn't kill Chin, Billy."

Rossi raised his right arm and blotted his lips with the sleeve of his robe. "Anything you say, pal. But keep the dough."

He turned to stare out the window. Laura Aguera was standing at the side of the swimming pool. The sun's reflection on the water made it look like crushed diamonds.

"It's hot out there, Tomb. Only a lizard could live in this heat all the time. That's a pretty lady you got there."

"Speaking of pretty ladies, I saw Sherri Dawson."

"She's alive?"

"Alive and kicking, Billy."

"What'd she say? Where is she?"

"She said that she's sorry she set you up. She had no choice. Kan Chin was going to kill her if she didn't cooperate with him."

A line of saliva was forming at the corner of Rossi's mouth. He wiped it away with his robe sleeve again. "I figured that. Where is Sherri? Back at my house?"

"No. She's taking a trip, Billy. Around the world. She wants to get away from everything. I have a hunch she'll be giving you a call when she comes back."

Tomei wondered how much truth there was to his story. His last vision of Sherri Dawson was when she had killed Kan Chin. Would she contact Rossi again? He doubted it. When he'd returned to Rossi's house and checked the master bedroom, he'd found that all of Sherri's clothes and jewelry were gone.

Rossi grimaced and with apparent great effort raised his right foot from the wheelchair footrest. "Look at this, Tomb. A robe and paper slippers. Man, I never thought I'd end up like this."

"You'll be fine," Tomei assured him. "A little rest, then you'll be right back in business."

"Wanna bet?" Rossi said, then laughed. "That's one bet I don't want to handle. Ester tells me the same thing. She's a sharpie. Dealt blackjack at the Sands. Dated Sinatra a couple of times. She likes this damn heat. I'm trying to talk her into coming back to San Francisco with me."

Tomei got to his feet. "I've got to get going, Billy."

"Take the envelope, Tomb. Live it up. Hit the ta-

bles. Get lucky. It takes money to win money. Remember: The less you bet, the more you lose when
you win."

Tomei waved to Laura. She waved back and smiled.
"I've been luckier than I deserve to be, Billy. I don't
want to push it."